To

Barbara

The Genesis Chamber

Best Wishes

The Authors

Simon Beighton & Paul Devlin

Would jointly like to thank Lt. William 'Bill' Gordon for always being available for guidance and advice. Our respect and thanks goes to the Law Enforcements Officers of the Orlando Police Department who daily lay their lives on the line to protect and serve.
"Courage – Pride - Commitment."

Also, thanks to Ken 'The Ghost' Scott who mentored us through the process of writing our first book. An accomplished author in his own right, Kens works can be found on his website: www.kentheghost.com

Simon Beighton

To Chunkz, we did it pal, "just sayin!"

Paul Devlin

To my loving wife, Charlene, for your endless patience and encouragement.
My boys, Kyle and George
And finally, "Kev," your mind fascinates me.

You can contact the authors on Facebook – Beighton Devlin
Or by email - BeightonDevlin@yahoo.es

Dedicated:

To all the families and friends of missing persons who day by day wait in hope.

Cover design by Simon Beighton & Paul Devlin

The Genesis Chamber

Chapter 1

The darkness gradually enveloped the isolated cabin until the host was satisfied it had seemingly disappeared into the dense surroundings. He had chosen the location knowing that it had not been used by its owner for many years. In fact, the only people to have set eyes on his "special place" were his guests, and they weren't going to tell anybody where it was located, or what happened there.

He took the wolf mask from the box and studied it intently, taking a comb from his pocket to restyle a little of the facial hair so that everything was just perfect. It had to be that way.

He grinned as he pulled it on to cover the top half of his face, and got more than a little aroused as the soft latex brushed his skin. He reached for more candles, aware that he would need just a little more light to illuminate the sparsely furnished interior. The candles were ready; everything was coming together nicely. It was now time for music. He walked over to the vinyl record selection and stood for a moment, considering his choice. He leaned forward and eased out a sleeve, taking care to read the words on the back cover. He nodded to himself subconsciously as he delicately removed it from the sleeve and placed it on the player. With one click the record began to spin and the needle automatically lowered onto the vinyl. The haunting sound of Etta James filled the cabin and blocked out the natural night sounds of the forest and the swampland beyond.

He lingered for a moment as he gazed hypnotically towards the ceiling and then closed his eyes, as if in a trance. As the unforgettable lyrics of "At Last" filled his head, he let his mind wander.

The boy was running as fast as he could, trying his best to follow the trail in the dense forest. He'd stop every now and again to check that the trail was still there and to make sure he wasn't still being chased. He leaned back against a tree, breathing hard. His whole soul cried out 'no more!' but he knew he had to carry on. And after just a few seconds he took off again, running blindly through the undergrowth.

Stray branches and thorns cut into his bare chest, drawing blood, which blended with the droplets of sweat and of course the salty tears that flowed freely. He sensed he was being followed, and couldn't help stopping far too often to listen for sounds that would indicate that. But all he could hear was his own exhausted breathing and his heart pounding so loudly he thought it was going to break out of his chest.

He wiped a bloody hand across his face. He tried his best to clean it on his dirty jeans, and after convincing himself it was hygienic enough, began to try and wipe the tears and the blood and the grime from his eyes. He could see a little better now and his heart skipped a beat as he realized he could see car lights in the distance. Had he made it out of the woods? He was so exhausted, but found a little more strength as a surge of adrenalin kicked in. He would keep going, make it to the main road, and try to flag down a passing car. The police would help; they always did. After all, that was their job, and he would tell them everything.

He ran again, so close, so close to the main highway he could almost touch it; he could smell it. Car exhaust fumes, carbon emissions, diesel oil; pollution had never smelled so good. So good he broke out into a smile as he slowed down and jogged towards the hard shoulder. A shape loomed up ahead, the form of something... an animal...a man? He didn't want to run now; he slowed down to a walk...a hesitant walk. And then he stopped. Something was preventing him from going any further. His legs turned to jelly and he froze to the spot. And yet something strange was happening. The shape, the form was getting bigger. He was aware of an inner tremble—panic setting in. The shape was coming towards him, ever nearer. He wanted to turn and run back into the forest but his body wouldn't obey the instructions from his brain. It was too late—the man was on top of him now, within touching distance. A bolt of fear shot through the boy when he recognized the face.

He whimpered, "No, please no,"

The man roughly grabbed the boy by the arm and dragged him away.

The sound of the needle repeatedly scratching at the end of the record brought the wolf out of his trance. He cleared his throat, pressed *repeat* on the player, and slowly drifted towards the kitchen to put the finishing touches to the meal.

You smiled, you smiled
Oh and then the spell was cast
And here we are in heaven
For you are mine...

The petrified child was dressed in a red cape, naked from the waist up and fidgeting with fear as the plate was placed in front of him by the man in a menacing wolf mask.

His food would remain untouched.

He looked across the table at the other man, who had just started to eat. His mouth was visible, but from the tip of his nose up it was covered by a grotesque pig mask topped by a red baseball cap. He ate greedily and far too quickly; the noises emanating from his mouth were not unlike swine at the trough. He switched his attention from his plate for a second, waving a fork in the air.

"C'mon, boy," he said. "Eat up. You've got a long night ahead of you; you need some energy."

The man didn't bother to empty his mouth when he spoke, and bits of half-chewed food flew from his mouth as grease ran down his chin and congealed into the folds of his second chin. Even the wolf man looked on in disgust, and the boy couldn't help thinking the inside of his mouth resembled his mother's washing machine on wash day.

"Why are you k-k-keeping me here?" he stuttered, then broke down and sobbed like the child that he was.

The wolf waited until the boy had composed himself, and spoke in a soft voice. "You've heard of Jesus, boy?" His Southern drawl was thick.

"Yes, sir." The boy sniffed.

"And you've heard about the story of the Last Supper?"

The boy hesitated. "I, I think so. Is Jesus going to come and help me?"

The wolf raised his voice a decibel or two, clearly a little angry. He looked at the pig, who continued to shovel more food into his mouth, and let out a deep sigh.

"I wouldn't quite say he was going to help you, boy. But can you remember a man called Judas in the story of the Last Supper?"

"Yes, sir." the boy said. "He betrayed Jesus."

"Good, that's right," said the wolf. "And Pontius Pilate, can you remember him?"

"Yes, mister." He took a sharp intake of breath. "He was the Roman who killed Jesus."

For a moment the child wondered if giving the correct answers in this bizarre form of quiz would be the key to his escape.

The man in the wolf mask nodded as he forked a morsel of meat into his mouth. The boy looked on as he chewed, glancing at the pig occasionally. The pig man had now cleared his plate and looked on eagerly in the direction of the wolf, as if waiting for an instruction.

But he waited. He waited patiently until the wolf finished his meal, arranged his knife and fork neatly in the middle of the plate, and removed his paper napkin from his collar, using it to dab at the corners of his mouth.

"The Last Supper," he said, as he looked at the pig and pointed to him. "That's Judas over there, the betrayer." He poked himself in the chest. "And me?" He laughed out loud. "I'm Pontius Pilate, the executioner, if you like."

A broad grin spread across his face below the mask. The boy was confused.

"And me?" the boy said. "What about me?"

"You," said the wolf. "You are the chosen one."

"Jesus?" the boy questioned.

"That's right, boy… you can play the part of Jesus."

Wolf turned to the pig. "It's time."

"Yeah, boy, it's time." Pig got excited and burst into a serious of grunts and squeals.

The wolf glared at the pig in disgust. "Stop!"

Pig instantly fell silent. The wolf slowly looked between them.

"I've had enough of this fucking charade." The obvious Southern drawl had gone.

A few hours later, the wolf man pulled his white van over on the remote road and got out. It was his practice to drive at least forty-five minutes to and from his lair. This was not only to make sure he was not being followed by anyone, but also to make his guests believe they were farther away from the designated pick up and drop off points, in case they tried to find their way back and turn up uninvited. He opened the rear doors and stared silently at his blindfolded passenger, who sat on an upturned crate in the corner, twitching nervously. His travelling companion was his guest from earlier, the one who had been wearing the pig mask.

"Get out," the wolf ordered.

Pig man stood up cautiously until his head made contact with the roof of the vehicle, then stooped a little, and edged his way to the back of the van. When he reached the open doors he sat down and cautiously dangled his legs out of the van. As soon as his feet made contact with the road surface he pushed himself up, swaying slightly as he regained his balance. "Can I take this blindfold off now?" He pointed to the material covering his eyes.

"No." The wolf smacked his hand down, causing him to stumble backwards into the seated position in the back of the vehicle.

"W-w-w-what happens now?" he asked, as the wolf pulled him back to his feet. The nervousness in his voice made him sound quite pathetic.

Wolf leaned in as close as possible to whisper in his ear. "We never see each other again. That's how this works." He quickly moved around the trembling man to close the door.

"Oh. Okay." Pig nodded, beads of sweat on his forehead staining the material of the blindfold as he nervously moved his head around, as if trying to track the mysterious figure. The double clunk sound of the van doors closing behind him made him jump; he had obviously misjudged his attempt at following the wolf using only his hearing.

"When you can't hear the engine," Wolf whispered only millimeters away from the pig's face, "take the blindfold off. Not a moment before. Do you understand?"

"Y-y-yes," he stuttered.

The aggressor nodded to himself. Satisfied his instructions had been absorbed, he got in the van and pulled away without turning the lights on. This was another one of his rituals; he couldn't afford to have one of his guests removing their blindfolds and seeing the number plate as he drove away. His tracks had to be covered, and nothing left to chance. That was what made his operation so appealing to the people he dealt with. The security of complete anonymity was the nature of his business.

He watched the pitiful figure get smaller and smaller in the rearview mirror as he drove into the darkness until he could no longer see him. Then, and only then, could he turn the lights on and go and complete his part of the covenant.

***

The isolated cabin was illuminated by the returning van. The headlights briefly reflected in the windows, sending a beam of white light sweeping across the surrounding swamp. The wolf exited the vehicle and stopped outside the front door. He stood motionless, looking around, listening to the natural, eerie sounds of the swamp. A few minutes passed before he was content there could be no one around in such an isolated place at that hour of the morning. He entered quickly, locking the door behind him.

Inside, he cleared the dining table of the dishes that had been left earlier that night, and removed the record from the player and delicately put it back in the cover before returning it to its rightful place on the shelf. Pleased that the place had been restored to the way it was before his guests had arrived, he turned the lights off in each room as he walked through the building until he reached the solid metal door. He paused and put his ear on the door, listened for a few seconds, then opened it.

Wolf stood in the doorway, his figure casting an elongated shadow deep into the room, and stared at the naked, lifeless body of the boy lying face down on the table. The only visible signs of the hellish ordeal the youngster had been through were the hand-shaped bruises on his neck where the wolf's grip had been so tight, five vertebrae had been crushed.

The menacing figure stepped through the doorway, allowing the light from the outside room to completely fill the inner chamber. He circled the table a few times before removing the restraints from the victim's hands and feet.

The wolf was tired. It had been a long night, and there wasn't much time left before the sun would rise, shedding new light on the outside world. He gently wrapped a white sheet around the body, lifted the boy in his arms, and carried him through the darkness of the building to the front door, where he stopped and lowered the body enough so he could unlock and open it.

The sounds of the swamp's creatures immediately filled the cabin. Again the wolf stood in the doorway, listening. After a few moments he stepped outside and walked towards the jetty.

Stepping into the old wooden rowboat that was moored at the end of the pier while carrying a body had become second nature to him; he had done it many times before. He placed the body at the bow, then sat on the wooden seat and calmly rowed towards the middle of the swamp until he was happy he was at the point where the dark, murky water was at its deepest.

He sat looking at the body, making sure there were no signs of life. He didn't want that, at all. He had to be one hundred percent certain, so he uncovered the boy's face. For a brief moment he thought he saw a tear running down the left cheek. He was mistaken; a trick of the light. Not wanting to prolong the moment any longer, he lifted the boy into his arms and gently lowered the body into the cold, black, inky water.

"Didn't your parents ever tell you not to go with strangers?" He spoke in a calming but slightly patronizing voice.

He stared at the body as it was slowly submerged into the darkness of the water below, never to be seen again.

Chapter 2

Andy Cooper rolled over to look at the clock on the nightstand. Through squinted eyes he focused on the time: 6:56 a.m. He rolled back over and placed his arm around Kim, his loving wife.

"Four minutes before it goes off," he informed her.

"Mmmm." She smiled and snuggled into his chest.

This was a routine he'd gotten into. He liked to just lie there, feeling the warmth of her pressed against him, knowing the alarm was about to go off but not wanting to wake up completely. Sometimes he tried to count the seconds in his head to see if he could predict the exact moment when the peace would be shattered. But not that morning; that morning he lay there, enjoying the serenity of being semi-consciousness. He knew the next four minutes would be over too quickly, so he pushed his head harder into the pillow.

Was it really Monday morning already? His weekend had been an enjoyable few days. On Saturday the couple had taken Jen, their teenage daughter, to Universal Studio's theme park. Despite his complaining, he actually loved the place. If truth be told, he loved all theme parks. He wouldn't let anyone know that he was really a child at heart, although he suspected his wife might already know. Then, on Sunday the small family unit had hung out at the house. He had done a few chores around the place before an impromptu afternoon BBQ. That evening he had run a couple of errands before returning home with pizza. All in all, it had been a pretty good weekend. He was starting to wonder how many more weekends he would be able to have like that before his daughter would deem it "too geeky" to spend time with her parents on the weekend.

Beep, beep, beep, beep.

There it was. That annoying sound that he hated so much. He reached out and hit the snooze button without opening his eyes.

"I'll start the coffee." She yawned as she got out of bed and put her robe on.

"Thanks, babe," he said, and continued to lie there, enjoying a moment's silence.

At thirty-eight years old, Andy had forced himself into this morning regimen after joining the police force, following in his father's footsteps. *It's a discipline that comes with the job*, his father told him. *Get used to it,* which he did, with surprising ease.

With those words of wisdom resonating in his head he opened his eyes, stretched his body, got out of bed, and made his way to the bathroom to shower. By the time he came back to the bedroom the curtains had been opened, flooding the room with bright Florida sunshine. He dressed in his usual white shirt, tie, and trousers, and went to the kitchen to get breakfast. He found his wife pouring the much-needed kick-start to the day, the morning coffee.

"Do you want breakfast, honey?" she asked, without turning away from the coffee machine.

"No thanks, babe. I'm meeting Maria at Coop's." He looked around the breakfast room. "Where's Jen?"

"She's still in bed," she answered, and passed him a mug of piping-hot coffee.

"What?" His agitation was apparent. "She does know she starts work with Chris today, doesn't she?"

Kim immediately turned round and raised her hands,

gesturing for him to calm down. "Honey, it's okay, I'll get her there on time."

"Maybe so." He started towards their daughter's bedroom. "But she needs to be awake before she gets there." He reached the door and knocked twice. "Jen, come on."

"Go away, it's too early!" a muffled voice shouted from inside.

He huffed and opened the door, slightly vexed. "Jen, get up. You've got to be at Uncle Chris's office at 9:00 a.m."

"Dad!" his offspring protested, and pulled her duvet over her head.

"Get up, young lady," he insisted.

"But, Dad, it's school break!" she argued.

"Yes, and you're going to spend it working." He paused for a second and changed his tone to try and diffuse any argument that may be arising. Then, he tentatively took a few steps into her room. "Look, Uncle Chris has gone out of his way to give you this chance. Not everyone has the opportunity to get this kind of experience for free, *and* get paid for it."

"Other kids get to enjoy their summer vacation, but not me!" she snapped and sat up.

"You'll thank me for this in a few years." He wasn't going to back down.

"But—" she persisted.

"I'm not going through this again, Jen. Now get dressed and be ready to leave as soon as possible," he ordered, and left the room, closing the door behind him before his daughter could answer him back.

"You're so fucking anal," she muttered under her breath, but loud enough so that her father could hear her.

"Clock's ticking, Jen!" he shouted back, as he walked

into the master bedroom where Kim was choosing her clothes for the day. "That went well."

"Why, what happened?" she asked, placing a blouse on the bed.

"Apparently I'm 'fucking anal'." He gestured quote marks, two fingers on each hand.

She sighed and dropped her shoulders, as if she was exhausted. "Oh no, I can't cope with you two arguing all the time."

Seeing she wasn't in the mood for another confrontation, he gently grabbed the lapels of her robe and pulled her towards him. "Come on, honey. I just want her to have a chance when she leaves school. And if it means spending time gaining experience now, then I can put up with a little bit of teenage attitude."

She snuggled into his chest. "I know, but she does need to spend some time with her friends."

"Yeah, you're probably right." He kissed her on the forehead, placing his hands on her shoulders and held her away from him, looking her up and down. "Did I mention you're looking mighty fine this morning?"

"In this robe? Don't change the subject." She looked at him with great cynicism.

"Would I do that?" He sheepishly smiled. "I'm just paying my stunning wife a compliment."

She carried on getting her clothes ready while he went to the bedside drawer and got out his hip holster and clipped it to the right-hand side of his belt. He then retrieved his gun, clipped the magazine into place, and holstered it. Finally, he clipped his police badge to the left side of his belt.

"I've got to get going, honey. Make sure she gets there on time," he pleaded, as he grabbed her round the waist to kiss her good-bye.

"I will," she assured him. "And stop worrying about her, she'll be fine."

A peck on the lips from her husband brought a smile to Kim's face.

"I know," he said, and gave her a cheeky pat on the backside, grabbed his jacket, and walked to the front door with her following close behind.

"Good-bye, Jen!" he shouted over his shoulder, and stopped when he heard her bedroom door open.

"Go to hell!" she shouted, and slammed the door closed.

That wasn't the response he expected. "Love you too, sweetie!" He shrugged and winked at his distraught-looking wife.

As he made his way to the car with his jacket slung over his shoulder, he spotted his ever-annoying neighbor from across the street waving at him.

"Morning, Jeff," he said through a forced smile.

"Morning, Andy." The over-enthusiastic neighbor waved.

The detective smiled to himself as he remembered overhearing his neighbor confiding in one of his guests at a recent BBQ he was hosting, fantasizing about being the cop across the street with the hot wife and loving daughter. At the time it had vexed him, but on reflection, he was quite flattered at the fact that someone else wanted to be him.

"How are you today?" Jeff continued. "Are you ready to haul ass on the bad guys?

"I'm fine today, Jeff. Always ready for what the criminal community has to throw at me." He smiled broadly at him as he opened the rear door and hung his jacket on the hook inside before quickly glancing at his watch. "Got to go, I'm running a bit late."

"Oh, okay. You have a good day." He awkwardly waved.

The detective couldn't help noticing that his neighbor looked a bit rejected at his lack of enthusiasm to stop and chat longer.

"You too, Jeff," he said as he got in the car, closed the door, and looked in the rearview mirror. The sight of Jeff returning to his front door reassured him that it was safe to leave without him having to stop while his neighbor leaned through the window aimlessly chatting about nothing. So he started the car, reversed out of the driveway, and headed off to meet his partner at the diner.

Twenty minutes later, after negotiating the increasing early-morning traffic, he pulled the car into the parking lot of Coop's Diner. He parked next to a few squad cars and made his way towards the entrance. The sound of a car entering the parking lot caught his attention. He knew by the reckless way the car was being driven it could only have been his partner, Maria Hernandez.

Maria swung her car into the nearest available space and got out.

"Morning, Detective Cooper!" she shouted.

"Morning, Detective Hernandez." He smiled back.

He held the door to the diner open for her and as she passed, he caught the distinct smell of stale alcohol. Andy made no effort to hide his disappointment in his partner.

"Good night last night?" he said sarcastically.

Maria stopped and turned around, embarrassed, and she tried to change the subject.

"You've changed something." She proceeded to look him up and down. "Your hair; you got your hair cut." She huffed. “Jeez, Andy, you look more like Chris than ever now.”

Before he could challenge her about the alcohol, she turned away and continued into the diner, leaving him looking slightly incredulous.

Detective Maria Hernandez was fast becoming the talk of the force due to her hard-drinking lifestyle, which surprisingly didn’t seem to interfere with her detective skills. At twenty-nine she was one of the youngest female officers to make detective in the Orlando PD, but her off-duty activities we’re becoming more and more disturbing.

Once inside the diner, they walked past a table of uniformed officers eating breakfast. One of the officers nudged the other sitting next to him and nodded at the female detective. He immediately sat up straight with a confident smile.

“Hey, Buenos Días, María. Fancy a few shots? Muchas fiestas chica?” he said playfully.

She stopped and looked him straight in the eye. “If it wasn’t for this mother of all hangovers you’d be hearing two shots right now, one for each fucking testicle.”

She continued towards her seat as the other uniformed officers showed their appreciation for her witty comeback with a round of applause.

To save face, the officer grabbed her by the forearm. “Don’t be like that, Maria.”

Without breaking her stride, she snatched her arm away. “It’s Detective Hernandez, and go fuck yourself.” She scowled and left the officer red-faced as he was verbally ridiculed by his eating buddies.

Maria didn’t stop at their usual seats, she just carried on walking.

“Hey, where are you going?” her partner inquired.

“Order me a coffee while I go to the john, will you?” she

answered over her shoulder, and continued towards the bathroom.

"Okay, but the ladies room is that way." Andy pointed in the opposite direction.

She stopped and looked at the "Gents" sign above the door she was about to go through, then looked back at the puzzled male detective.

"Yeah, I know." She paused for a moment, as if contemplating heading towards the other bathroom. "What the hell." She shrugged. "It's all the same to me." Then disappeared into the bathroom.

Andy smiled to himself and sat in his usual seat at the counter. He was about to shout his coffee order when he spied one of the uniformed cops approaching him.

"Andy, can I have quick word?" the uniformed cop asked nervously.

The detective turned his seat sideways to the counter so he could face the officer. "Sure, what's up?"

The uniformed cop moved in closer and lowered his voice to a whisper. "Last night, we were called to a disturbance at O'Leary's Bar."

"Oh yeah?" The ranking officer looked bemused, but knew exactly what was coming next.

"Yeah, when we got there we found Detective Hernandez drinking shot after shot after shot." The uniformed cop looked around to see if anyone had heard what he said.

Andy looked him in the eye. "Was she on duty?"

The cop looked more nervous. "No, but—"

"What's the problem then?" He cut him off.

The cop took another look round. "The problem was the two guys she laid out on the floor."

"Oh." This got his attention, and he looked around towards the bathroom door to see if Maria was coming. The uniformed cop did the same.

Satisfied the coast was clear, the uniformed cop continued. "Apparently they had a dispute about the best recipe for fajitas."

Andy sat back in his seat, smiling. "You're kidding me, right?"

The cop looked a little agitated. "No. Look, Andy, if she carries on like this we're going to have to arrest her and she'll lose her badge. We managed to talk the guys out of pressing charges, but as you know, this isn't the first time this has happened. Maybe you can have a word."

"Well, she does know her fajitas; but you're right," Andy conceded, and stopped smiling. "Leave it with me; I'll have a word."

The cop looked relieved and smiled before taking the opportunity to have a slight dig at the female detective. He checked the bathroom door again, then got closer to Andy.

"We've also heard she likes a corn dog or two." He sniggered and looked at the other cops for approval.

"Oh yeah?" He put his hand on the cop's shoulder. "I'll be sure to send her over when she comes back so you can ask her yourself."

The cop stopped sniggering immediately. "No, you don't need to do that." He shifted uncomfortably and leaned further in. "Seriously, as a friend, you need to put a chain on that puppy."

"Yeah, thanks for the heads-up." Andy nodded in appreciation and the cop made a hasty retreat.

His attention was drawn to Beth, the waitress, who had finished cleaning the tables. She waved her hand as if fanning her face as she approached, and gave him a quick peck on the cheek as she squeezed past him to get behind the counter.

"Morning, Andy, what can I get for you?" she asked, in her usual cheerful manner. Beth had been the only waitress at the diner since Coop took over, and a faithful one at that. Something the retired cop was only too keen to point out if anyone had a complaint about the service there.

"Good morning. Can I get two large coffees please?" He strained to see into the kitchen. "Is he in?"

"Who? Coop? He's in the back. I'll get him for you." She poked her head through the serving hatch to the kitchen. "Coop, Andy's here!" Then she produced two large mugs from under the counter and placed them in front of the waiting detective. She reached to the coffee machine, retrieved the half-full jug and filled the two mugs. "Enjoy. Coop will be through in a moment." She smiled and continued with her chores.

Coop entered through the swinging door leading to kitchen. "Morning, son."

"Morning, Dad. You okay?" He greeted his father with a quick hug over the counter.

"Fine, you?" He nodded as he positioned himself in front of his son and leaned on the counter.

"All's good with me," he replied.

"You still getting grief from Jennifer?" Coop smirked.

"Oh, you've heard," Andy sighed.

"I'm an ex-cop and her grandfather; of course I've heard." He winked as he straightened up.

The younger of the pair went into defensive mode. "I'm just thinking of her future. I don't want her to end up in a dead-end job or even worse, a cop."

"Hey, being a cop is not a bad thing," his father reminded him. "It's done right by you and me so far."

"Here it comes." Andy sat back in his chair, getting agitated at the thought of another lecture.

Coop looked around and leaned back on the counter, placing his hand gently on Andy's shoulder in an attempt to reason with his son. "Look, all I'm saying is that Jennifer needs to grow in her own time. Making her spend summer vacation working is taking away some of the time she should be spending with friends." He removed his hand. "I know you mean well, and I kind of agree with you, but you need to cut her some slack. Give her some downtime from the classroom before you lock her into a boardroom—"

"Parental guidance from you? Really?" he sarcastically cut his father off.

"Hey." He raised his hands as if surrendering. "I'm only saying."

Andy took a breath and calmed down. "I'm sorry, Pops, just feeling a bit stressed over the whole thing."

"Stressed over what thing?" Maria asked.

The sudden appearance of Maria returning from the bathroom surprised Andy. He signaled to his father not to say anything. She looked at them suspiciously, then shrugged her shoulders and sat on the stool next to her partner. She took one look at her coffee and stood on the footrest of her stool, enabling her to lean over the counter and fumble around on the shelf underneath.

Coop slapped her hand away as she scowled at him. She sat down in her seat, glaring at the retired cop as he retrieved a bottle of Tylenol and placed it on the counter in front of her.

"Is that what you're looking for?" He smiled.

"You're a lifesaver." She snatched at the bottle.

"What else can I get for the best-looking detective in the state of Florida?" he asked.

"A reason to live." She popped the lid off the bottle and dropped two tablets into the palm of her hand. "Failing that, just keep the coffee coming." She launched the tablets into the back of her throat and washed them down with a large gulp of coffee.

"That bad, huh?" He turned to his offspring and smiled. "How about you, son, what can I get for you?"

Andy glanced sideways at his partner and winked. "I'll have one of your finest Southwestern omelets." Then he gave his father a devilish nod and risked another glance at Maria. "Don't overdo the egg base; leave it nice and runny, just the way I like it."

The female detective glared at him. "Seriously? How can you eat that shit at this time of the morning?"

"Because I wasn't out drinking till six this morning," he quipped.

"Six fifteen," she said sarcastically.

"You need to slow down there, girlie," Coop interjected. "Burning it at both ends doesn't agree with this job. Take it from an old pro."

"Thanks for the advice, old man." She took another slurp of coffee. "Spare me the lecture though."

Andy gave him a sarcastic smile. "Seems like your advice isn't welcome anywhere today. It's falling on deaf ears."

"Hey." He raised his hands in defense as before. "I'm only saying." Then he took a step back, reached under the counter, pulled out a notepad and started scribbling. "Andy, can you do me a favor?" He ripped the page out of the pad and passed it to his son. "This kid from the neighborhood went missing the other night. His mom asked me if I could get someone to chase it up. If you get a chance, will you look into it for me?"

"Yeah, sure." He took the note, had a quick look at the

name, and put it in his pocket.

“He’s probably holed up at one of his friends’ places getting bombed, but you never know.” Coop reached for a few dirty cups and started to head back into the kitchen.

“Thank fuck I’ve got no kids,” Maria huffed. “Nothing but a pain in the ass.”

“You should speak to Andy about that.” He shouted over his shoulder, “I’ll go get your breakfast, son.”

Before Andy could reply, his father had disappeared into the kitchen. “Yeah, thanks for that, Dad. You should listen to the old man,” he said, turning to his partner. “You’re going to burn out before you’re thirty if you don’t slow down.”

“Bite me,” she sniped back as she extended her right arm and raised her middle finger within inches of his face.

Chapter 3

Andy and Maria arrived at police headquarters and made their way towards the homicide department. They passed Lieutenant Jack Regan, who stopped in his tracks as the smell of stale alcohol filled the air. The lieutenant turned to face the detectives.

"Cooper!" he shouted. "A word in my office, please. Alone."

The detectives turned around as their superior disappeared into his office.

"Uh oh." She shrugged. "Sounds like he's on one of his power trips again."

"I'm guessing he can smell stale alcohol." He looked at her and raised his eyebrows.

"What?" She sniffed her jacket. Her face flushed with embarrassment.

"Here." Andy passed Maria the piece of paper Coop had given him earlier. "You go and look into this while I see what he wants."

Andy started towards Regan's office. "Freshen up while you're at it. You stink like you've been more than a little intimate with a bottle of Jack Daniels."

She scowled at him as he disappeared into the lieutenant's office.

Regan had sat behind his desk by the time Andy entered the office. "Close the door and sit down," he ordered. The detective closed the door and slowly sat in the chair opposite. "What's going on, Cooper?"

"Boss?" he said, with a puzzled look on his face.

"Hernandez." He leaned forward on his desk. "She looks like shit, and smells like she's been sleeping under a bridge."

"That is a very real possibility, sir." He laughed.

"It's not good. It doesn't look good for the department, and it certainly doesn't look good on you." He pointed at Andy. "She's your partner, for Christ's sake."

"She might look like a sack of shit but…" He shifted in his seat and cleared his throat. "It doesn't interfere with her work."

"Maybe so, but for how long?" Regan opened a file on the desk and started flicking through its contents. "How many times have we seen this behavior from her?"

"She's just letting off a little steam—"

"Well, that steam could result in this department being brought down if she compromises an investigation due to her nocturnal activities!" he snapped.

"I hear what you're saying, boss." The detective tried to calm his superior down. "I'll have a word."

"Make it soon." Regan closed the file and sat back in his chair.

Andy noted the name on the cover of the file: Maria Hernandez. The lieutenant had obviously been checking up on his partner.

"Now, down to business." Regan interlaced his fingers across his chest. "How is the investigation going with these gangbangers shooting up my town?"

"Slow, boss. You know how it is with these guys; they smell a cop and they clam up." Andy shrugged. "They like to deal with things their way."

Regan paused for a moment. "Step it up. We need to draw a line under this before some innocent bystander gets caught in the crossfire." He smiled and leaned forward onto the desk. "Although, if it were left to me, I'd round them all up, stick 'em in a room and let them shoot it out till they were all dead."

The detective smiled at that thought. "Failing that, boss, what do you suggest?"

"Let's get a few more cars and uniforms on the streets." He opened another file and started writing some notes. "Make more of a police presence, to reassure the public we're making some effort." He closed the file and handed it to Andy. "You head it up for me."

Andy got up and took the file. "Will do."

"One more thing." The lieutenant stopped him as he reached the door. "Leave Hernandez in the office. Let her sober up away from the public eye." He opened another file and buried his head in it. "That's all," he added, without taking his attention away from the paperwork he was looking through.

Andy left the office and headed for his desk.

"What's happening?" His partner met him on the way.

He hesitated and took a breath. "Maria, I've got some bad news for you."

"Uh oh, what's Lieutenant Buzzcut been crying about now?"

"Lieutenant Regan wants you to lay off the sauce." He dropped the file on his desk and faced her.

"Yeah? What's new? I thought you said bad news."

"I did." He braced himself. "He wants you on desk duty till you sober up."

"Desk duty!" Visibly agitated, she pushed past him. "Are you serious? I'm going to rip him—"

He managed to grab her by the wrist. "Maria, he's right." She turned back to him with an incredulous look. "Look, you're a good cop, but you're drinking your career into the toilet," he pleaded with her. "Take this as a warning. If he was the real bastard that you think he is, he could have taken your badge by now. But he's giving you some breathing space." She looked back towards the lieutenant's office. "Why don't you stay here and look into that missing kid for Coop? He'd probably appreciate a quick response on it," he reasoned with her as he released his grip.

"Yeah, perhaps you're right," she conceded, and sat behind her desk.

"Okay." Andy breathed a sigh of relief. "Let me know later how it goes." He started walking towards the briefing room.

"Hey, whoa, slow down." She stood up. "Where are you going?"

"I've got to head up the investigation on the gang-related shootings." He didn't stop. "Regan wants more cars and uniforms on the street to act as a deterrent."

"Great. You get to kick ass and I get to kiss ass." She sat down, deflated.

Andy stopped as he felt the vibrations from his cell phone. He retrieved it out of his pocket, checked the text message, and put it back in his pocket as he turned back to his dejected partner. "I've got to go. Drink coffee, keep your head down, and I'll catch you later."

He ignored her despondent look and continued to the briefing room. "I want all detectives in the briefing room now!" he shouted to the other officers in the office.

Maria sat helplessly as she watched her partner enter the briefing room, followed by the other detectives. For the next hour she tried to peek through the briefing room window to see what Andy was organizing. Finally, the door opened, and all the detectives left and headed off in different directions.

"How are you feeling?" Andy showed his concern as he approached her.

"How do you think I'm feeling?" she snapped. "My ass is going numb. But on the upside, I'm getting the feeling back in my head."

His attention was grabbed when the phone on his desk rang. He immediately picked up the receiver.

"Cooper . . . When . . . ? Get some units there, ASAP. I'm on my way." He slammed the phone down. "Gotta go."

"What's going on?"

"There's been another gang shooting," he informed her, as he wrote the address down on a notepad.

Maria jumped up and opened the drawer of her desk to retrieve her weapon. "Now that's what I'm talking about."

"Hey, where are you going?" He put his hand up to stop her.

"We've got a shooting to go and investigate." Her enthusiasm was apparent as she holstered her weapon.

"Not you," he protested. "You stay here until the lieutenant thinks you're fit enough to be back among the public."

"You're shitting me, right?" Her eagerness quickly turned to anger.

"No." He moved closer to her. "Listen, if it looks like I'm going to need backup on this, I'll call the lieutenant and tell him I need you. That way you get out of here without pissing him off."

She frowned and looked like she was considering what he was offering. Then, her frown dissipated. "Okay, thanks. You'd better call, though."

"And you'd better sort your shit out so we don't get into this situation again." He turned to leave. "Use this time to look into that thing for Coop."

She sat back down behind her desk, looked around at the now-empty office, and started to look on her computer for any information leading to the missing kid.

***

In a district on the south side of downtown Orlando

known as Little Haiti, Andy Cooper turned the corner and immediately saw the police tape. The scene had been cordoned off not long after the incident the night before, but had been left until the forensics team had arrived to process the evidence. He pulled the car up as close as possible and watched the swarm of activity for a moment. Forensics, in their white suits and face masks, were busy collecting anything that would tell them what happened. Uniformed officers were canvassing local resident's houses for witnesses.

He took a last gasp of the cool air inside the car before getting out into the already stifling Florida heat. He decided it was too hot for his jacket, so he left it in the car. As he approached the tape, a uniformed officer lifted it for him to pass.

"What have we got here?" he asked, surveying the scene in more detail.

The uniformed officer led him around the scene by pointing. "One male adult here, one male adult and one male minor in the doorway to the house. CSI's doing their thing now, sir."

"There's a kid involved?" He looked shocked.

"Yes, sir." The uniformed cop pointed back to the house. "Just inside the doorway over there."

"Damn." He shook his head in disbelief and walked over to the first body, which lay half on the sidewalk and half on the street. Next to the body there was a .38 Smith & Wesson and a red baseball cap, which had rolled a few feet away after the victim had fallen. There was a forensics officer taking a few photos.

The detective watched as forensics rolled the body over, took more photos, and did a search of the body. The only thing found was a mobile phone in his jacket pocket. "Any ID on this guy?" Andy asked.

The CSI placed the cell phone in a clear plastic bag and

sealed it up before placing it in his evidence box. "None whatsoever, Detective. I'm going to print him now and run them through our database."

"Let me know when you have something." Andy looked up at the house. The front door was open, and he could see the body of a white Haitian male slumped in the doorway. He looked back to the forensics guy. "Are we clear to go in the house?"

"We're all done in there, sir, just waiting for you to give the go-ahead to remove the bodies."

"Thanks." Andy gradually made his way up the steps to the front door. As he ascended, he stopped as the body of what he guessed to be a twelve- to thirteen-year-old boy came into view. Andy sighed and continued. A uniformed officer stepped into the doorway from inside the house.

"Detective Cooper. Homicide." He moved his forearm away, allowing the officer to see his badge. "And you are . . . " He looked at the name badge on the uniform. "Wilson. Okay, Wilson, what are we looking at?"

Wilson took out his notepad. "We haven't got much at the moment, sir. This place belongs to Ilyas Surin." He pointed at the body of the male adult. "A known Haitian drug dealer and gangbanger. Lives here with," he pointed to the body of the boy, "his thirteen-year-old-son."

"Well, that accounts for these two." The detective nodded to the body outside. "I suppose we'll have to wait for forensics to come up with something on the guy in the street. Are we lucky enough to have any witnesses?"

"We're canvassing the neighborhood right now, but you know what it's like around here." Wilson pointed to a house directly across the street. "The old woman over there told us she heard shouting, looked out of the window, and saw a guy on the sidewalk either pointing or waving a gun at Surin. The kid appeared and tried to drag him back into the house. Surin's gun went off. The guy outside started firing like a maniac and tried to run. Surin fired one last shot and dropped our mystery guest."

Andy quickly surveyed the scene again. "Hmm… What's your take on this?"

The uniformed officer pondered for a second. "If I was a betting man, I'd put money on this being a straightforward drug deal gone wrong, sir."

"Yeah, that's what I'm thinking." Andy patted Wilson on the shoulder. "Finish up and get the reports to me as soon as possible."

"Yes, sir."

Andy descended the steps and took a long, hard look at the body on the sidewalk before getting back in his car and heading back to the station.

***

Maria jumped up and ran towards Andy when he entered the office. "Thanks for the call, partner."

"What?" he asked, caught off guard.

"You were supposed to call the lieutenant and get me out of here!" she pushed.

He held his hands up in protest. "No. What I said was if I couldn't handle it I would call the lieutenant and tell him I needed you."

"And?"

"It was a straightforward drug deal gone wrong." He put his hands down and continued to his desk. "Only tragic thing about it was a young kid got caught in the crossfire."

"A member of the public?" She was visibly disturbed by the news.

"No." He sighed as he sat down. "The drug dealer's son. Looks like he was trying to drag his dad back into the house and got hit."

"Shit!" she gasped, as she sat opposite him. "Do we

know who the shooter is?"

"Was. And no. No wallet or ID on him." He shook his head and started to fill out a report sheet. "Forensics is running his prints at the moment. We've got a witness whose version of events supports the theory of a drug deal gone wrong."

"Sounds boring." She suddenly sat upright and looked excited. "You should see what I've got."

"Anything interesting?" He didn't look up from his work.

"Hell yeah!" She picked a small pile of papers up. "This kid that Coop asked us to look into. He's not the first. I checked with missing persons. And they told me that, get this, there have been eighteen twelve- to thirteen-year-old boys gone missing in the last two months."

Andy instantly looked up at her. "How many?"

"Eighteen," she emphasized. "In two months."

"Any leads?" he quizzed.

She shook her head. "None, all still open cases."

"There's no bodies?"

"No." She passed a few pieces of paper to him. "There's an average of one hundred kids that go missing in the whole state of Florida every month, which I am quite alarmed at. But, for eighteen to go missing in this area alone in such a short time isn't right."

"Yeah, you're probably right." He nodded. "But, without any bodies, it's not our department." He passed the papers back to her. "You're going to have to throw it back to missing persons."

"What?" She snatched the papers back. "Are you fucking serious? Have you seen these figures? This could be huge—"

"Look, Maria." He cut her short. "We've got enough on at the moment with all these gang-related shootings. And as you know, I'm temporarily without a partner—"

"These aren't numbers that someone has plucked out of the air," she persisted. "According to the National Center for Missing and Exploited Children, the state of Florida ranks third in the nation for reported missing persons, most of whom are children—"

"Enough!" he shouted. "I hear what you're saying, but like I said, we're homicide, not missing persons. The last thing we need is to be taking the workload from another department. We're already stretched." He returned to his paperwork. "And if you don't sort your shit out, we're going to be down another detective permanently."

Maria looked at the paperwork in her hands and reluctantly put it in a folder. "Okay, I'll tell Coop we checked it out and it's being dealt with by the relevant department."

"Now you're thinking." Andy signed the sheet he was filling in and put it in a file. "Come on, I'll give you a lift back to the diner for your car. I've just got to stop at Chris's on the way."

"I still can't believe you made Jen go to work there," she jibed.

"It's for her own good!" he snapped back at her.

"Well, I think—" she began.

He held his hand aloft and cut her short. "You are in no position to think, let alone advise me on my daughter."

She defensively held her hands up. "Hey, in the words of Coop, I'm only saying."

"Well, if you keep only saying, you'll be walking from here." He stood up. "Come on, let's get out of here."

She stood up and watched him head towards the elevators. With his back turned away from her she quickly picked up the folder containing the information she had found, and hid it under her jacket before rushing to catch up with him.

Chapter 4

The traffic was already stacked up as the detectives drove out from the parking lot of police HQ. It took over twenty minutes to drive the normal ten minute-journey but, eventually, they pulled up outside AppTech, the software company owned by Andy's identical twin brother, Chris. They entered the futuristic, glass-fronted building and were immediately greeted by the head of security, John Sinclair, at the reception desk.

"Good afternoon, Detectives Cooper and Hernandez." He smiled as he tapped on the keyboard in front of him and opened the visitor's book on the counter for them to sign in. "How are we today?"

"Fine thanks, John," the male detective responded, and signed the book. "How are you?"

"Everything is fine." He checked the signature, then slid the book to the female detective, who signed it without hesitation. "Would you like me to buzz you up?"

"Is Chris in his office?" Andy asked.

"Just a moment, I'll check," he said, punching a few digits on the keyboard to bring up the security camera in his employer's office. "Yes, he's at his desk," he confirmed, and reached under the counter to pass two 'Visitors' badges to the guests. "Just pin these on and I'll let you through. Don't forget to hand them back when you leave."

He located the release button under the desk and buzzed them through the turnstile before escorting them to the elevators, where he pressed the call button for them.

"I'll see you shortly." He gave a semi-bow before he returned to his desk.

"Jeez, he's a strange one," Maria said, looking at her partner as the glorified receptionist walked away.

"You think everyone is a bit strange." He leaned closer to her. "Although this time I think you might be right. Flashlight cops always are, aren't they?" He winked.

"You got that right. I'll tell you who else I don't like—concierges!" She shook her head. "Something very wrong about those guys. They all seem to know too much about everything."

"You really are a trusting soul, aren't you?" He laughed.

The ding from the elevator signaled its arrival. The doors opened, and as they boarded, he reached out and pressed the number five button.

"Mark my words, those guys will run the world one day. Wouldn't surprise me if they're behind the new world order." She stood back and watched the numbers over the door ascend as they travelled to the corresponding floor.

Her partner looked at her, observing her whole demeanor. Sometimes he was unsure if she was drunk, winding him up or, if she was that weird that thoughts like that were in her head.

"Concierges? Running the world?" He looked incredulous.

"Oh yeah; always tip them well. You don't want to be on the wrong side of them when they make their move," she said as a matter of fact.

Ding. The elevator had arrived at their chosen level and the doors slid open. She exited without looking at her partner, who stood open-mouthed.

"You are one seriously fucked up individual," he said as he snapped out of his daze and followed her down the corridor.

He had almost caught up to her when his phone rang. Stopping to retrieve it from his pocket, he studied the screen for a moment. "You go ahead!" he called after her. "I've got to take this."

She waved a hand over her shoulder in acknowledgement and was a few feet away from Chris's office when she heard a scream coming from inside. She turned to call after her partner but he had gone. Taking a moment to assess the situation, she drew her weapon and was edging her way to the office door when she heard the distinctive voice of Andy's daughter.

"Don't shoot, don't shoot!" Jen sounded scared.

The detective looked down the corridor, hoping to see her partner coming, but he was nowhere to be seen. "No time to wait," she muttered under her breath.

She edged closer to the door, getting herself in position, and strained to hear what was happening in there. She had been to the office several times before, which gave the advantage of knowing the layout of the place.

A quick glance down the corridor confirmed there was no sign of her partner. She took a deep breath and burst through the door, instantly scanning the room to assess the situation.

Andy's brother, Chris, was sitting behind his desk, with Jen immediately behind him. Both had their arms raised above their heads. A young unidentified male wearing a red baseball cap stood between Maria and the suspected hostages, pointing what appeared to be a rifle at them. In one swift motion she was on him, violently grabbing him from behind and putting him into a headlock as she thrust her weapon under his chin.

"Drop the gun and don't you fucking move," she snarled through clenched teeth.

"Maria! No!" Jen protested, waving her hands.

"Maria, it's okay." Chris jumped from his chair. "Please put the gun down," he pleaded.

The female detective tried to comprehend the situation as she looked over to the software executive and noticed he was smiling. *That is not the reaction of someone who has had a firearm pointed at them,* she thought. Bemused by his unperturbed attitude, she glanced at the weapon the suspect was holding. It only took the briefest of moments to realize it was a toy gun, a Nerf gun.

The suspect had begun to tremble, which resulted in his employer erupting into a fit of laughter. "Please, please, don't shoot. I'm putting the gun down. It's only a toy," he pleaded.

"What the fuck is going on here?" Maria said.

The door to the office suddenly flew open behind them. Andy entered, pointing his weapon at the female detective and her prisoner. He must have heard the confrontation from the corridor. The look of anguish on his face when he saw his daughter quickly turned to relief.

"Maria, put the gun down. He works here." Andy ordered. "It's okay, that's Martin Miller, he works here."

She glanced over her shoulder at her partner, then back to the detainee before releasing her grip and re-engaging the safety on her firearm. Miller fell to the floor, breathing heavily.

"Would someone please tell me what the fuck is going on here?" Maria exclaimed, with adrenalin still coursing through her veins.

They were all startled by the sight of Sinclair rushing into the office, slightly out of breath. "Is everything all right, Mr. Cooper?"

"Fine, John," the software executive assured him. "Just a little misunderstanding."

Jen moved from behind her uncle and came around the desk. "We're role playing for a new app, Maria."

"What?" She looked confused.

Chris chuckled loudly and adjusted his thick rimmed glasses which had slid down his nose. "This is brilliant; we should be catching this on camera!"

"We are, Mr. Cooper," the security chief informed him. "Here, let me show you." He edged his way over to Chris's desk, keeping an eye on the female detective. "It's all been captured on the security system. That's how I knew there was a problem."

"Really?" His employer looked at Maria and pointed at the man shaking on the floor. "In that case, shoot him."

The color drained instantly from Miller's face. "No!" he screamed, holding his hand up, sending Chris into uncontrollable laughter which, in turn, sent Jen into a giggling fit.

Maria failed to see the funny side of the situation. "You guys are fucking freaky." She frowned at them.

"This is how we work here." The executive composed himself. "Someone comes up with an idea for an app, and we role play it to see if it works. And I have to say, after today," he smiled broadly, "I think it's safe to say, this one is a winner."

Andy put his weapon back in its holster and sighed as he nodded to his partner, who looked at Miller's trousers and noticed he had wet himself.

"Oh." She awkwardly indicated to the damp patch. "Sorry about that. You might want to go and change."

Miller looked down and noticed his predicament, then glanced at Jen. Embarrassed, he sprang to his feet and rushed out of the office.

"Oh, that is just priceless." Chris laughed out loud. "Although, I don't think we can actually put that in an app, can we?" He directed the question at Sinclair.

"As much as I'd love to say yes," he shrugged, "I don't think the lawyers would be happy."

"I'm joking." He laughed and removed his glasses to wipe his tear filled eyes with a handkerchief he had produced from his pocket. "Although *America's Funniest Home Videos* might be interested in seeing the footage."

Andy put his hands on his hips in disbelief. "So, I send

my daughter here to learn, and this is what you do, play games?"

"Calm down, bro," his sibling said. "This is how the whole process works. You want her to learn everything, don't you?"

"Yes, but I didn't expect it to be like a kindergarten." He fumed. "What type of app is this anyway?"

"Oh, it's just a first person shoot 'em up," Chris explained. "We have a client who manufactures laser guns for the leisure industry, and wants to incorporate an app that registers when the laser makes contact with the screen. A mobile Laser Quest, so to speak."

"So you just stand around playing games all day?" the detective persisted.

"Dad!" Jen stepped in. "It's not like that. I've been learning all sorts of things today."

"Oh yeah, like what?" He turned to his daughter.

"Look, I'll show you," she said with great enthusiasm, and got her notebook out to show him. "Martin showed me the basic binary codes for starting a program off. Then Uncle Chris took me to lunch—"

"Lunch?!" He cut her off and turned his anger back to his brother. "Do you take all your staff to lunch?"

"Only the special ones." He winked at his niece.

"I told you, no preferential treatment." He pointed his finger at him. "How is she ever going to learn?"

"Andy, stop." Chris waved his hands in a calming motion. "I promise I won't give her any more preferential treatment."

"Fine!" Jen snapped, thrusting her notebook back its folder. "Thanks, Dad. You just can't help yourself, can you?" She stormed out of the office.

Her uncle signaled to Sinclair to follow her, which he did, leaving Maria looking slightly awkward in the presence of the two feuding brothers.

"I'll go get her in the car." Maria broke the silence. "We'll wait for you there." She moved swiftly towards the door. "See you later, Chris."

"Erm . . . before you go. Maria." He stopped her before she could get out of the door. "I'm throwing a BBQ at my house this weekend for family, friends, and AppTech employees. We've just acquired a rival software company in a takeover so we're celebrating. Everyone is invited, so you're more than welcome to come along."

"Thanks, Chris." She nodded. "I'll see you there."

"Excellent." He beamed. "Oh, one more thing. There's likely to be a few water pistols there, so leave your gun at home. Don't want you getting overzealous again." He laughed again.

"Very fucking funny!" She gave him a sarcastic look and left.

Chris walked over to his brother and placed his arm around his shoulder. "Come on, bro, Jen needs a bit of fun in her life," he said as he started leading him out of the office.

"I know," Andy sighed.

"Wanting the best for her is only natural." He continued in what was bordering on being patronizing. "Listen, I'll treat Jen the same as the other staff during the week, and this weekend I'll treat her like any uncle should treat his only niece." They stopped walking and he turned to face his brother, placing both hands on his shoulders. "Come to the BBQ, and make sure you and Kim are ready to relax. Stay over and we can share a few brewskis."

"Yeah, you're right." He exhaled in defeat. He knew Chris had made a fortune out of his powers of persuasion in the boardroom, as well as the ability to control a situation to his advantage. "I could do with some stress relief. Thanks, bro. Promise me though; Jen's the same as the other staff."

"I promise. Now go and make it up with her, and make sure she's here bright and breezy in the morning." He guided Andy out of the door. "Tell her she's got a lot to learn from Uncle Chris. Now give me a hug."

Andy succumbed to his brother's positive influence and they hugged. "Thanks, man. See you in the morning." He patted him on the back and walked towards the lift.

"Will do." He smiled as he watched his brother leave. "Hey, give Kim a kiss for me."

Andy waved his hand in acknowledgement and disappeared into the waiting elevator.

Satisfied his brother had gone, Chris quickly glanced at his watch. When he saw the time he fumbled to retrieve his cell phone from his inside jacket pocket, dialed a number and returned to his office while waiting for the call to connect. "Franco… How far away are you? Andy is just leaving the building. Take your time; if he sees you here he'll get suspicious… Okay, Sinclair will let you straight through. See you in fifteen minutes."

He disconnected the call, sat behind his desk, and waited for his mysterious guest to arrive.

Chapter 5

The sun had disappeared below the horizon, sending the secluded cabin into relative darkness. Inside, the wolf placed another record on the player and listened intently as the words of Ella Fitzgerald singing "Every Time We Say Good-bye" drifted through the cabin, sending him into another trance.

Every time we say good-bye, I die a little,
Every time we say good-bye, I wonder why a little,
Why the gods above me, who must be in the know.
Think so little of me, they allow you to go.

He stood looking towards the ceiling and dared to sway in time with the music as he let his mind drift.

"No, please no!" the boy remonstrated as the man grabbed him by the upper arm and dragged him away.

"You know the rules, and you know the punishment," the man scolded.

Before he knew it the boy was face down on a table, his naked buttocks exposed, unable to escape due to the vice-like grip on the back of his neck from the man holding him down. He screamed and pleaded for forgiveness, but to no avail. The punishment and the pain continued to the point where the boy passed out.

The wolf suddenly snapped out of his dream-like state by the sound of the needle clicking at the end of the record.

Disappointed that he had missed one of his favorite songs, he pressed the replay button and continued with the ritual of preparing a meal before sitting with his guests.

The boy's whole body trembled with fear as he sat naked from the waist up, apart from the red cape draped over his shoulders, just staring at his food. Sitting opposite was a man wearing the evil pig mask worn by previous guests.

"Come on, boy, eat your food," pig man grunted.

The wolf glared at the pig with a feeling of utter contempt, then turned his attention to the boy. "Do you read the Bible, boy?" he asked in his thick Southern accent.

"Excuse me, sir?" the boy whimpered.

"You heard the man; do you read the Bible, boy?" Pig squealed again.

"Shut up!" the wolf snapped, clearly vexed by the pig interrupting his moment. "Eat your food."

The pig shrugged away slightly and carried on eating.

"Do you read the Bible?" the host addressed the boy again.

"No," he replied.

"Well, that's the end of that conversation. Eat up," Wolf ordered, and proceeded to consume his food in silence. When he had finally finished, he placed his knife and fork neatly on his plate, took his napkin and dabbed each corner of his mouth before throwing it back on the table, then looked between his two guests. "Let's do this," he growled.

There's no love song finer
But how strange the change from major to minor
Every time we say good-bye.

***

Sometime later, the wolf watched as the lifeless body of the boy drifted into the dark, inky-black water of the swamp. Satisfied his deed had been done, he turned the rowboat towards the cabin and casually rowed.

Chapter 6

The next morning, Andy and Maria were sitting at their usual places in Coop's Diner, drinking coffee and waiting for their breakfast to be delivered. Andy's face lit up at the sight of his father exiting the kitchen with his Southwestern omelet. He didn't hesitate; as soon as the dish hit the counter, he dug in.

"Mmm… Just like Dad used to make," he sarcastically mumbled between mouthfuls.

"Very funny," Coop replied, and turned his attention to Maria. "So, have you shot any Nerf gun-wielding nerds today, Detective?"

"Hilarious. Is everyone a fucking comedian today? I wonder where you heard about that?" she sniped, and glanced in her partner's direction.

"Hey, don't look at me." He held his hands up as if surrendering.

His father laughed and patted her on the shoulder. "Yeah, I have two sons, remember?"

"I take it Chris had great delight in telling you about our, errr . . ." the male detective placed two fingers under his chin mimicking, a gun, "hostage situation."

Both father and son started to laugh at her actions. She swung her seat sideways to face Andy.

"Yeah, right, you guys keep laughing it up and I'll shoot you right here, right now." She swung her seat back to face the counter. "Nerf gun or not."

Coop composed himself. "I'd love to have seen it. That guy is a bit of a weird one." He moved forward to lean on the counter. "Tell me, did he really piss himself?"

"Like a newborn baby. Hey, he probably drew mud as

well." The broad smile on her face signaled she was joining in with the fun, and all three laughed out loud.

Andy stopped laughing and cleared his throat. "Speaking of pissing, I need to go to the bathroom."

They both watched him disappear into the bathroom., Coop waited a few seconds then he leaned in closely.

"What did you want to talk about?" he whispered.

She quickly glanced around the diner to see if anyone was close enough to hear what she was about to tell him. "Yeah, listen. I checked with missing persons, and he's not the only kid that's gone missing lately." She spoke softly.

"Really?" He sounded shocked. "Tell me more; how many?"

"There's been eighteen kids between twelve and thirteen years old gone missing from the local area in the last two months. All male. And they're only the ones that have been reported missing." The volume of her voice got louder as she conveyed the information.

"Jeez, that's a lot of kids." He nodded towards the bathroom. "What's Andy doing about it?"

"He told me to throw it back to missing persons." She shook her head.

"Why?" His anger was apparent.

"He figures our hands are tied. If there are no bodies, it's nothing to do with homicide. Besides," she shrugged, "we have a lot going on with these gang-related shootings. Bodies take priority."

"Yeah, sounds right for the modern police force. They'd rather spend time looking at bodies that aren't going anywhere than looking for kids that are possibly alive. Bureaucratic BS." He slammed his clenched fist on the counter, which caught the attention of some of the diners. He looked at the concerned parties and waved a hand in the air to signify everything was all right, then continued his conversation. "It winds me up. I remember when being a cop wasn't about meeting targets, it was about solving crimes and protecting the public." He poked his finger on the counter to emphasis his point. "To protect and serve."

"Times have changed, Coop. It's all about the paperwork and trying to not get sued by the people we're trying to help" The sarcasm in her tone was unmistakable.

He rubbed his chin as if in deep thought. "Maybe I could have a quick look into it myself."

She suddenly sat up with the enthusiasm of a puppy waiting for a stick to be thrown. "Ooh. Is this one of the famous Coop hunches?"

"Well, I don't think you need to be Sherlock Holmes to work out something's not right here." He looked around the diner at all the customers. "Besides, it will give me a break from all this for a little while."

"So what's the plan, and how can I help?" She began to get louder again as she spoke.

"Well, I'm not sure yet, but taking a look at those files would be a good place to start, I would imagine. Is there any chance you could—"

"Consider it done." She cut him off mid-sentence. "I'll get them to you within the next day or two. Anything else you need?"

"Yeah, just one thing." He checked the bathroom door again. "For the sake of family harmony, why don't we keep this between you and me?" He winked.

"I'm with you." She acknowledged with a wink.

The sight of the bathroom door opening and Andy returning made Coop straighten up and reach for the coffee pot. "Can I get you guys a refill?" He nodded towards coffee mugs on the counter.

Maria shoved her mug away. "You got anything stronger?"

"Seriously?" Andy quickly checked his watch as he returned to his seat. "It's nine thirty in the morning. We'll have some more coffee please, Dad."

Coop grinned at Maria as he retrieved the pot from the machine and proceeded to fill his son's mug. Before he could make any attempt to fill Maria's mug, she reached out and put her hand over it to stop him.

Andy gently nudged her. "You should drink more coffee."

"That shit gives me the shakes," she said, pointing towards the coffee jug.

"Opposed to the shit you were drinking till what time this morning?" her partner goaded.

"Not now," she protested.

The gentle jibing was interrupted by Coop. "Did you two get your invite to Chris' thing this Saturday?

"Yep," Andy acknowledged. "You and Ma going?

"Hell yeah, we'll be there. Your brother sure knows how to throw a good BBQ," he said. "Will you be making an appearance, Maria?"

"Well, I haven't thought of an excuse to get out of it yet so yes, I will probably be there," she answered, with just a hint of sarcasm in her tone.

"Well, if you do come, just remember that this is a friendly, family BBQ." The male detective paused and shared a grin with his father before continuing. "There will probably be water pistols a-plenty, so in the interest of public safety, it's probably best you leave your service weapon at home."

The father and son burst into laughter.

"You guys really are too fucking funny. Have you been working on this double act for long?" She looked annoyed, but quickly joined in with the laughter.

Andy swallowed another mouthful of coffee. “Come on, let’s get to the office. See you later, Dad.”

He threw a twenty dollar bill on the counter and made his way to the door. The female detective quickly jumped up and followed.

“See you later, Coop.” She gave the retired cop a knowing nod and tapped the side of her nose.

“You guys have a good day.” He smiled. “Take it easy out there.”

Andy waved his hand in the air to signal his acknowledgement as Maria pushed past him to open the door for him. As they exited the diner she glanced back at Coop; both nodded in recognition of their little secret.

Chapter 7

The aroma of what would undoubtedly be the best cuts of meat on the grill, along with children's laughter and adult conversation filled the afternoon air. Chris Cooper didn't do anything in halves, and at a large banquet-style table the Cooper family, along with all the AppTech employees, sat around eating steaks, drinking champagne, and generally having a good time.

Everyone was enjoying the full amenities that his multi-million-dollar mansion had to offer. Andy was distracted from a conversation with his wife by the sight of Maria's car being driven somewhat erratically up the long, sweeping driveway leading from the secluded road to his brother's designated parking area. Instinctively he knew that his partner was going to be the worse for wear. He swiftly excused himself from the table and went to head her off. He reached her vehicle as she stumbled out of it and grabbed her by the upper arm to lead her away from the gathering.

"What the hell are you doing?" he chastised his partner.

"What's the fucking problem now?" Maria slurred, and snatched her arm away from his grip.

He tried desperately to keep his rising anger in check. "The problem is, this is a family-friendly BBQ and you turn up driving like Mario Andretti. To top that, you're wasted."

"Fuck you! What's a party without a few drinks?" she sneered. "Besides, if I have to spend an afternoon with kids, there is no fucking way I'm doing it sober." She started laughing at her own little quip then turned away, aimlessly looking for the bar.

Andy spotted her service weapon in the holster clipped

to her belt behind her back. He immediately grabbed her arm again and swung her round. "I told you not to bring that here," he growled through gritted teeth and unclipped the weapon.

"Orlando Police Officers are required to carry their firearms at all times." She tried to grab at the gun but he swiftly moved it behind his back. "I'm only following strict policies," she persisted.

"Those policies are kind of null and void if you're too hammered to shoot straight due to alcohol intake." He turned her around to face the other guests, who were unaware of their minor confrontation, and pointed. "Now, unless someone is smuggling any water guns in their swimsuits, I think we'll be okay," he said, mocking her.

"You are fucking hilarious at times. But right now is not one of those moments." She scoffed at him, and continued to look around. "If you want me I'll be by the complimentarys. Where are they?"

He let out a heavy sigh in frustration. "If you mean the bar, it's over that way. Please take it easy."

She focused on the bar and started walking towards it, then suddenly stopped and turned back to her vexed partner. "Can I have my gun back?"

He brought the weapon into view. "I'll tell you what. I'll keep hold of this, and you can have it back on Monday when we get to the office."

"Fuck you." She gave him a disgusted look before continuing on her quest for refreshment.

Andy, seething with anger, looked around at the partygoers to see if anyone had witnessed their encounter. The guests appeared to be completely oblivious. He paused for a moment, and decided the best place to put the weapon would be in the glove box of his car. As he walked towards his vehicle he heard the familiar voice of his brother over his shoulder.

"Is everything all right, bro?" Chris inquired.

"Yeah, everything is fine. Just a minor disagreement with that ever-happy partner of mine." Holding her gun aloft, he continued, "I'm securing this in my car so we don't have a repeat of the incident in your office."

"Oh, now that is a shame; that's the only reason I invited her," he said. "Listen, I have a state-of-the-art security system and one of the best safes money can buy. Why don't you put Rambo's geek worrier in there?"

The detective took a second to consider his brother's offer. "Okay, that seems a better idea. At least I know there's no way she can get to it in there."

The brothers walked towards the house. Once inside the sprawling mansion, they ambled through the marble-floored entryway towards Chris's home office, where he keyed in a passcode on an electronic keypad positioned on the wall next to the door. The red LED light switched to green and the door unlocked. The brothers entered, and the homeowner walked straight to a six foot by three foot mirror that was mounted on the wall, then pressed a hidden switch located behind the frame. The mirror glided to one side to reveal the door to his safe.

Andy surveyed the office, taking in his brother's many academic certificates adorning the walls, along with the trophies for various business achievements and numerous family photographs. He centered his attention on a particular photo and moved in for a closer look. The photo had been taken many years earlier, depicting the two brothers with Coop at the family fishing lodge. Andy smiled.

"You know, it's been years since we were there," he said, pointing at the photo. "We should do it again."

Chris entered a code on the keypad. The electronic beep and the sound of the locking mechanism disengaging indicated the safe was opening. Two more beeps and the safe door opened slightly. He walked over to join his sibling to contemplate the photo for a few moments. "You're right, we should." He tapped the photo. "Just the three of us, like old times. The old man would love that. They were great days."

"Maybe we could take a ride up there in that new Porsche I saw in the garage?" Andy nudged his brother.

"Oh. You saw that?" His face beamed with excitement. "Isn't she a beauty? Miller bought one and kept telling me how great it was, I have to admit, it is an awesome machine."

The look on his brother's face reminded Andy of their childhood Christmas mornings. Chris had always been far more excited than he was about opening their presents while he had favored the occasion itself, the family time together, as opposed to the materialistic giving and receiving of the gifts. There they were, years later, and the same sentiment was still at play.

He was nonetheless highly impressed by what his twin brother had achieved. The house, the cars, the big boy's toys and Amber, the model-esque trophy wife. "You know, bro, I'm incredibly proud of what you've achieved and the lifestyle you lead." There was no hint of jealousy as he spoke; he was just stating facts. He let his gaze wander around the office, allowing his mind to drift.

Andy dropped down a gear and the Porsche growled as he pushed the accelerator pedal hard to the floor. His adrenalin coursed through his veins as he swerved in and out between the traffic. He started laughing and looked to Amber in the passenger seat. Her hair flowed behind her like a flag in a strong wind whipping back and forth. Her loose-fitting blouse revealed her oversized, perfectly formed artificial breasts every now and then when the wind caught the collar.

Andy took his right hand off the steering wheel and gently placed it on Amber's exposed thigh. She gasped and looked at him before joining him in laughter.

They continued laughing as he continued to swerve in and out of the traffic.

"Andy… Andy…. hey, are you listening?" Chris snapped him out of his daydream by nudging him with his shoulder.

"Oh, sorry." He cleared his throat. "I, err… was just remembering the good times we had with Dad at the cabin."

"I was saying, I would trade all of this with you tomorrow." The entrepreneur waved his hand around, pointing at various things in the office. "Sure I have all the toys, but there is still a large void in my life. This is all…" He paused and looked skywards. It was obvious to Andy that his brother was searching for the right word to use. "Façade!" he suddenly shouted. "A fucking façade! It's just all smoke and mirrors."

"You all right, dude?" Andy looked puzzled, and noticed his brother's eyes had reddened as tears began to form.

"Not really." Chris sat on the leather couch. "I just keep overcompensating for us not having kids." He paused to take a breath. "I keep telling myself that this latest purchase will make up for it and, being honest, it will—for a short while." A tear started to roll down his cheek as he continued. "Then you suddenly realize it's just a car, or just a new TV, then it isn't long before the emptiness returns."

Andy was momentarily speechless. The bond between the identical twin brothers was strong, but Chris's bluntness had taken him a little by surprise. They had broached this subject before but not in such a direct manner. He had known for some time that they were trying for children, but he had no idea just how much it was affecting his sibling. He regained his composure and offered some reassuring words.

"Come on, buddy, it will happen eventually. You just

have to stick with it." He sat next to him, placing an arm around his shoulder. He saw an opportunity to inject a bit of levity into the conversation.

"Let's face it." He continued patting him on the back. "All the practicing will be fun. And another thing; when you do become a dad, you'll have to say good-bye to that Porsche in favor of a station wagon. Believe me, brother, when you get woken up at 5:00 a.m. to change a diaper, you'll be longing for these days of relative freedom."

A smile emerged on his brother's face. "Yeah, you're right. I guess I just must have had more beers than I thought. Sorry for offloading like that. I didn't realize I needed to get that out." He used the back of his hand to wipe the tear from his cheek.

"No need to apologize, bud," he comforted him. "You know I'm always here for you." He looked up at the photo, then back to Chris. "Hey, listen, we should definitely make that trip. And let's do it sooner rather than later."

"That's the best idea you have ever had." Chris inhaled sharply, waited a moment, and let the air out slowly. He slapped his hands on his knees, and stood up quickly. "Come on, let's get back to the party."

Andy stood and looked closely at his brother's face, his reddened, glazed eyes were the only indication he had been crying. "I mean it, bro, it will happen for you." He wrapped his arms around him to give him a caring hug. "I love you, man."

Chris patted him on the back. "Thanks, man."

"Come on, let's put this in the safe and get back out there." He waved Maria's weapon slightly aloft and walked over to the safe, placed the gun inside, and closed the door. "Does this lock automatically?"

"Just push the red button and it does the rest for you," Chris replied.

Andy pushed the red button and listened as the mechanisms locked into place. He returned to his sibling, put his arm around his shoulder and together, they left the office to re-join the party.

As they passed through the large double French doors leading into the garden, his attention was immediately drawn towards Maria, who was at the bar. He thought about going over to her, but he'd had enough of problem solving for one day, so decided instead to head back to the table.

***

"Scotch!" Maria ordered in her usual abrupt manner when she'd had a few drinks. She placed one hand on the bar as she swayed backwards and steadied herself.

The bartender shot her a look of annoyance. "Certainly, madam, would you like ice?"

"Ice?" Maria looked sternly at the bartender. "Are you serious? Did I ask for it diluted? No, I don't want fucking ice," she growled.

As the bartender turned to open the bottle of Scotch, Coop approached the bar and sidled up next to Maria

"Hey, pretty lady, do you come here often?" Coop asked jokingly.

"No, with the service in this place I would be a teetotaler." She glared at the bartender, who was still struggling to open the fresh bottle.

"By the way," she said, turning to face the retired cop, "I have those files in the car that you asked for."

He glanced around to see if anyone had overheard and moved closer. "Maria! Keep your voice down! This is meant to be just between us two, remember?"

"Shit! Sorry, old man, that's my bad." She looked around at the guests. "I don't think anyone heard me anyway. Except for numb nuts here," she slurred, pointing at the flustered bartender. "And he will be a corpse in the next three minutes if my Scotch is not in front of me."

"I find it hard to believe that people think you have no charm." Coop grinned at her.

"I know, old man; it's a complete mystery to me too. Anyway…" She looked around and lowered her voice. "What do you want me to do with these files?"

"Swing by the diner in the morning." He winked at her. "We'll have a look through them together. Make it early, before the place gets busy."

"Early? On a Sunday? Come on, Coop, give me a break!" She looked totally bewildered by his suggestion as the bartender placed her Scotch on the bar in front of her.

"Should I order my next drink now to give you time to get it ready?" She sneered at him with more than a hint of sarcasm. The bartender didn't answer; he went to the other end of the bar and busied himself.

"You wanted in on this, and if you really want to work with me then we do it *my* way." He emphasized, "And my way means I need you clean and sober."

"Come on, old man, cut me some slack; it's the weekend!" she pleaded.

"Those are the rules, take them or leave them. If you're in, be at the diner at 8:00 a.m. tomorrow. If not, drop the files off at your convenience, and I'll do it on my own." His stern look told her there was no point in arguing with him.

"All right, pops, you've got yourself a date. See you in the morning." She picked up her Scotch and got up to walk away. After a couple of steps she stopped and turned back to him. "In the meantime, do you have any objections to me enjoying whatever it is this little soiree has to offer?"

"Well, that's what I intend to do, so as long as you're at the diner for eight and you're in a fit state to do some proper police work . . . " He nodded at the drink in her hand. "Then what you do in between now and then is of no concern to me."

Coop grabbed his drink and walked to re-join his family; she followed closely behind. As they approached the table, Chris looked up and smiled. "What have you two been up to?" He inquired.

His father spoke before Maria had a chance to open her mouth. "Would you believe it Andrew, she's been bugging me for the secret of my Southwestern omelet recipe."

The inebriated female detective looked more confused than everyone else at the table as she tried to keep up with his story. The brothers glanced incredulously at each other then directed their attention back to their father.

"Erm, dad," Chris smirked, "I'm Christopher and that young man over there is your other son, Andrew."

His brother gave him a sarcastic wave of acknowledgement. "Hi. It's me."

The elder looked from one to the other; obviously trying to work out which of his sons was Christopher. "Well put your damn glasses on boy," he said in an attempt to redeem himself, "how the hell are we supposed to tell you two apart otherwise?"

"Are you wearing contacts bro?" Andy asked, his brother nodded. "I would have thought with all this money you have floating round you would have at least afforded to have your eyes lasered instead of…"

"I'm thinking of it." His brother cut him off.

"Oh good Lord, if you get that done I'll never be able to distinguish between you guys." Their father said sarcastically.

"Like I was saying," the detective continued, "if you spent your money on things that mattered…"

"Are you jealous of one or two little luxuries I've afforded myself?" The executive said modestly.

"Little luxuries!" Andy exclaimed looking at the main

house and around the expansive garden. "All I'm saying brother is, can a new Porsche make sure your health is intact or even more so, your families health. Priorities." He tapped his index finger on the table as if making his point then sat back in his seat leaving the party in an awkward silence.

"I don't think your eyesight really matters in this case Andy." Coop broke the silence. "Your vision is gonna be pretty much blurred if you drive a car that goes naught to sixty in a few seconds."

The partygoers began to laugh at the dry wit of the elder man causing the detective to concede.

"Very funny dad." He smiled. "Hang on, Maria Hernandez wants a recipe for something that isn't a cocktail? No, come on… seriously. What were you talking about over there?"

"He is being serious," she interjected. "I'm all about the omelets; can't get enough of those bad boys."

Andy's skepticism was apparent as he looked at her. "Do you even own a frying pan?" he huffed, and decided not to push the point. "I just don't see you as a domestic goddess. Dirty Harry with a spatula?" Then putting on his best Clint Eastwood voice he went on to mock her. "I know what you're thinking; did I use three eggs or four eggs? Question is, you feeling lucky, punk? Go ahead, punk, make my omelet."

Everyone at the table laughed at Andy's impression, and even though she was the brunt of his joke, Maria began to laugh too. "Fuck you, partner." She smiled as she fired off the comment.

As the laughter died down, Maria looked around the table and devilishly decided to sit next to Miller.

Meanwhile, Coop sat himself next to Chris, who was at the head of the table. "So, son, what is this party in honor of, anyway?" he inquired.

"Well, thanks mainly to Miller down there," he pointed at his employee, who held his hand up and gave a shy wave, "I've just acquired a new business for an unbelievably low price, and now AppTech stands to make a very tidy sum from the deal. So," he smiled broadly, "I thought I would spread the wealth with the people who made it all possible." He gestured with his hands at everyone in attendance.

"That's my boy." His proud father patted him on the shoulder. "Smart, and never forgets the people who are important to him."

"You taught me well, Dad." He looked at his father. "You always said—"

"A king is only as good as his legions. Treat them well and you will reign for a long time," the elder interjected.

"In that case," Chris rose from his seat, his glass of champagne in his hand, "I propose a toast." He raised his glass. "To my legions; my trustworthy staff, my loving family, and to the future of AppTech. Thank you, everybody. Cheers."

Everybody raised their glass and joined in the toast. Then one by one they began to applaud their king, who sat down and, to Andy, he seemed to revel in the adoration.

For a while the party continued. The conversation flowed, as did the alcohol and food. Andy noticed the Scotch had really taken hold of Maria; she was getting audibly louder and more obnoxious as she held court with the AppTech staff, reciting her version of events in the boss's office a few days earlier.

"So, I've got my Glock pressed up against his temple, begging this fucker to move so I can put a hole in him." As she spoke she was slapping Miller on the knee to emphasize who she was referring to. "Next thing I know he's pissed himself right in front of the boss."

She laughed while the programmer looked very

uncomfortable; his face had gone rosy red with embarrassment. Every guest's attention was now drawn to the conversation.

"All right, Maria, it's time to let it go. Leave the kid alone now," Andy chastised his partner.

"It's all right, he knows I'm only joking. Don't you, piss quick," she said as she again patted him on the knee.

Miller moved awkwardly and grimaced. It was clear to everyone that he was not in any way enjoying the moment. An awkward silence cloaked the event until Chris came to the rescue. He signaled to the waiter.

"Can we get refills on the champagne all around?" he ordered in an almost regal tone. The waiter hurried away. "Right, can someone please turn the music up? This is meant to be a party!" He ordered cheerfully. "Maria, how about you and I get the dancing started?"

He stood up and walked towards her, extending his hand in her direction. Andy watched the scene unfold; bracing himself for the tirade of abuse that he was sure would flow from her mouth. Instead, what happened next shocked everyone.

She reached out and grabbed Chris's hand. Then, with her other hand, she grabbed Miller and dragged him along. As they made their way to the poolside, which was the designated dancing area, the embarrassed programmer kept looking over his shoulder. The nervous look of uncertainty on his face brought a few stifled laughs from the people still seated.

Coop stood up and took Catherine's hand. "Come on, they say there's safety in numbers. Let's go keep that poor boy safe."

Gradually, everyone stood up and made their way to the dance area. Even Andy got up after a little gentle coaxing from Kim.

The party continued into the early evening, until one by one they all left.

Chapter 8

Coop sat alone at the end of the counter in the diner, reading the morning paper. He looked around at the early-morning customers, who were mostly cops refueling their caffeine levels. He looked at his watch; eight thirty-four.

"Damn you, woman, punctuality is a virtue," he muttered to himself.

He looked out of the window and saw the familiar sight of Maria's vehicle pulling into the parking lot and intently watched her slender frame extract itself from the masculine muscle car. She began to make her way into the diner but suddenly stopped after a few steps, cursed, and slapped herself on the side of the head. Then she turned and headed back to the vehicle. Once there she impatiently opened the door, leaned in, and retrieved a pile of files. As she closed the door, a few documents fluttered to ground as they fell out of the folder. Cursing again, she quickly scooped them up and walked briskly into the diner. As soon as she entered she caught sight of Coop waving her over.

"I said eight a.m.!" he snapped. "Not eight thirty-six, not seven forty-nine; eight a.m." He banged his finger down onto the table to emphasize his point.

"Not entirely my fault, old timer," she said in a dismissive tone. "Those fucking do-gooder sons of yours are to blame." He looked quizzically at her as she continued. "Get this. Apparently, I was far too wasted to drive home last night after the party, so they made me take a cab. As they had already taken my gun, I couldn't protest too much." He grinned as she started getting louder and her tone became more aggressive. "So, at seven a.m. I ordered a cab to go back and pick up my vehicle and service weapon from Chris's house," she ranted. "Seven fifteen the rat bastard turned up and proceeds to drive like Miss Daisy. I eventually got to Chris's at about seven forty and was told by the maid that Mr. and Mrs. Cooper were still sleeping, and she does not have access to the safe. I did tell her who I was, but she point-blankly refused to get Chris. So I had to jump in the car and high-tail it over here."

Coop looked to be studying her; she was visibly agitated by retelling the tale. "So, it took you just under an hour to make a twenty-five-minute journey?" he inquired.

She erupted into full flow, her eyes growing larger as she raged on. "Not quite; we have our wonderful colleagues of the Florida Highway Patrol to thank for that. I was trying to make up time so I put the pedal to the metal and those fuckers caught me doing seventy-five; bastards." She pulled out her speeding ticket to show him.

He began laughing and gestured for her to sit down. She placed the files on the counter then sat down, while he signaled to Beth to bring two coffees. "Well, I'll let it slide just this once; but it's the first and last time, do you understand?" he said in a stern voice.

"Roger that. Do you know anyone at FHP who can get me out of this?" She waved the ticket at him.

"That's your problem. You sort it out." He nodded towards the files. "Let's get down to business. What have we got here?"

"These are the files on all of the kids that have gone missing in the last two months." She looked at him. "You must know someone at FHP; you know everyone."

He dismissed her last comment and nodded at the files once more. "So, does anything spring out at you?"

She took the top file, opened it up, and flicked through

until she found a paper that she had made notes on. "Nothing individually, but there is an average of 100 kids who go missing every month in the state of Florida." She paused and looked at him to see if he was taking the information in, then returned to the statistics on the paper. "However, according to these files, over the last two months there has been an average of thirty kids aged between ten and fifteen who've gone missing within a fifty-mile radius of here alone."

"Are you sure?" He looked directly at her. "That seems like an awful lot of kids to just disappear."

"That's just the tip of the iceberg. According to a paper published by the MCN—" "And the MCN is…?" he interrupted.

"The Missing Children's Network," she responded, as if he should have known that. "It's some charitable organization that puts out flyers in an attempt to locate runaways."

He nodded at her as if giving her permission to continue.

"Anyway, according to those guys, only twenty-one percent of missing kids get reported," she finished.

He looked thoughtful; it was as if he was trying to comprehend the scale of what she had told him. "So, let me make sure I'm clear on this. You're saying this figure of thirty kids could be as many as one hundred and fifty kids missing?" He looked genuinely shocked.

She held her hands up. "I'm not saying anything. I'm just telling you what I've learned." Her tone had a hint of smugness about it.

"That's a hell of a lot of kids. I can't believe that no alarm bells are ringing at the precinct." He paused to compose himself and looked around the diner.

A young family caught his attention; he watched them enjoying their breakfast. The baby, no older than two, was laughing as the dad made silly noises while the mother cradled the child in her arms. All three started laughing.

Coop turned back to Maria. "Well, I think we need to do some digging on this." He pointed to the young family. "We owe it to people like that to make sure they can let their kids play in a safe environment." He paused, then absently said, "One hundred and fifty kids a month; how is that even possible?" He shook his head in disbelief.

"I know, old man, it's fucking shocking. So, what are 'we' going to do about it?" she asked.

He looked thoughtful again. "I think the best plan of attack is for you to leave these files with me and let me go through them thoroughly, see if I can see something you might have missed." He placed his hand on top of the files. "Am I all right to hold onto these?"

"I had a feeling that's what you would want, so these are all copies. You can have them as long as you want, as long as nobody knows; fucking data protection." She grinned at him.

"All right. While I go through these, can you find out if there are any ongoing investigations on any of these cases? If so, find out the status of the investigation." He had switched to cop mode, and looked to be enjoying having something to get his teeth into, even something as unimaginable as this.

"It's going to take me a couple of days to chase this up, old man." She stopped and looked a little flustered, as if trying to find the courage to ask something.

He must have picked up on this unusual behavior. "Anything else?" he asked.

"Well, just one thing." For an instant she looked like a vulnerable girl, a look that was rare for her. She looked like she was summoning the courage to ask for something. Then, she retrieved the speeding ticket from her pocket and held it up in front of him. "Seriously, do you know anyone at FHP?"

He began laughing and snatched the ticket out of her

hand. "Leave it with me. I'll take care of it."

Maria stood up and kissed Coop on the cheek. "Thanks, old man. I'll get straight on this first thing. It's going to make things a little difficult as I have to be secretive, but I'll try my best." She pulled a five dollar bill from her pocket and threw it on the counter. "If that's all, I'm out of here. Sec you tomorrow." She smiled at him and turned to walk away but before she had taken three steps he called after her.

"Hey, Hernandez." She stopped and turned around. "That's some damn good police work you've done."

"Hell yeah, it is." She gave a beaming smile, turned towards the door and walked off.

Coop shook his head, laughing to himself; he watched her get into her vehicle and exit the parking lot before turning his attention back to the files. He chose the top file, opened it up, and began reading. He stopped when he saw the name at the top of the page.

Sergeant Simon Percival. He looked again in disbelief, then under his breath he muttered, "Son of a bitch."

Chapter 9

The atmosphere was less tense in the isolated cabin as the wolf decided which record he thought would be appropriate for the moment. He delicately let his finger touch the spine of every cover as he moved his hand from right to left along his prized vinyl collection, then suddenly stopped and moved back a few records to retrieve his choice. He perused the cover for a moment and gently slid the vinyl disc out, blew off any possible dust, and placed it on the player. With the push of a button, the arm mechanically moved across and lowered the needle onto the record. The sound of an acoustic guitar filled the cabin, followed by the haunting voice of the late Johnny Cash singing "Hurt."

I hurt myself today
To see if I still feel
I focus on the pain
The only thing that's real
The needle tears a hole
The old familiar sting
Try to kill it all away
But I remember everything

Wolf mouthed the words as he entered the kitchen, picked up two meals that had been prepared, and made his way into the dining area. He placed one meal in front of his guest, then seated himself opposite to him. His guest wore the usual pig mask and red baseball cap, and waited patiently for the host to sit before starting to eat.

"Do you like Johnny Cash?" Wolf asked.

"Take him or leave him," the guest nonchalantly replied before putting his cutlery down. "So, how does this work? What's with the masks and caps?"

Wolf put his cutlery down. "The masks are for safety. If you don't know who I am, you can't mistakenly identify me if something goes wrong and you are detained by the authorities."

The guest acknowledged the reasoning with a nod. "Good thinking. But you know who I am."

Wolf nodded. "You have been specially chosen because of your previous activities. Now, listen very carefully."

Wolf picked his cutlery up and proceeded to cut his steak into small pieces. "I will give you a description of the desired target. You will make contact and bring him to me. Then you will have the pleasure of whatever gets you off. After that you can leave."

"What about the kid?" The guest continued eating.

"You don't need to know what happens after you leave; just be certain that you will never see that kid again." Wolf put a piece of food in his mouth and stared at his guest. "Do you have a problem with that?"

The guest shifted in his seat. "No."

"Good." Wolf put his cutlery down again, wiped his mouth and stood up. "Would you like a drink with your food?"

"Do you have any beer?"

"Certainly." Wolf made his way into the kitchen, opened the fridge, grabbed a beer and returned to the dining area.

I wear this crown of thorns
Upon my liar's chair
Full of broken thoughts
I cannot repair
Beneath the stains of time
The feelings disappear

You are someone else
I am still right here

He placed the beer in front of his guest and returned to his seat. “Are you a religious man?”

“Take it or leave it.” The guest opened the beer and glugged half the bottle.

“You don’t really care for much, do you?” Wolf stabbed another piece of steak and put it in his mouth. He was losing patience with his guest.

“Are you not having a beer?” the guest quizzed.

“I don’t normally, but, seeing as this is a special occasion and we have come to an agreement about our little venture, I think I will join you.” Wolf stood and made his way to the kitchen. “You know, I thought you were the right guy when I read about you.” He raised his voice as he went into the kitchen so he could be heard.

“Oh yeah?” The guest was puzzled. “How did you read about me?”

The wolf returned with a beer in his hand. “I have a knack for gaining access to the police database. Don’t you just love computers? There’s a whole world of information at your fingertips.”

The guest looked impressed by the Wolf’s admission. “When we’ve finished with the kid, maybe you could help me out.”

“Really?” Wolf sat back in his chair and let his hands drop into his lap.

“Yeah, if you can hack into the police database, maybe you could erase all my records for me,” the guest said hopefully.

“Oh, I’m sure I could do that for you,” Wolf confidently responded.

“Now that’s what I’m talking about!” The guest dug into his food again.

"Please excuse me; I think I left something on in the kitchen." Wolf slowly walked past the guest, glaring at him as he shoveled the food into his mouth.

Once in the kitchen, wolf leaned against the sink for a moment. He took a sharp intake of breath and started back to the dining area. "You know, there's something you can do for me in return."

"Me? Help you?" The guest continued with his food. "How?"

Wolf walked briskly behind his guest. "You can help Detective Hernandez find me."

Before his guest could react, the wolf placed a gun onto the back of his head and fired a single shot into his skull. The force of the shot pushed the guest's head straight into his food, shattering the plate and sending his baseball cap flying across the table. The wolf stood back and watched as the pool of blood slowly spread across the table, and continued to mouth words to the song which was coming to the end.

I will let you down
I will make you hurt
If I could start again
A million miles away
I would keep myself
I would find a way

"Oh, and don't worry." Wolf stepped forward and bent down to whisper at the lifeless body. "I will erase all your records. *That's* the way this whole thing is going to work."

Chapter 10

Early on Monday morning Andy drove along, tapping his finger on the steering wheel in time to Lynyrd Skynyrd's "Sweet Home Alabama" while Maria sat beside him, looking out of the window. In the back seat, Jen sat looking at her phone and making exasperated sounds every so often as various messages came through.

Andy was enjoying the fact that he didn't need to make conversation, giving him the opportunity to listen to the soft rock station he had recently stumbled across on the radio, and had been his only pre-set station ever since. His moment of inward serenity was broken when his partner turned to look at him with a slightly vexed look.

"So, the first time ever I actually want some breakfast is the one day you decide to pick me up from home?" she said, with a hint of anger in her voice.

"Quit moaning. We need to drop Jen at the office, so this seemed the easiest solution," he said, dismissing her outburst. "Besides, you've missed breakfast for the last ten years. I don't think one more morning is going to kill you."

"It might not kill me, but I might kill you." She scowled, and formed the shape of a gun with her right hand, then dropped her thumb to indicate pulling the trigger.

"Oh, yeah, you might want a real one of those things." He pointed at the glove box. "Yours is in there. I swung by Chris's on the way and picked it up." He suddenly swerved to avoid a car that had stopped in the middle of traffic. "Damn tourists!" he shouted at the car and blasted the horn.

One of his pet peeves was the way tourists drove in

Orlando. Aside from the residents of every other state in America descending on the Sunshine State to see the famous house of the mouse, tourists from all over the world came to town, which made driving tedious, as far as he was concerned. Lost people paying more attention to the paper map supplied by the car rental companies than to the actual task of driving really bugged him.

"You know, they should pay more attention to the road. It's just plain dangerous, stopping like that for no reason," he stressed to his partner as he pointed out yet another example of bad driving.

Maria rolled her eyes; she ignored his usual Monday morning rant about the traffic problems in Orlando, and dove into the glove box to retrieve her treasured service weapon. Instinctively she dropped the clip out of the handle and examined the top bullet.

"Hmm…" She appeared perturbed.

"Something wrong?" He looked at the weapon.

She rolled the top bullet slightly with her thumb. "No. It's okay."

Before he could say anything else she quickly replaced the magazine, readied the chamber, set the safety on and holstered the weapon. "So, Jen." She turned to face the obviously displeased teenager still huffing at the messages on her cell phone. "How is this work thing going for you?"

Jen dropped her phone into her lap. "It's not as bad as I thought it was going to be. I'm mainly working with Martin. He's a fun guy to be around. Plus, Uncle Chris is cool, too. In fact, everyone has been really nice to me."

She smiled, then picked her phone up. But before she got a chance to look at the latest batch of messages that she had received, the female detective continued.

"Just be careful around that Miller guy; there's

something about him I just don't like," she said.

Andy, who rarely agreed with his partner, especially when she was advising his daughter, quickly jumped in on the conversation. "Listen to her, sweetie." He nodded in his partner's direction. "That's a good cop's instinct at work right there."

Maria looked to be taken aback at him agreeing with her. She looked at him for a second, then leaned over to purposely whisper loud enough for Jen to hear.

"You wish I had pulled the trigger the other day, don't you?" she joked.

"Oh… I'm sorry if I'm giving off that impression." He said this with heavy sarcasm in his voice.

"Dad!" his daughter exclaimed. "Martin is all right. He's a nice guy when you get to know him, and I'm learning lots of stuff from him."

"Martin is a geek, and I don't like him," he said, making eye contact with her in the rearview.

"I have to agree with your dad on this, Jen. There is something very 'off' with pee wee." The female detective jumped back in on the conversation.

"Thanks a lot, Maria. I thought you of all people would be on my side." Jen sat back into her seat with a pout on her face.

"I *am* on your side, kiddo. Hey, in the words of your grandpa . . ." She held her hands up to mock the retired cop's surrendering pose. "I'm only saying."

All three of them laughed at her impression of Coop. As the laughing subsided, Andy pulled into the AppTech parking lot. They exited the vehicle and made their way to main reception, where they were greeted by head of security, John Sinclair. He smiled pleasantly at the trio from behind his desk as they approached. "Good morning, Detectives. Jennifer. How are you all this fine morning?" he asked with a beaming smile that made Andy wonder if he practiced it in the mirror at home.

"Good morning, John," he replied. "I didn't see you at the party on Saturday; I thought you might have been there."

"Well, I was there. Although not physically. I was there in spirit. Shall we say, overseeing the proceedings?" He laughed at the joke that only he seemed to get.

Maria looked at the security-expert-come-receptionist, then turned to her partner. The confusion was apparent on her face as she turned back to Sinclair. "What the fuck are you talking about?"

The head of security was noticeably annoyed by her abrupt tone and returned her stare. "I was here all weekend putting the finishing touches to Mr. Cooper's latest home security addition," he announced proudly.

"Is he still speaking English?" she asked, as she turned to Andy, who grinned at just how rude his partner could be without really even trying.

It was part of the reason she was such a good cop. She had the ability to cut straight through all the bullshit that criminals would tell her. It was also part of the reason people took an instant loathing to her when they first met her. He was pretty certain that not being liked didn't really matter to her, either. If people didn't like Maria Hernandez, then fuck them. That was her motto, and he believed she meant it.

"Do you mean you were putting some cameras up?" Although a straightforward question, the tone she used to ask it made it sound like she was belittling him.

Sinclair shifted uncomfortably in his chair. "If you want to break it down like that then yes, I was installing cameras. However, it is a little more complicated than that. This is a state-of-the-art security system we are talking about here."

"Security cameras," she repeated.

"Well, you were missed, wherever you were," Andy

interjected, sensing that this conversation needed to end before she got angry. "Is Chris in his office?"

Sinclair shot the female detective a scornful look, then turned back to Andy. The big welcoming smile instantly returned to his face.

"Yes, sir. Mr. Cooper arrived about twenty minutes ago." His fingers went to work on the keyboard in front of him. "He is currently in his office." Without taking his eyes off the computer screen, he reached into a drawer in his desk, pulled out three visitor's badges, and placed them on the countertop. "If you would care to put these on," he stood up, "I will escort you up, as I have to see Mr. Cooper anyway."

"I bet that's the highlight of Chris's morning." Maria continued staring at the enthusiastic receptionist.

Jen's face flushed with embarrassment. "We only need two passes, John. I have mine already."

"Of course you do, how absentminded of me." He tapped a few times on the keyboard, then picked up an iPad from the desk, swiped the screen, and looked back to the computer screen again. "I just have to sync everything up before we go in case someone comes while I'm away from my post… Okay, shall we head up?"

The female detective raised her eyebrows, but refrained from saying anything. Sinclair strode purposefully towards the elevators, checking over his shoulder every few steps to ensure the trio were following him. Once there, he swiped his pass key and the elevator doors opened immediately. All four boarded, and the escort pressed for level five. The doors closed, and they were on their way up.

Ding. They had arrived at the fifth floor and the doors opened. The security expert stepped to one side to allow the others to alight, then hurriedly pushed past them, almost quick-marching towards Chris's office, where he knocked on the door but didn't wait for permission to enter. He swung the door open and held it for the others to enter. When they were all in the office, he closed the door and stood behind everyone.

Chris looked up from behind the large desk in his very spacious office and smiled when he saw who was standing in front of him. "Good morning! How is everyone today?"

Jen rushed over to her uncle, sat on his lap, hugged him, and gave him a quick peck on the cheek, which drew a raised eyebrow from the female detective as she looked on.

After they had all exchanged pleasantries, Sinclair approached his employer. "Sorry to be so forward, sir, but can I just show you the new surveillance and spyware I've installed? It's just that I have left the front desk unattended, so I need to get back quickly."

"Sure, come show me what you've done." Chris eagerly waved him over.

"Right, well, first of all, I updated all the existing security protocols that were in place. Then I installed a few new ones to cover a few backdoor loopholes I detected. I actually made a whole new program, which is quite a nice bit of software. We should think about marketing it." He paused for a response from the CEO but received nothing. "It detects any outside threat," he continued, looking slightly vexed. "Then it plants a virus in the system that is attacking ours, allowing us to trace it to the source. The best bit of all is that the hacker has no idea the virus has been planted."

He looked around, smiling like a child on Christmas morning, clearly looking for some sort of praise for his hard work.

What he got was Detective Maria Hernandez. "Fuck me! Rain Man is going off again. Is he always like this?" She directed the question at Chris, who went to the defense of his head of security.

"Go easy, Maria, John here is the best in his field at what he does." Chris gave his employee a reassuring smile.

"I don't understand the need for all this security," she said, as she looked around the office at the two cameras and the bank of screens that all had live video feeds from different locations. "Surely this is overkill for a few computers?"

"It's not the computers," the security expert interjected. "It's the information stored on them that is invaluable." He moved to the bank of screens, pointing to draw everyone's attention to them. "Housed in this building is a myriad of databases containing some of the most advanced and original gaming ideas the world has ever seen. Other gaming companies will stop at nothing to get a glimpse of what goes on inside these walls. The threat of a cyber-attack is far greater than any other, so we have to have in place the most stringent of security systems to—"

"Forget I asked." The female detective put her hand up to stop him. "Life is too short to listen to you going on and on. I'm guessing you're single?" She frowned at him, but before he had a chance to answer she turned and walked away. "I can't take any more of this shit. I'll wait by the car, partner."

Andy placed his hand on Sinclair's shoulder. "I think you lost her at *myriad*. Hey, Chris." He turned to his brother. "Just wanted to say thanks again for having us over last weekend. We had a great time."

"Yeah, it was fun. We should do it again soon." He smiled.

"Listen, I'd better get going. I don't like leaving Maria for too long on her own," he said and pointed at his daughter. "Be good, and have a nice day. I'll pick you up on my way home."

Jen jumped off her uncle's lap and gave her father a hug.

"No need, bro, I can drop her off when I leave," Chris

offered.

"Well, if it's not too much trouble, that would be better for me," he replied.

"Nothing is too much trouble for my favorite niece." He winked at the teenager.

"Thanks, buddy, I'll catch you later," the detective said as he left the office, escorted by Sinclair, who was anxious to get back to his desk.

Andy left AppTech through the main doors and immediately saw Maria waiting by his car. He had nearly reached her when his attention was drawn to the sound of loud music, and the unmistakable roar of a high-performance sports car's engine. He looked around and saw a bright-red Porsche 911 convertible heading towards him. The car swung into the space next to his at a rate of speed that he found excessive.

The detectives watched as the roof unfolded from the trunk and stretched into place. The windows simultaneously closed, sealing the car and protecting it from the early-morning sun.

Andy didn't recognize the driver at first; the red baseball cap that had the peak pulled down towards the wearer's nose obscured his face.

The door opened and the driver got out. He closed the door gently and pressed the security button on the key fob; two electronic beeps signaled the car was locked. The vehicle owner raised the peak of his cap slightly. They immediately recognized Martin Miller.

"Morning, Pee Wee," she said in a mocking tone.

The programmer lowered his head as if shying away when he saw who was talking to him.

"Maria!" her partner barked, stopping her before she ripped into the nervous-looking Miller. "Leave the kid alone!"

She edged towards the geeky-looking programmer; the

look of terror became more apparent as she got closer. With her nose no more than an inch away from his, she reached up and lifted his red baseball cap, staring at him for a couple of seconds. "Boo!" she shouted.

The geek flinched and jumped back a few feet, almost falling over the hood of his car as he stumbled. He managed to keep his footing by placing one hand on the windshield to steady himself.

"Enough!" Andy shouted, temporarily stunning Maria and making Miller stumble back even further.

Before he knew it, Chris's prize employee had slid the length of the hood of his new car and was sitting on the concrete, his face flushed with embarrassment.

The male detective rushed over to help him up, offering his heartfelt apologies the whole time while Maria was obviously using every piece of self-control to stop herself from laughing out loud.

"Thank you, Detective Cooper," Miller stuttered, as he pulled him to his feet.

"No problem, Martin. Are you all right?" he inquired, with genuine concern.

"Yes, I'm fine, thank you. I'd better get into the office." He scurried away. "Have a good day, Detectives."

"Hey, Miller!" She called after him. "We'll catch up real soon, you and me."

He didn't turn around. Instead, he just picked up his already rapid pace and kept going.

"You really are a piece of work, Maria," Andy said as he turned to face his partner. "You know, maybe Jen is right; he seems like an okay kind of guy. Just a little geeky." He started to make his way back to their vehicle. "Just for once can you try and get through a day without upsetting anybody?"

"I could try." She smiled. "Now can we please go and

get some breakfast?"

They got in the car and headed out of the parking lot. After travelling a few blocks in silence, Maria turned to Andy.

"They all seem very friendly in Chris's office, don't they?" she quizzed.

By the tone of her voice he knew she was leading up to something, so instead of cutting her off, he let her continue.

"I mean, all that hugging. That's surely not normal, is it?" she continued.

Andy took his eyes off the road for a brief second to glance at her. He was unsure if she did actually have a hidden agenda, or whether she was just questioning normal human interaction. "I think that it's quite normal," he said, returning his attention to driving. "Believe it or not, there are some people out there who actually like the company of other people."

"I couldn't be doing with that hugging shit," she said nonchalantly, and gazed out of the side window.

Andy didn't pay much attention to what she had said. He dismissed the comment as something she must have inadvertently said out loud instead of keeping it as a thought in her head.

***

"At last!" Maria broke the silence when Andy swung the car into the parking lot at Coop's Diner. "I'm so hungry I could eat a piece of three-day-old road kill."

"Nice. I know it's probably the first day you've not been hung over in God knows how many years, but road kill?" He looked incredulously at her.

They both got out of the car and entered the diner. Coop had already placed two coffee mugs on the counter and had nearly finished filling them when they sat on their usual seats. Maria noticed the 'hangover kit' he had prepared next to her coffee. Without hesitation she picked it up, leaned over the counter, and deposited it on the shelf.

"What's going on, Maria?" Her partner looked shocked. "No hangover on a Monday? Are you all right?"

"I'm fine. Just thought I might give this sobriety thing a try." She lifted her mug and took a sip of coffee.

"Really?" He glanced at his father, then back to her. "And what, or should I say *who*, has brought on this change to central Florida's most hardened party animal?"

"What makes you think there's a person involved?" she asked, putting her mug on the counter.

"I know you, Maria Hernandez," he persisted. "Nothing comes between you and your favorite nocturnal activity, unless someone has found a way to that heart of stone of yours."

"Fuck you, partner." She flicked her middle finger at him.

"Come on, girlie, you're among friends here. What's going on?" Coop reached over and gently nudged her hand. She looked at him and realized what he was trying to do as he flicked his eyes towards his son.

"Oh… Okay… There might be someone who has shown me the light," she said coyly, while giving the retired cop a little grin.

"Well, you kept this quiet!" Andy sat back in his seat and turned sideways to face her. "When do I get to meet him?"

She picked up her mug and shrugged in an attempt to dismiss the question. Andy looked like he was set to continue his probing but was cut off by his phone ringing. He quickly got the phone out of his pocket and checked the display.

"I have to take this. Dad, the usual for me." He stood and tapped her on the shoulder. "I will be back to finish this conversation. You won't get away with it that easy."

He walked towards the door, answering the phone on the way, and stepped outside for some privacy. Coop watched as the door closed behind his son, then turned to Maria and leaned over the counter to get closer to her.

"I've had a look through those files." Coop's voice was almost a whisper. "Any chance you can come here after your shift? There are a few things I need to take you through."

"Yeah, my car's at home, so when Andy drops me off I'll come straight back here," she said with enthusiasm.

"It's really that easy to get a date with Florida's hottest detective?" He stood up, mimicking a shocked reaction. Her face flushed when he winked at her.

"Well, that depends on who's asking, and at what time of night they approach me." She smiled at him.

"Are you flirting with me, Detective Hernandez?" He toyed with her.

"You son of a bitch," she giggled. "You started it."

"Are you sure about that?" He continued, "Listen, I'd better get going on Andy's breakfast. Do you want anything, or is that a stupid question?"

"Would you believe that I'm starving?" She posed the rhetorical question then continued. "Give me the same as Andy, and a strong coffee, please."

He looked at her and grabbed his chest, pretending that the shock of her ordering food had sent him into cardiac arrest.

"Very fucking funny, old man," she scowled.

He held his hands above his head in a surrendering pose. "Hey, I'm only saying." He pointed at her. "That's the first time in all the years you've been coming here I've known you to order breakfast." Then he leaned forward and gently held her hand and gave a warm smile. "It's good to see you looking after yourself." He patted the back of her hand and headed into the kitchen. "Two Southwestern omelets and two coffees, coming up."

Andy returned from his phone call and took his seat next

to her. He leaned on the counter with one elbow and rested his head on his hand, studying her for a second, waiting for her to speak. She didn't, so it was up to him to break the silence.

"All right, what's going on with you?" He knew the best way to deal with her was to not skate around anything you wanted to discuss with her. Go straight in, get the information you want, and get out. Hopefully without a bullet wound.

"Someone may have pointed out that I need to slow down a bit. Don't blow this out of proportion, partner, it's no big deal." Her dismissive tone made him even more suspicious and determined to get to the bottom of this sudden change in her.

"I've been telling you this for years and you've never listened." He sat up off the counter and took a sip of his coffee. "This 'someone' must be some piece of work to get you to pay attention so quickly; I would like to meet him or her."

He looked for a reaction, but she didn't respond. She just kept looking straight ahead, as if ignoring him. Coop came out of the kitchen and placed some cutlery and condiments in front of them. Without warning, Maria spoke.

"Yeah, I guess he is kind of special. Very wise, and my God is he hot." Maria risked a sly grin at the older man before continuing. "We haven't slept together yet, but I just know he will be dynamite between the sheets."

Andy screwed his face up in mock disgust. "Enough! You're going to put me off my breakfast."

"I thought you wanted the details?" She laughed.

Coop walked back into the kitchen with a confident smile on his face to collect their order, then re-emerged seconds later followed by Beth giving him a hard time about her not being employed as a cook. The diner owner rolled his eyes and smiled at the detectives.

"Two Southwestern omelets," he announced, as he placed the food on the counter. "Made by Beth's fair and beautiful hands."

He raised his voice as he spoke and looked over his shoulder towards Beth, who shot him an exasperated look.

"How about those coffees, old man?" Maria asked.

Before he got a chance to retrieve the coffee pot from the machine, a loud beep followed by the dispatcher's voice came over Andy's police radio attached to his belt. The dispatcher was requesting any available detectives to respond to a scene not far from their location. Andy picked up the radio, pressed the button, and responded that they were on their way.

"You have got to be shitting me?" Maria almost shouted.

"You heard it, partner. Time to go to work. Let's roll." The male detective stood up. "Dad, we have to go. Put these on my tab and I'll pay you later."

Maria slowly rose from her seat, shoveling as much food in her mouth as she could. She eventually threw her fork down on the counter and took a final gulp of her coffee. She waved at Coop and rushed to catch up with Andy.

***

The crime scene was only a short distance from the diner, and they arrived there in under ten minutes. Andy parked alongside the four police cruisers that were in attendance, along with the crime scene van. The whole area had police tape sealing it off, making it unclear at first exactly where the crime had occurred. They got out of the car and walked towards the tape.

"Morning, Detectives." A uniformed officer stood guard to make sure no unauthorized people could pass greeted them.

Andy recognized the cop from a previous crime scene.

"Hi . . . Officer Wilson, isn't it?" Andy asked, while still looking around the area.

"Yes, sir," the cop replied.

"This is Detective Hernandez." Andy pointed at his partner.

Maria nodded her head at the cop, who acknowledged her with a brisk nod.

"So what are we looking at here, Wilson?" Andy asked.

"If you follow me, I'll show you." Wilson held the tape up.

The detectives stooped under the tape and waited for Wilson to lead the way.

"This way." Wilson held his hand out in the direction of an alley.

Maria and Andy followed a few steps behind him, taking in as much of the surrounding scene as possible without stopping and making notes.

The alley walls were covered in graffiti, letting anyone unfortunate enough to wander into the area know the region was under the control of a local gang. There was an overbearing odor of urine. The familiar sight of a CSI officer wearing a white boiler suit taking photos of something on the ground hidden behind a dumpster indicated they had reached the scene. As the detectives got closer, they could see that the target of the camera was the body of an adult male.

"Are we okay to come closer?" Andy queried.

The CSI officer stopped taking photos and looked at them. "Sure. I'm just taking some last shots."

Both detectives knew the CSI from previous investigations as Jack Palmer. Neither Maria nor Andy found him particularly interesting or funny, but they both agreed that he was a brilliant Crime Scene Investigator. If any clues were to be found here, undoubtedly Palmer would find them.

The trio exchanged pleasantries before getting down to business.

"What have you found, Palmer?" the female detective asked in her usual direct way.

"Still preliminary, but I'm pretty confident the cause of

death is due to the large hole in the back of the victim's head." Palmer looked up as if expecting some kind of reaction from the detectives but they just stared at him with deadpan expressions. He coughed nervously and continued.

"The victim was bound, gagged, and shot at point-blank range with a 9mm in the back of the head." He paused as if gathering his thoughts. "Time of death I would guess at around 2:00 a.m. Obviously, I'll know more when I get the coroner's report."

"Bound and gagged, eh?" Maria reiterated. "Execution style?"

"Any ID on him?" Andy asked.

"No ID, but I'm confident I'll be able to get something on him quite quickly. Judging by the tat's he was a gang member, so he'll undoubtedly have a record." The CSI turned to the detectives. "There is one other thing. This isn't the kill site. The body was dumped here."

"Are you sure?" She looked Palmer in the eye.

"Hundred percent," the CSI replied with confidence. "There's no blood spatter, and the pooling from the wound would be a lot more. This dude lost most of his juice somewhere else."

"Any clues to the location of the primary site?" Andy quizzed.

Palmer shrugged. "I've got to get the body back to the lab and see if there's anything I can find, but that's all I have for you at the moment. As soon as I get anything more I'll give you a call."

"Thanks, Palmer." The male detective nodded, then turned to his partner. "I recognize those tats. They're Surin's gang."

"I thought they looked familiar. Regan is going to love this; gangbangers with bullet holes all over the city." She looked around the alley and the surrounding area. "Good place to dump a body. No houses overlooking. I'd imagine canvassing the area would be pointless."

"Do it anyway," Andy ordered Wilson. "See if anything turns up. If it does, let me know immediately." He took a moment to scan the area. "Come on, partner; let's go for a coffee."

"Coffee!" she exclaimed.

"Yeah, coffee." He signaled for her to follow him. "There's a guy a few blocks away who keeps his ear to the ground. If you need to know what's happening around town, Randell is the man you speak to."

"Randell?" She looked quizzical at him. "We've been partners for years, how come you never mentioned this guy?"

"Theres a lot of things I've never told you." He smiled at her. "Come on Maria. One of the main rules of being a Detective is never show your full hand."

***

Five minutes later, Andy stopped the car outside a single-story building. The only indication that its purpose was a diner was the large double window that was used as a serving hatch. A dreadlocked black male leaned out of the open window, shouting lewd comments and wolf whistling at a young woman who was passing by.

"Wow, he's a real charmer, isn't he?" Maria said as she got out of the car.

"Be nice," Andy warned, as he walked around the car and smiled at the dreadlocked male.

"Detective Cooper!" the man shouted in a heavy Haitian accent. "How is my favorite enforcer of the law? And who is this vision of beauty that is with you?"

"Randell, my man. How is the fast food trade?" They shook hands.

Andy knew Randell's food joint was just a front for his drugs trade. He was a low-level dealer so they left him alone in exchange for any information that he had on the area they called Little Haiti.

The Haitian knew everyone and everything that happened in the area, and that was far more valuable to the detectives than busting him for dealing a bit of weed to some college kids.

"I need some information, Randell." He leaned on the sill. "Oh, and two coffees."

"Two coffees coming right up." The vendor clicked his fingers at someone in the kitchen. "Can I get you anything else?"

"I've just come from a crime scene a few blocks away," Andy proceeded. "Not a pretty sight. I've got one of Surin's crew dumped in an alley with a bullet hole in his head."

"I don't know anything about that, Detective. I just sell rice and beans," he said with a smug mile on his face as he turned to Maria. "And hot Haitian sausage is always available."

"Is this fucking guy for real?" She glared at him.

"She's got spice of her own, I like her! She's feisty," he said, then pretended to take a bite out of her.

"She!" the female detective emphasized, disgusted at his act of chauvinism, "also has a 9mm Glock with ten in the mag and one in the pipe. If you do that to me again I will empty the fucking lot into your dick. Do I make myself clear?"

"I like her. I like her a lot." He laughed loudly.

"Believe me when I tell you she will shoot you." Andy's abruptness brought his laughing to an instant and sudden end.

"Now, I'll ask you one more time." The detective leaned in close to him. "And what you say next will determine whether or not I call the DEA and have them rip this shithole you call a diner apart." He grabbed Randell's collar and pulled him through the window far enough for his feet to leave the ground. "Am I making myself clear?"

The Haitian nodded his head with vigor, acknowledging he understood the threat. Andy released his grip, letting him regain his footing inside.

"Again, what do you know about Surin's gang?" he asked, as he brushed the Haitian's collar back into place.

"No need to come down on me like that, Detective Cooper. You know I'm always happy to help the good guys." He lowered his voice and lost some of his accent. "Truth is, I don't honestly know what is going on." Randell looked genuinely terrified as he continued. "I've got a feeling that something big is going down." He took a good look around to make sure no one could hear him. "My guess is an internal power struggle for leadership. At the same time, rivals are trying to take advantage of a leaderless gang."

"That makes sense," Maria interjected, still eyeing up him as if she was deciding whether or not she should shoot him.

"Randell, I'll level with you. I don't want to send hordes of units down here, but you're not leaving me many options here." Andy spoke slowly and concisely to really make sure his point was getting across. "Spread the word that this needs to stop before an innocent gets caught in the crossfire. Because if that happens, every law enforcement organization in the state will descend upon you, and that won't be good for business."

"Okay, okay, okay." The vendor stood back. "I'll spread the word; but you have to believe me, this is nothing to do with me, and I have no influence over these guys."

"I believe you," the detective reassured him. "Just work with me on this, and everything will be fine."

"Hey, I got your back, Detective Cooper." The heavy accent had returned. Then turning to Maria, the vile chauvinist returned. "You sure I can't interest you in some spicy Haitian sausage? It's my own special recipe."

“No, thank you.” She looked him up and down in disgust again. “I need something substantial. Come on, Cooper, let’s get out of here. I need to leave before someone else gets shot.”

“Call me soon, Randell!” Andy shouted over his shoulder as they got into the car.

“Can we please go eat now? After a morning of dead and horny Haitians I’ve definitely worked up an appetite.” She glared out of the window at the grinning Haitian as they drove off.

“Sorry, partner, we’ve got to head back to the PD and give Regan the situation report,” he said, reveling in the moment. “We can go for an early lunch though.”

“Gee, thanks, pal. At this rate I’m not going to make it to lunch,” she complained.

“Quit bitching!” he snapped. “This is what it’s like in the world of sobriety. Deal with it.”

“I think I liked you more when I was hammered,” she sniped back.

“I’ve got news for you, partner,” he said, as he swung the car into a left turn. “I’ve always been this way. It’s your perception of things that has been distorted for the last ten years.”

“Just get me to the office so I can at least try one of those Twinkies out of the vending machine,” Maria huffed, as she turned to look out of the window.

They travelled the rest of the journey in silence.

Chapter 11

When the detectives entered the station, they were greeted with the usual Monday morning scene of 'weekend warriors' being released after spending the night, or nights, in the cells.

These were the people that held respectable jobs during the week. People from every walk of life. Office workers, manual laborers, even tourists who had intended to go out on a Friday or Saturday night for a few drinks and found themselves having to be bailed out on Monday morning.

Every cop hated Monday morning for this reason, along with the smell of vomit, urine, and the detergent used to clean up the mess that filled the whole place. It was not the most pleasant place to be at the beginning of the week.

Andy looked around at the chaos. The desk sergeant, an old friend of his family, Sergeant Simon Percival, was trying his best to organize everything. He seemed to be the only person who wasn't running around like a headless chicken.

He was dealing with a man who looked to be in his early thirties and sported a fresh black eye, split lip, and bruised cheek. A woman, who Andy presumed was the man's wife, kept interrupting to express her anger at her husband as he tried to answer Percival's questions.

Andy, a married man himself, felt a little sorry for the poor guy. He knew the cuts and bruises would be long healed before the nagging stopped.

Percival glanced up from the feuding couple for a brief moment, as if trying to summon a little more patience out of thin air. He saw the detective over the crowd and gave him an acknowledging nod, then rolled his eyes before smiling and returning to deal with the couple.

The detective smiled to himself; he sometimes missed not wearing the uniform. The respect it brought. The power it gave. The way people would come up to talk to him in the street. He sometimes longed to return to those days, especially when he was working a difficult case; but today was not one of those days.

He signaled to his partner to follow, and they pushed their way past the booking desk to the door marked 'authorized personnel only,' where the female detective punched the code in to unlock the door. Andy, the true gentleman that he was, held it open for her to pass through before taking one last look at the chaotic scene before closing the door. As he followed Maria to their office, he smiled to himself again. *Yes, this is definitely not one of those days,* he thought. The image of his graduation day at the academy suddenly flashed into his mind. His thoughts had drifted a little far. He didn't notice that his partner had stopped in front of him until it was too late and he bumped into her.

"I'm sorry," he apologized.

"It's fine." She steadied herself against the wall. "You okay? You were somewhere else then. Did you hear what I said?"

"Yeah, I was—"

"Andy, seriously, I need to eat something." She walked away. "I'm going to go to the cafeteria and risk something from there. Do you want anything?"

The thought of the omelet he'd had to leave at the diner, coupled with the smell of the booking area had left him feeling a little sick. "No, I'm good. Maybe get me a soda though. I have a funny taste in my mouth."

"You should eat breakfast," she scolded. "It's the most important meal of the day. I read that somewhere."

"Wow, reading *and* eating? This new guy is really doing a number on you, isn't he?" he joked.

"Bite me! You want something or not?" she asked.

"Just a soda. We'll get lunch after we've briefed Regan," he answered, and continued towards homicide. "Hurry up. I'll see you in the office."

She watched him walk away, and as soon as he was out of sight she headed away from the cafeteria in the direction of the CACU, the specialized Crimes Against Children Unit. Taking another quick look over her shoulder to make sure he had gone, she scurried around the nearest corner.

Andy got to the office, but before he had chance to get to his desk, Lieutenant Jack Regan bellowed across the office.

"Cooper! My office, now!" The detective turned to see the obvious look of anger on his superior's face. "And where is that partner of yours?"

"Good morning to you too, sir," Andy said with a broad smile. But the scowling glare told him not to push his superior too far. "Yes, sir, coming right away, sir." He briskly made his way to the private office. The lieutenant had already sat behind his desk by the time he entered.

"Shut the door and sit down, Cooper!" he barked.

The detective hesitated for a second, then closed the door and sat opposite the lieutenant. He braced himself for the almost certain onslaught of anger.

"What the fuck is going on in my city?" Regan's tone was more aggressive.

"Boss?" He looked puzzled.

"Gangbangers shooting each other I can stomach, as long as they do it on their own patch and no innocent bystanders get caught in the crossfire. But from what Palmer tells me, this was an execution-style shooting." The superior frowned, his face getting redder. "This is Orlando, not the fucking Bronx!" he blasted, then took a moment to calm down. “The chief is going to be getting it in the ass from the mayor, which means I’m going to be getting it in the ass from the chief. Now, guess who’s next in line to get it in the ass from me?” Andy looked uncomfortable and shifted in his seat. “This needs to end, and end fast. If the press gets hold of this, tourism will take a dive and we’ll all be sweeping empty streets for a living.”

“Sir, with respect, this shouldn’t even be our case.” The detective went into defensive mode. “Gang-related issues should go to Organized Crime. Just because there’s a few bodies doesn’t make it Homicide. We haven’t got the resources to deal with this.”

Andy knew he had a valid point. He also knew the head of the Organized Crime Unit was the chief’s son-in-law, and there was no way they would have an unsolvable crime on their desk.

“From what I can gather,” he continued before the lieutenant could get a word in, “since Surin’s death, everything has gone crazy down there. My sources tell me there is an internal power struggle to lead the gang, and other gangs are taking advantage of the situation. In short, sir, and using the phrase Hernandez used, it’s a clusterfuck.” He sat back and waited for Regan to respond.

The lieutenant pondered for a moment to take in as much of the information as possible. “You’re right about it being the Organized Crime Unit’s.” He nodded. “But for whatever reason, we’re stuck with it.” His anger had subsided. “So we need to nip this in the bud. We generally turn a blind eye to most things and give those fuckers plenty of space to do what they want, then this happens. What do you think about flooding the area with marked units?”

“I’ve already hinted to my sources that that is exactly what will happen if they don’t sort it out quickly.” The detective gave a reassuring smile. “Maybe just send a few extra units down there over the next couple of days to show we’re serious. Not so much flood the area, but a few more than normal. The Haitians will get the message that we’re not playing around.”

Andy spoke with a great deal of confidence, so much so that his superior had almost completely calmed down from his agitated state. “I’ll go make a few calls; organize a few extra sweeps of the area. If the bodies continue to pile up, then we go in hard.” Andy looked at Regan for confirmation.

The lieutenant put his head in his hands and after a moment’s silence he looked up at the detective. “All right.” He sat back in his chair. “Emphasize to your contact I don’t want any more bodies, and I certainly don’t want any more executions.”

“Done,” Andy confirmed.

“Make sure they know we’re watching closely, and we will not hesitate to call in the heavy artillery if this continues,” he stressed, then nodded as if dismissing him.

“Consider it done, sir.” The detective hesitated. “Is there anything else?”

His questioned was ignored and he sat in an awkward silence for a few seconds, watching the ranking officer, who had buried his head in a large pile of paperwork.

“Close the door on the way out,” Regan ordered, without looking up.

Andy slowly rose from his seat and made his way out of the office, closing the door quietly behind him. He walked to his desk, sat down, and sighed. Today had turned into a day that he missed the uniform.

Chapter 12

The late afternoon/early evening rush hour in Orlando seems to last till midnight. It starts around 4:00 p.m. with the white-collar workers finishing work and making their way home as fast as they can before the assorted theme parks prepare to wind down for the day. This is when the second wave of traffic begins. Exhausted parents and tired children making their way back to their temporary homes as quickly as possible to recharge their batteries for the next day.

Maria sat in a queue of traffic that slowly edged towards a set of lights that didn't stay on green long enough for more than a dozen cars to go through. She looked at the vehicle next to her; it was obviously a rental car.

She took comfort in the cold environment she sat in and gently lowered her hand towards the center console, to reassure herself that her service weapon was within easy reach. She always placed her gun in the same place in anticipation of any road rage incidents that might flare up, which became more frequent as the summer heat escalated and the patience of frustrated travelers diminished.

The light changed to green, and the flow of traffic moved forward with some haste, everyone trying to pass through before it changed back to red. Maria accelerated, getting as close as she could to the vehicle in front. This time she was going to get through the light, and kept an eye on it as they got closer. The car in front began to brake so she slammed her hand on the horn, which made the driver in front look in his rearview mirror. She shooed him on with her hand, and after checking the light was still on go, he accelerated away. The light flicked to red as she passed through and sighed with relief.

She pulled the vehicle into the parking lot of Coop's Diner and stopped in the nearest available space. Before getting out, the ever-cautious detective made a quick check by looking around the parking lot. She did this out of habit, checking that there were no possible threats from anybody hanging round. There was always a risk of opportunists waiting for the right moment to strike on an unsuspecting person and relieve them of their valuables. Satisfied there was no such threat, she holstered her weapon, exited the vehicle, and made her way into the diner.

It was unusually quiet in the diner, considering Coop's was "the" place to go for her work colleagues. She couldn't see any cops, just a few civilians having a drink and chatting away.

Coop was at the end of the counter. She couldn't decide if he looked frustrated, angry, or completely bored as he tried to make sense of the stack of receipts in front of him, emitting the odd grunt as he peered through the reading glasses that balanced on the end of his nose.

"Hey, old man." She grabbed his attention as she approached and joked, "You must be getting old if you need readers."

"Oh… hey, Maria." He looked up, took his glasses off and waved them over the slips. "I'm just going through all this crap. I hate paperwork. Working out what stock I need to order, how much I have to pay the good old IRS, have I got enough left to pay the mortgage. I tell you, it's a nightmare."

"Your son owns a huge software company. Can't he make a program that does all this for you?" She nodded at all the paper.

"He did offer," he sighed. "But I just don't like computers. Don't trust them; never have, and never will. Everything is computerized these days. As much as I hate paperwork, I hate computers more."

"Now I know where Andy gets it from," she quipped.

A look of confusion came over the old man's face but he didn't say anything.

"So, where are we at on our project?" She spoke quietly, not wanting anyone to overhear her.

"Tell you what." He pointed to the coffee machine. "Why don't you pour us some coffee while I put this away? Then we can go over our project."

She pushed past him behind the counter and started pouring the coffee while he started gathering all his papers.

"Don't you be making a mess out there, young lady!" Beth startled Maria as she popped her head through the serving hatch.

"Oh… hi, didn't know you were here. I'll try not to," the flustered detective said, and quickly wiped up the coffee she had just spilled.

Coop had placed all the loose receipts into a folder and slid it under his arm. He stood up and moved behind the counter, grabbed a mug of coffee, and signaled to Maria to follow him.

"Beth, hold the fort. I've got some business to go over with Detective Hernandez here," he called over his shoulder as they walked through the kitchen to his office.

"Sure, no problem. I'll do everything," the obviously agitated waitress replied with her usual hint of sarcasm. "You need me to stick a broom up my ass so I can sweep up while I work, too?"

"No." Coop looked blankly at her as he unlocked the office door and held it open for Maria to enter. "You can do that later. For now, just serve anybody that wants a drink or something to eat."

"Gee… thanks," she huffed, as she threw a cloth onto the nearest worktop and disappeared into the restaurant area.

The retired cop smiled and followed his young protégé

into the office. He closed the door and locked it before depositing the file from under his arm into the top drawer of his desk. He patted his trouser pockets as if looking for something. A puzzled look followed by a 'eureka' moment signaled he had remembered where he had put his glasses, and retrieved them from his shirt pocket.

"Here. Put your coffee down and give me a hand." He waved her over to a large filing cabinet. "I'll push, you pull."

Maria grabbed one side of the cabinet and pulled as hard as she could while he pushed with one hand. The unit slid along the wall with surprising ease, revealing a hidden door. Coop unlocked and opened it, then reached inside for the light switch and turned it on.

"Go on in, I'll get the drinks." He nodded.

The female detective slowly edged her way into the room, open-mouthed. The wall opposite the door was covered floor to ceiling with corkboards. Photos from the files she had left with him were pinned to the boards. Names, ages, and addresses were scribbled on notes beneath each picture. Some of the photos were linked with red lines drawn by red marker.

The other walls in the room were partly hidden behind piles of boxes and folders. A photocopier sat on a small desk next to the door.

"Fuck me, old man! Are you in the CIA? What the hell is this place?" She was astounded.

"This is my *private*, private office." He grinned. "You like what I've done with the place?"

"You really are a dark horse." She looked around in amazement. "Who else knows about this room?"

"Including you and me? Two people, and that's the way I'd like it to stay if it's all the same to you." He winked at her.

"Hey, my lips are sealed." She held her hands up. "I don't think anyone would believe me anyway. And for the record, you're freaking me out here." She turned a full three hundred sixty degrees. "This…" She waved her hands around. "This is all a bit much."

"Everyone needs their own space. Anyway, shall we?" He walked towards the desk.

"What's all this stuff?" She looked closer at the labels on the boxes.

"They're old cases." He handed her coffee to her. "Shall we get down to business?"

He grabbed a foldaway chair that was leaning against the desk and placed it in the middle of the room, facing the corkboards.

"Pull up a box." He nodded.

"No thanks." She turned her attention to the photos pinned to the boards. "I'll stand for this. Here…" She reached into her pocket and pulled out a few sheets of folded paper, unfolded them and passed them to him. "I went to the CACU earlier and spoke to the guys there."

"What's this?" He took the papers and perched his glasses on the end of his nose.

"The top sheet is the names of the cops that work in the unit. They only have three guys to deal with all this shit, and one of those is on a secondment to a federal investigation. That leaves the other two stretched thin." She pointed at one of the names. "This guy seems to know his shit. And, as a side note, he's kind of cute."

"Are you using your charms on someone else?" Coop peered over his glasses, appearing to be hurt by Maria's interest in another man. "You're breaking my heart here."

"I said that he was cute, not that I was fucking him." She nudged him. "Please, concentrate. Underneath is a list of the kids that have turned up. According to him, there's a network of hostels and safe houses where these kids hole up." She grabbed the empty metal waste bin from under the desk, turned it upside down to make a seat and sat next to him. “Now, federal law requires that these places report any minors that turn up on their doorstep immediately to the authorities.” She paused to sip her coffee.

“Makes sense,” Coop agreed. “Go on.”

“The problem is, if they report a kid who then returns home the next day, the hostel is still left with a mountain of paperwork.” She tapped her index finger on the papers he was holding. “This costs time and money. So what they tend to do is leave it a couple of days before reporting them, to make sure that they are genuine runaways and not your everyday teenager throwing a hissy fit.”

Coop stopped her by holding his hand up. “So you’re telling me that because of this bureaucratic BS it’s difficult for the good guys to do their job effectively and efficiently?”

“Exactly. How fucked up is that?” She pointed at the papers again. “Anyway, these are the kids that have either returned home or are located in hostels. Eight of them are in the files I gave you. Well, on your corkboards now.”

He handed the papers to her and walked to the wall filled with the information. “Read them out so we can eliminate them.”

She read out the names of the kids that had been accounted for while he carefully took down the photographs and notes for each of them.

When they had gone through the list, he took a couple of steps back and looked at the remaining photographs. Maria stood up and joined him. The pair stood there in silence, looking at each photo individually.

“What are your thoughts?” she asked, not taking her eyes off of the boards.

He looked thoughtful for a few moments, then pointed to one of the pictures.

"Take that one down for a second," he requested. "And those two."

She obliged and removed the three photographs.

"Now, come and stand back here," he ordered. "Have a look at what we have left. Tell me what you see."

Maria stared blankly at the boards, trying to figure out if her mentor had actually spotted something, or if he was just testing her. Either way, she was failing to see anything in the photos.

Without speaking, he stepped forward and started rearranging the pictures. He put all of them next to each other on one board in a single line and stepped back again.

"*Now* tell me what you see," he said, while studying the photographs again.

"Holy sweet mother of God!" She exclaimed. "All these kids look pretty much like each other. Fair hair. Similar ages. Similar height and build. Fuck, they even look similar facially." She looked at him open-mouthed. "Tell me you're seeing this, too."

"I am." He frowned and got closer to examine the pictures in more detail. "But, there's something else."

"What?" she inquired.

"These kids look familiar for some reason." He glanced from picture to picture. "I wonder if there's anything linking these kids. Dig out their files."

She spread the files out on the desk so she could see all of the names. "Okay, who do you want first?"

"James 'Jamie' Straite." Coop read the notes he'd made. "Does it say where his last known sighting was?"

She quickly checked the report sheet. "Yeah. Last seen at the bus terminal on Americana Boulevard."

"Check the last known sightings of the others," he demanded.

Maria quickly went through the files, noting that all the missing kids were last seen at bus terminals.

"Mother fucker! That's it; they all went missing around bus terminals." She was excited by her discovery.

"It's more than that. All the routes end at the same type of place." Coop scribbled on a piece of paper and stuck it on the board above the photos. "Here." He pointed at the note. "Theme Parks."

The female detective stepped forward, glancing from picture to picture, and then to the note above them. "You have got to be shitting me." Her mind raced as she tried to comprehend the gravity of the discovery. "This could be huge. We have to take it to Regan."

"Slow down there, we don't have anything concrete yet. This could all be coincidental," he said, curbing her enthusiasm. "Let's just take a bit of time here and go over everything again before we start raising the alarm."

"Coop, I don't think this is a coincidence. It's in the reports." She waved the files in his direction. "Granted, this has been overlooked, but I shouldn't have to remind you that I am a serving officer and you know the rules, I have to report this."

"You went to Andy with this and he didn't want to know; he passed it over. This is our case now, and until we have something concrete to offer him, then this stays between us. Am I clear on that?" The retired cop's whole demeanor changed. He was no longer the friendly diner owner. Standing before her was the intimidating, hard-nosed cop that he once had been. Almost snarling, he looked at her.

His penetrating eyes actually made her feel slightly uncomfortable. The reputation he had was renowned around the department for this kind of thing, but it was the first time she had witnessed it first-hand. It became clear to her why he had his legendary status.

"Okay. Firstly, you need to calm the fuck down. Don't be getting in my face like that or I will put you down." Her words were not a threat. "Secondly, if you ever speak to me like that again, I *will* put you down." She paused and glared at Coop, who suddenly looked a little embarrassed by his outburst. "Thirdly, I'll hold back reporting this until we have more to present to the lieutenant."

She didn't raise her voice, staying cool, calm, and collected as she laid down her rules to him. This tactic worked when confronted with any form of conflict. Staying extremely composed and using threatening terms had an incredible impact on the person it was directed at.

He bowed his head for a moment and when he looked up, the anger had gone from his eyes. He was back to the loveable Coop again.

"Sorry, Maria," he said with sincerity. "I thought you were going to take this away from me. It's the first thing in years that's got my juices flowing, and the thought of not being able to see this through… well... I'm really sorry."

"Forget about it." She opened her arms and moved towards him. "Come here, give me a hug."

He sheepishly accepted a hug from her and gave her a peck on the cheek.

"Listen," she said as they separated. "It's getting late, and I need my beauty sleep."

"Okay. You get out of here. I'll just tidy this up a bit." He walked to the door and unlocked it, then led the way to the door to the kitchen area, and unlocked and opened it.

"See you tomorrow?" She patted him on the shoulder as she passed.

"You bet." He smiled and watched her till she went into the restaurant area.

He stood leaning against the door for a few moments,

and then went back into the office to continue studying the evidence on the corkboards.

Chapter 13

"Please, mister, can I go home now?" the boy asked nervously.

He sat opposite an obese man who was sweating profusely and sloppily eating his food, while glaring at the boy from behind the pig mask concealing his face.

The wolf pointed at the boy's plate with his knife. "Eat your food, boy," he demanded in his usual Southern drawl, which wasn't as prominent as previous occasions at the cabin. "This man wants you to be full of energy."

"Yeah, full of energy," the obese pig spluttered, before taking another mouthful of food.

The boy's whole body visibly shook underneath the red cape he wore. A tear slowly trickled down his left cheek. The host leaned forward to peer under the red hood that cast a shadow over the upper part of the boy's face.

"Please don't cry. Be brave," he said in a reassuring tone. "Listen to the words of this song." He put down his cutlery and sat back, closed his eyes, and lifted his head towards the ceiling, letting the words of Billie Holiday singing "God Bless The Child" drift through his mind.

Money, you've got lots of friends
They're crowding around your door
But when you're gone and spending ends
They don't come no more
Rich relations give crusts of bread and such
You can help yourself, but don't take too much
Mama may have, Papa may have

But God bless the child that's got his own, that's got his own

"I don't understand, sir," the boy whimpered.

Wolf opened his eyes and looked at the boy. "Never mind. Have you ever read the Bible?"

"Yes, sir." The boy looked up enough to reveal his tear-filled eyes.

"Are you familiar with the story of the Last Supper?" the host continued.

The boy didn't answer. He burst into tears.

The wolf looked at the pig and stood up. "Let's not prolong this for the poor child. Bring him."

The pig threw his cutlery down and reached out to grab the child.

"No!" The boy shrugged away but, for a man of his size, the pig leapt out of his seat with remarkable speed, managing to get ahold of his prey.

Unable to stop his momentum, they crashed to the ground and wrestled for a moment before the sheer strength and weight of the pig subdued the terrified boy. The wolf stormed over and helped the pig to his feet and held the kid down with a well-placed foot on his chest.

"You finished?" he snarled at the breathless man.

"Y-y-y-yeah." The sweating man gasped for air.

"Then quit playing round and let's get this done." He took his foot from the boy's chest, pulled him to his feet, and shoved him into the waiting arms of the pedophile, who immediately put him into a headlock.

"No, please! Leave me alone!" the boy pleaded. "Let me go! I promise I won't tell anyone."

"Shut up, boy!" Pig shouted, as he struggled to follow the host, who led them to a curtain. He swiped it to one side, revealing a door.

"What's in there?" the kid screamed.

"In here is the reason you shouldn't have disobeyed your parents when they told you not to go with strangers," the wolf hissed as he swung the door open, allowing his 'guests' to see inside.

The sight of what was in the room sent the kid into a struggle to get free from the sweaty pig's grip but it was useless; the grip visibly tightened.

The wolf bent down to look the boy in the eye. "Welcome to the Genesis Chamber, kid."

The pig dragged the boy into the chamber followed by the Wolf, who closed and locked the door behind him, leaving the mellow tones of the song filling the interior of the isolated lodge.

Here just don't worry about nothing cause he's got his own
Yes, he's got his own.

When the record finished the continuous *click, scratch, click* was the only sound that could be heard in the log cabin. Whatever went on in the Genesis Chamber could not be heard from the outside. Every sound was swallowed up by the sound-proofed walls.

Chapter 14

Andy was awakened by the alarm going off. He fumbled in the darkness for the snooze button and gave it a deliberate push to silence the annoying sound, then rolled over, hoping for a cuddle or, time permitting, a little more from Kim. His wanting turned to disappointment when he realized he was alone, so he reluctantly pulled the covers back and left the comfort of his king-sized bed.

After a quick shower he dressed, grabbed his gun from the bedside cabinet, holstered it, and headed downstairs to the kitchen. The unmistakable aroma of grilled bacon greeted him. As he entered the dining area, he saw his wife by the stove.

Jen sat at the table, a plate of half-eaten food in front of her. It was a scene of domestic bliss, something that Andy hadn't seen for a long time.

He stopped and adjusted his tie. *What the hell is going on?* he asked himself. A cooked breakfast, a smiling wife, and a normally grumpy teenage girl sitting and eating with a smile on her face. His cop instinct told him he was about to walk into an ambush of some kind, one that would inevitably cost him money. He surveyed the scene one more time, and briefly wondered if he had time to make a break for the car and get the hell out of there.

"Good morning." He greeted the two women in his life with a great degree of apprehension. "And to what do I owe this pleasure? Have one of you crashed my car, or am I writing a check for something else today?" Andy laughed nervously.

"Honey, don't be so cynical. You're turning into a very distrusting, grumpy old man," Kim teased.

"Yeah, Dad, I agree with Mum on that," his daughter affirmed.

"So, my car is in one piece, and neither of you want money from me?" he asked with caution.

"God, Dad! There really is no pleasing you, is there? I get up early, show enthusiasm for the job you wanted me to do, and you still find fault," the perplexed teenager ranted. "And why would I need money from you when I've just got my bonus from work, anyway?"

"I wasn't complaining darling, I was just saying…wait, you got a bonus?" He wasn't sure if he was shocked, angry, or proud at that moment. "You've only been there two minutes and you got a bonus already?"

"Yes. Quite a large one, too," she said smugly. "Mum said we can go to the mall this weekend so no, I don't want your money. I just wanted to have breakfast with my dad. Looks like I was expecting too much."

Andy looked embarrassed; his daughter's words left him feeling awkward.

"I'm sorry, sweetie. I didn't expect to see you up so early." He desperately tried to fix the situation. "I really am pleased for you. My little princess is growing up. Tell you what; how about we all go to the mall on Saturday. And by way of an apology, I'll take us all for dinner on the way back."

"That sounds like a great idea," Kim butted in. "It's been too long since we all went for a meal together."

Jen looked up at the ceiling as if considering the offer. "Sure." She smiled and nodded her head in acceptance. "As long as I choose where we eat. There's this new restaurant everyone is raving about."

"Deal!" He high fived his daughter. "Hey. This restaurant, it's not that dodgy place they call Coop's, is it?"

"Ooh… I don't think Grandpa would be pleased if he heard you talking about his pride and joy like that." The youngster winked at him.

"Jennifer Cooper!" he exclaimed. "Are you trying to bribe a police officer?"

All three laughed.

"Right, young lady, are you ready?" He grabbed a piece of bacon and quickly scoffed it down. "Sorry, sweetheart. I appreciate the breakfast, but I'm going to have to leave to drop this clever girl off and get to roll call." He put his arm around his offspring.

"No, Dad, it's okay." Jen continued eating her breakfast. "Martin is picking me up."

"Martin?" he quizzed. "As in Miller?"

"Yes, as in Martin Miller. He's just moved into a house nearby so he said I can get a ride with him." She smiled at him reassuringly. "He'll drop me off, too, so you don't have to worry."

Before he had a chance to object, a car horn beeped outside, followed by the sound of screeching tires and the distinctive sound of a high-performance engine being revved filled the air.

"That'll be him now. Got to go." She jumped off her stool, dropped her mobile into her handbag, then went to the mirror by the front door and applied some lipstick. "I'm out of here; see you tonight."

"Erm. Excuse me." Kim stopped her as she reached for the door.

Jen turned around to see her mother signaling for a kiss by tapping her index finger on her cheek.

"Oh, yeah, sorry." Jen rushed over and kissed Kim on the cheek, then went back to the door.

"Hey, what am I, chopped liver?" Andy called after his daughter. "Where's my kiss?"

Jen doubled back, nearly dropping her bag as she did so. He bent down slightly to receive his good-bye kiss on the cheek, and before he had a chance to thank her, she was out of the door.

Curiosity got the better of him, so he followed his daughter out of the house and watched as she approached the vehicle. The roof on the new Porsche was in the process of folding away so the occupants could take advantage of the glorious weather that was forecast for the day.

Miller was being the perfect gent by holding the passenger door open. She gave him a hug and a peck on the cheek before getting into the car. He made sure she was safely inside, then closed the door and walked around the back of the car to get in the driver's door. Andy looked on as they settled into their seats and fastened their seatbelts.

"Good morning, Martin!" he shouted.

The computer programmer looked over and waved. The nervous look and the forced smile let Andy know he had the young man's attention.

"You drive careful now. That's precious cargo you're carrying there!" the doting father said assertively, and turned his body so the driver could see he had placed his hand on the handle of his gun. "I'd hate for anything to happen to her."

Miller's reluctant smile turned to a look of terror. Satisfied he had got his message through, Andy kept his hand on his gun as the red convertible reversed out of the driveway.

"See you later guys." His daughter smiled as she waved.

He smiled and nodded at her, then felt a slap on his arm. He jumped and looked around, not realizing his wife had been standing behind him the whole time.

"That was just mean." She grinned.

"What? I'm just a concerned parent," he joked, as he turned to his wife and grabbed her around the waist to pull her in for a kiss. "You know, now that I don't have to drop Jen off, I have twenty minutes to spare."

"Well, I don't, so you're going to have to hold that

thought until later." She pushed him away and headed back into the house.

The rejected husband sighed, shook his head, and followed his wife indoors. When he got inside he noticed that she had cleared everything away from the breakfast table.

"Hey, what happened to my bacon?" He scanned the kitchen.

"You said you had to go and it had gone cold. It's in the trash if you want me to dig it out," she joked, as she busied herself to get ready to leave the house.

"No thanks." He was ready to leave, so he picked up his car keys from the worktop and kissed her. "As tempting as that sounds, I think I'll decline and just head over to Coop's. By the way, I will be holding that thought until tonight."

The impish grin on his face made Kim's cheeks flush red. Even after all these years he still knew how to make her feel special.

"Get out of here. Go protect and serve." She gave him another kiss, then turned around to pack her laptop in its carry case.

"I'll see you later, babe." He took one final look at her, then left.

***

His journey was an unusually pleasant experience. For once, no bad drivers had pissed him off, and the image of a terrified Miller driving away from his house kept Andy smiling. That, coupled with the soft rock that emitted from the car's speakers, had put him in a very good mood indeed.

The Eagles "Life in the Fast Lane" was blaring out as he pulled into Coop's. He knew that song would be in his head for the rest of the day as he entered the diner, singing it under his breath. He was pleasantly surprised to see Maria sitting at the counter.

A half-eaten stack of pancakes and a coffee cup about to be refilled in front of her told him that she had been there for some time. Coop looked up as he finished pouring Maria's coffee.

"Morning, son. How are you today?" he asked with his usual enthusiasm.

"Pretty good this morning, Dad." He sat next to his partner. "Can I get the usual, please?"

"Sure. Coming right up." He filled a mug with piping-hot coffee and placed it in front of the new arrival before going into the kitchen to prepare his breakfast.

"Morning, partner." The male detective nodded at his colleague, who was shoveling pancakes and bacon into her mouth like it was her last meal.

She nodded in his direction and continued eating.

"Seriously, what is going on with you?" He looked closer at her. "No red eyes. You're up early, showered, eating a hearty breakfast." He sniffed the air around her. "You don't smell of alcohol. I'm not sure I even recognize you anymore."

She swallowed the mouthful of breakfast she had been chewing.

"Well, you better get used to it." She took a sip of her coffee. "I kind of like not feeling like shit every morning."

The old man returned from the kitchen and placed his son's breakfast on the counter.

"What do you think, Dad? Will this new, improved Detective Hernandez last?" He didn't take his gaze off of her.

"You know, son, I think it will." He gave her a little wink.

She finished chewing on the last mouthful of food and swallowed it, wiped her mouth with a napkin, and let out a bellowing belch.

"That was fantastic, Coop," she said with genuine

enthusiasm.

Her partner gasped and feigned a look of complete disgust. "You really are something, Hernandez."

Before she had a chance to retort, her phone rang. She checked the caller ID and jumped up from her stool. "I've got to take this. Be right back," she said over her shoulder as she went outside.

"So, what do you think of this new Maria, Pops?" Andy asked, and continued to watch her through the window.

"I like it. She'll make a great cop; great instinct and plenty of balls. I'm glad she's not throwing it all away because of the booze. And let's face it, son," he tapped his index finger on the counter to emphasize his point, "We have seen many a good cop that has done just that."

Andy nodded in agreement. Both men had indeed seen it too often; good cops who, due to the stresses of the job, had hit the bottle and found it hard to give up, often resulting in broken homes. Ironically, the only thing that was left in their lives was their job.

"Well, I hope she does stick to it because the lieutenant is just waiting for an excuse to get rid of her," he confided in his father. "He knows she's a good cop, but all he sees at the moment is her being a total liability."

"Jack's a fair man. If she sorts herself out he'll be the first to forget about her misgivings," Coop said, and nodded his head as if agreeing with himself that what he was saying was true.

They fell silent as the female detective returned. Andy started to attack his omelet with vigor. He hadn't realized how hungry he was until that first mouthful kick-started his taste buds, sending the signal to his digestive system that something good was on its way.

"Everything all right?" Coop asked, referring to her

phone call.

"Yeah. Just family stuff," she said, a little downbeat. "You know how it is."

"I sure do. Family can be a real pain in the ass," he said, and glanced at his son, who looked up from his food but kept quiet.

There was an awkward moment as Andy looked into his father's eyes, waiting for another sermon on how bad he had been as a teenager, something his dad always came up with at the most inappropriate times. He waited in anticipation to defend himself. The moment seemed to last forever until the elder of the two burst out laughing. The detective sighed with relief and went back to his omelet, completely devouring it before gulping down his coffee.

"You ready to roll, partner?" he asked Maria as he pushed his plate across the counter.

"Sure. You go get the car started and I'll take care of the check." She pulled out her purse. "What do we owe you, Coop?"

"Hey, I am definitely liking this new you. I'll be in the car." He nodded to his dad. "See you later, Pops."

The retired cop watched his son leave the diner before leaning in to Maria. "So, what did the child unit say on the phone?" he asked, lowering his voice.

"How the hell did you know that's who it was?" she asked accusingly.

"I didn't until now." He grinned. "The oldest cop trick in the book. You still have much to learn, young grasshopper." He winked and then laughed to himself.

"You rat bastard!" She smiled. "Anyway, they said another kid went missing last night."

"Is this one going to be of interest to us, or is he just another runaway?" he asked, almost whispering.

"He fits the profile of our other kids. That's all I have for now." She looked out of the window to check that Andy was in the car. "Look, I've got to go. I'll swing by after work. Hopefully with more details."

"I'll be here," he confirmed.

The detective threw down a twenty dollar bill on the counter "Will that cover breakfast?"

"Plenty." He picked the money up and put it in his shirt pocket. "See you later."

"Thanks. I'll see you later, Pops." She turned and scurried out of the diner to join her partner in the car.

As Coop watched the car peel out of the parking lot, he grabbed the phone from the counter and dialed a number. "Hey, Herb, it's Coop. Listen, old friend, I need some information. Are you going to be around in about an hour?"

Chapter 15

The booking area of police HQ was completely empty except for a cleaner who was buffing the floor with a large industrial polisher. It was a complete contrast to the chaos of Monday mornings. The sound of Andy and Maria's footsteps echoed around the booking area. As they approached the front desk, Sergeant Simon Percival looked up from his computer screen.

"Good morning, Detectives." He waved as they passed. "One moment, I'll buzz you in."

"Morning, Percy; how's the wife?" Andy inquired.

"Still a pain in my ass, but, aren't all women?" Percival winked at him as he reached under the counter and pushed the button to release the lock on the door to the office area.

Andy looked at Maria, expecting her to burst into a tirade at the sexist comment, but she seemed oblivious to what had been said.

"I've got to say it again." Andy nudged her. "I really do like this new you."

"What?" She looked mystified.

"Percy." He nodded towards the desk sergeant. "If anyone had said something like that to you this time last week we would be mopping up the blood by now."

"Said what?" she asked, looking back at Percival.

"That… about women… are you okay?" He tilted his head to one side and looked at her with a look of curiosity.

"Me?" Maria looked back at him. "I'm fine. I, err… just can't be bothered this morning."

She continued to the Homicide Office with Andy trailing

a few paces behind. The curiosity was still evident on his face as he rubbed his forehead.

They reached the office, but before they got to their desks they were stopped in their tracks by a familiar, thundering voice.

"Cooper, Hernandez. My office. Now!" Regan bellowed across the room.

The detectives looked at each other. Maria rolled her eyes and gestured with her hand for Andy to lead the way. Regan was perched on the corner of his desk by the time they entered the office. He signaled for the detectives to take a seat. They shuffled to their seats like a pair of school kids who had been summoned to the principal's office.

"Right, where are we with the investigation into the execution?" the lieutenant asked.

"Randell can't give us a name on this—" Andy was cut short.

"Can't or won't?" his superior demanded.

"I'm fairly sure if he had a name for us, sir, he'd give it up." Cooper sat back in his seat with confidence. "He has nothing to gain by keeping any information from us. He also knows I would never sell him out."

"I don't like that slimy bastard, and I certainly don't trust him." Regan shifted around on the desk as if he was trying to get more comfortable as he spoke. "Go lean on him some more. I want you to be one hundred percent certain he's not holding back on us."

"I agree. He is a horrible little weasel fuck," Maria said as a matter of fact. "But Andy's right, sir. Randell doesn't know anything. He strikes me as the type of guy who would sell his own mother out for a plate of refried beans. If he had any information he would have told us yesterday."

"We'll head back down there later and talk to him again.

Knock on some other doors." Andy looked for approval from Regan.

The lieutenant pondered for a few moments in silence.

"Worst-case scenario is the Haitian community will see we're doing something about this." Cooper continued.

"All right, that sounds good to me. Take a couple of uniformed units with you to let people see we're all over this." He paused for a second. "Are we still marking this down as a gang-related execution?"

"I can't see it being anything else at this time." Andy looked to Maria for confirmation.

"It seems that way to me too, sir," she agreed.

"I'm going to level with you guys. The mayor has got wind of this and there's a shitstorm rolling downwards. The chief has a meeting with the commissioner and the mayor tomorrow morning. He wants something positive to say." The lieutenant looked deflated. "Guys, I need you to get me some good news on this, and quick."

"We'll head straight down there now, sir," Andy reassured Regan, and signaled to Maria. They stood up, ready to leave.

"Just one more thing." The lieutenant stopped them. "Have we got a name for the John Doe at Surin's place?"

"Not yet. Forensics has had no luck with his prints," Maria informed him.

Regan stood and walked around his desk. He fanned a few files that were stacked next to his phone and studied them for a few seconds.

"Okay. New plan of attack." The lieutenant sat in his chair. "Andy, you get down to Little Haiti. Kick some doors down. Make some noise; lots of noise. Take four marked units and partner up with Zamora." Before he could finish doling out his orders, Maria interrupted.

"Hang on; what about me? I want to kick doors down!" Maria exclaimed.

"No. I want you to head to forensics and find out who this mystery guy in the Surin shooting is. He might be more connected than we first thought." Regan started filling in a requisition sheet. "If the execution is in retaliation for his death, then we need to know who the hell he is."

Before Maria had a chance to object, Regan thrust the completed form in Andy's direction.

"Let me know when you have something for me," he said, without looking up from the paperwork he was reading. "Close the door on your way out," he added.

They left the office in silence, and closed the door behind them. They had only taken a few steps when Maria started on Andy.

"Come on, partner, can't you talk to him?" she pleaded. "I should be there with you. This is what I do."

"For once I actually agree with you. This is right up your alley," Cooper agreed. "But I've seen that look on his face before. He won't change his mind, so it's pointless asking."

Andy showed genuine disappointment that he wouldn't have his partner with him in Little Haiti. For all of her faults, he knew that Maria was exactly the kind of backup you needed in situations like this. Little Haiti was a notorious hotspot, and things could flare up and escalate very quickly.

"This is bullshit!" Maria's frustration was apparent.

She sat behind her desk and reluctantly started checking on her computer for the latest information on the Surin case when she noticed the piece of paper that Coop had originally given to Andy.

"Hey, if it looks like it's going to go bad down there, make sure you call me." She picked up the note. "I'll be there in a heartbeat."

"Will do." Andy nodded as he put his bulletproof vest on. "In the meantime, keep your head down, and try not to piss anyone off, especially Regan."

He checked his weapon and radio. "I'll call you if I need you."

"I'm on my way to Forensics." Maria stood up. "Call me on my cell."

"Will do," Andy acknowledged as he started to leave.

"Hey, partner!" she shouted after him. "Be careful."

He waved his hand in the air and headed for the door.

***

Andy returned to the office later that afternoon and found Maria busy tapping away on her keyboard. He noticed eight to ten files neatly stacked in her 'Out' tray, and only two in her 'In' tray. There was also a file open on her desk that she was taking notes from and logging them into the police database.

"Wow, you've been busy." He pointed to the files in the out tray. "You've gone through all these?"

Maria had been so engrossed in her work she hadn't noticed her partner returning and was quite startled when he appeared next to her.

"Hey, you scared the shit out of me! Didn't anyone ever tell you to never sneak up on a cop?" She looked at Andy for an apology.

He gave her a grin and nodded in the direction of the paperwork, giving her a cue to tell him what she was up to.

"Yeah, I've needed to get through these for a couple of weeks now." She continued, "So today came in handy, really. How did you get on?"

"It was as we thought; nobody is talking. I don't think the marked units helped." He sounded deflated. "The people in Little Haiti simply don't like or trust cops."

Andy went over to his desk and took off his bulletproof

vest before sitting down and starting his report for Regan.

"What about you? Anything on the John Doe?" he asked.

"I went to Forensics; they got nothing on the prints and are still waiting on the DNA results." She flicked through the files in the 'Out' tray and retrieved the one for the Surin case.

Maria opened the file and thumbed through the pages until she found what she was looking for.

"The cell they found at the scene was a drop phone. No numbers on the call log, but there were a couple of messages in a media app. I've got Palmer trying to make sense of it." She looked up from the file. "It looks like the guy was involved in some kind of delivery."

Maria was very matter of fact as she went through things, only listing the important parts. It was a common cop trait, to alleviate any confusion when giving details on the progress of a case.

"Well, that backs up the theory we had at the scene. A drug deal gone wrong." Andy tapped his pen on the desk while he thought through what Maria had presented to him.

"I'll write it up later and wait for Forensics to come up with a name for us. Good work, partner." He gave her an approving nod and continued to fill in the Little Haiti report sheet.

The detectives busied themselves with their paperwork until Andy abruptly threw down his pen and checked his watch.

"Hey, listen, I'm going to shoot over to AppTech and check up on Jen." He stood up and threw his jacket over his shoulder. "I'll swing back here later and pick you up when I'm done."

"Is everything all right?" she asked.

Andy thought for a second. "Not sure. Miller picked Jen up this morning in that Porsche of his. There's something about that guy that just doesn't sit right with me."

"Holy shit, a young girl getting picked up in a Porsche by a guy with loads of money?" She paused and looked Andy in the eye.

"I'm sure you're worrying about nothing," Maria added sarcastically.

Andy scowled at her.

"I'm joking!" She forced a broad smile. "Listen, I haven't been to the gun range for a week or so, and I could do with some target practice. Do you want me to come with you and have a little firearm workout session with Pee Wee?"

Maria looked at Andy with no expression on her face. He was fairly sure she was joking.

"No, you stay here. I just want to check it out and have a word with Chris to see what he thinks of this guy." He continued to look at Maria, trying to work out if she was joking about shooting Miller or not.

"Okay, but don't worry about picking me up. I'll get a lift home when I've finished up here." Maria gestured at the files on her desk. "You go sort Jen out."

"Are you sure?" Andy said with enthusiasm.

"Absolutely," she confirmed.

"Maybe I could take her for dinner on the way home. Spend some quality father- daughter time together." He glanced over at the lieutenant's office. "Can you cover for me with Regan? If he asks, tell him I've gone back downtown?"

Andy pouted and gave her the puppy dog eyes.

"Okay, okay." Maria dismissed Andy with a wave of her hand. "Now go, get out of here. I'll see you at Coop's in the morning."

Andy started to leave, then stopped and walked back to Maria's desk.

"One more thing. You were joking about using Miller as target practice, right?" He looked puzzled as he waited for an answer.

"Of course I was joking, partner!" She laughed. "You know I would *never* do anything like that."

The sarcastic tone in her voice left Andy even more unconvinced than before. Still looking confused, he turned and left.

As soon as he was out of sight, Maria opened her desk drawer and pulled out another file. She quickly glanced around the office to make sure Andy hadn't come back, then returned her attention to the closed document, opened it, and began reading.

Chapter 16

Maria entered the diner and spotted Coop talking to two uniformed officers who she vaguely recognized.

"Hey, Coop." She grabbed his attention as she approached.

The two officers looked and nodded at her.

"Good evening, ma'am," the taller of the two greeted her, then turned back to Coop. "Better get back on the streets. See you later, Cap."

Even though Coop had been retired for some time, the cops who came to the diner still addressed him by the title given in his last position.

"You guys have a good evening." Coop shook their hands. "Stay safe out there."

"Sure will, Cap." The shorter one mock saluted as he walked away.

Both officers touched the peak of their caps as they passed Maria. "Ma'am."

"You guys take care," she acknowledged.

"Come on." Coop picked his coffee up and nodded towards the kitchen. "Let's get some privacy."

When they entered Coop's 'inner sanctum,' Maria was rendered speechless. Gone were the boxes that had previously been piled against the walls. They had been replaced with corkboards that were filled with extensive details of each of the missing kids, all fitting the profile, and all looking very similar to each other.

"Wow!" she exclaimed. "You've been busy, old timer."

"Less of the 'old timer,' if you don't mind." He stuck his

chest out and posed to show off his physique. "There is plenty of life left in this old dog."

"My mistake, you're a regular Adonis," she mocked. "Anyway, what have you come up with?"

"Well, I think I've found a pattern." He paused for a second, and then shook his head. "The problem is, it's very weak. It might not be a connection at all."

He stopped and looked at the boards.

"And the more I think about it, the weaker it seems." He sighed and continued to study the evidence.

"Well, seeing as I'm here, how about running it by me anyway?" She sensed he doubted himself, so gave him a reassuring smile.

"Don't patronize me." Coop grinned and walked over to the desk.

"All right, here goes." He picked up a notebook. "I've cross-referenced all the information we have on these kids. We already worked out that they were riding the buses, right?"

Maria nodded.

"Now, on the days these kids went missing, they were all quiet days at the particular parks the buses were heading for—"

"Quiet days?" Maria interrupted. "What does that mean?"

"Different parks are quieter on different days of the week," Coop said.

The puzzled detective wrinkled her face, not really knowing what he meant.

"You mean like Christmas holidays and stuff?" Maria asked.

"No." Coop opened a drawer in the desk and pulled out a map of central Florida. "Look here. For example, the second Tuesday of every month is the best time to visit Sunny Glades, because it's usually quieter, so the lines for the rides are shorter."

He pointed on the map at the Sunny Glades location, then pointed at another park.

"Now, if you go to Aqua Splash here. Every Monday and Thursday there are a lot less people in the park than the rest of the week." He looked away from the map to Maria. "Are you with me?"

She stood gawking at the map for a few seconds.

"One quick question." She looked at Coop. "How the fuck do you know this?"

"I thought everyone who lived in Central Florida knew this stuff. Besides, there are books you can buy with all this information in them." He pointed at his desk. "I have the latest copy there."

"Somebody wrote a book about that?" Maria shook her head. "That's unbelievable. Somebody actually took the time to note all this statistical shit and wrote a book about it?"

She picked the book up and quickly flicked through it before throwing it back onto the desk.

"Anyway, continue," she requested, and turned her attention to the boards.

"Well, all these kids went missing on the quiet days of each of the parks." Coop walked past the boards, tapping the notes with his index finger on each one. "They all disappeared between 5:30 and 7:30 p.m., which would suggest that whoever is taking these kids has some sort of routine. A job or something that ties them up till that time of the evening."

Coop paused and narrowed his eyes as he looked up to the ceiling. He stood silently for a moment, then shook his head, as if dismissing whatever he had been thinking.

"Now, I want an unbiased opinion." He picked up a small pile of folders and gave them to Maria. "I haven't had a chance to process these files. You look through and see where those kids went missing. Check the days and times, then cross-reference them with that book. If I'm right about the quiet days, this is a major lead, and could give us a rough time and location for the next possible snatch."

Maria opened the first file and laid it on the desk, then grabbed the book. She looked eagerly between the file and the book and started making a few notes. One by one she worked her way through the documents, getting more enthusiastic as each file was closed. After several caffeine fixes, numerous expletives, and a lot of arm shaking to wake up sleeping limbs, the last file got closed, and she stepped back.

"Fuck me, old man!" she blurted out in amazement. "You were right! These kids all went missing in the same time frame, and on the quiet days of the parks they were heading to."

Her mind raced as she tried to analyze the whole situation. Why were the kids going missing at those times? Was it an office worker on his way home? Why only the quiet days? How did he know those were the quiet days? Was he a theme park employee? Every question she asked herself led to another.

"What do you think, old man?" Maria asked, as she turned to study the boards again.

Coop took the photos out of the files that had just been scrutinized and pinned them on the boards.

"I have to admit, I thought you were off the mark with the quiet day theory, but this looks like the real deal." Maria joined Coop in looking at the new faces on the boards.

"You know I should take this to CACU and see what they think." She didn't have any conviction in her voice.

Firstly she had to convince Coop that passing it over was the right thing to do. And secondly, she really didn't want to turn this over to someone else just yet. She looked upon the legendary retired cop as a genius, and liked working with him. It wouldn't take much to convince her not to report this.

"Let's just keep it between us a little while longer," he

pleaded. “I have an idea I want to try out.”

Maria thought about it for a few seconds. She was intrigued as to what his idea could be.

“Okay. Run this idea by me.” She sat on the chair and waited to be convinced not to go to the CACU.

“I’m going to go through this again and see if there is a more definitive pattern.” Coop turned to face her. “If I can come up with something solid, we may be able to stop another kid going missing, and nab the perp at the same time.”

She sat looking at him, not completely convinced.

“Come on, kiddo. I know I can blow this wide open!” Coop implored.

“I have to be honest. I do think you have stumbled onto a credible connection here.” She stood up. “So, I’ll hold off reporting this—for now.”

Coop let out a sigh of relief. “Now you’re thinking.”

“One thing; are you working on the assumption these kids are alive still?” Maria inquired.

“Until a body turns up, yes. That’s the way we should conduct this investigation.” Coop rubbed his face in his hands. He looked tired. “Right. First thing in the morning, I’m all over this. If I come up with anything I’ll message you.”

He started tidying the paperwork on the desk, preparing to leave.

“Make sure you do. If this is accelerating as fast as we think it is, we need to jump on it,” she affirmed.

“I may even ride a few of these buses to see if anything jumps out at me.” He picked up a bus schedule from the desk and studied it.

“What? Is that wise?” she asked.

“Sure. What can happen?” Coop shrugged and put the schedule in his wallet. “It’s a while since I’ve been in the field.”

“May I remind you that you’re a *retired* cop?” She got in

his face. "Retired!"

"Hey, look, some of the best evidence is found while re-enacting a situation." He dismissed her comment.

"No. Coop—" She was cut off by him raising his hand.

"This is how I do things." His voice was harsh. "I'll be fine. I promise if I see something of interest, I'll call you immediately."

"Okay. But be careful, and make sure you call me," Maria conceded.

"Thanks for your concern, but I've been doing this longer than you've been out of diapers." He smiled. "Now give me a hug and get out of here."

He opened his arms and Maria stepped in for a hug.

"I'll swing by in the morning for some breakfast," she said as she stepped back.

"If you don't see me, don't ask for me." He winked. "If Andy's with you and gets suspicious, he'll be straight on the phone to Cathleen. I don't need the grief."

"Gotcha." Maria winked. "I'm out of here."

She waved and left the office. Coop finished tidying the files on his desk and took one last look at the boards. Every pair of eyes of the missing boys stared back at him. There was a heavy silence in the room as he stood, mesmerized. Then, as if someone had pushed a 'go' button on him, he turned the light off and locked up for the night.

Chapter 17

"Damn heat," Coop muttered to himself as he sat at the back of the bus.

He reached into his pocket and retrieved a handkerchief, wiping the sweat from his brow before returning it to his pocket.

The air conditioning on the bus he was riding seemed to be working intermittently, and when it was working, the air was barely cold.

This looked like it was going to be another fruitless journey, as he had ridden so many buses the past few days, with nothing of any significance to report to Maria. Thankfully, no more kids had been reported missing, so he told himself he would do it for just two more days before returning to the drawing board to come up with another plan.

His mind wandered as he thought how much of a setback it would be if he had read this whole thing wrong. He also hated the thought of handing this case over to some young desk jockey who, in his opinion, had no idea or experience on being a true policeman.

The bus jolting to a halt to pick up and drop off passengers snapped Coop out of his thoughts. He focused on the open doors and counted four adults off and what appeared to be a family of two adults and three children get on.

The father shepherded the two youngest children to the nearest available seat before sitting behind them, with the mother next to him. The third child didn't stop and sit behind them. Instead, he continued to the seat in front of Coop and slumped into it.

The retired cop stared at the back of the kid's head. His

mind began to race. This kid fit the general description of the others on the boards in his office

He leaned diagonally forward slightly to get a glimpse of the boy's face, and took a good look before sitting back. He leaned on the armrest and rubbed his chin while looking out of the window, trying to decide if this was what he had been waiting for.

"What should I do?" he said quietly under his breath.

The boy seemed anxious. He kept checking the cell in his lap, every so often flipping it over and looking at the screen before shaking his head and returning it to the face down position.

The bus came to another stop and a few passengers alighted. Coop's attention was immediately drawn to the only person who got on. The new passenger was pretty much nondescript. Male, five ten, roughly two hundred pounds. He was wearing a Khaki shirt, matching trousers, and a distinct red baseball cap.

Every instinct Coop had told him something was not right with this guy.

Using his peripheral vision so it appeared he was gazing out of the window, he watched the man walk up the aisle towards the back of the bus. He looked at the boy for a moment before sitting two rows in front of them on the opposite side of the bus.

Coop disguised taking a look at the male by taking his handkerchief out of his pocket again and wiping his brow. He noticed the guy was typing a message into his cell so turned his attention to the boy. After a few seconds he heard the familiar sound of a cell phone buzzing while being on silent. The kid flipped his cell over.

He had obviously received a message and read it.

This is it, Coop told himself. *This has got to be the son*

of a bitch.

A mixture of excitement, apprehension, and tension started to course through his body.

He continued to survey the reactions of the boy and the unknown male as the bus got fuller at each stop, getting closer to the theme park.

"Last stop before Sunny Glades, everybody!" the driver announced, pulling up to a stop.

With all his senses aroused, he focused his vision directly towards the driver so he could keep one eye on the male in the red cap and the other on the boy. He didn't want to get caught and spook either one of them. He was close, so close. He could feel it.

The other passengers on the bus started to gather their belongings, preparing themselves to get off the bus and into the theme park as quickly as possible to take advantage of the last few hours before the park closed.

This is the end of the line. Surely they're getting off here, he convinced himself, and decided it would be best to get off before anybody else so he could position himself at a safe distance, just enough to keep up the surveillance while he contacted Maria.

He walked down the aisle of the bus, holding onto the back of the seats as he passed to steady himself, purposely knocking into other passengers and apologizing as he went by. To everybody else on the bus he looked like an infirm old timer, but Coop knew what he was doing. When he got to the front of the bus he held onto the rail behind the driver and fumbled in his pocket for his glasses.

"Excuse me, sir," he addressed the driver with his glasses balanced on the end of his nose. "Did you say Sunny Glades?"

"Sure did, mister," replied the cheerful driver.

"Oh my." Coop peered through the windshield. "I appear to have gotten on the wrong bus again."

"Are you sure, mister?" The driver quickly glanced in the rearview mirror.

"I'm certain." He looked towards the back of the bus. "How far away from the Aqua Splash Park are we?"

"It's about seven miles east of here." The driver now looked a little concerned for the old man standing behind him.

"Oops. I'm supposed to meet my daughter and the grandkids there." Coop fumbled for his cell. "I'd best ring her to come and pick me up."

He searched through the contacts on his cell and pressed the call button to connect to Maria. The final stop was getting closer.

"Oh, hi, honey," he stuttered when she answered.

"Coop?" She sounded surprised. "What's with the honey shit?"

"I've made a bit of a mistake again, sweetie." Coop winked at the driver through the rearview mirror. "I know I was supposed to meet you at Aqua Splash but I got on the wrong bus and now I'm at Sunny Glades. Can you bring the kids and pick me up?"

"What the hell are you talking—" Maria's angst was clear.

"That's right, honey. Sunny Glades." The bus came to a halt at the park entrance. "Oh, one moment. We're here. Don't hang up."

All the passengers stood up and filed down the aisle towards the exit. The doors opened, and Coop led the way for everyone to disembark. One by one everybody got off the vehicle and raced towards the entrance.

"Are you onto something?" Her tone had changed.

He knew he'd got her attention.

"Yes, that's right, sweetheart." He turned and waved at the driver as the boy wandered past him. "I'll wait by the main entrance for you."

"Okay. I'm on my way." Maria almost shouted down the phone. "Don't do anything till I get there."

"Thank you, sweetie." He wandered around, trying to stay between the kid and the guy in the baseball cap, who was a few steps behind, all the while trying to give the impression of a lost and confused old man. "Oh, and hurry. I don't want to miss out on any precious time with the kids."

Coop disconnected the call and noticed the kid had stopped by a water fountain. He watched as the boy bent down and quenched his thirst, then he diverted himself towards a bench that was positioned at the side of the gates leading into the park and sat down.

The guy in the baseball cap had gone. Coop sat back on the bench and rested his arm across the back so he could still see the boy while casually scanning the area for his suspect.

The kid suddenly reached into his pocket and pulled out his cell. Another message? He pushed a button and replaced the phone before walking towards one of the parking lots.

Coop's instincts kicked in again.

Why would a kid turn up at a theme park and head towards the parking lot? his conscience shouted.

He waited till the boy was a reasonable distance away before scanning the area again. Still no sign of the suspect. The kid rounded a corner and was out of sight. Coop sprang from his seat and hurried after him. He reached the corner in seconds and peeked around it.

The guy in the baseball cap was talking to the boy as they walked. He placed a hand gently between his victim's shoulder blades and started guiding him to a secluded part of the parking lot.

Coop quickly scanned the area. He looked back towards the main entrance, then in the direction of the boy. Both the kid and the suspect had disappeared from sight.

"Fucking idiot!" he chastised himself, and quickly reassessed the situation.

His phone buzzing in his pocket brought him back to the reality of what was about to happen. He knew it was Maria, so didn't feel the need to check before answering.

"Where are you?" he snapped.

"I'm about three minutes away!" she shouted over the sound of screeching tires. "What's happening?"

"I lost them." Coop started moving in the direction his quarry was heading.

"What? Where are you now?" she asked with some urgency.

"I'm heading towards the parking lot west of the main gate." He picked up his pace.

"Okay. I'll be there—"

"I see them." He cut her off.

Coop had spotted the suspect and the boy walking along a line of trees that shielded the parking lot from the park. He watched as they moved away from the trees and started weaving their way between vehicles that were parked.

"Coop, what's happening?" she pressed.

The kid suddenly stopped and stepped backwards. Without warning, the suspect grabbed the boy by the shirt and put him in a headlock. A struggle broke out and they fell to the ground near a van.

"Maria, you'd better get your ass here!" he demanded. "This is going down now!"

"I'm nearly there!" she shouted. "Keep them in sight, Coop. Don't do anything till I get there!"

"Too late!" He hung up and raced towards the van,

taking his .38 Smith and Wesson revolver out from its shoulder holster as he ran.

He raced between the vehicles and saw that the boy was face down on the ground, kicking and wriggling, with the suspect straddling him, trying to subdue his victim. The kidnapper produced a rubber nightstick and raised it high above his head, readying to land a knockout blow.

"Freeze! OPD! Drop your weapon and let the kid go!" Coop shouted.

The kidnapper immediately got up and dropped the nightstick on the ground before raising his hands in the air.

"Don't you fucking move!" Coop growled, as his adrenalin rushed through his body. He hadn't felt like this for years. The rush of catching a criminal in the act was something he always relished. The suspect stood frozen to the spot, looking towards the ground, his face hidden by the peak of his cap.

"Lace your fingers behind your head and get on your knees!" Coop ordered.

Without making a sound, the suspect put his hands behind his head and lowered himself onto his knees.

Coop flicked his eyes between the suspect and the kid.

"You okay, kid?" he asked.

The boy flipped over onto his back, his eyes wild with fear as he stared at his attacker.

"Hey, kid! Get behind me!" he shouted.

The petrified boy snapped out of his daze and scrambled backwards, not taking his eyes off of the suspect until he was level with his savior. Then, without any warning, he sprang to his feet and ran off as fast as he could.

Without taking his aim from the mystery man, Coop quickly looked around in an attempt to follow the kid, but all he could see was the boy's head bobbing up and down between the vehicles as he scurried away before he vanished behind the line of trees.

"Kid! Come back! I'm a cop!" He shouted, and turned back in time to see the captive attempting to get up.

"Stay down or I will shoot you," he snarled.

The suspect froze for a moment, then lowered himself back down onto his knees, still keeping his head down, hiding his face.

The sound of squealing tires told Coop the cavalry were on the way. He looked towards the entrance in time to see Maria's car narrowly missing a white van that was leaving the park. Her car slid sideways for a brief moment. He could see her spin the steering wheel to correct the vehicle. Flashing police lights behind the front grill signaled backup was there.

He looked back at the suspect, who was motionless. Coop waved his arm in the air to let her know where they were.

Maria brought her car to a screeching halt and jumped out. She looked at Coop, who nodded to the suspect. Without breaking her stride, she took out her cuffs.

"Don't move!" she ordered, as she clamped one cuff around the suspect's left hand. "Bring your hand behind your back."

The suspect lowered his hands behind his back, allowing her to cuff the other hand. She grabbed him by the shoulder and pulled him to his feet, then pushed him face down onto the hood of the nearest vehicle.

"I think you can put that pea shooter away now," she said to Coop as she patted the suspect down, looking for any weapons.

Her partner looked at her sarcastically before activating the safety catch and replacing it in his shoulder holster.

"Pea shooter my ass," he quipped. "You can't beat a good, old-fashioned .38. It's never failed me."

"Where's the kid?" She looked around

"He ran off in that direction. He's long gone." Coop pointed at the line of trees. "At least we got this piece of shit."

Maria finished searching the suspect and pulled him up off the hood.

"He's clean." She pulled his cap off to reveal his face. "What's your name?"

The suspect remained silent and stared at the ground.

"Where's your ID?" she pressed.

Still no response. She looked at Coop.

"He was about to knock the kid out with this," he said, as he picked up the cosh with his handkerchief.

"Okay. Get on your knees," she ordered the suspect.

The suspect lowered himself onto his knees again. The female detective grabbed him by the shoulder.

"Now, I'm going to lay you face down," she said.

She lowered him down so he didn't harm himself. "Stay there and don't fucking move. You so much as twitch and I'll shoot you for resisting arrest. Am I making myself clear?"

The suspect didn't acknowledge. He just lay there.

Maria stood up and walked towards Coop, pushing him a few steps back so she could speak to him out of earshot of the suspect.

"I'm going to call this in. Do you want to take my car and get out of here?" She lowered her voice. "It will be one less thing for me to explain to the lieutenant and Andy."

He looked a little frustrated and peeked over her shoulder at the suspect.

"I will get this fucker back to the station and see what he has to say for himself," she assured him, as she took the cosh from him, taking care not to compromise any forensic evidence on it.

"Okay. Call me if you need picking up after work," he conceded.

Maria tossed her car keys to him.

"See you later, kiddo." He winked and made his way to her car.

"Hey, old man!" She called after him. "That's some good police work."

He waved his hand over his shoulder in appreciation. Maria turned back to the suspect, got her phone out, and dialed dispatch.

Coop jumped into her car and as he pulled away, he got his phone out of his pocket and pressed speed dial number 2.

"Hey, I need a favor, and I need it now . . ."

Chapter 18

Sergeant Percival methodically tapped the letters on the keyboard, only pausing to peer through his thick-rimmed glasses at the computer screen to make sure he had entered the information correctly. Although he had been the booking sergeant for many years, he had never mastered the technique of typing with more than one finger. His attention was drawn away from his work as the sound of footsteps echoed around the empty booking area. Detective Hernandez had entered via the rear door, followed by a handcuffed male wearing a red baseball cap. Two uniformed officers had a firm grip on the suspect's upper arms as they led him to the desk sergeant.

"Good evening, Detective Hernandez." He smiled, and then looked past her at the suspected felon. "And what have you got for me here?"

"Assault and attempted abduction of a minor." She looked at the suspect, who continued to stare at the floor. The peak of his cap made it difficult for anyone to get a good look at his face.

The booking officer banged his open hand on the desk. "Well, bring him closer and let's get him booked in."

The female detective grabbed the miscreant by his shirt and pushed him forward. When he was close enough, Percival leaned over the desk and snatched the cap from his head. The force of the garment being removed in an unduly manner unbalanced the kidnapper, sending him even further forward. Had it not been for Maria grabbing his arm to pull him back, he would have ended up face down on the desk.

"Let's take a look at this pretty face of yours," the

sergeant said in a condescending voice.

The suspect attempted to bury his face into his chest and turn away, but Percival reached out, cupped his chin, and lifted his head to get a look at him.

"Oh, you really are a pretty boy, aren't you?" he mocked. "Our other guests in the holding cell are going to really enjoy your company."

Maria did her best to contain a smile, and managed to compose herself before speaking.

"Is it okay if I leave him here while you do the paperwork?" She pointed to the ceiling. "I have to go upstairs and explain this to Lieutenant Regan.

"Certainly, Detective. I'll look after him." Percy grinned.

"When he's booked in, can you place him in an interview room?" She grabbed a piece of paper and wrote her extension number down. "Call me on this line."

"Certainly, Detective. It could be a while yet though." He paused with a big grin on his face. "I mean, you know how I like to be very thorough with my cavity searches before putting any prisoner in an interview room."

"Of course, Sergeant." Maria enjoyed the intimidation tactic, especially as the perpetrator looked increasingly uneasy with each comment. "I wouldn't want you to rush your process, so please be extra methodical on this."

She winked at Percival, then headed for the homicide office.

***

The Homicide Department seemed eerily quiet. The officers present were occupied with their individual cases. Some talked on their phones. Others filed reports and logged information into the police database. A relaxed atmosphere had descended upon the usually active workplace. Maria had only taken a few steps into the office when the silence was shattered.

"Hernandez!" Regan's voice bellowed over the entire department, causing the other detectives to jump out of their mellowed states.

The lieutenant stuck his head out of the half-closed door. "My office! Now!"

She stopped in her tracks and rolled her eyes, exasperated at the fact that she had not even got to her desk to prepare a report before being summoned to the head honcho's office.

She sighed and let her shoulders drop, then turned and made her way to what she thought was almost certainly going to be an ass-whooping, convinced the lieutenant wouldn't give her the chance to explain herself. She glanced at the other detectives as she passed them. All watched as she entered the private office and closed the door behind her.

"Sit down, Hernandez," her superior ordered, without looking up from the file he was studying.

She sat and anticipated the onslaught.

"So." He flipped the file closed and looked up at her. "I hear you're taking your own cases now?" he said.

She decided that offense was the best form of defense, and prepared herself for a shouting match.

"Sir, I did—" She had barely started before Regan cut her short.

He held one hand in the air to stop her talking. "Before you say something you will regret, Detective, I need to tell you that what you have done today is some damn fine police work."

Maria was stunned. She blinked in disbelief. *Did I just hear right?*

She began to relax but kept her guard up, in case the lieutenant had another go at her. The sound of someone else in the room clearing their throat surprised her. She shifted around in her seat to see Andy sitting in the corner.

Confusion set in. What was he doing there? Does this mean he knows about Coop?

She casually nodded at her partner, who acknowledged her with a reassuring smile.

"The details we have are sketchy." Andy stood up and placed his seat next to her. "What exactly are we looking at here?"

Maria hesitated for a moment, looking between the lieutenant and her partner.

"Basically," she proceeded with caution, "I caught the perpetrator in the midst of trying to snatch a kid. During the arrest the kid got spooked and bolted, so we don't have his account of the incident. I've got uniforms out looking for him."

"What do we have on the suspect? Any priors?" Regan inquired.

"He's not talking, sir. I'm hoping we'll find out when Booking runs his prints. Until we get them, we have no positive ID," she answered.

"Has he lawyered up yet?" Andy asked, as he stood up from his seat.

"No." Maria's frustration began to show in her voice. "This fucker is literally saying nothing."

"Right." Regan clapped his hands together in a show of enthusiasm. "This is what's going to happen. As soon as he is processed, I want you two in an interview room with him." He pointed at the senior detective. "Andy, Maria has the lead on this. You back her up. Get him talking, and make it quick. I need you two back on the streets, concentrating on these gangbangers."

"No problem, sir," Andy answered.

"Now, get out of my office, the pair of you." Regan pointed towards the door. "Hernandez, don't make a habit of doing stuff like this."

He signaled for her to leave, then buried his head in a file on his desk.

"Yes, sir." Maria nodded, thankful that she still had her job.

Both detectives left the lieutenant's office and headed for the booking area.

"So, you kick the sauce, start eating, and become super-cop?" Andy teased as they walked.

"Can I just ask how you guys found out so quickly and, more to the point, why are you here, anyway?" Maria stopped.

"Ah." Andy stopped and turned to face her. "Your 'new partner' called me from the scene. I was in the car on my way home. He said I had better get back here and give you some support."

"So much for him keeping it quiet," she said with a hint of sarcasm.

"He was just worried you would walk into a shitstorm so asked me to clear a path for you," he said, trying to defend his dad.

They walked on.

When they reached the booking area, they saw Percival with the phone pressed against his ear. He happened to glance around and spotted the approaching detective.

"Well, that explains why I was getting no answer," he said, replacing the phone on its receiver. "Your suspect is in interview room three." He paused and peered over his glasses. "Still not talking."

He pushed a few keys on his keyboard, and the printer in the corner whirred into action.

"Palmer has taken his prints and swabbed him for DNA. He's also taken his phone to examine," he continued, as he went to the printer to retrieve the booking sheet.

The ever-thorough sergeant examined the document in

its entirety before handing it over.

"There we are." He smiled. "He's all yours. Interview room three."

"Thanks, Sarge." Maria took the paper in one hand and quickly tapped the side of her temple with index and middle finger in a mock salute.

Andy leaned in to have a brief look at the booking sheet.

"You ready?" He looked at his partner.

"Let's go nail this bastard!" she replied with confidence.

***

When the detectives entered the interview room the suspect sat bolt upright, causing the short length of chain on his handcuffs to snap tight on the arms of the chair. He sat with his back to the door so had no idea who had entered. He fidgeted in his seat, seemingly unable to get comfortable due to his restraints.

The interviewers closed the door and silently walked around the table to sit opposite him. Maria placed a file on the desk, sat back, and crossed her legs in an apparent relaxed state while she studied her subject for a few moments.

Andy leaned forward, rested his elbows on the desk, and began to twirl his thumbs around each other behind his interlaced fingers. The silence in the room fuelled the growing tension, which made the suspect fidget more as his eyes flicked from one interrogator to the other. Even though the air conditioning was turned to full, beads of sweat began to appear across his brow.

The situation stayed the same for what seemed like an eternity until the psychological pressure the detectives applied forced the antagonist to break the silence.

"Let me save you a lot of time here. I have nothing at all to say," he said nonchalantly, and returned his gaze to the floor.

"We can sit here all night." Maria sighed and leaned forward. "But let me tell you this, the longer you keep quiet, the worse it's going to be for you."

She noted the threat seemed to have no effect on the unperturbed suspect, who continued his mute-like state. She flipped open the file and was about to continue when she was interrupted by a knock on the door.

The door opened enough for Palmer to pop his head around and wave a piece of paper in their direction. "Sorry to interrupt. Detective Hernandez, can I have a word outside please?"

The female detective was vexed by the sudden interruption, but nonetheless relished the thought of having some evidence that might bring this investigation to a conclusion. She closed the file and stood up without taking her gaze off the suspect.

"I'll leave you in the capable hands of Detective Cooper," she said, as she moved towards the door. "Feel free to make a statement when it suits you."

Palmer held the door ajar for Maria to pass, then closed it and led her into the observation room so they could watch the perpetrator and Andy through the two-way mirror. She folded her arms and stared at the suspect through the glass.

"Okay, what have you got for me?" she asked, as Palmer closed the door and stood next to her.

"Nothing. We've run his prints through our local database, but there's no match," he replied.

She unfolded her arms and snatched the paper out of his hand to take a quick look at it. "Have you run them through the national database?" The anger in her voice was apparent.

"Yes. Again, nothing. We're reaching out to Interpol, but that's going to take some time," he informed her. "Is he talking?"

"No. He reckons he has nothing to say." Maria was trying to stay calm. "What about the phone?"

"There's no calls in the log but, there is one message. It's on a social media app and was sent from someone called Genesis. It appears to be in some kind of code. I'm running that through code-breaking software now." Palmer shook his head as he took the paper back from her. "If he doesn't start talking, this is going to drag on."

"Okay, I'm going back in. Let me know if anything turns up." She took one last look into the interview room before leaving Palmer to get back to his side of the investigation.

When she returned to the room, she noticed Andy had stopped twirling his thumbs. He sat motionless and stared menacingly at the suspect who, in Maria's opinion, looked terrified. His whole demeanor had changed. He no longer stared at the floor. The color had drained from his face, and his wild eyes glared back at his interrogator. Sweat ran down his face and neck and stained the collar of his shirt. More sweat stains on his back and armpits led her to believe her partner had threatened him with something. Rather than question what had happened, she decided it was the right time to get the interrogation under way properly. Armed with a new piece of information, she sat on the corner of the table next to the suspect.

"Who, or what, is Genesis?" she quizzed.

The perpetrator snapped his gaze away from Andy and fixed it on Maria. His mouth gaped at the mention of Genesis.

"Oh, touched a nerve, have we?" She stood and moved around the table to sit opposite from him again. "Are you ready to start talking now?"

"I haven't done anything wrong," he protested.

"You were in the process of kidnapping a minor." She pointed her index finger at him. "You were caught with a cosh in your hand about to crack his head open."

He shook his head. "No, he attacked me. He came at me from behind and I managed to get the weapon off him."

“Our witness tells a different story.” She picked the file up and opened it.

Maria gave the impression she was reading a document. The suspect stared at her with his mouth open.

“Our witness says you made contact with the boy on the bus with your phone. Then you arranged to lure him away from public view before you attacked him when he tried to get away from you—”

He closed his mouth and gulped. “I would like my lawyer now.”

“Of course you would, you piece of shit.” She closed the file and threw it on the desk. “We’ve checked your phone. You deleted the messages to cover your tracks, didn’t you?”

“I want my lawyer now.” He stared at the floor, dismissing the detectives.

“Well.” She swung her arm up to look at her watch. “They’re busy, so if that’s the way you want it, you’ll have to go into holding for the night. I would advise you to get some sleep. Maybe when you wake up you’ll feel a little more cooperative.”

She picked up the file and signaled to Andy. They left the room without further communication and went straight to the booking area.

***

“That fucker wants to lawyer up, Sergeant. Can you put him in a cell overnight?” Maria asked Percival as she approached the desk, with Andy a few paces behind.

He hadn’t noticed the detectives entering the booking area as he was sat hunched over a pile of paperwork, which had landed on his usually orderly booking station. ‘A tidy desk is a sign of a tidy mind’ was his regular citing when asked by numerous colleagues why he spent most of his day shifting things around to exactly the right position, sometimes by mere millimeters, before sitting back with a satisfied look that everything was in its place.

"Best put him in isolation for his own safety," added Andy.

"Still not talking?" he asked, as he picked up the forms he had been studying and tapped on the desk between his hands to straighten them up before depositing them into a folder. "Let me see what suites we have available."

He pushed his glasses up the bridge of his nose with his index finger and peered at the computer screen, then started tapping away on the keyboard.

"We'll leave it with you, Sarge." Andy nodded to his partner to follow him. "Call Maria on her cell if and when he decides to start talking."

"I take it there's no rush for the lawyer," the sergeant asked sarcastically.

"None whatsoever!" Maria called over her shoulder, and continued to follow Andy out of the station.

Before they reached the parking lot, Maria suddenly stopped. She had suddenly realized she didn't have her vehicle with her.

"Andy, I need a favor," she said in a pleading voice.

"After what you've done today, just name it, partner." He gave her a wink.

"Thanks. Can you drop me at Coop's? I need to thank him personally for ratting me out, and he's got my car," she said, only half-joking.

"Sure, come on." He waved at her to follow him. "But, take it easy on the old man. He probably saved your ass in there tonight. Going solo on an unauthorized investigation can lose you your badge. If he hadn't called a favor in from Regan you wouldn't be coming to work tomorrow."

"I know." She smiled and quickened her pace to catch up with her partner. "But I'm still going to kick his ass for being a snitch."

"Yeah, right." He laughed as he opened the car door and looked across the roof at her. "Don't let the old timer fool you. He could probably take me *and* you on without breaking into a sweat."

"Now that you mention it, he is kind of ruggedly fit for his age." She winked and got into the car before Andy could make any comment. He just smiled and got in.

Chapter 19

It was busier than normal in the diner. Numerous cops filled the place, getting their caffeine fix. Some chatted about the game on TV the night before, some recited mildly humorous stories of their careers, which always ended with their colleagues forcing out a laugh in mock appreciation. The detectives had been forced to occupy a booth, as their regular seats were taken. Maria had managed to get halfway through a stack of pancakes while Andy devoured his usual omelet when Coop approached them.

"Sorry I missed you last night, Maria," Coop apologized. "It had been a long day so I just left your keys with Beth."

"That's okay, Judas," she fired back. "I figured you just wanted to get out of my way. Lucky for you I have been calmed by these pancakes." She waved her fork in his direction. "So, I have decided to forgive you."

"I was just making sure you got the backup you deserved," he replied sheepishly. "By the way, I've shredded those files."

"Files?" Andy looked up from his breakfast with a mouthful of half-chewed food.

"Just a bit of research, son." He gave him a reassuring pat on the shoulder. "Nothing for you to worry about."

Andy sat back and shifted a suspicious look between the two of them, then swallowed his food and continued.

"You really are a pair of mavericks, aren't you?" he said as he sat forward, taking his turn to wave a fork at his father. "If Mum finds out that you have been working a case she will be at the divorce court faster than you can say no prenuptial."

"Yeah, you're probably right." He laughed and leaned on the table to deliver a menacing look. "Lucky for me she won't find out. Will she?"

Andy averted the glare and returned to his food. "Not this time. But make sure there isn't a next time, please, Dad. I don't like lying to Mum." He lifted his head and made direct eye contact with his father. "Especially when I agree with her."

"I can't promise, son," he said, as he pushed himself up off the table. "You know what it's like when you've been in the job." Then, not taking his eyes off him, he held his hands up in his familiar mock surrender pose. "Hey, I'm just saying." He winked at Maria.

"You're unbelievable, Dad," he said, shaking his head and returning to his breakfast.

Maria and Coop laughed at Andy's disbelieving attitude to their antics. The laughter was cut short when the sound of Hootie and the Blowfish singing "I Only Want To Be With You" filled the air. The female detective jumped out of her seat and struggled to retrieve her cell from the pocket of her figure-hugging trousers.

"My bad. Keep meaning to change this ringtone," she apologized. The flustered expression on her face altered to adopt a more serious manner as she checked to see who was calling her. "It's the station."

She flipped the phone open. "Hernandez…"

The instant look of concern on her face grabbed her breakfast companion's attention.

"What?" she said, exasperated. "When?"

Coop and Andy looked at each other and shrugged before returning their attention to Maria.

"Okay, we're on our way." Maria disconnected the call and stuffed her cell back into her pocket. "We have to go. Now!"

"What's happened?" her partner asked with a worried

look.

"Our suspect is dead." She threw a twenty dollar bill on the table.

"Holy shit!" The retired cop fumed. "Are you serious? How?"

"Apparent suicide in his cell." She tapped Andy on the arm. "We have to roll."

"How can this happen?" Coop seethed. His rage was becoming more visible as the seconds passed.

"No idea," she replied, as she started towards the exit. "CSI are on scene. I'll let you know as soon as we have some answers."

"See you later, Dad." Andy waved over his shoulder as he pursued his partner out of the diner.

***

As they entered the short corridor that led to the holding cells, the detectives were momentarily halted by the coroner slowly pushing a gurney bearing their suspect in a zipped-up body bag. They stood against the wall and watched as the corpse passed by. Andy tapped Maria on the arm and pointed to the cell.

"Come on. Let's see what happened." He peeled away from the wall and entered the cell, followed by his partner a few paces behind.

The scene took her breath away. "What the fuck?" she gasped.

Sergeant Percival was leaning against the wall just inside the door with his thumbs tucked over his belt. He acknowledged his colleagues with a silent nod as they passed. CSI Palmer was busy taking photos of the scene. The usually pristine white corner of the cell furthest away from the door had been turned red. Blood spatter could be seen covering a large area of the adjoining walls and ceiling. A hefty pool of congealed blood seeped towards the center of the room, letting them know where the perpetrator had been found.

"Careful where you stand. I'm not quite done here," Palmer instructed, while he kept shooting the scene.

The detectives scanned the floor and moved near Palmer's equipment case.

"Is here good?" Andy inquired.

The CSI glanced over and nodded, then continued snapping away.

"What happened?" Maria asked.

"Looks like suicide," Palmer said nonchalantly. "The tearing of the skin on the neck around the jugular suggests a self-inflicted frenzied attack."

"What with? I thought all sharp objects were taken from prisoners?" she remarked.

"They are." The forensics expert ceased photographing the area, switched his camera off, and checked where he could place his feet before carefully stepping backwards until he was next to them.

He replaced the lens cap on his camera and put it in its case, then retrieved a zipped-up evidence bag that contained a blood-sodden screw.

"I found this on the floor. Preliminary checks match the scarring and puncture wounds on the suspect's neck." He nodded in the direction of the bed. "It matches the type used in the bed frame. There's one missing from under the right-hand corner nearest to us."

"Wow. That's a smart design." Maria's anger materialized in the form of sarcasm.

"These are old frames," Palmer informed them. "The new ones are completely different. It's like space-age technology. They're a solid structure with zero removable elements which eliminate—" His enthusiastic reciting was brought to an abrupt halt when he looked at the detectives and found them staring blankly at him. "Anyway, I'm done here. Like I said, preliminary findings are that he used this screw."

He bent down to put the evidence bag in his equipment case and closed it up. As he stood up, he pointed to the pool of blood. "I have to say, to pierce his jugular in this manner, he must have really hated the room service here," he said with a wry smile

Andy and Maria stared at him, motionless. The momentary silence added to the somber atmosphere in the room

"Anyway." Palmer shattered the hush. "I will confirm everything when I get back to the lab and have concluded my tests."

"Wasn't anybody watching him?" Maria turned to the desk sergeant.

"We did a complete search on him before putting him in here, plus, he wasn't down as a possible suicide risk," Percival said in defense, and removed his cap to scratch his head. "I've never had anything like this on my watch. I just can't believe it."

"You couldn't have known." Andy put his hand on the sergeant's shoulder to offer some comfort.

"What about CCTV? I'm curious how he managed to do this without drawing attention to himself," commented the female detective.

"There's no CCTV in the cells. Human rights took care of that," Percival replied cynically.

"Fucking do-gooders!" She made no attempt to contain her anger. "I wanted this bastard to pay for what he's done. Justice for those poor kids. This coward piece of shit took the easy option."

"I hear what you're saying." Her partner turned to her. "But let's keep our heads clear on this. There's probably going to be an internal investigation—"

Andy was cut short by the lieutenant appearing at the

cell door, who stopped to survey the scene before entering.

"Holy fuck, it looks like a battle scene," he said with a sigh. "What have we got here?"

"Palmer is writing it up as suicide, sir. But he's still got tests to do before giving us full confirmation," the senior detective answered.

Regan scanned the scene again for a few seconds. "Well, I guess we can draw a line under this investigation." His line of vision followed the blood spatter up the walls till he was straining his neck to check the 'damage' on the ceiling. "It looks like he took his own life rather than face life in prison as a child molester. That's admission of guilt enough for me."

"He took the easy way out, Lieutenant," Maria said in an irritated tone. "There's no justice here."

Her superior drew his gaze away from the ceiling. "Don't beat yourself up, Hernandez. You got him off the streets, and let's face it, this way we know he won't be re-offending anytime soon." The lieutenant returned to looking around the cell. "Well, clear up the paperwork on this and get it on my desk before IA starts chewing my ass."

"Just one thing, sir. We've still got no ID on him," stated Maria.

"Hmm. Leave it as John Doe for now, and see what crops up. Maybe somebody will report him missing at some point." Regan turned and exited the cell with some haste. "Reports on my desk as soon as possible, Hernandez," he barked, as his footsteps could be heard travelling down the corridor.

"Come on, let's get back to Homicide. I'll help you with the paperwork, then lunch is on me," Andy offered.

"You have a deal. I just want to go to CACU and let them know the situation." Maria was disheartened by the whole thing. "I'll meet you upstairs."

***

As she entered the CACU, Maria was a bit overwhelmed as to how quiet the office was. She considered under the circumstances of the past twenty-four hours that the place would be buzzing with activity. Instead, there was only one officer, who had his head down, trudging through an extensive pile of paperwork stacked on his desk in front of him.

"Hey. What the fuck is going on here?" Her voice shattered the sedate environment. "Where is everyone?"

"Excuse me?" The officer snapped his head up to see the female detective closing in on him.

"Where are all the other investigators?" she pressed.

"If you mean my colleagues," he twiddled with his pen between his index fingers and thumbs, "They are out on visits to various hostels and safe houses, checking the new arrivals so they can be crossed off our ever-increasing lists of missing children." His matter-of-fact attitude took Maria by surprise. "Can I help you, again?"

"Yes," she retorted. "Don't you know what happened last night in the holding cell?"

He looked blankly at her. "I'm sorry, I must have missed that memo."

"Yesterday we caught a perp in the act of abducting a kid," she informed him. "Last night he took his own life in the cell."

"Oh, that?" The sarcasm in his voice annoyed her. "Yes, I heard about it."

"So what the fuck? Why aren't you all over this?" Her agitation made him smile.

The officer raised his hands in a calming manner. "Look." He stood up. "Detective Hernandez, isn't it?" He held his hand out for her to shake it.

She was taken a bit by surprise with his attitude, but

reluctantly shook his hand.

"I'm Detective Travis." He smiled as they shook hands. "Pleased to meet you, again."

"Likewise," she replied.

"Now." He signaled with his hand for her to sit. "Take a seat, and I'll let you know how we do things down here."

Maria took a moment to calm down, and slowly lowered herself into the seat beside her.

"Sorry, it's been a shitty morning." She sighed. "I was all set to bury that fucker this morning."

"It's a shame you couldn't have got some more information out of him." He tried to console her. "You never know, he may have helped clear some of our backlog."

"Didn't even get his name; he wouldn't say anything." She looked at the floor and sighed again.

"Well, feel free to check out our wall of shame." Travis pointed to the wall directly behind her. "Anytime you want to track down one of those guys and bring him in, help yourself."

She twisted her head round to see a wall full of mug shots, and instantly got out of her seat to inspect the photos.

"What's this then?" she inquired while she perused.

"All those guys have previous convictions for sexual-related crimes against minors, and, get this . . ." He joined her. "All of them are in this area."

"You mean these guys are on the streets?" Maria exclaimed.

"Absolutely," he said with confidence. "They do their time, and they're out. Personally, I don't think they get long enough inside."

"Our guy last night had no ID, no prints, nothing." She shrugged and continued looking at the pictures. "We're waiting on DNA results to see if he shows up on any database locally, nationally or internationally."

"These guys on here," he tapped his finger on the wall, "they're just the ones that have priors. God alone knows how many are out there who haven't been caught yet," he added. "I bet your guy was a first-timer. That's why he got caught."

"I know I could have got him to talk given a little more time." She continued to walk along the wall, inspecting the mug shots of each face as she passed. "Maybe you could help me out here. When we get a name on our guy I'll pass it over to you. He may be a known associate of one of these guys."

"That'll be good." He looked her up and down as she walked further away from him. "Maybe we could discuss it over a drink, or maybe a bite to eat one eveni—"

"Fuck me sideways!" Maria shouted, cutting him off mid-sentence.

"I'd be happy with just a dinner date . . ." He looked puzzled at her.

"Who is this guy?" Maria tapped her index finger on the photo with some force.

He moved next to her and took the picture down. "Seaton, Charles James. Why?"

"That's him." She glared at the image. "That's the guy I arrested yesterday."

"The suicide?" he asked with alarm.

"Yes!" Her eyes were wild.

"But I thought you said the guy wasn't in the system?" He looked closer at the picture.

"He isn't." She snatched the mug shot from his hand.

"He must be. All these guys have a record." He waved his arm, indicating every picture pinned to the wall. "All have prior convictions, so they should be in the system."

He suddenly turned away from her and walked towards a bank of filing cabinets.

"Give me the reference number on the back," he called

over his shoulder.

Maria read out the number while he looked through the relevant filing cabinet and pulled out a file.

"Here we are." He flipped the file open and walked towards his desk. "Charles James Seaton. Forty-three years old from South Carolina. He's got numerous misdemeanor convictions for robbery and assault, and served three years of a five-year sentence for child molestation. Been out eight months."

He sat behind his desk and started typing on his keyboard. A bewildered look developed on his face. He feverishly entered more information into the computer.

"This can't be right." Travis sat back in his chair and thoughtfully rubbed his chin. "If he's on that wall, he should be in the system. But he isn't."

"Why the hell isn't he?" Maria demanded.

"I have absolutely no idea," he said, closing the file and passing it to her. "It's lucky my boss is old-school and insists on making hard copies of everything on the wall or we would have nothing."

She took the file and began reading through it. "Son of a bitch! I need to show this to my lieutenant. Can I borrow it?"

"Not a chance." He jumped up and reached over the desk to snatch the document back. "But, I'll gladly photocopy the entire file for you." He gave her a broad smile.

"Great." Her anger subsided as excitement took over. "Can you just photocopy the cover page and the photo now? I'll collect the rest later."

"Sure," he agreed, and went to the copier. "Give me an hour to get the rest done."

Travis copied the requested documents and passed them to Maria. She snatched the paper from him and rushed out of the unit.

"I'll be back in one hour!" she shouted, as she

disappeared into the elevator.

***

When Maria exited the elevator she was so engrossed in studying the information she had received as she made her way to the lieutenant's office she didn't notice Officer Wilson walking towards her.

"Detective Hernandez! Have you got a minute?" Wilson caught her attention in time to stop her from bumping into him.

"Not now, Wilson, I'm in a rush." She tried to sidestep to get around him.

"It's about the kid that ran away from the scene yesterday," he persisted.

She stopped dead in her tracks and spun around. "Have you found him?"

"Not exactly—"

"Look, I'm really busy," she interrupted, and continued to her destination. "Tell me when you've found him."

"I've been showing his description around and I think I know where you can find him!" he shouted after her.

She stopped again and slowly walked back to Wilson.

"How sure are you?" she asked, trying to contain her newly piqued excitement. "I'm fairly confident he'll be at Richmond Park at some point." The officer took out a notepad from his shirt pocket and flicked through the pages until he found what he was looking for.

"Ah, here we go," he continued. "He's a latchkey kid—"

"A latchkey kid?" she queried.

"Yeah. You know. A latchkey kid." He looked at the detective for a moment before explaining. "Their parents are never around so they leave the kid with a key. That way he can let himself in and out of the house after school."

"Really?" She was astounded. "They're never home

when he gets in from school? What the hell goes through these people's minds?"

"Believe me, Detective," he continued with confidence, "This isn't an isolated incident. This kind of thing goes on all over the place. Most modern-day parents have to take on two, maybe three jobs to make ends meet."

"Jeez. I had no idea." She shook her head, trying to comprehend what she had been told.

"So, from what I hear, he spends most of his time hanging out at the park. Goes by the name of Ronaldo," Wilson concluded.

"Ronaldo." She looked puzzled. "Are you sure it's the right kid? The description I have doesn't sound like a kid from South America."

"It's his street name. He's always got a soccer ball with him," Wilson answered, with the smugness of someone who was expecting the question. He ripped the note from the pad and passed it to her. "Here, take this."

"Thanks, Wilson, I owe you one." She took the note and tapped the cop on his shoulder, then continued her rushed walk to the homicide unit.

***

Andy Cooper had been entering information into his computer for some time when Maria burst into the office.

"Whoa, there. Where's the fire?" he joked.

"Follow me. You need to see this." Maria waved the paper she had got from Travis and signaled for him to follow her to the lieutenant's office. She knocked on the door and opened it immediately. Andy sprang from his seat and rushed to his superior's office.

Lieutenant Regan, obviously startled by the sudden invasion of his private space, sat upright and scowled at the impatient female detective.

"Hernandez! We've talked about this. You knock, then wait before—" He was cut off mid-sentence by her.

"Sorry, sir, no time for formalities." She thrust the documents in front of him. "I've got something on the suspect."

Regan took the copies from her and started inspecting them.

"What's going on?" The senior detective entered the office and closed the door behind him.

"I've found something," She waved her finger at the papers in her superior's hands with great enthusiasm. "The suicide guy's name was Charles James Scaton. He's got previous, and he has only been out for eight months after serving time for sexual molestation of a minor," she blurted before taking a breath.

"Where did you get this information from?" Regan looked up and passed the documents to Andy.

"The CACU. They have the originals. They have a wall of shame down there, and that's where I spotted our guy." She took the copies back from her partner. "But, here's the kicker; when we ran his name again, it still came back with nothing."

"How can that be?" Andy joined in.

"No idea." She held her hands out in a disbelieving manner. "I had a feeling that we were trying to close this case too quickly.

"What made you think that?" the lieutenant asked.

"When we were in the interview room, sir, the only time the guy lost his composure and looked nervous was when I asked him about a name that was on his phone." Maria shook her head. "My instinct is telling me that this is not over."

"Psychic powers now?" Andy belittled his partner.

"Not at all. Just a feeling." She was defensive and slightly affronted by her partner's words. "We need to find out more about this guy, and why he wasn't in our system."

"I agree with her," Regan interjected. "If there's a glitch in the system, it needs fixing as a matter of priority."

"There's something else." She looked between the two men. "I have a lead on the kid that fled the scene."

"Where is he?" Andy snapped.

Maria became agitated by her partner's attitude.

"He hangs about at Richmond Park." She looked at Andy in an attempt to work out where his brashness had come from. Was he angry because she wanted to investigate this further? Did he want to get back to investigating the gangbangers?

"Okay." The lieutenant sat forward in his seat and placed his elbows on the desk. "Cooper, you get down to the Cyber Unit. Tell them to look into why this guy hasn't turned up on a search. I'll call their lieutenant to let him know you're on your way and will be waiting for an answer." He pointed at Maria. "You, get a uniformed unit and head down to this park. Do not come back without that kid. Do I make myself clear?"

Both detectives nodded in acknowledgement.

"I want to put this case to bed as fast as possible. Now go." He waved his hand, dismissing the pair from his office.

As she closed the door to the lieutenant's office, Maria decided to confront her partner about his attitude. She was about to call after him but noted he was heading straight out of Homicide, and judging by his brisk walk, it would be better to leave it till later. *He must be having trouble with Jen again,* she thought.

Although her orders were to take a uniformed unit to Richmond Park, she decided that taking Travis would be a better option. Having a cop trained to deal with delinquent children seemed more of an advantage to her.

When she got to the elevator she saw Andy waiting. Seizing her opportunity, she walked briskly to confront him about his mood. As she got closer the door opened so she quickened her pace. They entered the elevator together. Before she had a chance to say anything, he broke the silence.

"Listen, Jen has a big presentation tonight at AppTech; it's a big deal to her." He glanced at her with an expectant look. "Would you be able to swing by and show her some support? I can pick you up if you want."

So that's what's wrong with him. He's stressed about Jen's presentation.

"Of course I'll come, if for no other reason than to make sure you don't have a heart attack," shc replied.

Ping. The elevator halted and the door slid open.

"This is me." He exited and turned to face her, putting his hand on the door so it couldn't close. "See you back here around five?"

"Sure." She smiled. "See you later.

"Thanks." He returned the smile and stepped back, allowing the door to close.

Alone in the elevator, she felt relieved she hadn't upset him. That was one less thing to worry about on a day that was turning out to be quite eventful already.

Ping. The doors opened again and she headed to the CACU.

***

Travis had put the last document into the copier when Maria entered.

"You done yet?" she asked as she approached.

He looked over his shoulder and smiled.

"Detective Hernandez, good timing." He retrieved both the copy and original document from the machine a placed them into their relevant folders. "I've just finished."

She took the file and had a quick scan through it and smiled. "Thank you. Are you busy now?"

"Nothing that can't wait, why? What have you got in mind?" he asked with a mischievous grin.

She narrowed her eyes as if weighing him up.

"Okay, whatever that is," Maria waved her hand around his face, indicating the grin, "stop it now. I need backup looking for a kid, and as it is your alleged field of expertise, I thought I might take you along."

"Say you want me and you need me and I'm in," he teased.

"How about I agree not to shoot you right here, right now, if you come?" She squared up to him.

"You drive a hard bargain." He put a finger on his chin and looked towards the ceiling in a mock thinking pose. "Okay. I'll come. But I know the real reason you asked me."

His contemptuous tone was beginning to get under her skin. She also knew that asking what he thought her reason for asking him was almost certainly a license for him to make some other innuendo towards her, so instead of acknowledging his comment, she simply nodded.

"Good. Grab your shit and let's roll," she said.

"Yes, ma'am." He saluted. "I do like forceful women."

Although she found him a little annoying, she couldn't help but raise a smile. He quickly grabbed a few things from his desk drawer, then ran over to the door to hold it open for her to pass through.

Chapter 20

The incessant midday sun beat down in Orlando, a reminder to everyone why it was known as the Sunshine State. But, it wasn't bothering Maria and Travis, who were in the relative comfort of the air conditioned car they had picked up from the car pool. They had parked by the main entrance to Richmond Park and watched for the latchkey kid for three hours, with nothing that had spiked their interest. Contrary to how stakeouts are portrayed in movies, the reality is that these operations are invariably drawn out, tedious, and not for people who lack patience. The conversation between the officers had dried up over an hour earlier; well, for Maria it had. He still kept trying to ignite a spark of a conversation every now and again, and had even suggested playing a game of eye spy to alleviate the boredom. The look she gave him quickly dispelled that idea.

"So, are we going to get lunch soon? There's a great sub shop about a block from here. The meatballs are amazing." He persisted in his attempt to get some form of conversation going.

"We are on a stakeout, not a picnic," she responded curtly.

"Yeah, but we have to eat. It will only take five minutes." He rolled his head around to alleviate the stiffness in his neck and shoulders.

"What if the kid comes during that five minutes?" she replied.

"Then we get him when he leaves." He leaned forward to try and draw her attention away from staring at the park entrance. "I like meatballs."

“Shush!” She grabbed the binoculars that were nestled in her lap and craned her neck as she looked through them.

A group of five boys and two girls made their way along the sidewalk and into the entrance. Satisfied that none of them matched the description of the kid they were looking for, she placed the binoculars back on her lap.

“What’s your favorite sub? No, let me guess.” Travis looked at her and tapped his chin with his finger. “Everyone likes meatballs, but I can’t see you dealing with the mess of meatballs.” He looked up at the roof of the car. “Got it! Philly cheesesteak; definitely a cheesesteak kind of girl.” Travis had the look of a man who had just won the lottery as he faced forward and looked in the vanity mirror of the sun visor.

“Will you please just shut the fuck up?” she snapped. “This might be a game to you, but I take my work seriously, and I’m trying to look for this kid. I can’t do that with you constantly talking shit in my ear.”

“Well, that is clearly the case,” he said, still looking in the vanity mirror. “Because if you could multi-task, you would have noticed the kid with the soccer ball approaching the gate from behind us.”

He turned to look at her with a smug look that made her use every ounce of self-control not punch his face. She frowned at him before quickly turning around and saw a kid fitting the description, bouncing a soccer ball as he approached the park.

“That’s got to be him,” she said. “Come on, let’s grab him.”

“Wait for him to enter the park. There’s only one way in and out. Once he’s in, he’s ours.” He picked up the handheld police radio and squeezed the transmission button. “Unit two four to base, requesting a marked unit to Richmond Park.”

“What the hell are you doing? We don’t need backup to grab a kid!” she said indignantly.

"I've just told you there is only one exit. If we have uniforms on the gate and he runs, they can get him. I do not want to run in this heat." He opened the door and got out, then popped his head back in. "Are you coming?"

"You're starting to piss me off," she snarled, as she opened the door and got out.

"Hey, wait till you get to know me," he said, checking the traffic before they crossed the road. "I can be a real charmer."

They watched the kid disappear into the park before scurrying across the road. A marked police unit pulled up as they got to the gates. Two uniformed officers exited the vehicle and placed their night sticks into their utility belts. Maria flashed her badge that she had cupped in her hand to let them know who she was.

"Detective Hernandez," she informed them, as she clipped her badge back on her belt. "This is Detective Travis."

Both uniformed officers acknowledged them by touching the peaks of their caps and nodding.

"What's the problem, Detective?" the taller of the officers asked.

"We need you to watch the gates." Travis led them to one side of the entrance so they couldn't be seen from inside the park. "We're trying to detain a kid. He's white, about twelve years old with shoulder-length, mousey blonde hair, wearing white and red Bermuda shorts and a Brazilian soccer shirt."

"And he's got a soccer ball with him," Maria added.

"Yes," her new partner confirmed. "This is the only way in and out of here, so we're going to go in and attempt to grab him in there. If he runs and gets away from us we want you to be ready to grab him here."

"What's this kid done?" the second officer asked.

"Nothing. He ran from an attempted assault before we

could question him. So he's obviously going to be a bit spooked if he makes us," she told them.

"Okay, ma'am." The taller officer nodded. "We'll position ourselves on either side of the gate."

"Shall we?" Travis looked at her and nodded towards the gate.

Inside the park, the detectives casually scanned the area, looking for their target as they meandered along the path. Maria was taken by surprise when she felt Travis's hand slip into hers. She snatched it away and stepped sideways.

"What the fuck are you doing?" She glared at him.

"Just taking a walk in the park with my fiancée." He smiled at her. "Don't want to give the kid a head start. If he makes us before we see him… well… you know what'll happen."

"We can walk without contact," she said, as she walked on.

He shrugged and ran a few paces to catch up with her.

"Am I right about the Philly cheesesteak?" he asked, while trying to keep up with her brisk pace.

"Just keep an eye out for the kid." She was angry with herself that this guy could so effortlessly get under her skin.

"Maria." He grabbed her upper arm to stop her. She spun around and looked at his hand on her arm. "Listen, if you continue storming around the park like this he's going to make us before we get any further."

She sighed and looked up at him.

"I'm sorry," she said calmly. "I'm just a bit tense with all this shit that's going on. We've got execution-style killings, gang-related shootings, and now all these kids going missing. This place is getting like the wild…"

Maria drifted off as she looked over Travis's shoulder.

"Hey. Are you okay?" he asked with a look of concern.

“There he is.” She grabbed both of his hands and held them so they appeared to be a couple having an intimate chat.

“Where?” he inquired, without turning around.

“He’s about fifty yards over your right shoulder,” she informed him.

The kid stood with one hand holding onto the chain-link fence separating the park from the basketball area, his soccer ball resting between his hip and his other arm. He was so engrossed in watching about a dozen teenagers taking turns playing one on one that he didn’t notice the detectives approaching him. They had separated so they could come at him from different angles, reducing the chance of him making a run for it.

“Hey, kid!” Maria said loudly to get his attention. “We need to talk to you.”

The kid jumped and spun around to see adults approaching him. He quickly looked between them with squinted eyes and made a step forward, but Travis moved sideways to block his exit. With a look that told the detectives he had resigned himself to the fact that he wasn’t going anywhere, he stepped back against the fence.

“I’ll scream for help if you don’t back off,” the scared youth said as he continued to switch between them.

Maria pointed to her badge clipped on her belt. “Take it easy, kid, we’re the good guys.”

He held his hand up to shade his eyes from the blinding sun. “I ain’t done nothing,” he professed, when he realized who the approaching adults were.

“We never said you’ve done anything wrong,” Travis reassured the frightened youth. “We just want to talk to you.”

“Yeah, well, I don’t want to talk to you, so leave me alone.” He pushed himself off the fence and tried walking past the cops, but the male detective put his hand out to stop him.

“Listen, we only want to talk to you. It’ll only take a few

minutes." He looked at Maria, then back to the kid. "Are you hungry? Do you like subs?"

The kid looked confused by the question and glanced at Maria, as if he wanted clarification.

"Sorry, kid, he is obsessed with sandwiches." She shook her head. "He's been asking me the same thing all morning."

"Yeah, I like subs," he answered, squinting his eyes again as he looked up to the male officer.

"Okay, how about this. The three of us go to the sub shop around the corner. We buy you a sandwich. We have a talk, and then you can go. What do you say?" Travis asked.

The kid considered the offer. "If you throw in a soda, you got a deal." He extended his hand out to shake on the deal.

"You drive a hard bargain, kid, but you've got a deal." The male detective shook his hand. "By the way, this is Detective Hernandez." He nodded towards his partner. "And I'm Detective Travis."

"I'm Brad," said the boy, looking a lot more relaxed. "But everyone calls me Ronaldo."

"Come on, Brad," Maria said, as she put her hand on his shoulder. "Let's go and get you that soda."

***

"You guys get a table and I'll get the food," Travis suggested as he made his way to the counter.

Maria and Brad sat opposite each other in a booth by the window and waited for their sandwiches to arrive. It wasn't long before they were joined by their companion, who placed a laden tray on the table and slid onto the bench next to the boy. He started distributing the contents of the tray between them.

"I figured you were a meatball kind of guy, Brad, so here you go." He placed a sub in front of the boy before sliding another over to his partner. "Philly cheesesteak for the lady," he said sarcastically.

"Take it easy, Prince Charming," she retorted.

"I was right though, wasn't I?" He looked for confirmation of his choice.

She smiled and started to unwrap her sandwich. "We'll see."

"I knew it," he said confidently.

"Okay, kid, time to talk." She pulled out her small notepad from her back pocket, leveraging herself against the back of the seat to do so. "Firstly, what's your full name?"

She flipped the notepad open and pulled out the pen that was held inside the ring binding of the book. Brad eyed her and the notebook with suspicion.

"Bradley Lloyd," he said, then took a bite of his sub.

"Okay, Bradley Lloyd." She wrote his name down. "We want to talk to you about what happened at Sunny Glades the other day." Maria looked at him.

The boy froze and stopped chewing his food. His eyes grew wide. "I wasn't there."

"Don't bullshit me, kid. We have a reputable eyewitness who says you were there." She pointed her pen directly at the nervous boy. "So, what were you doing there?"

Brad glared at the pen, then looked up at the female detective. He slowly put his sandwich down and started to stand up. "This has been great, it was nice meeting you both, but I want to go now." He slid sideways and nudged Travis to let him out, who obliged by sliding along the bench.

"You stay right where you are, Detective." She pointed the pen at him and looked back to the boy. "Kid, you sit your ass back down and start talking." She slammed the pen on the table. "Now, what were you doing there?"

"You can't make me stay here. I have rights," the boy said indignantly.

"Rights? You want me to tell you what your rights are

right now?" She leaned over the table to get a little closer to him. "You have the right to start telling me what I want to know. If not, then I have the right to get my colleague here to phone social services and have you put in foster care within the hour."

"You can't do that," he pleaded, and cowered into the bench.

"I'm the police, kid, and I can do whatever I want. Now, for the last time, what were you doing at the theme park?" Maria glanced in Travis's direction.

He sat motionless, holding his sandwich in his mouth ready to take a bite, his eyes wide open with the look of someone in total disbelief.

Brad sat back in his seat. "Man, you're a hard bitch." He shook his head.

"And then some." She picked the pen up and readied herself for more writing. "Now start talking."

"Okay, I was there to meet this TV producer guy." He shuffled in his seat. "He wanted to make a film about my soccer skills."

"Had you met this guy before?" Travis joined in the questioning, albeit a little more gently.

"Not exactly." He shook his head.

"How exactly then?" Maria was becoming impatient.

"I got talking to him on an app. I sent him a short video of me doing some keep me ups and other ball tricks—" He was cut short.

"What type of app?" Travis interrupted.

"The one on my phone." He looked at the male detective.

"What's the app called?" Travis interrupted.

"Chat Around Me." Brad went in his pocket to retrieve his phone. He started pressing the screen, then offered it to the detective to have a look. "It lets you chat and meet people within a certain distance of you."

Maria peered across the table to try and get a look at the app. Unable to see it, she reached into her pocket and got her phone out and brought up the photo of Seaton on the screen.

"Is this the guy you met?" she asked, as she held her phone so Brad could see the image.

"Yeah, that's him," he replied, as he bowed his head to look away.

"Kid, you have no idea how lucky you were." She shook her head. "This guy is a convicted child molester. Didn't your parents ever tell you not to talk to strangers?"

"Yeah, but he seemed on the level." He sat back and crossed his arms.

"Okay, talk me through what happened from when you got off the bus," she continued, in a more soothing tone.

He looked around, and then sat more upright in his seat.

"I got to the park and waited where he told me to. Then he came over to me and asked me my name. Then he said we were going to go to the studio." He looked back and forth between the two detectives, and then fixed his vision on Travis. "But we headed for the parking lot, and that's when I became suspicious."

"Why did you get suspicious?" Maria asked.

"I've been going to that park for years. I know the studio part is in the opposite direction," he said.

"Smart kid." Maria nodded in approval. "So then what happened?"

"The closer we got to the parking lot, the more I knew something wasn't right. So I told him I didn't want to go any further and that I was going home. That's when he grabbed my arm and tried to drag me." He paused, and swallowed hard as he fidgeted in his seat. "Then out of nowhere this crazy old guy appeared, waving a big gun. The guy let go of me so I ran."

"You did the right thing, buddy." Travis rubbed the boy's head.

"I've told you everything. Can I go now?" He looked pleadingly at Maria.

"Just a couple more questions." She scratched the side of her face. "The whole meeting, was it set up using this app?"

"Yeah, everything was arranged on that." He started to stand up and nudged his seating companion to allow him to leave.

Travis looked at his partner for confirmation. She nodded after taking a moment to assess if she had the information she needed. The boy started to push his way out of the booth.

"One more thing." She put her hand on the table to stop the boy. "Does Genesis mean anything to you?"

Brad thought for a second. "Nope, can I go now?"

"Before you go." She took out her wallet and retrieved her business card. "Take this. If you ever need anything, you call me." She handed him the card. "And, kid, stay off that app for the time being."

Brad looked the female detective up and down, then he gave her a little smile.

"You know, for a hard bitch, you're kind of all right." He held her card to his forehead and saluted, then left them.

She watched the boy leave, then noticed her partner was disbelievingly looking at her.

"What?" she exclaimed.

"I see you have a very unique way of talking to kids," he said sarcastically.

"Worked, didn't it?" She shrugged and took a bite of her sub. "Mmm, that's a nice sandwich," she said with her mouth full.

"Philly cheesesteak," he confidently announced with a

big smile. She swallowed her food. “I also have the knack of punching people in the face who irritate me.” A sudden look of euphoria appeared on her face. “Hey, do you think we would be able to get a list of users for this app from somewhere?”

“I have no idea, that’s not my department.” He drew a large mouthful of soda through his straw and gulped it down. “But from what I do know of these things, you’ll probably find that a large percentage of the people registered on this app will be using a fake ID and e-mail account to set them up. Especially the kind of people we’re dealing with at the moment.”

Maria made a few notes on the pad as her partner spoke when she suddenly remembered something and looked at her watch.

“Jeez, look at the time.” She hurriedly closed her notepad.

“Are you okay?” Travis asked.

“Yeah, I promised Andy I’d attend Jen’s presentation at AppTech.” She finished putting her things away and stood up to leave. “I’m late. Look, you’re going to come with me.”

He finished his drink. “Sure, can you drop me off later?”

“Yes.” She scurried towards the exit. “Come on. I’m late enough without you trailing your sorry ass behind.”

She reached for the door when her phone rang and stopped her. She checked the screen and answered the call.

“Hey, Palmer, what can I do for you?”

“I’ve just done my preliminary report on Seaton,” the voice on the other end informed her. “It appears it wasn’t suicide.”

“What?” she exclaimed in disbelief. “Are you telling me this was an accident?”

“No, Detective Hernandez,” Palmer continued. “I’m telling you that I’m ninety-five percent sure this was murder.”

Chapter 21

Maria stood rooted to the spot in stunned silence.

"I'm sorry," she said in disbelief. "Can you repeat that?"

"I said Seaton was murdered," Palmer confirmed.

She continued her silence and slowly looked up at Travis, who was trying to listen to the conversation.

"What?" he mouthed at her, but she just stared at him through incredulous, wild eyes.

"What makes you say it's murder?" she continued.

"I found beige fibers around the back of the head and neck. This would indicate that he was put into a sleeper hold. It's a classic wrestling move to render your opponent unconscious," he explained.

"So what you're telling me is someone went into his cell unseen, knocked him out, shredded his jugular, and walked out of the station completely unnoticed." She sighed.

"That's what it seems like," he agreed. "There's also the entry wounds. Whoever did this took particular care to make it look like suicide, but made a huge mistake."

"How so?" she interjected.

"The initial entry wound, which was the fatal one, was at an angle that would have been impossible if it was self-inflicted. So I can deduce it was made by the attacker," he said with confidence. "The following wounds were self-inflicted—"

"Wait!" Maria interrupted. "You said he was unconscious—"

"If you'll let me finish, Detective Hernandez." Palmer began to sound irritated by the disruptions. "I was about to say self-inflicted in a fashion. The screw was then put between the victim's index finger and thumb and thrust repeatedly into the neck to make it look like suicide."

"Sick bastard. Have you told Regan?" she asked the forensics expert.

"Yes. He's ordered a second examination. I've organized it for first thing in the morning. It'll be carried out by another examiner, who is unaware of the circumstances so we can get an independent judgment. He's also got someone going through the CCTV from the entire station to see if they can spot who went near the holding cells."

"Okay, so we have to wait till tomorrow to see what they find?" she asked.

"Pretty much so, Detective," he replied. "If you like, I'll call you when we start the second examination."

"Yes, please do." She nodded to herself. "And Palmer, thank you."

"No problem, Detective." He disconnected the call.

The information she had just received raced around her head, leaving her momentarily mentally paralyzed.

"Are you okay?" Travis asked, bringing her out of her trance.

"What?" She blinked, coming back to reality.

"Are you okay?" he asked again.

"No. I mean, yes," she flustered, and quickly looked at her watch. "Come on, we have to get going. I'll tell you in the car. This case just got even stranger."

***

After they had negotiated Sinclair at the front desk of AppTech, they arrived in the conference room just as Jen made the final comments of her presentation.

" . . . So, in conclusion, we see this latest piece of software as the next big thing to hit the market, which will take AppTech to the next level in mobile applications, a concept that we are all very excited about. Thank you all for the hard work you have put into this product, and thank you for making AppTech the fantastic company that it is." She picked up her notes and tapped them on the podium between her hands to straighten them before putting them in a leather folder and zipping it up. "Thank you for your time."

Jen stepped sideways from behind the podium and curtseyed. The crowd all exploded into a rapturous round of applause, and one by one stood to give her a standing ovation. She was obviously overwhelmed by the response; her cheeks had flushed red.

Chris walked onto the stage followed by Miller, who carried a large bouquet of red, yellow, and pink flowers. He kissed his niece on both cheeks before taking the flowers from his star programmer and presenting them to her, then stood back and encouraged the audience to offer more adoration. As the applause continued, she cradled the bouquet in her right arm and waved her left hand in appreciation before slowly leaving the stage for her uncle to say a few words of encouragement to the entire AppTech staff.

Peering over the crowd, Maria spotted Andy, Kim, and Amber at the front, all holding their arms open to proudly envelop their "little star."

"Ladies and gentlemen, if I could just have your attention for a few moments." Chris stepped behind the podium and waved his outstretched arms to signal for everyone to return to their seats.

The attendees slowly sat in their seats and prepared themselves for the boss's rallying speech.

"Thank you." Chris cleared his throat. "I would like to take this moment to reinforce what my niece has said." He pointed at her in the front row before waving his hands across the rest of the staff. "Each and every one of you have put a lot of hard work into this latest project, and it's about to pay off. Thanks to all of you, AppTech is well and truly on its way to being the leading mobile software company in the United States."

The applause erupted again, forcing him to pause until it had died down.

"This was my dream when I first set up this company, and today only proves that if you put the time and effort into your dreams, anything is possible." He paused for a moment. "So, to show my appreciation for everything you people are doing, this weekend starts early. You can all take Friday off, with pay." He looked proudly at his staff as again they erupted into rapturous applause. "Now go, enjoy the buffet and champagne."

He stepped down off the stage to be greeted by Andy, Kim, Amber, and Jen. Maria watched in slight agitation from the back of the room as they hugged and chatted among themselves with beaming smiles while members of the staff took the opportunity to shake Chris's hand and congratulate his niece on her performance. She wanted to tell Andy about the latest developments, but didn't want to cast a dark cloud over the occasion. She let out a small sigh of relief as they joined in the flow of people filing towards the exit.

"About time, too." She glanced at Travis, who had stood just over her right shoulder, and something caught her eye.

A familiar face; one she knew, but couldn't immediately put a name to it. The man stood motionless, watching the Cooper family from behind dark glasses with great intent as they moved towards him.

He was dressed in an immaculately tailored Prussian blue suit with a contrasting electric-blue tie that rested on a crisp white shirt. His matching electric-blue handkerchief was neatly folded in the breast pocket, accessorized by the gold tie pin, gold cufflinks and what she guessed were easily thousand-dollar shoes. This guy not only had money, but also class. He looked eerily menacing, but not as menacing as the two stooges that flanked him. They, too, were dressed in immaculately tailored suits to fit their muscle-inflated torsos. Maria surmised that black was their favorite color. Everything was black. The suit, shirt, satin tie and handkerchief, socks, shoes, and finally the black sunglasses.

As she scanned the stooge nearest to her she noticed the tell-tale bulge under his left arm. This guy was armed. Bodyguards, she told herself. Then it hit her. The guy. It was Franco Baresi.

"Fuck me," she muttered under her breath. "What the fuck is he doing here?"

"Who?" Travis looked in the direction of the mannequin-type trio.

She was about to tell him but was cut short.

"Glad you could make it," Andy said as he approached.

"Hard day. I'll tell you later." She dismissed the sarcasm and pushed past him to congratulate Jen "Well done, kiddo. Sorry I missed most of it."

"Thanks, Maria," she gushed. "Don't worry, I'm used to having people not be there for me when they say they will." She paused and nodded towards Andy. "My dad's a cop, so you learn not to get your expectations raised."

"Hey, a cop's life is not an easy one." Maria smiled. "I know for a fact your dad always tried to attend everything that he got invited to."

"You see, honey, I told you I was busy." He winked at his partner in appreciation. "Maria will tell you how things are in this job. And if you don't believe her, Grandpa will always be keen to tell you a few stories about when he turned up late after Grandma left his dinner on the table."

"And those stories should be left for another time," Chris interrupted, as he pushed past his brother. "What did you think of my prodigy, Maria? You could be looking at the next vice chairman of AppTech here." He put his arm round Jen's waist and squeezed her.

"I wouldn't say that, Uncle Chris." Her face flushed again. "It's only my first presentation."

"And what a perfect presentation it was." He beamed. "You are going to go far in this business, sweetie, don't you forget it." He looked over to Franco Baresi, who nodded to him.

"Now, if you'll excuse me, I have to attend to something."

Maria was about to ask him about the app when he let go of his niece and started to move away. She watched as he went over and greeted Baresi with a kiss on each cheek before shaking hands with his companions. She was surprised by the public show of friendship between them.

Franco "Frankie" Baresi was, and had been for a long time, a well-known figure in the underworld of central Florida, notoriously heading up the Baresi mob, which had links to numerous criminal activities including extortion, bribery, narcotics trafficking, and rumored murders. None of these accusations had ever been proven in the many court cases the authorities had managed to subpoena him for.

"Hey, Andy, is that who I think it is?" she asked her partner, while not taking her eyes off them.

"Uncle Frank?" he said nonchalantly.

"Uncle Frank?" She looked at him with raised eyebrows.

"Yes, he's an old friend of the family. He and Coop go back a long, long way," he informed her.

"You do know he has a history?" she stressed.

He leaned in and lowered his tone while watching if Franco was keeping an eye on them. "Have you ever heard of the saying, 'Keep your fiends close and your enemies closer'?" He looked her in the eye. "Sometimes things like that work, and are best kept that way."

"Does the lieutenant know about this?" she continued.

"Yes, he does." He stood back and watched as Chris and Franco finished their conversation. "Let's just leave it there, shall we?"

Before she could say another word, Chris gently took hold of Jen's hand and started to guide her towards the mob boss.

"Jennifer, Uncle Frank would like to have a quick word about your presentation." He pushed her over to her meeting.

Maria watched as she was affectionately greeted by the boss and his bodyguards. She was taken aback slightly by the whole thing. How could a family with such close connections to the law be able to fraternize with the 'enemy,' so to speak? *I'll get to the bottom of this later,* she told herself.

"Chris, sorry to bother you." She grabbed his attention. "I have a question to ask."

"Sure. Fire away," he cheerfully answered as he watched his niece.

"We're in the middle of an investigation and have come across a mobile app called 'Chat Around Me.' Have you heard of it?" she queried.

He took his attention away from Jen and looked at her. "Heard of it?" He laughed. "Of course I have. It's one of ours."

"One of yours?" She had to stop herself from asking the plethora of questions, but realized this was neither the time nor the place. "Listen, I know you're busy now, but would it be okay if I came by tomorrow to have a chat about it?"

"Of course." He smiled. "Drop by anytime. I'll be here all day."

"Everything okay?" Andy interrupted.

"Everything is fine. Although, I could do with a quick word with you, just to bring you up to speed on a few things," she added.

He narrowed his eyes as if trying to work out what she was about to tell him. "Sure, shall we go outside?" He nodded towards the door.

"Chris, I'll call your secretary in the morning to make an appointment," she said, as she turned towards the exit.

"No need, just come by whenever you want," he replied.

"Okay, thanks," she replied, and as she passed Jen she reached out and placed her hand gently on her upper arm. "Hey, well done, again. I'll catch up with you soon."

"Oh, thanks, Maria." Jen turned from her conversation. "Maria, have you met Uncle Frank?"

She glared at the mob boss through his dark glasses. "No, I've never had the pleasure."

Franco stepped forward and offered his hand to be shaken. "Detective Hernandez, I've heard so much about you."

The hackles on the back of her neck rose. She shunned the offered hand. "Please excuse me. Jen, I have to speak to your dad." She maintained eye contact with him while she walked towards the door.

As she walked through the double doors to the corridor Travis caught up with her.

"Hey, are you okay?" he asked.

"Yeah, I'm fine." She dismissed his question and continued walking. "Come on. Let's get out of here."

Once they were in the corridor they looked around them to see if they could be overheard.

"What's going on?" Andy asked, and pointed at Travis. "Who is he?"

"Oh shit, sorry, this is Detective Travis from CACU." She held her hand out indicating her new partner, and then waved her hand towards her usual partner. "Travis, this is Detective Andy Cooper."

The two men shook hands.

"So, what's going on?" he repeated.

"We found the kid," she said.

"Fantastic! So that's it then, case closed?" He looked at the pair.

"Far from it. I think this thing is far from being closed. The kid was contacted using the app I just asked Chris about." She paused. "I think this thing is a lot bigger and a lot more organized, and I still have questions about who or what Genesis is."

"Really?" he exclaimed. "What are your thoughts?"

"I'm starting to lean towards an organized pedophile ring." She looked straight into his eyes.

Andy was visibly shocked by what he had been told.

"There's one other thing." Maria looked down and shuffled her feet like a child about to be chastised.

"What?" he asked

"Seaton." She paused. "It wasn't suicide. He was murdered."

"What?" he almost shouted, then looked around to see if he had been heard. He rubbed his forehead. "Murdered while in police custody? By whom?"

"Don't know; I just had a call from Palmer telling me that the initial wound couldn't have been self-inflicted," she said.

"This is not good." He shook his head. "Regan is not going to like this."

"He already knows," she informed him. "He's ordered an independent secondary examination and has someone going through the CCTV footage from the station."

"When is the next examination?" he continued.

"First thing in the morning. Palmer is going to ring me

so we can go in on it." She looked at Travis. "Do you want in on this as well?"

"Sure," he confirmed. "I'm more than intrigued about this case now."

"Okay," Andy said. "So what's the plan?" He looked at Travis, then back to Maria.

"I'm going to go grab some dinner and have an early night. I have a feeling that tomorrow is going to be a long day." She smiled. "One thing is for sure. I certainly picked the wrong week to quit the booze."

"Okay, I'll meet you at Coop's in the morning and make a plan of action." He shook his head again and rubbed his face with his hands. "Murdered in the cell . . . the press are going to crucify us."

"Yeah, we'd better keep this quiet for now." She tapped Travis on the arm. "Come on. We're out of here." Then she looked back at Andy. "See you at Coop's." She walked towards the elevator.

Travis extended his hand to Andy. "Nice meeting you."

"Likewise." They shook hands, and Travis walked in a hurried pace to catch up with Maria. Andy went back to the party.

She had reached the elevator and was impatiently pushing the button.

"You know what? Screw it; I need a drink," Maria said, as Travis got closer. "You want to join me?"

"I don't usually drink on a school night." He looked at Maria's face. "However, I don't think one would hurt."

"Okay, just one. I need a clear head for tomorrow anyway," she conceded.

As the two detectives boarded the elevator, Sinclair stepped around the corner. He had been listening to the entire conversation further down the corridor. He waited for the doors to close before he got his phone from his pocket and made a call.

“I need to see you. I have something you’ll be interested in… The usual place, tonight at nine.” He disconnected the call and headed for the elevator.

Chapter 22

"Are you okay? You don't look well," Andy said to Maria as he sipped his coffee.

"Just tired." She shrugged. "I've been up most of the night running this case through. I can't make any sense of it." She rubbed her eyes then took a mouthful of her coffee, staring at him intently. He had turned up at the diner a considerable while after she had arrived. So much so, she had actually finished her breakfast before he had even showed. When he did get there he walked in as if he didn't have a care in the world and sat next to her. The only words he had muttered were asking Beth for a drink, and then he just sat there, staring straight ahead, silently. She put it down to being a tad tired after probably celebrating Jen's achievement the night before. Or was he struggling with the case as much as she was?

"I thought you were back on the sauce for a moment there," he added, bringing her out of her thoughts.

"Oh, no. I had one beer last night. I'm not going to lie to you; I came close to really kicking back and having a party." She finished her coffee and pushed the cup to the end of the counter, awaiting a refill. "But I didn't!"

Coop appeared right on cue carrying a fresh pot of coffee. "Morning, son. The usual?" he asked while filling her cup.

"Morning, Dad." He raised his right hand to his forehead and mock saluted his father. "Yeah, the usual please."

He wrote the order down, ripped it from the pad and put it on the hatch to the kitchen.

"Special for Andy, Beth!" he shouted through to the

kitchen, then turned back to the detectives. "So, any news on our dead suspect yet?"

Maria put her head in her hands, then swept her hair back while taking in a deep breath. "It's a complete clusterfuck, old man." She sighed. "The guy wasn't in the system. I spotted his photo on the wall of the kids unit, found out his name. Then I got a call last night from forensics telling me it wasn't suicide. He was murdered."

"You have got to be shitting me?" Coop stared, open-mouthed. "In the holding cells?"

"Yeah, tell me about it," Andy said in a disbelieving tone.

"How could that happen?" He looked genuinely flabbergasted.

"We're trying to find out," she said despondently. "Second examination is getting underway soon, and Regan has people reviewing the CCTV footage now." She shook her head. "Someone must have seen something."

"You'd think." He grabbed a mug and filled it for himself.

"Anyway, how did you get on with the tech geeks?" She turned to Andy.

"Oh, yeah, they examined logs and databases and found the whole system had been breached from a remote IP address." He looked at his father and then back to her. "The thing is, it was so clever that we would have never detected it unless we did a search for the individuals." He took a sip of coffee. "Luckily you did, and found there was a serious problem. They suspect that other files were deleted too, so they're trying to weave their magic and restore it somehow."

"Can they find out who hacked in?" she asked.

"They doubt it. It was bounced about from server to server. If they can catch the hacker in the act they might have a chance." He shrugged. "But after-the-fact tracing is going to be nearly impossible. There's also a possibility that whoever is doing this is setting it on a timer. Now that's some smart shit."

"Jeez, get you with the computer talk," she scoffed, and winked at Coop.

"Hey, don't let my son kid you. He knows more than he lets on." He smiled, then shook his head. "I can't believe it. How can a prisoner get murdered in a cell?"

"Don't know, but I'll tell you, this case is getting stranger by the day," she said.

"Tell me, who was on the booking desk?" he asked.

"Your old amigo, Percival." She took another gulp of her coffee.

"Percy?" He looked startled then glanced at Andy, who shifted uncomfortably in his seat.

She glanced from one to the other, waiting for an explanation to the sudden change in their manner. The elder began to drum his fingers on the counter in obvious agitation while the younger avoided making eye contact with either of them.

"Am I missing something here?" Maria asked.

"As you know, Percy was my partner for a while." Coop paused and cleared his throat. He looked around and then leaned forward and lowered his voice. "We got a call out one night to a domestic disturbance. A drunk guy had gone a few rounds with his wife, who was six months pregnant." He paused again. Telling this story obviously vexed him.

"They also had a four-year-old boy. The boy had woken up when he heard the screams from his mum. He started shouting at the guy to stop. He slapped the kid to shut him up; quite a few times. When we arrived the woman and kid were outside waiting in the front yard. They were pretty badly beaten. The husband was asleep in a chair in front of the TV." He took a deep breath and rubbed his face.

"Go on!" encouraged Maria.

"Well, we surveyed the scene, and Percy told me to watch the woman and kid outside while he secured the suspect. I can't be sure what happened inside the house that night. What I do know is that guy was in intensive care for five weeks. He had severe brain damage and ended up having some kind of seizure that finished him off," he concluded, and stared at the counter.

"Shit!" she exclaimed. "I'm not saying the guy didn't deserve a beating, but . . . " She huffed and shook her head. "It would have been better if he'd been put away and suffered inside. Now *that* would have been justice served. What happened after that?"

"Percy was cleared by internal affairs for lack of evidence. He claimed the guy woke up as he tried to cuff him and all hell broke loose." He looked her straight in the eye and tapped his index finger on the counter to emphasis what he was saying. "Something wasn't right about his story. You think you know someone, but… I never rode with him again after that night."

"So let me get this straight." She sat upright. "Are you saying Percy could have done this?"

Coop shrugged and looked at Andy, who was still avoiding eye contact.

"It would explain how someone could have done this without being detected," she started to convince herself.

"Hey." He stood back and held his hands up. "I'm only saying."

"Yeah, well, you 'only saying' may give us a starting point on this." She tapped Andy on the arm. "What do you think?"

"I can see where you're going with this, and I agree with both of you, but…" He turned to face his partner. "You're going to have to be very careful with this. If you start making accusations against a cop of Percy's status, you'd better be ready for some serious backlash if you're proven wrong."

"I hear you, partner." She turned to him as if readying for a confrontation. "But this is now a murder case. I know what Seaton was, but we needed to get to the bottom of this Genesis thing before that happened to him. There are kids' lives at stake here."

"I know," he said, holding his hands up to calm her down. "We just need to tread very carefully here."

"I have to agree with him on this, Maria," Coop said calmly. "If you want my advice, go to Regan first, and let him know what your thoughts are. Hey, if you don't want to take the heat for this, tell him you got it from me."

She sat back in her seat and looked from father to son, thinking of her plan of action.

"Okay," she said finally. "Thanks for the advice, old timer. Andy, you're lead detective here. I'll go with what you think is right."

"Good." He sighed. "We'll go and see Regan after roll call and let him know our thoughts."

"I can go with that," she agreed.

"Now, Dad, can I have my breakfast?" Andy pleaded.

"Coming right up, son," he said, as he disappeared into the kitchen.

Chapter 23

"As you are all aware, the entire floor around the holding cells is off limits due to the ongoing forensic investigation." Sergeant Percival peered over his thick-rimmed glasses at the occupants of the squad room.

There was an unusually strange tense but somber atmosphere in the entire station. The word had rapidly spread about the murder of a prisoner, which left small groups of officers whispering among themselves, all trying to draw conclusions as to what had happened, and who had perpetrated the crime.

"What do you think?" Maria nudged Andy, who was busy studying the report sheets he had been handed on the way in to roll call.

"What?" he said, looking up from the documents and scanning the room to see what she was talking about.

"Percy." She nodded towards the sergeant. "Do you think he did it?"

"Hey." He leaned in to lower his voice. "Keep your voice down. If you start throwing accusations around like that you could ostracize yourself before you know it."

"I want to get to the bottom of this!" she snapped back in a harsh whisper. "Do I have to remind you, someone went into that cell and murdered a suspect?"

"I know! But we need to get some facts first, and not jump to a conclusion because of what Dad said." He quickly looked around to see if anyone was listening. "Let's talk to Regan first."

"Okay." She stared at him. "But if he agrees, I want first

crack at Percy."

He looked at her for a moment before nodding his head.

"So, until either Lieutenant Regan or I give you the all-clear, no one is permitted in that area," Percival continued. "All suspects brought in for holding will be processed here, then transported to the nearest available holding facility." He picked his notes up and placed them in a folder. "Any questions?" He looked across the room waiting for a query. "No? In that case roll call is over. Have a good day and stay safe, people."

A low hum of muttering voices filled the room as everyone started filing out to proceed with their duties.

"Cooper and Hernandez!" Percival shouted. Everyone stopped and turned their attention to the detectives, who looked at the sergeant. "Lieutenant Regan wants you in his office immediately."

"Come on. Let's get this over with." Andy started to push his way past some of the officers, and Maria followed.

***

When they got to the lieutenant's office, Andy hesitated before knocking. He took a breath and rapped on the door with the knuckle of his index finger.

"Come!" Regan barked from inside.

He opened the door and stepped aside, allowing his partner to enter. She glared at him as she passed. Regan was pacing in an agitated manner back and forth behind his desk. His hands were perched on his hips, holding his jacket open. He stopped and pointed at the seats in front of his desk, signaling for them to sit. They had hardly settled into their chosen seats before he began his tirade.

"What the fuck is going on?" he bawled as he walked over to the door and slammed it shut, before undoing the top button of his shirt and loosening his tie. "How the hell can someone be murdered in a allegedly secure unit? *My* secure unit!" he emphasized, and continued pacing back and forth.

"Sir—" Maria tried to make a statement.

Regan marched around his desk and stood over her with a menacing scowl, his hands still on his hips. "I haven't finished yet, Hernandez."

"Sir," she said apologetically.

"Internal Affairs is going to be crawling all over this within a couple of hours, and once the press gets wind of it, all hell is going to break loose!" He dropped his hands off his waist, walked back behind his desk, and flopped into his chair. He then retrieved a handkerchief from his pocket and wiped the thin layer of sweat from his forehead.

"Sir," she said with some hesitation. "We may have a person of interest that we want to talk to." Maria shifted in her chair.

"Who?" he asked, as he sat forward with interest.

"It's…" she started, but was cut off by Andy.

"It's someone we want to eliminate from our inquiries first, sir," he said, as he looked at her with a frown.

"We, er…" She stalled for a moment and took a breath before blurting out, "We want your permission to question Sergeant Percival, sir."

"Percival?" Regan exclaimed. "What the hell has he got to do with this?"

Maria shot a quick look at her partner, hoping he would help her out, but he stared at the lieutenant. She turned back to her superior.

"Taking into account that Sergeant Percival was on duty when the suspect was murdered, and…" She glanced at Andy again. "I have reason to believe that he has assaulted a suspect on a previous occasion, which may have resulted in the death of said suspect."

Regan looked outraged as he looked at the senior

detective. “What is she talking about?”

“Sir.” He cleared his throat. “Coop told her about the incident when Percy was investigated by IA.”

His eyes closed, and a look of realization came over his face.

“I knew it.” He was exasperated. “I told him one day this would come back and bite him in the ass.” He sat forward and pointed his finger straight at her. “He was cleared of any wrongdoing. Internal Affairs concluded that the guy resisted arrest, and Percy did what he needed to do.”

“We just need to talk to him, sir,” she said in a pleading tone. “You must see that he needs to be interviewed.”

Regan sat back in his chair and clasped his hands together in front of his mouth in a prayer fashion. He tapped his index fingers together as he appeared to be in deep thought.

“Okay, you can talk to him.” He pointed at Andy. “You, and you alone,” he emphasized, then shifted his attention to her. “You—you have until the end of the day to bring me something that will give me a reason not to hand this back to missing persons—”

“Sir,” she interrupted, and sat forward to lean on the front of his desk. “This is about kids—”

“I know,” he cut her off. “But if no other bodies turn up then it’s not our problem, so hand it off.” He paused as she huffed and threw herself back in her seat. “Look, Hernandez, I’ve got a murder scene on my doorstep here. IA is going to be here any second and, like I said, when the press get wind of this, we’re most certainly going to get shut down.

“Lieutenant, this isn’t kids absconding from home,” she insisted. “This is something big. I know it.”

“That’s why you need to get me some results on this.” His tone had changed to a more calm one. “I’m as intrigued as you are. But our workload is stacking up here, and the last thing we need is to be down a detective." He slowly eased himself back into his chair and took another moment to think. "If Percy didn't do this—and we are working on the assumption that he didn't—then we direct all our attention to finding out who did before IA gets here, upsetting everyone. So, Andy, talk to him. Clarify the situation for your partner, because I'll tell you now, Maria." He glared at her. "Percy is a good cop, not a vigilante killer." Regan pointed to the door as a signal for the detectives to leave. "Now go, and don't come back until you can make me smile with some positive information."

They left the office and walked through the squad room towards the elevator.

"Let me know how you get on with Percy," Maria said.

"Will do." Andy pressed the call button for the elevator. "What are you doing?"

"I'm going to go grab Travis and head to AppTech," she said, as the elevator doors opened and they both stepped in. She pressed the button for the ground floor and lower ground floor. "I'm taking him in case I need to talk to the kid again afterwards."

"Regan is right, you know," he said. "Percy is a good cop, not a killer."

"Well, we'll see if he pops up on the CCTV," she said in a sharp tone.

Ding. The elevator came to a halt and the doors opened to mayhem. The entire reception area was flooded with people bustling and shouting at Sargent Percival.

"What the…?" Maria exclaimed.

"There's Hernandez!" someone shouted from the melee.

"Shit," Andy said under his breath. "Press!"

Everyone's attention was drawn to the two detectives who were still standing in the elevator. The crowd shifted towards them and they were blinded by a wall of camera flashes.

Before they could react they had microphones and digital recorders thrust in their faces.

"Detective Hernandez!" A suited male edged further forward, getting his microphone as close to her as possible. "Can you confirm that a suspect you brought in has been murdered while in police custody?"

"How the…?" She was stunned by the sudden appearance of the press and that they knew what had happened.

"No comment," Andy said, as he pushed the recording device away from her and started to push the advancing crowd back.

"Do you have any suspects, Detective Cooper?" the reporter persisted.

"I have nothing to say," he replied, as he pushed harder to get the entrance to the elevator clear so he could shut the door. He reached over and pushed the button and stood in front of Maria until the doors had closed.

"How the fuck did they get wind of this?" She glared at him.

"I have no idea, but you need to get out of here before they find you." He leaned back against the wall of the elevator. "Listen, go and do what you need to do and get back as soon as you can."

"What about you?" she asked.

"I'll go back up and get rid of them for now," he said. "Then I'll talk to Percy and get some answers from either him or from the CCTV. I'll call you when I've got something."

Ding. The elevator came to a halt again and the doors slid open to relative silence.

"Thanks, partner," she said as she exited.

"Hey!" he shouted after her. She turned to face him. "Make sure you come back with something that can sort of justify bringing that guy in, or we're fucked."

She didn't speak; instead she just looked at him for a moment, then nodded and walked on to the CACU.

***

"Hey, Travis, you want to come do some more *real* police work?" Maria shouted across the office as she approached him.

"And a very good morning to you, too," he said, looking up from his computer. "What's happening?"

"We've got to go to AppTech to ask Chris Cooper about this app Ronaldo mentioned," she replied. "And I've got to get out of here. The press are crawling all over the place upstairs, asking about Seaton's death."

"What?" he said with genuine surprise. "How the hell did they find out so quick?"

"That is what I would like to know," she said. "Someone must have leaked it from here."

"What makes you say that?" he inquired.

"Come on." She gave him a disbelieving look. "It's not rocket science. The people at the station are the only ones who know about it. Probably some dirty cop trying to earn a few extra bucks."

"I hope you don't think it was me," he said, looking straight at her.

"Nah, you're a desk jockey. You haven't got the balls for that sort of thing." She smiled.

"Gee, thanks." He looked around the office. "Give me ten minutes to finish this off, then I'm pretty much done here," he added.

"Okay, I'll just have another look at your wall of shame here," she said, and wandered over to the wall to inspect the photos.

He watched her closely, paying special attention to her backside as she stood in front of the wall.

"Travis." She spoke without turning around. "Quit looking at my ass, or I will put a hole in you."

"Yes, ma'am." He smiled and went back to his work.

She continued looking at the rogues gallery. Her attention was drawn to one face in particular. She leaned closer to get a better look and snatched the picture off of the wall. She held it close to her face, glaring at the image.

"Holy sweet mother fucking Jesus Christ!" she shouted out.

"You know, you should have been a nun." He glanced up from his screen. "What is it?"

"This guy?" She held the photo up so he could see it. "Who is this guy?"

"I told you, the name is on the back." He went back to the screen.

Maria brought the photo down to look at the name on the back.

"Hector Tobin," she said aloud. "Run that name for me."

He fervently tapped away on his keyboard, then looked bemused. He frowned and went to work on the computer again. "Nothing is coming up."

"Not another one," she said, not wanting to believe what he had said.

"Afraid so," he confirmed. "I have a hard copy here, though. How do you know this guy?"

"He's dead. He was executed in an alleyway. I left uniform to ID him. This is obviously the reason they've had no luck." She studied the photo again. "Can you grab the file? I have to show my lieutenant, and don't give me that crap about needing to copy it. We don't have the time."

***

They walked up the four floors to Homicide via the rear stairwell to avoid being caught by the press in the reception area, and marched straight to Regan's office. With the file under her left arm she knocked and entered without being invited in. The lieutenant was sitting, leaning on the table with his elbows, the phone pressed against his ear. He held a hand up to stop them from speaking, then pointed to the seats on the other side of his desk.

"Yes, Commissioner," he said firmly into the phone. "As soon as I find out, sir, you will be the first person I call." He disconnected the call and looked directly at Maria. "I see our chat about just walking into my office really sank in with you."

"What?" Maria was momentarily confused. Then the light bulb went off. "Oh yeah, sorry about that. But I have something that could justify keeping me on this case."

He pointed at Travis. "Who is this, and why is he in my office?"

"Travis. He's with CACU," she absently said. "Anyway, look at this." She slammed the file down on his desk. "I've got the body you wanted."

"Tell me you didn't shoot someone." He slowly picked the file up.

Travis tried unsuccessfully to stifle a laugh at the lieutenant's comment. She glared at him.

"You're not helping here," she snapped at him, then returned to her superior. "No, sir, not yet." She looked at the detective, who nervously shifted in his seat. "That is the guy from the alley. Hector Tobin. He's another convicted child molester, and another one not in our system." Maria sat back and folded her arms confidently.

He opened the file and quickly scanned the initial rap sheet, then studied the photo.

"You have all these guys on hard file?" he asked Travis.

"Yes, sir. My boss is old-school," he replied. "Insists on everything being backed up."

He continued browsing through the file while they sat in silence, waiting for a response. He eventually sat back in his chair and started stroking his chin, as if pondering the situation. Then he suddenly sat forward.

"Okay." He tapped his finger on the file. "Two previously convicted pedophiles that have been erased from our system can't be a coincidence." He stopped and perused the file again. "Our hands are tied with Seaton. Internal Affairs is going to take over on that, possibly even bringing in the feds if they suspect an inside job. But with this one . . ." He tapped the file again, emphasizing it was the case that he was talking about. "This one, I can give you a green light on."

"Thank you, sir," she said with obvious relief. She had been anticipating this moment, and was pleased her persistence had paid off.

"Here's what we do." He pointed at her. The enthusiasm in his voice gave her encouragement. "You officially work on this as a separate investigation until something else turns up that conclusively links the two cases. That way we keep this one away from the feds."

"Roger that, sir." She approved of his tactic.

"I'll keep the feds off your back until you come back to me," he assured her. "But this isn't an open-ended thing, Maria. I need something quick, so keep me up to speed on your movements."

"Yes, sir, I will." She smiled. "I'm going to head to AppTech."

"AppTech?" He looked surprised. "Chris's company? What have they got to do with this?"

"I have a few questions about an app that belongs to them," she informed him. "The kid we interviewed yesterday told us he was contacted via this app on his cell phone. If there is a pedophile ring behind these kids going missing, this could be how they're luring them into a meeting."

The lieutenant raised his eyebrows and looked impressed. Her instinctive thought process had obviously captivated him.

"Okay. That's good enough for me." He nodded. "Is there anything I can do to speed this along?"

"Actually there is, sir." She glanced at Travis, who had sat in silence. "Could you get onto the tech geeks? Maybe if you light a fire under their ass they might be able to give us some answers as to who breached our database."

"I'll see what I can do." He asked as he closed the file and passed it back to her, "Anything else?"

"Well, if you don't mind, Lieutenant," Travis interjected. "Could you square it with my boss to come to your department on secondment while I'm helping out?"

"Do you need him?" he asked Maria.

"We wouldn't be here now without these hard copies, sir." She looked at Travis, then back to Regan. "I'm certain he'll be an asset to this investigation."

"Okay." He extended his arm and they shook hands. "Welcome to the team. Now go, and keep me updated on this, Hernandez."

"One more thing, sir," she said as she stood up. "Can you let Andy know what's happening?"

"I'll bring Cooper up to speed when he's done with Percival," he confirmed.

"Thank you, sir." She nodded to her new partner to leave. "Come on. Let's get over to AppTech and get this thing moving."

Chapter 24

The ever-vigilant John Sinclair greeted them as they entered the reception area of AppTech.

"Good morning, Detective Hernandez." He looked at Travis and half-stood, reaching over the desk to offer his hand. "And…"

"This is Detective Travis," Maria said curtly. "We're here to see Chris."

The pair shook hands. Sinclair lowered himself back into his chair, looked at his computer screen, and started typing. "Can I ask what this is regarding?"

"Official police business," she said abruptly.

"Do you have an appointment?" he nonchalantly asked.

"Look, we haven't got time for this." She placed her palms on the desk and leaned forwards to face off with the security expert. "I was told by Chris that I don't need an appointment, so can you just tell him we're here and let me know where I can find him?"

Sinclair raised an eyebrow and kept eye contact with her. He pressed a button on his phone then put in an earpiece.

"Mr. Cooper, I have Detectives Hernandez and Travis here to see you . . . very good, sir."

He tapped the phone, removed his earpiece and retrieved two visitors' passes from the top drawer of his desk. "Mr. Cooper is in his office," he said, as he handed them over. "He's expecting you."

As Travis took his pass, he leaned forward to have a closer look at Sinclair's name badge.

"John Sinclair." He said the name aloud, as if

memorizing it. “Thank you very much, John Sinclair.”

“No problem, Officer,” he said, bemused by the detective’s tone. He kept watching them as they made their way to the elevator.

“What was that about?” Maria inquired as they walked.

“What was what about?” He pressed the call button when they got to the elevator.

“That whole ‘John Sinclair’ thing,” she said, waiting for the doors to open.

“Not sure,” he said, as he glanced back to the reception desk. “I recognize his face but not the name. I just wanted to make sure I had read it right.”

Ding. The elevator arrived and the doors slid open. He held his hand out, allowing her to enter first.

“That’s very chivalrous of you,” she said sarcastically.

“Why is he even here?” he asked, as he joined her in the elevator.

“I asked the same question.” She laughed. “Apparently he’s some kind of super nerd when it comes to protecting computers from hackers.” She leaned in closer and lowered her voice. “He sits behind that desk all day watching everything on his CCTV monitors.” She pointed at the security camera in the top corner of the elevator. “I don’t like him.”

Ding. They arrived at their floor and the doors opened. Maria exited the elevator, closely followed by Travis, and they walked the short distance to Chris’s office. When they got there, the door was slightly open. The sound of playful giggling grabbed her attention. She looked inquisitively at Travis. Without knocking, she tentatively pushed the door open and peered around it to see Chris sitting behind his desk, typing away on his computer. Jen stood behind him with her arms wrapped around his neck, her head gently rested on his. They were being entertained by whatever they were watching on the screen.

"Not interrupting anything, are we?" Maria coughed.

Jen immediately stopped smiling and stood up away from her uncle, who continued smiling and waved them in.

"Not at all, come in, come in," he said, as he tapped on his keyboard and gestured for Jen to go to the coffee machine. "Would you care for a drink? Coffee maybe?"

"Yes, coffee, black for me," the female detective confirmed.

"And how about your friend?" he asked, looking at her partner.

"Oh, excuse me," she apologized. "This is Detective Travis, from the CACU."

"The what?" he inquired.

"Crimes Against Children Unit," Travis answered. "And I'll have the same please."

"Certainly. Two black coffees please, Jen," he said as he stood up. "I'll have a Jasmine tea please, honey." He walked around the desk and signaled for them to take a seat on the sofa. "Please, sit."

The detectives sat where they were requested, and Chris sat opposite them. Before they could ask their first question, their drinks were placed on the coffee table between them.

"Thank you, sweetheart." He smiled at his niece and patted the seat next to his. "Come sit here."

She shyly sat next to him and looked at the two officers staring at her.

"Now then," Chris cheerfully said. "What can I do for Florida's finest this morning?"

Maria sat forward and picked her coffee up. "We need to ask you a few questions about this app, 'Chat Around Me'."

"Sure, fire away," he said, as he sack back and cradled his tea in his left hand.

"We need to know how it works," she stated.

"Oh, it's quite simple, really. It uses the phone's built-in GPS to scan a pre-determined radius, allowing people to chat with other users in that local area." He sipped his tea.

"Can the users chat about anything, or are there specialized chat rooms?" Travis interjected.

"Both," Chris replied, as he placed his cup on the table and straightened his jacket, sitting back in the seat. "The main page is a general chat room. Then, for example, if you want to talk about your favorite bar, you have the facility to open up a separate chat group with the name of the bar. This will be displayed in the general chat forum, allowing users who are interested in it to join the group."

"Is there some sort of registration? Say, for instance, do people have to use their real names and provide their ages?" she asked.

"They can create a user name, like a nickname, in the chat rooms, but they have to provide a proper name at registration." He paused and looked at both detectives. "Can I ask what this is about?"

"And is there any way of verifying that information?" she continued.

"Not really." He looked concerned. "Is there something wrong with the app?"

"Are there any other security features on this app?" Travis dismissed the question and continued.

"Security features?" He leaned forward in his chair. "Regarding what?"

The male detective sat forward and clasped his hands together while resting his elbows on his knees. "Well, for example, would a terror cell be able to set up a private chat group and organize a strike without being monitored?"

"Holy shit!" Chris spluttered. "Is that what happened?" He became very animated. "We have a keystroke logger installed on it that sets alarm bells ringing if keywords are used. Let me get the developer in here." He pushed himself up out of the chair and walked briskly to his desk, where he frantically pushed buttons on his phone.

"Miller," the electronic-sounding voice answered.

"Oh, Martin, can you come to my office immediately?" he said urgently.

"Yes, Mr. Cooper," the voice replied. "Right away, sir."

Click. The call was disconnected, and Chris returned to the meeting. "Miller will be able to answer all your questions about terror attacks."

"Slow down, Mr. Cooper—"

"Chris," he interrupted. "No need for formalities here, Detective Travis."

"Okay, Chris," he said, holding his hands up, gesturing to slow things down. "I never said that's how it had been used. I was asking, is it possible?"

"I, err…" He rubbed his forehead, visibly worried by how the interview was going. A gentle tap on the office door drew his attention away. "Come," he ordered.

Miller entered, carrying his prized tablet. When he saw the detectives he was visibly shaken by their presence. Maria noted he was wearing his usual beige shirt, beige trousers, and sneakers. A red baseball cap was pulled down just far enough for anyone looking at him to not see his eyes. *Is this the only clothing this guy wears?* she asked herself.

"Ah. Now here's the man you need to talk to," Chris said, waving his finger at the programmer. "Martin, come and join us. The detectives have a few questions about Chat Around Me."

Miller hesitantly sat in the chair at the head of the coffee table between Maria and Chris. He placed his tablet on the table and sat back. The worried look on his face told her she wouldn't have any problem getting information out of him.

"Morning, Pee Wee." She wasted no time in putting the geek under pressure. "Tell me, is this the entire collection of your wardrobe?" she asked, looking him up and down.

Miller bowed his head, allowing the peak of his cap to cover more of his face.

"Oh, come now, Maria, play nicely. He's here to help you." Chris was quick to defend his star developer.

Maria glanced over to Travis, trying to work out how much information to part with at this stage. Figuring that she needed results and answers quickly, she decided to tell them what she needed and why.

"We're working a case at the moment, and it appears that this app of yours is being used to arrange meetings which are resulting in the abduction of minors." She directed the information at Chris.

"So it's not a terrorist plot?" He sighed. "Wow, that's bad. Kids being abducted? This is terrible. But, being honest, I'm relieved it's not terrorists."

"Yeah, I'm sure it's a massive relief to all the parents out there, too," Travis said, throwing a look of disgust at the boss.

"Sorry." He held his arms up. "I really am. I wasn't thinking." He shook his head. "Obviously this is terrible. We'll help any way we can."

"Okay. Let me tell you that according to a kid that was nearly abducted, the meeting was set up using this app." Travis sat back in his seat and looked at the programmer. "So, Miller, tell me about the app. Does it have any security features built in to prevent this sort of thing from occurring?"

"When we were brainstorming this idea, we did have concerns over this kind of event happening." Miller paused and moved awkwardly, crossing his legs and leaning towards Chris. "Although to be honest, our major concern was terrorists using it. So we installed some security features aimed specifically at that area."

"I don't follow." Maria looked at him with curiosity.

"We contacted the NSA, who sent a guy down from Langley to consult with us. He advised which keywords we should be looking out for—"

"So if someone typed in jihad, bomb, and al Qaeda in the same sentence, alarm bells would start ringing?" she interrupted.

"Exactly that!" he exclaimed.

"What happens if that occurs?" Travis joined in.

"It automatically gets sent to the NSA to analyze." He shrugged. "How they deal with it is up to them. It's in their hands."

"Okay, that explains the terrorist element. What about pedophiles? What safeguards are in place against them?" She pointed an inquisitive finger at him.

"Unfortunately, without someone actually typing 'I'm a pedophile would you like to meet me after school,' there are very few keywords we can pick up on that can differentiate between something sinister and a perfectly innocent exchange," he said apologetically.

"Are all the messages sent stored anywhere other than the actual phone?" the male detective jumped in again.

"Sure, we store all the messages on a database in our mainframe here." Maria noted he looked please with himself. "At the moment we have the capacity to store them for one hundred days, but, as the popularity of the app grows, we won't be able to store them for that long." He looked at the two detectives.

"Can we have a look at some of the old messages?" she asked, turning her attention to Chris.

"Absolutely, Maria. I told you we are here to help in any

way we can." He paused and took a deep breath. "All you need is a court order, and you can look to your heart's content."

Maria was taken aback; her eyes widened. "I thought you said you were going to help us!"

"Come on, Maria; you know me. You know I would help, and I'm offering to help, but we all need to be covered here." He leaned forward and interlaced his fingers while leaning his elbows on his knees. "Just bear in mind that anything you found without a warrant would be inadmissible in court anyway. We have had dealings with law enforcement before," he added.

"Okay." Travis looked back and forth from Chris to Miller. "What if we were to give you some names? Would you be able to look and tell us if it's worth our while getting a warrant?"

"That's still a very gray area." He thought for a moment and glanced at Miller. "How about this; you give me the information you have on the messages you want to look at. Then, when you get the warrant, call me, and I'll personally make sure that all the information is waiting for you when you get here." He sat back in his chair. "Honestly, that is the best I can do, and I think you both know it."

"Okay, thanks for your help." Maria realized her words may have sounded sarcastic. "Sincerely, Chris, thank you."

"Yes, thank you, Chris." Travis stood up and shook his hand before offering it to Miller, who didn't move.

The detective bent down to take a look under the peak of the red baseball cap. He hesitated for a moment, then moved a little closer.

"Hey, have we met before?" he asked.

"I don't think so." Miller dipped his head further and stood up to leave. "I'll be in my office if you need me, boss." He scurried out of the office as quickly as possible.

"Nice meeting you, Martin Miller!" Travis shouted after

him, emphasizing the name as if saying it in full to make sure he remembered it later.

Maria noticed what he had done and glanced at the disappearing programmer, then back to her partner, before turning her attention to Chris and Jen.

"Thanks again, Chris," she said as he stood up. "By the way, Jen, great presentation yesterday; well, what I saw of it."

"Thanks, Maria." Jen blushed.

"Okay, we'll get out of your hair and leave you to..." She waved her hand at Chris's desk and computer. "Whatever it is you were doing."

"Give Dad a kiss for me," Jen said with a cheerful smile, as they walked towards the office door.

Maria stopped in her tracks, causing Travis to nearly bump into her. "How about I just say you said hi?"

"That will be fine." She laughed. "See you soon."

They continued to leave, but Travis stopped before they reached the door.

"Oh, just out of curiosity, Chris, how long has Mr. Miller worked for you?" he inquired.

"About eighteen months, why?" he asked.

"Just like to know all the facts." He shrugged. "Thanks again. Nice meeting you both." He gently nudged Maria to continue and they left the office.

***

"Okay, spill the beans," Maria demanded, as she put her seatbelt on and fumbled to get the key in the ignition. "What was all that about with Miller?"

He turned slightly in his seat and leaned against the car door. "Well, I thought Sinclair looked a little familiar, but that Miller guy . . ." He paused. "I definitely recognize him. I'm pretty sure I recognize him from one of the files in the office."

She was about to start the car but stopped and stared at

him, open-mouthed. “You have got to be fucking shitting me!”

“No.” He shook his head. “I’m pretty certain that’s where I’ve seen his face before.”

“If that’s true, Andy is going to go ballistic.” She started up the car. “His daughter hanging out with a sex offender will not sit well with him at all.” She shifted the car into gear and drove away.

Chapter 25

It had just turned midday by the time they got to the CACU. As usual, the office was empty, a fact that hadn't escaped Maria's attention. She began to think that Travis was the only officer assigned to the department.

"How come you're the only person I ever see in this place?" she asked Travis.

He had already got to the row of filing cabinets and was busy frantically running his fingers along the files in one of the drawers.

"I told you, we're only a small unit," he answered, without taking his attention away from his search. "The other guys spend most of their time in court or taking statements, leaving me here alone to do most of the dog work."

Maria made her way over to the wall of shame and casually scanned the pictures. "I still can't believe all these fuckers are on the loose," she muttered to herself.

"Got it!" he shouted, as he pulled a file out of the drawer and waved it in the air. "Miller, Martin." He flipped the file around and tapped his finger on the name to show her. "I knew I had seen that guy."

"Mother fucker." She glared at the file as she marched over to take a look at it with him. "What is he in the system for?"

He flipped the file open and went straight to the charge sheet. "It looks like he was just unlucky."

"Yeah, the prisons are full of guys like that; you know, the ones who are just unlucky," she said with heavy sarcasm.

"Seriously though." He laughed. "It says here he was caught having sex with an underage girl, but he wasn't even a full year older than her. He got charged with statutory rape even though the act was consensual."

"Unbelievable." She shook her head and tutted.

"It's not that unbelievable. I mean, let's be honest; quite a few of us could have been charged with the same thing," he answered,.

"True, but I meant it's unbelievable that Pee Wee found someone to have consensual sex with him in the first place." She smiled.

"Ouch! That's a bit harsh!" He grinned back at her.

"So what happened? How long did he get?" Her curiosity was well and truly pricked.

"The judge showed leniency after a plea from the girl's parents. His name was to be kept on record for ten years, then destroyed if he didn't reoffend," he explained.

"Hmm." She thought for a moment. "I think I should hold off telling Andy for a while. But, I will have a quiet word with Pee Wee and let him know he needs to stay away from Jen."

"You really think Andy would beat the shit out of the guy?" he asked.

"Let's just say it's a risk I would rather not take." She looked at the file and studied the photograph of the youthful-looking Miller. Then she glanced at her watch. "Hey, the courthouse will be closed for lunch by the time we get there. How about you put that away and we get some lunch. We'll apply for the warrant later."

He closed the file and returned it to the cabinet before scurrying along to catch up with her, paying particular attention to her backside again and smiling.

***

They opted for a booth and slid into their seats opposite each other. Maria looked around, deep in thought.

“What’s wrong?” Travis asked.

“I was just thinking I seem to spend half of my life in this place,” she said, and continued scanning their surroundings.

“There are worse places to spend your time,” Coop said, as he approached the table with his customary beaming smile. “Besides, you add a bit of glamour to the place,” he added, as he placed two empty mugs on the table and filled them with piping-hot coffee.

“Hey, old man.” She looked up and returned his smile. “Do you know Detective Travis?” She paused and held her hand out in the direction of her partner. “He’s the one helping me with this case.”

“Yeah, I saw you at Jen’s presentation yesterday but didn’t get a proper chance to introduce myself.” He put down his coffee pot, wiped his hand on his apron and offered his hand to Travis. “How is the case going?” he asked, as they shook hands.

“We think we have another connection. It’s to do with an app the perps are using to message the kids and set up meetings.” She paused, not wanting to give away too much information, as she was sure it would only confuse the old Luddite. “So, anyway, after we leave here, we’re heading to the courthouse to get a warrant to go through the files at AppTech.”

“AppTech?” Coop repeated.

“Yes,” she confirmed. “The app is one of theirs. We wanted to look on their database to see if we could get a lead from the messages that have been sent—”

“And Chris is making you get a warrant?” he interrupted, and reached inside the pocket of his apron to get his phone.

Maria put her hand on his to stop him from retrieving the phone.

“Chris made a valid point. Without a warrant, any evidence would be inadmissible, you should know that,” she said calmly. “He has promised to be fully cooperative as soon as we have a warrant.” She squeezed Coop’s hand. “He does want to help but, he wants to do it the right way.”

Coop released his grip on the phone and nodded his head in agreement. “Smart kid, always was.” He stuck his chest out a little, like any proud father would. “So, what’s the plan now?”

“Well, after two of your world-famous Southwestern omelets, we’re going to apply for a warrant. Then we’re going to head to Seaton’s place and see what we can turn up there.” She removed her hand from Coop’s and gave him a wink. “See, old man, I’ve got this covered.”

“In that case, two omelets, coming right up.” He picked up his coffee pot and walked off.

“How come you didn’t tell him about Miller?” Travis asked.

“Because as nuts as Andy will go when he finds out,” Maria smiled and kept her eye on Coop as he went behind the counter, “it pales in significance to what Coop would do if he knew his only granddaughter was hanging out with a sex offender.”

“Yeah, I’ve heard about his temper from a few of the old timers at the PD.” He sipped his coffee. “So, what’s the next stage of the plan?”

Maria looked at him thoughtfully. She was trying to come up with something that what would get the case moving along. “Until we get that warrant, there isn’t a great deal we can do. And to be honest, I’m not sure that it will turn up anything.” She sighed.

“Let’s hope Andy has come up with something.” He tried to lift her spirits.

“He would have called if he had something.” She sighed again. “I’ll call him when we leave here and get a situation report.” She seemed to drift off into thought again. “Why can’t we just catch a break on this bastard?"

Travis looked at her. "I'll tell you what; you're looking a little stressed. Why don't we apply for the warrant, go and canvas the Seaton neighborhood, then let me take you to dinner, somewhere different."

She glared at him.

"Hey, I'm only saying you look like you could do with some downtime," he said, in an attempt to calm her down. "A bit of 'you' time. Relax, have some nice food, and maybe a glass of wine, or two."

She pondered for a moment. "Okay, let's see how it goes with the warrant first. Then I'll let you know about taking me out for dinner."

"There you go." He smiled.

"Just to make things clear," she pointed at him, "this is not a date. You make any wrong moves and I will shoot you where you stand. Clear?"

"Absolutely." He smiled broadly.

"You know, you're showing qualities I like in a work partner." She smiled.

***

Maria let out a slow, relaxing sigh as she took in the intimate surroundings and soft lighting of Dino's Italian Ristorante. The quiet and low-key atmosphere served to enhance the romantic senses, and indeed, over the years, the place had seen many a nervous prospective groom go down on one knee.

"I did warn you not to get any ideas; this is not a date." She pointed her fork at him with a half-smile.

He had just taken a mouthful of carbonara, which he chewed and swallowed as quickly as possible, no doubt in an attempt to defend himself against her insinuation that he had other things on his mind.

"I have no idea what you're talking about." He gulped.

"I just love the angel hair pasta here. It's the best in town." He reached out and took a swill from his glass of Chianti to wash down his hastily eaten food.

She raised an eyebrow. "Glad we're clear." She, too, grabbed a mouthful of her Chianti. She had hardly put her glass down before he was ready with the bottle to refresh her drink. She was slightly enamored by this show of chivalry, something she had never been treated to before. "So, tomorrow we pick up the warrant, and go over the cell records at AppTech."

"You know I've had an idea about the phones," he said, as he placed the bottle back into the ice bucket.

"Oh yeah?" she smirked. "Please do enlighten me."

He swept his tongue across his front teeth. "Well, there is a way of finding out the last locations of the kids' cell phones by tracing back through the cell towers."

"Really?" she asked, as she held her glass midway to her mouth. "How?"

Travis smugly held his glass and smiled. "It's not that complicated." He sipped his wine. "I'll take you through it in the morning. This is supposed to be chill time."

"Okay, but first thing in the morning we're on this." She picked up her glass and held it out to make a toast with him. "You know what? We may make a detective out of you yet."

He picked up his glass and tilted it towards hers. "Here's to good friends, good colleagues, and a good first date." He smirked.

As the glasses were about to touch she pulled hers away. "This is not a date!" She smiled again and touched glasses.

Chapter 26

Maria and Travis got to the office early the following day. They got straight to work on his theory. She stood next to him, making notes as he typed away on her computer, looking for the information that would give them the kick-start they needed. They were hard at work when Andy strode purposefully, almost marching, into the office.

"Where the hell were you?" he demanded.

Maria looked up from her notepad. "Morning, partner." She smiled, sensing his bad mood. "Before you start all your hollering, check your cell." Then she dismissed him and went back to writing on her pad, leaving Andy to fumble in his pocket to find his phone.

When he retrieved it, he pressed a button to illuminate the screen and focused on the message alerts, then turned his attention back to Maria.

"My bad," he said sheepishly. "I must have accidentally put it on silent."

Grinning, she looked back at him. "Bet you feel pretty stupid right now, don't you?" she teased.

"Bite me." He broadly smiled, drawing a laugh from his partner. "I tried calling you last night to give you an update."

"Oh… I, err…I was busy last night," she replied, slightly burying her face in the notepad.

Travis smiled a 'cat that got the cream' kind of smile. Andy leaned forward slightly to get a closer look at him and raised an eyebrow. The new detective caught sight of him out of the corner of his eye, stopped smiling, and continued typing on the computer.

"Okay, so what are you doing now?" he asked, turning back to the female detective.

"Well, Travis had an idea that seems to be panning out, so far," she said, and bent down to take a closer look at the current information on the screen.

The senior detective put his hands on his hips as if waiting for an explanation. No one spoke for a moment. "Are you planning on sharing the idea, or should I just wait for the police report?" he asked, sounding a little dejected.

She put her pen down and held her hands up apologetically. "Sorry, partner. Travis had the idea of trying to locate the last known location of the phones of the missing kids."

Andy rubbed his chin, giving her the impression he had no idea what she was talking about.

"Okay." She faced him to talk him through it slowly. "Basically, there are cell towers all over the place that 'ping' your mobile." She paused to let him take in the information. "Anyway, the closest tower to you will ping your cell. These pings are all stored on a database so you can basically tell what time a phone went past what tower." She paused again to make sure he was following her. The confused look on his face made it clear to her she was not explaining it well. "Okay, let me try this." She pointed at the computer screen. "By looking through this information, we can determine where the kids' phones were when they were last active."

"Wow," he exclaimed. "That's a bit Big Brother, isn't it? So, what's the outcome?" he asked.

"We've compiled a list of some of the missing kids and tracked their cells through the towers, and found quite a few in the same place," she said, obviously pleased with the results.

"Really?" He seemed surprised.

"Yes. We're just checking these last few, then going to CACU to go through some more files down there." She paused.

"Hey, I forgot to ask, how did the interview with Percy go?"

"Not well." He ran his hand through his hair. "He was very defensive at first." He walked over to his desk as he spoke. "And he was genuinely upset by the whole thing. He knew he would be the chief suspect and that his past would be brought up." He sat behind his desk and turned his computer on. "Anyway, I took his statement. Then I checked in with Palmer for a TOD. He gave me a two-hour window. In that time frame, Percy has an iron-tight alibi."

"So what's next?" Travis asked from behind the computer screen.

Andy scratched the back of his head as he looked at the younger detective. "Well, after his alibi checked out, I went back down to the tech guys to get them to search the security camera footage from the night of the murder."

"I thought we weren't allowed to have cameras in the cells?" Travis inquired.

"They don't, but I figured the perp had to get in and out of that area somehow, so he would be on cameras around the cells." He looked at his cell phone, which was still in his hand, before placing it on the desk.

"I guess that stands to reason." The younger detective nodded.

"This is where it gets weird, though." Andy leaned on the desk and looked directly at Maria. "When the geek squad went through all of the footage from that night . . ." He shrugged his shoulders and sat back in his seat. "It had been wiped."

"You have got to be fucking kidding me!" She looked slack-jawed at her partner. "How the f—"

"I know," he cut her short. "I left them trying to see if they could somehow retrieve it. But they're already snowed under trying to retrieve the deleted files from the security breach." He shook his head. "I think this is what *you* would call," he pointed at her, "a clusterfuck."

"Something is very wrong here." She frowned, trying to process the information. "This can't be a coincidence."

"I'm inclined to agree with you. Anyway, while the geeks are at work, I'm going to head down to forensics and see what's happening with the Hector Tobin case. Then I'm going to go canvas the scene, see what I can find out."

"Tobin!" She exclaimed. "He's on the wall of shame in CACU.

"Holy Shit. Are you sure?" He asked.

"Absolutely," she glanced at Travis, "spotted him straight away."

"Well in that case," he continued, "do you want to come with me?"

"No. I, err…" She glanced at Travis, then back to Andy. "I think we're on to something here. I wouldn't mind following this up if you can manage without me." She gave him the puppy dog eyes look that had been very successful in the past.

"Sure. So what's your plan?" he asked.

"Like I said, a large percentage of these phones' last known location was from the same tower. Meaning they were all in the same area." She tried to dumb it down for her tech-shy partner.

"What's the location?" he asked.

She beckoned him over to a map of Orlando that was adorning a full wall of the office and pointed at a specific point. "This is the tower."

Andy looked closely at the spot she was referring to. "Right next to the airport?"

"Exactly." She nodded. "This makes me more concerned."

"What are you thinking?" He continued staring at the map.

"It's looking like they snatch the kids and fly them out. That's the assumption we're working on." She looked at Andy. "Unless you have a better theory?"

"For what purpose though?" He looked skywards.

"Well, they are blue-eyed, fair-haired boys. Perhaps they're trying to build the master race again." She shrugged her shoulders.

"That's a bit farfetched." He looked across the entire map and scratched his head.

"Personally, I think with the ages of these kids, it rules out adoption," Travis interjected, as he joined them at the wall.

"Leaving us with what?" Andy asked.

"Working on the assumption that these kids are being flown out of here? First option is the child slave trade. Second option is they're in a pedophile ring." He paused. "If I was a betting man, I would put my money on the pedophile ring."

"Why not the slave trade?" Her curiosity was obvious.

"Well, these kids all look the same. No need for them to all look the same if they were in the slave trade. It doesn't matter what they look like as long as they can work." He began to explain his theory. "These boys are what are traditionally considered 'good-looking.' It may not even be a ring. It could possibly be just one guy living out a fantasy who wants a fresh supply of young boys. Once he's had his kicks he moves the kid on and gets a new one. Hence the reason they all look similar."

"So, what kind of a guy would we be looking for?" she asked, knowing that he was a trained profiler. That fact had come to light during their conversation on the previous night.

"Well, obviously a male, and quite well off. I would say married, with either no kids or a recent addition of a baby." Travis walked away from the map and sat back behind Maria's desk.

"Okay, so I get the rich part," she said, as she made her

way back to her desk. "He would need to be able to fund an operation like this. But, why the wife and no kids or a recent baby though?" Maria asked.

She was genuinely interested in this kind of thing, and had often considered taking the police profiler course herself.

"He would be married and appear to have the perfect family life. If he has no kids he'll be trying to fill a void, expressing his fatherly love onto these kids, if you will—"

"Fatherly love? The sick bastard!" she said in disgust.

"In his head, he'll be able to justify it," he added.

"You said he could have had a recent addition?" Andy asked.

"Well, it could be that he has had these urges for some time and, if he has a child in the house now, he could be finding it hard to fight those urges." He sat back in his chair.

"So, is he collecting these kids?" She was puzzled.

"No, like I said before, he could be at the top of a pedophile ring. Once he's done with them, he passes them down, or sells them to the rest of the group." He paused. "Of course, he could be killing them when he's done with them, too. We just don't know at this stage."

"I know it's a terrible thing, but this profiling thing is really fascinating to me." She put her pen in her mouth and gently chomped on it.

"So, what do we do now?" Andy asked. "This is your case, Maria. How do you want to play it?"

"I know this is a long shot, but I want to send Travis over to the airport to see if he can locate those phones." She looked at him for confirmation. He nodded his approval.

"I'll chase up the geeks and Palmer on my way to canvas Tobin's neighborhood if you want," the senior detective offered.

"That would be great," she agreed. "I think this theory is our best so far. I'm going to go through the flight manifests for the times that the phones went dead, and also try to find any connection between our dead guys and the airport."

"Good thinking. I'll use that line of inquiry on Tobin's family and if I get time, Seaton's family, too." He nodded.

"Great. If either of you find anything, or if you need backup, call me," she ordered.

Travis shut down the computer and stood up while Andy went to his desk and retrieved some files before he headed out of the office.

"I'll call you later," he said, as he waved his hand in the air and left.

Travis straightened the files they had brought up from the CACU and he, too, headed for the door.

"Let me know how it goes," she said to him.

"Will do." He smiled.

She looked thoughtful. "Hey!" she shouted after him, and grinned as he turned around. "In fact, you can tell me at my place tonight. You bring the pizza."

"Yes, ma'am." Travis smiled broadly and did a mock salute.

***

After leaving Homicide, Andy went straight to the tech department, but to no avail. They were frantically trying to retrieve the files that had been deleted and trace the CCTV footage. Unable to get any satisfactory answers, he proceeded to Forensics, where he met with Palmer. But they, too, were working flat out to get answers. He left with no more information than earlier.

He was in his car heading to interview the Seaton family, a task he was not looking forward to. He was fairly certain there would be a hostile environment waiting for him which, he conceded, was understandable, owing to the fact that their loved one had been murdered in police custody, and now a cop was asking them questions. He was working out in his head how to handle the situation when his phone rang. He looked at the screen, 'Regan.'

"Good morning, sir." The awkward silence on the other end of the line made Andy very nervous. "What's wrong, boss?"

"Where are you, Andy?" the lieutenant said abruptly.

"I'm on my way to interview the Seaton family, sir," he answered in an official tone, considering his superior's curtness.

"You need to get your ass back here, immediately!" he snapped.

"Is there something wrong, boss?" Andy hesitantly asked.

"You bet your ass there's something wrong." He paused. "I've just had a call from Palmer. He's found a ballistics match for the Surin shooting, and I've told him to double check his findings." He went silent.

The detective waited for a moment. Nothing, just silence. "Lieutenant? Are you still there?"

"There's no easy way to say this…" He paused again. "The ballistics report shows a ninety-seven percent match for a police-registered service weapon."

"A service weapon?" he exclaimed. "Whose weapon is it?"

"You're not going to like this. It's registered to Maria Hernandez. Now get back here," he growled. The line went dead.

Chapter 27

Palmer was waiting in Regan's office when Andy walked in. The two men looked up at him as he entered. He slammed the door behind him.

"You have got this wrong!" He burst into a tirade, pointing his finger straight at Palmer. "I don't care what the report says, this is bullshit!"

Regan stood up behind his desk. "Detective Cooper!" he shouted. "Calm yourself down right now!"

But it wasn't going to make any difference. Andy was furious, and he wasn't done berating the poor CSI just yet.

"You've made a mistake. No way is Hernandez involved," he said through clenched teeth.

"Detective, I won't tell you again, back off," Regan ordered.

Still visibly angry and sneering at Palmer, Andy took a few deep breaths, put his hands behind his head, and interlocked his fingers. He managed to calm himself a little.

"Sorry, sir." He dropped his hands down by his side and looked at Palmer. "CSI Palmer, I apologize."

Palmer nodded at him. "Look, I don't want to be the bearer of bad news. Protocol dictates that I should report this to Internal Affairs, but I brought it to the lieutenant first." He looked down at his shaking hands. "I don't want to get Maria in trouble; I'm just doing my job."

"I know, Palmer. I'm very sorry." He sighed and placed one hand on his hip and gestured a calming motion with his other. "I just can't accept that Hernandez would be in any way accountable for this."

He knew the guy was only doing his job, and he also knew it was only a matter of hours at the most before Internal Affairs was involved, and Maria would be instantly suspended. Plus, with the murder of Seaton, a suspect she had brought in, she could be in serious trouble if they found the slightest reason to charge her.

"How long have we got before you have to notify Internal Affairs?" He looked at the CSI.

"Palmer is taking the rest of the afternoon off," Regan answered.

"What? I am?" Palmer looked surprised.

"Yes, you're taking the rest of the day off because you're not feeling well." Regan spoke slowly and nodded his head with each word to make sure that Palmer was following his intent.

"Oh, that's right." He coughed an over-elaborate cough. "I feel terrible! Probably one of those twenty-four-hour bugs." He looked at Regan, who nodded to confirm his diagnosis. "Yeah, I should be back at work tomorrow at 9:00 a.m." It was more of a question than a statement.

"Yes, I think a twenty-four-hour bug looks like the illness we've got here. Obviously I would imagine the first thing you'll do tomorrow when you return is check in with me to see if you missed anything that may need reporting to our good friends at Internal Affairs?" Regan led him.

"Yes, sir, that's exactly what I'll do." He coughed a loud and obviously fake cough again. "I'd better get going home and get tucked into bed."

"See you in the morning," said the lieutenant.

"Get well soon, buddy," Andy added. Palmer turned to leave and as he reached the door he said, "Hey, Palmer. Thanks, I owe you one."

Palmer coughed again. "I have no idea what you're

talking about." He winked at the detective and left the office.

Andy turned his attention back to Regan. "How the hell do I get her out of this?"

"Quickly is all I can suggest." He picked up a file and tossed it to him. "It's a positive match, Andy. I'm not sure you can help her on this."

Andy sat down and started to read through the report. It was pretty damning evidence, but he continued. Suddenly he was hit with a thought.

"She didn't do this," he said, snapping his head up to look at his superior.

"So you keep saying, and I'm inclined to agree with you. But, IA will need a little more convincing. They might even need some proof," he said cynically.

"I have the proof." The detective stood up, then stopped. The realization that clearing Maria would implicate his brother left him momentarily confused.

Regan looked at him with expectation. "Come on, I'm waiting. What's your proof?"

"The night Surin was shot, Maria didn't have her gun." He looked down at his feet. "It… it was in a safe." He paused. "In my brother's house."

Regan stared at him, open-mouthed. "Are you fucking kidding me?"

"Wish I was, sir." He rubbed his forehead. "I put it in there myself."

"Well, this just gets better and better." Regan shook his head. "Clear your partner and implicate your brother. This is a big day for you, Cooper."

"I can't see Chris doing anything like this," he said, shaking his head. "He literally doesn't like getting his hands dirty. There has to be an explanation."

"Well, we need to come up with one ASAP." Regan

leaned over his desk.

Andy took a moment to think. "Chris has a state-of-the-art security system, so maybe he caught something on camera," he said with some excitement. "I'll head over and talk to him, see if I can look at the footage from that night."

"Okay." The lieutenant sat back in his chair. Then he stood up abruptly. "I think I'd better come with you on this." He stopped. "Just in case it comes down to a question of the investigation's integrity, it's best if I'm involved."

"That makes sense, sir." He nodded. "We can go over to AppTech now. The head security guy there can access Chris's home system from there."

Regan grabbed his gun from his desk drawer. He checked the chamber and holstered it. "Let's make a move."

***

Reagan and Andy walked into AppTech and were greeted by Sinclair.

"Good Morning, John. This is my lieutenant, Regan." He gestured towards his superior. "We're here to see Chris."

"Good morning, gentlemen." He shook hands with the lieutenant, then started pressing buttons on his keyboard. "Mr. Cooper is in his office, sir. I'll inform him that you're here."

"No need, John. In fact, would you be able to take us up?" Andy asked. "We need your help on something."

"Really?" His voice rose, and Andy could detect the excitement in his voice. He quickly filled out two name badges and handed them over. "Follow me, gentlemen." He pressed some more buttons and picked up a tablet before guiding them to the elevators. "Can I ask what you need my assistance with?"

"We'll explain once we're with Chris," the detective answered.

***

Ding. They exited the elevator, and Sinclair led the way

to Chris's office. He knocked, then entered without waiting for a formal invitation. "Sorry to disturb you, sir, but you have visitors."

Chris was alone in the office, which suited Andy; he didn't want to have the forthcoming conversation in front of Jen. His brother sat behind his desk with his face buried in the computer screen. When he popped his head up, the detective noted how tired his sibling looked.

"Heeeyyyy!" He smiled broadly as he got up and walked around the desk to greet them. "Lieutenant Regan, nice to see you outside of your office." He shook the superior officer's hand, then hugged his brother. "Please, take a seat." He guided them to the sofa. "Can I get you some refreshments? Coffee? Something a little stronger?"

"Sure, coffee, cream with no sugar for me please, bro," Andy requested, as he took his seat.

"And how about you, Lieutenant?" Chris inquired.

"Coffee, black, no sugar. Thanks, Christopher." Regan nodded and sat next to the detective.

"Fine." He turned to Sinclair. "Can you sort the drinks out for our guests, please, John? And I'll have one of my herbal teas." The security expert nodded, and went to the coffee machine to prepare the drinks. "Now, what can I do for you?"

"We have an awkward situation," Andy started.

"Actually, it's quite a serious situation," the lieutenant corrected him.

"Ooh, sounds ominous," Chris said as he sat forward, leaning his elbows on his knees and clasping his hands together. Sinclair returned with the drinks and gradually distributed them on the coffee table in front of each of the meeting attendees. "Thank you, John, that'll be all."

"Yes, Mr. Cooper." He nodded and turned to leave.

"Actually, we need him to stay." Regan waved his hand

to stop him.

"I'm sorry, I thought you wanted to speak to me." Chris looked a little concerned.

"We do." The lieutenant was deadpan.

Andy shifted uncomfortably in his seat and looked at his brother. "We're here on official police business."

"Okay," he said with some apprehension, and looked suspiciously at the cops. "What's going on? Do I need a lawyer?"

"That depends on what you can tell us." The superior officer showed no emotion.

There was a heavy silence in the room. Andy watched as Sinclair slowly moved around the back of his brother and sat in the chair next to him, then looked at Regan, who nodded.

"Okay, this conversation does not leave this office for the time being." He looked at them to make sure they both understood. They nodded their heads. "Right. Maria's gun was used in a fatal shooting."

"What? Fuck me! She killed someone?" Chris shouted, resulting in his brother waving his hands to shush him.

"Well, I can't say that I'm at all shocked," Sinclair added in a smug tone. "It was only a matter of time."

"No, her *gun* was used; she didn't fire it." Andy looked at the head of security that, in his opinion, was looking rather conceited.

"So, what's that got to do with me?" his brother asked.

"It was the night of the BBQ at your house." He glared at Sinclair before looking at Chris. "The night we put it in your safe."

"I'm confused." He frowned. "How did that happen?"

"That's why we're here," Regan spoke up. He was eyeing up Sinclair, but diverted his gaze towards Chris. "Andy tells me you have a state-of-the-art security system with cameras everywhere at your house." Chris didn't speak, he just nodded at the lieutenant. "Can we have a look at the footage, and see if anyone went into the safe?"

"For sure, anything you need." He looked at his head of security. "John, can you set this up for them?"

"Absolutely." Sinclair jumped out of his seat and walked over to his employer's desk. "Can I use your computer, sir?

"Help yourself, John," he said, as he stood up and signaled to the officers to follow.

"It was definitely in the safe?" the security expert continued.

"I put it in there myself," Andy confirmed.

"And it was definitely locked after you put it in there?" he asked.

"I told him to push the quick lock button," Chris informed him. "The red one. Wouldn't it show on the log when it was opened and closed?"

"I'm just about to check that." Sinclair tapped on Chris's keypad and waited for a second. The screen flashed up the information he was looking for. "Hmm…"

"Have you found something?" the lieutenant asked, as all three gathered round to take a look at the screen.

"No. Wait, let me check again." He held his hand up to silence them, then continued to tap on the keyboard. "No, nothing. I checked the date and time, but it only shows that the safe was opened at fourteen twenty-two and closed at fourteen twenty-seven on the Saturday afternoon, and wasn't opened again until the following Monday morning at zero eight eleven."

"That's when I went to collect the gun," Andy told them.

He turned to the detective. "Are you certain it was Detective Hernandez's weapon that was used?"

"Forensics says the ballistics report give a match to her weapon," the lieutenant informed him.

“Can you check the CCTV footage for me, John?” Chris asked.

“That will take hours, won’t it?” Regan asked.

“Not really.” Sinclair went back to work. “I installed motion-sensitive cameras. They only record when someone enters and moves around the room.” After a few more entries on the keyboard, he pointed at the screen. “There, that’s Mr. Cooper and his brother on the day of the BBQ.” They all leaned forward to observe the brother talking in the office. “And there is the detective locking the safe. And there they are leaving.”

“I didn’t go into the office for the rest of the weekend,” Chris interjected, and smiled. “I was far too hungover after the BBQ to think of doing any work.”

“And there you are.” The security expert drew their attention back to the screen. “Mr. Cooper enters with Detective Cooper. Mr. Cooper opens the safe and passes the gun to his brother—”

“Yes, we can see all this, Mr. Sinclair.” The lieutenant stopped the running commentary. “But this doesn’t explain how someone got into the house, took the weapon, murdered someone, and replaced it without being caught.” He looked at Chris. “Apart from you, who else has access to the safe?”

“Well, just me and John here,” he answered.

“So that narrows things down considerably.” Regan turned to Andy.

“Wow, slow down, Lieutenant.” He held his hands up. “My brother is a computer programming geek—no offense, Chris—but he’s not a killer.”

“Okay, we’ve narrowed things down even further.” The superior officer put his hand on Sinclair’s shoulder.

“Hey, hey, hey!” he protested. “I was at the office all weekend. Here!” He feverishly pounded the keyboard. “Look, here is my signing in and out log on the database.”

All three looked closely at the screen.

"Do you live at AppTech, Mr. Sinclair?" the lieutenant asked.

"Mr. Sinclair is one of the best security advisors in the country, Lieutenant Regan." Chris came to his employee's defense. "One of his conditions when we approached him was that we provide living accommodation for him onsite. He has an apartment on the premises, but still has to log in and out every time he leaves the building."

"Convenient," Regan said with some skepticism. "Tell me, Mr. Sinclair, how easy would it be to manipulate these logs on your database?"

"In what way?" he asked.

"Could these logs be erased to cover up somebody's movements?" he pressed.

"I don't think you need to answer that, John," Chris interrupted. "Not without a lawyer present." He stepped between the lieutenant and his employee. "I think this interview is over now—"

"Hey, Chris, calm down. We don't need to get lawyers involved." Andy stepped in.

"No, no need for that just yet, Christopher." Regan straightened his jacket. "We're done here, Cooper. I'll see you in the car."

Andy had heard many stories about the lieutenant's knack of ruffling feathers and getting answers, but this was the first time he had witnessed him in action. He had to admit, he was impressed. He waited till his superior had left the office before turning to his brother.

"Pay no attention to him. He's pissed that someone was murdered in the station and wants some answers now." He comforted his sibling.

"Well, next time he wants to have a chat, tell him my

lawyers will be present." Chris put a hand on Sinclair's shoulder. "John's a good man. If he says he was here, then he was here. And I know I didn't take the gun out of the safe."

"Look at it from Regan's point of view, and let me point something out here, bro." He pointed at the security advisor, who stared at them. "If you can vouch for him, then you're framing yourself."

The startled look on his brother's face told Andy he had got his message across. He nodded, and left the office abruptly.

***

Regan was standing by the car, looking up at the AppTech building. He looked at Andy as he approached; neither spoke. They got in the car and the detective drove out of the parking lot.

"Are you going to tell me what the hell is going on here, Andy?" the lieutenant barked.

"Sir?" He glanced across at him, then back to the traffic.

"I've got kids going missing, gang shootings, prisoners being murdered in my station, and now your brother and his geeky little cop wannabe are lying through their teeth," he fumed. Andy couldn't answer. "I'll tell you now; I think we have a prime suspect in this case."

"Sinclair?" He glanced across again.

The lieutenant looked him in the eye. "Or your brother."

Chapter 28

Maria had gone over and over the flight manifests on the dates some of the kids had gone missing and had come up empty. She had failed make any kind of connection. As far as she could surmise, there was no distinguishing pattern at all, so decided that she needed another pair of eyes. As Andy was out of the office, and the lieutenant was nowhere to be found, she contemplated going to consult Coop. If anyone could find a connection, it would be the old man. And since she had stopped drinking so hard, she noticed that she got hungry around midday. Her thoughts drifted, and she thought about a cheeseburger she had seen a customer consume at the diner the previous day. That was it; her mind was made up. She stood up and proceeded to pack all the files away. Cheeseburger and fries lingered in her thoughts—oh and of course, the case.

With her files packed into her briefcase, she retrieved her weapon from the drawer, holstered it, and swung her briefcase over her shoulder. She was about to head for the door when she saw Andy and Regan enter. The lieutenant glanced over at her.

"Hernandez, come with me. Now," Regan ordered, and continued marching briskly towards his office.

"What's going on?" she asked Andy, who just signaled with his head for her to follow. "I've got stuff to do." Her words fell on deaf ears.

Reluctantly she took her briefcase off her shoulder, put it on her desk, and followed her partner into the lieutenant's office. The cheeseburger would have to wait a little while longer, she thought, as she entered. Regan was already sitting behind his desk, straightening his jacket and getting comfortable. Andy stood by the door and closed it as she passed.

"Sit down, Detective," the lieutenant ordered.

She could sense by his whole demeanor and abruptness that this was not going to be a pleasant conversation, so decided to remain quiet, and slowly sat in front of her boss. Her partner sat next to her.

"Does somebody want to tell me what the fuck is going on?" She looked at the two of them.

"We have a ballistics match on the gun that shot Tobin," Regan answered, then cleared his throat.

"Oh, please tell me we've finally got a lead in this case!" she said with some excitement.

"Kind of," Andy butted in. "The match came back as a positive match… to your gun."

The office fell silent as Maria just stared at Regan, stunned. Eventually she spoke. "There has to be a mistake. Palmer has fucked up somewhere."

Even as she said it she knew Palmer wasn't the kind of guy to make mistakes. She also knew that every guilty perp she had put away at some stage said this very same thing. And finally, above all of this, she knew she was innocent, and somewhere a mistake had to have been made.

"I didn't shoot anybody!" was all she could muster, as she switched her wild eyes between the two officers.

"We know." Andy put a hand on her shoulder.

"Don't patronize me, Andy. I did not do this," she snapped, and shrugged off his hand.

"I'm not patronizing you. We know you didn't do this." He sat forward in his seat and rested his right elbow on the desk while offering his other hand to her. "The shooting took place when your firearm was in Chris's safe, the night of the BBQ." He replaced his hand on her shoulder. "We're just letting you know because IA is going to be called in on this first thing in the morning. They're going to have to interview you, Maria."

"Well, that's just fan-fucking-tastic," she huffed, as she slumped into the seat like a sulking teenager. "I told you to leave me alone and let me have my gun." She paused for a moment to catch her breath and gather her thoughts. "You know, now I remember; when you handed it back to me that morning, the bullets didn't match up."

"What do you mean?" The lieutenant looked confused.

"It's kind of an OCD thing." She sulked. "When I load the bullets into the magazine, I always put them with the number nine showing at the top."

Both the officers looked completely baffled.

"Here, let me show you." She unclipped her weapon, dropped the magazine into her hand, and slid the chamber back to release the readied bullet in one fluid movement. "See? If you look at it from behind you can see the number nine every time." Her superiors examined the magazine, then passed it back to her. She put the loose bullet in the magazine, flipped it around so she could see the number, then slid it back into the weapon and readied it before engaging the safety and returning it to its holster. "That would explain why it was so dirty, too!" she exclaimed. "Mother fucker. So, who was it?"

"We don't know," Regan answered.

"What do you mean, you don't know?" She tilted her head to one side in a questioning manner.

"We've interviewed Chris Cooper and his head of security," he explained. "They took us through the security system at Chris's house. We checked the log on the safe. It showed the time of the safe being opened and closed, but the weird thing is, the log showed nothing until Monday morning, when Andy went to collect your weapon."

"What about the CCTV?" She looked at Andy.

"It works on motion sensors," he answered. "No one went into the office after we were in there on Saturday until I went back on Monday."

"So how the fuck has this happened?" she pressed.

"We're working on the assumption that the log was tampered with," Regan interjected.

"You mean someone erased the information?" She showed concern. "Could it be the same person who has infiltrated the database here?"

"We don't know until the tech department gives us some answers," he said.

"So, what happens now?" she asked.

"Well, Palmer is off sick today." Both men turned to her. "So this won't get reported until the morning. At which point, Internal Affairs will probably be in here, braying for your blood." Regan paused again. "Unless . . . the head of IA is a poker buddy of mine. I'll take him to dinner tonight. Explain the situation, and ask him to give me some breathing space."

"Do you think he'll go for it?" She sighed.

"It might buy us some time." He relaxed into his seat. "I'll tell him that as far as I'm concerned, you followed department procedures. Knowing you were going to be drinking in a non-hostile environment, with other cops present, you did the responsible thing and placed your firearm in the safe of a businessman of good character who was from a cop family." He nodded to himself. "Hell, even *I'd* believe you're a fucking angel after saying that."

"That's because I am, sir." Maria smiled in appreciation.

"Let me be perfectly clear on this, Hernandez." He sat forward, pointing his finger at her. "You need to get me some answers on this case, and fast." He looked at Andy. "Cooper will let you know my thoughts on a possible suspect. Now get out of here."

"You have a suspect?" she asked, surprised.

"Come on, I'll explain in our office." He stood up and guided her out of the office.

They walked over to their desks. Maria sat down, and Andy perched himself on the corner so they could chat.

"Okay." She looked at him in anticipation. "Tell me who Regan has in his sights."

"It's not good," he said, deflated. "He was questioning Sinclair about tampering with the logs and Chris went all defensive. He basically told Sinclair to say nothing until he had a lawyer present."

"So the lieutenant has got the hots for Sinclair?" She sprang forward like an excited child. "I knew there was something with that slimy—"

"No." He stopped her. "It's worse."

"What do you mean?" She looked puzzled.

"Think about it," he said. "If Chris is vouching for Sinclair and he lawyers him up, that puts Chris in the line of fire."

Maria sat gawking, trying to comprehend what he had just said. "You cannot be fucking serious."

"Unfortunately," he nodded, "I am. I told Chris to wise up, but we'll have to wait and see if anything develops in that direction."

"Well, I've been through the flight manifests from when some of the kids went missing." She tapped her briefcase and picked it up. "I'm going over to see if your old man can shed some light on this."

"Promise me you won't mention this thing with Chris to him," he pleaded.

"He's going to find out soon enough," she said, looking him straight in the eye.

"In that case, we need to take something to Regan to

take his mind off my brother." His phone beeped so he took it out of his pocket, flipped it open, and looked at the message. "All right. I'll get down to the tech department and tell them to look towards AppTech. They might be able to identify one of the IP addresses as one of theirs." He walked off, then suddenly stopped. "Call me later if you get anything. Regan needs to be kept up to speed. And one more thing; IA will be gunning for you no matter what the lieutenant says, so keep your head down." He nodded, and continued towards the elevators.

"Roger that! I'm just going to call Travis and see how he's getting on with finding the cells at the airport!" she shouted after him, but he had already left the office. She picked the phone up and dialed the number for Travis. "Hey, it's me. How's it going?"

"It's not going to be easy." He sounded tired. "I'm trying to get a fix by using two other towers to triangulate the position, but the restrictions of cellular use around the airport are hampering my search."

"Okay, keep at it," she told him. "When you've finished, give me a call. I have something to tell you."

"Ooh, that sounds a bit suspicious." He laughed.

"It's serious," she said curtly. "I'm going to speak to Coop at the diner, so call me when you're done and we'll meet up."

"Okay. Are you all right?" he inquired.

"Fine," she replied. "See you later." She put the phone down, picked her briefcase up, and left the office.

As she drove to the diner, she tried to work out what was going on. Why would someone break into Chris's safe to steal her gun? She was obviously being framed—or was someone trying to frame Chris? Why go to the trouble of returning the gun? The more she ran it around in her head, the less sense she made of it all. Maybe Coop could shed some light on it for her.

Okay, worst case scenario, he has no idea and can't make any sense of it either. At least her hunger pangs would be satisfied after a juicy cheeseburger. There she went again, thinking about food. "What the fuck is wrong with me?" she said out loud.

***

The diner was relatively quiet when Maria entered. She noted there were only six customers in the place, and not one of them was wearing a cop uniform. She took her usual seat at the counter. Beth walked out of the kitchen into the dining area carrying a coffee pot; a coffee pot that Maria was certain was surgically attached to the waitress's hand.

"Good afternoon, sweetie," she said, as a mug magically appeared in front of Maria and she started pouring. "What can I get you?"

"Cheeseburger, please," she requested.

"Do you want fries with that?"

"Please," she confirmed, and before she had a chance to say anything else, the waitress had gone into the kitchen. She looked around to see if she could spot Coop anywhere. "Is Coop around?" she shouted through to the kitchen, but got no answer so she waited patiently.

Beth returned shortly with the cheeseburger she had been craving most of the day. Her mouth began to salivate the moment she saw it. She stared wild-eyed at the fare as it approached, picking up her cutlery that was neatly wrapped in a napkin, which she swiftly removed before the burger was placed in front of her. She stabbed a few fries with her fork and eagerly placed them in her mouth. With her mouth full, she addressed the burly waitress.

"Thanks, Beth, I've been looking forward to this all day." She chewed and swallowed, and grabbed a few more fries with her fingers. She had decided against using the cutlery. "Hey, where's Coop?"

"Well, ain't that the million-dollar question right there?" she replied, as she took a cloth from the pouch of her apron and began wiping down the counter. "You know what that silly old fool is like; he thinks he's some kind of James Bond."

Maria stopped chewing and looked straight at her. "Do you mean he's working a case?"

The waitress held her cloth aloft. "He's always up to something. He says he isn't, but I know that look he has in his eye. I've seen it too many times over the years."

Maria swallowed the food she had been chewing, rummaged in her bag to fish out her phone, and dialed Coop. The call was answered almost immediately. "Hey, old man, what are you up to?"

"Oh, hi, I'm just working on something," he replied.

She picked up a few fries and began chewing them as she spoke. "Are you going to be long? I have some stuff I want to run by you."

"Listen, I've been working a hunch, and I think I've come up with something. I was just about to call you." He paused for a moment. "I've got a kid matching the description of the other kids, and I also have a guy acting a bit suspicious. Same MO as last time."

Maria froze. "You have another potential kidnap situation?"

"That's why I was about to call you. Can you get here?" he asked.

"Holy fuck, old man. Where are you?" She was panicked now.

"Sunny Glades Theme Park." He paused and lowered his voice. "Yeah, something is very wrong here. I think you'd better hightail it over."

"Stay put; don't do anything stupid. I'm on my way." She stood up and shouted to Beth, "I've got to go!" before throwing ten dollars on the counter and grabbing a bite of her burger.

"Hey, if you see that bum, tell him to get his ass back here. My shift finishes in an hour!" Beth yelled after her.

Maria raised her hand above her head and waved in acknowledgement. She rushed to her car and was soon racing to the theme park. Traffic was beginning to build up on the roads. She was pondering turning on the blues and twos but decided against it, opting instead to drive erratically in and out of the slow-moving traffic. Her phone rang. She pressed a button on her steering wheel, activating the hands-free.

Coop's voice came over the car audio: "Hey, get here now. It's going down."

Chapter 29

"What's happening?" Maria was frantic. The traffic was building up and becoming more congested. She quickly checked over her left shoulder and swerved the car into the outside lane, enabling her to jump another space in the ever increasing procession of slow-moving vehicles. She ignored the car horns that blasted at her.

"The guy I said was acting suspiciously has made contact with the kid and he's leading him towards the parking lot." Coop relayed the events as they were unfolding. "You'd better get here fast, Maria."

Taking the decision that this was an emergency, she flicked a switch on the center console, activating the blues and twos. "On my way. Stay on the line. I'm going to radio in for backup. Are you sure this is another abduction?"

"Roger that, it's exactly the same as last time." Coop said. "They're heading towards the Pink Flamingo parking lot."

With the sirens wailing and the lights flashing, Maria was making good headway. Cars were swerving out of the way to let her pass. She could see a clearing in the traffic and went for it. Managing to squeeze in, she grabbed her radio. "This is Unit Forty-one, requesting immediate backup at Sunny Glades Theme Park."

"This is dispatch. Roger that, Unit Forty-one." The metallic-sounding voice drowned out the roar of her engine as she accelerated. "All units in the vicinity of Sunny Glades Theme Park respond immediately to an officer in need of assistance."

"Coop, are you there?" she shouted into the hands-free. "I've got backup on the way. I'm about three minutes away. Do not do anything stupid."

***

The retired officer kept a safe distance while he followed the suspect and the kid to the parking lot. He noticed that the area had been taped off, indicating it was closed to the public. His quarry momentarily went out of sight as they rounded a corner. He scurried over to the corner and poked his head around. The suspect was guiding the kid with his hand placed between his shoulder blades. He appeared to be in deep conversation with the boy and gestured wildly with his free hand. If Coop didn't know better, he would think the guy was telling the kid a story as they walked towards the only vehicle in the parking lot. It was a white panel van.

He put his phone to his ear. "Okay, the guy is taking the kid towards a vehicle. A white panel van. Did you get that?"

"Copy that," she confirmed. "I'm entering the park now. I'll be there in a minute. Backup is five minutes out. Shit!" He heard the screeching of tires.

"What?" He took his eyes off the suspect for a second as he waited to hear from her. "What's wrong?"

"There's a detour." She sounded frustrated. "I'm going to have to go around the—"

"No time, Maria," he said with some urgency, and looked back at the suspect. They were nearly at the white van. "It's going down; I'm going to have to make a move."

"No. Wait for me! Do not. I repeat, do not make a move without me." He heard the sound of screeching tires again and the engine roar; she was obviously moving again.

He looked on in horror as the kid walked out of sight with the suspect. They had gone around the side of the van. *Decision time,* he told himself, and quickly scanned the area to see if anyone else was around, anyone who could offer some assistance. No one. He was alone with them.

Taking a deep breath, he un-holstered his weapon and rushed towards the van. He could see their feet underneath the van and surmised a struggle had broken out by the way they were seemingly dancing round. With no time to waste he rushed around the front of the vehicle.

"Freeze! Don't move! Let me see your hands!" he barked, as he edged towards them and brought the phone up so he could talk to Maria. "I've got the son of a bitch."

"Okay. Just hold him, I'm almost with you!" he heard her reply.

He stood about seven feet away from them with his gun trained on the suspect. As the perp put his hands up the kid edged his way along the side of the van, then, without warning, took off running.

"No! Wait! Come back!" Coop hollered after him. "I'm a cop!" He waited for a moment to see if the kid had stopped but no, all he could hear was the sound of his sneakers squeaking on the tarmac as he ran faster and faster.

Can't take my eyes off this guy, he told himself, but he wanted to see where the kid was running to so he could send backup after him when they arrived. He glanced over his shoulder for a split-second and something caught his attention out of the corner of his eye. Something moved. Was it the suspect? He whipped his head back towards him. It wasn't the perp.

Coop was startled by the sight of a wolf mask behind the suspect. His heart raced. Had he miscalculated the situation by being overzealous? What was that? He looked over the shoulder of the suspect and saw the muzzle of a nine millimeter pointing straight at him.

He tried to react, but everything seemed to be going in

slow motion. Before he could say anything into the phone he saw the flash from the gun. A feeling of surrealism overtook him when the gun fired; his hearing was muffled and his sight was blurred. The only thing he was completely certain of was the searing pain in his chest.

Through sheer instinct he pulled his trigger, firing a shot into the chest of the suspect, who fell against the side of the van and slid to the ground. He then tried to fire another round off at the wolf, but nothing happened. He felt numb. He couldn't feel the weapon in his hand. Something was wrong. He fell to his knees, dropping his weapon and the phone. His whole body felt heavy as he slumped to the ground, rolling onto his back.

The sound of his labored breathing and slowing heartbeat was all he could hear as he looked up at the cloudless blue sky. He started to drift.

"Coop! Coop!" Was that Maria's voice he could hear? He rolled his head to the left and saw the phone, which had hit the ground and bounced under the van. A shadow swept over him. He looked back towards the sky, but his view was blocked by the wolf mask.

He was kneeling next to the dying cop, staring silently into his eyes. Without making a sound, he gently grabbed Coop's hand and replaced his gun in it.

"What the fuck are you doing?" Coop managed to whisper.

"Shhh…" he hissed, and raised the hand to point the gun at the dying suspect a few feet away. Then he squeezed the finger on the trigger to fire a shot into the suspect's head, sending his baseball cap flying across the parking lot.

He's covering his tracks, Coop thought. With his last ounce of energy he reached up and grabbed the mask, ripping it off the killer's face.

Shock and terror engulfed his body as he stared wide-eyed at a face he recognized.

"Oh God! Not you!" was all he could muster with his dying breath.

The wolf replaced his mask and slowly stood up, all the time staring into the dying eyes of Coop. With no sign of emotion he raised his weapon and fired a shot into Coop's heart.

The distant sound of wailing sirens began to fill the air. He surveyed the scene for a moment, then placed his gun in the dead suspect's hand and calmly walked away, leaving the dead suspect and the lifeless body of James "Coop" Cooper behind him.

The Genesis Chamber

Chapter 30

The setting sun cast a burnt orange glow on the log cabin, making it look as though it was on fire to anyone passing by; but, nobody ever passed by. The gentle sound of the water lapping against the dock, the occasional splash from catfish playing just below the surface of the water, and the ever-present humming of bugs were the only sounds that broke the silence of the swamp. Inside, the mood was less tense than previous nights there.

The wolf perused his collection of vinyl records, performing his usual ritual of sliding his index finger across the spines of the covers before making his choice, finally deciding on his favorite, Ella Fitzgerald. He gently tugged at the cover and slid it from between the other records. He inspected the cover, then flipped it over to read the track list.

"Aha," he said aloud, and nodded to himself in appreciation of his choice.

He delicately retrieved the vinyl disc from the cover and

placed it on the player, lowered the needle, and stepped back to listen to the haunting lyrics of "Into Each Life Some Rain Must Fall."

Into each life some rain must fall
But too much is falling in mine

As the music filled the air, he slowly let his head fall back and looked towards the ceiling. With his eyes closed he gently swayed to the rhythm, lost in the moment.

Into each heart some tears must fall
But someday the sun will shine
Some folks can lose the blues in their hearts
But when I think of you another shower starts
Into each life some rain must fall
But too much is falling in mine

He suddenly took a sharp intake of breath and snapped out of his trance. There was work to be done. He walked to the kitchen and tended to a pan that was simmering on the stove. He examined the thermometer that rested in the gooey, bubbling liquid.

"It's time," he mumbled, and took the pan off the heat.

With a spatula in one hand and wearing an oven glove to carry the pan on the other, he made his way into the dining area, stopping every few steps to have a little dance on the spot. There were no guests that night; he was alone.

He placed the pan on the table next to a bust and flopped into the chair to face the cast. The atmosphere grew solemn as he stared at the sculpture in front of him. The lifeless features were barely recognizable, but he knew when he had finished his work that the mask would be an exact copy of a face he knew so well. His mind drifted again as he thought about the recent events that had led him to this point. He also knew that what was to come would take its toll on him. The cold-blooded slaying of the retired cop and the pedophile was one step closer to his goal. The vision of the bodies he left in the parking lot was etched on his mind.

Click-click... click-click... click-click. He snapped out of his daydream.

The record had finished playing and the needle bounced back and forth, waiting to be taken off the vinyl. He rose from his seat and switched the player off, sending the log cabin into a deathly silence. He returned to the sculpture, loaded the spatula with the goo from the pan, and started to apply it to the face. He stopped abruptly and dropped the spatula. What was this? he thought to himself. Beneath his wolf mask he felt the warm trickle of a tear rolling down his left cheek. Without taking the mask off, he slid his finger beneath it and wiped the tear away.

"Not long now," he said, as he picked the spatula up and continued to apply the mixture. "I hope the Cooper family will be able to handle what's coming."

Chapter 31

The John McMillan Cemetery was packed with mourners. Maria estimated around five to six hundred people. She also figured about four hundred of those were cops, or people with connections to the police. The sun beating down made wearing customary black attire extremely uncomfortable, and the formal ceremonial police uniform that she was currently wearing made her fidget now and again.

Although Coop had been retired for years, the top brass had made the decision that, because he had maintained a close affiliation to the police department and had been killed saving a kid from being kidnapped, or worse, that he should be buried with full police honors, including a twenty-one gun salute. Bracing herself for the first round of shots, she straightened up and tilted her head slightly back, but kept her eyes on the casket. Raising her white gloved hand in a salute as the salvo was fired, she found it hard to fight back the tears, and was grateful for the privacy that her Oakley wraparound sunglasses afforded her.

Her thoughts went back to that afternoon, and the sight of Coop lying on the ground. How she ran from her car trying to get to him as quickly as possible, to cradle him, to hold him. "I'm here," she kept saying to him, but he was gone.

The second salvo startled her and made her jump. The smell from the salvo reminded her of the stench of gunpowder that had been in the air.

The sound of the third and final salvo was too much for her. Still saluting, her bottom lip began to quiver. Tears now flowed freely down both cheeks. Through blurred vision she watched the plumes of smoke from the rifles drift away in the gentle breeze like a ghostly spirit leaving a body and vanishing into the atmosphere. She snapped her gloved hand away from her temple and returned her arm to her side to stand at attention. This was surreal to her. She had gone into a form of autopilot, and wasn't really fully aware of what she was doing. To lose a brother or sister in uniform was emotional for any cop, and she had in this situation, and so many times before—too many times before. But to lose someone who was so close to you was devastating, and this time it was more personal.

Her thoughts turned to Andy. She looked over at her partner. He was sitting next to his mom, Cathleen, staring at his father's casket. Jen sat next to him, sandwiched between her parents, who were trying to comfort their daughter, but she was inconsolable. On the other side of Cathleen sat Chris and Amber, both of whom were sobbing. Maria noted that the only two that were not showing any form of emotion were Andy and his mother. *It must be Coop's influence on them,* she thought to herself. "Never show your hand under any circumstances," he had once told her.

Andy, being a good cop, must have had that instilled into him from an early age. And Cathleen had been with the man forever, so she was bound to have picked up some of his legendary traits. Poor Cathleen. She had lost her life partner, and was still appearing to be strong for her family.

Familiar feelings began to return to her, the ones she had been experiencing ever since Coop's murder. The 'what if's,' as they were known. What if she had called Coop sooner? What if she had put the blues and twos on a little earlier? What if she had gone a different route that day? What if. What if. What if. *Stop!* she chastised herself inwardly. No matter how much she blamed herself, it wouldn't bring him back. She found herself staring at the casket again, covered with the stars and stripes.

The service came to an end, and the mourners began to disperse, all eager to get to the diner and pay their respects to the family at the wake. Maria stayed at a respectful distance as she followed the Coopers to their waiting vehicles. As Cathleen approached the lead vehicle, Maria noticed three dark-suited figures standing to the left. She blinked to clear her still slightly blurred vision and took another look. She was surprised to see Franco Baresi and his bodyguards. What were they doing here? And what surprised her even more was to see Cathleen break from the family and be enveloped by a hug from the known gangster, without so much as a batted eyelid from her superior officers in close proximity.

She watched intently as the pair embraced for a few moments, then Baresi signaled to Andy and Chris to join them for a group hug. Again, no one flinched at the sight of a top-ranking mobster embracing a leading detective and his family. Sure, it was a sad time and emotions were running high, but—

"You okay?" Travis interrupted her thinking.

"What?" She looked at him. "Yes, fine." She nodded and looked back at the group, who had separated and were heading for their vehicles. "Come on. Let's get to the diner," she said as she walked away, keeping her eye on Baresi. "I need a drink."

***

Maria and Travis stood away from the crowd, watching the mourners pass on their condolences to Cathleen and the rest of the family as they filed into the diner. The place was becoming pretty congested, and it wouldn't be long before the doors would have to be closed, and late arrivals would have to stay outside in the parking lot.

"Apart from when you were working with me," she broke the silence between them, "had you ever heard of Coop?"

"I've got to be honest." He sipped his drink. "I had heard a few stories. All good, and making the guy sound like a mythical legend."

"Yeah? Well, let me tell you. The guy was, and always will be a legend," she said, as if informing of a fact.

"Hey, you'll get no argument from me there." He waved his glass around. "You only have to look at this turnout for him to realize how special he was."

"Well, I can only hope I get to being half as good as he was…" She stopped talking when she saw Cathleen approaching.

This was the moment she had been dreading more than anything. Apart from Andy, she had not had a chance to speak to her or any of the family since the shooting. Her heart began pounding and she passed her drink to Travis, who respectfully stepped away a little to give them some privacy. The two women looked at each other for a couple of seconds. Maria's promise to herself that she would not break down in front of any of the family went straight out the window. She lurched forward and grabbed her, hugging her like she was never going to let go.

"I'm so sorry. Cathleen!" She began sobbing. "I feel so responsible for this; I shouldn't have encouraged him. You have to believe I never thought for one second anything like this would happen."

Cathleen broke free of the younger woman's grasp just enough to make eye contact. She gently cupped Maria's face, placing her hands on either side and wiping away her tears with her thumbs.

"Don't you blame yourself, child. That stubborn old fool would have found a way to get involved in something." She paused and smiled. "You know, he actually thought I didn't know when he was doing his private investigating."

"You knew?" she asked between sobs. A smile began to form as she thought about how Coop thought he was being clever by hiding those things from his wife.

"Of course I knew." She shrugged. "It bothered me at first, but then I realized, that was who he was. The only time he was truly happy was when he was working something." She stopped again. A different kind of smile formed. She moved in and lowered her voice. "Besides, when he was doing something, it was like he was alive again. It was like he was that young, virile cop I first met." She winked at Maria. "If you catch my drift."

Maria's cheeks reddened as the realization of what she was being told sank in. "Oh . . . I . . . erm . . . I see," she flustered.

Cathleen laughed. "Sorry, I didn't mean to embarrass you. It seems like an eternity since I last laughed." She removed her hands from the detective's face and placed them on her shoulders. "Thank you for that."

Maria had an awkward look on her face. She tried to avoid eye contact with the older woman by looking down at the floor.

"Could I ask one favor?" Cathleen asked.

"Of course," she said, looking up at her. "Anything you need."

"Well, first off, will you keep an eye on Andrew for me? He is not as mentally strong as he makes out. Plus, he's going to have to be strong for the girls. I just fear he may be storing his grief and have a meltdown at some stage." She sighed.

"Of course," she said. "Although I think he's tougher than you give him credit for."

"Oh, I know he's a tough and hardened cop, but, I know my son. And I know this will affect him more than he'll let on." She looked at Andy, then back at Maria.

"Well, I'll be there if he needs to talk," she reassured her.

"One more thing. My door is always open to you." She

swept her arm around the diner. "As, of course, is this place. Don't be a stranger, you hear?"

"Loud and clear." She leaned in and hugged her again. "You'll have to brick this place up to keep me away." The two women embraced and when they stopped, Cathleen again took Maria's head in her hands and kissed her on the forehead. Then she dropped her hands to gently hold the younger woman's hands for a second or two before giving them a squeeze, and walking off to face more mourners.

"That looked intense," Travis said, as he awkwardly stepped forward to pass her drink back to her.

"Yeah, it was." She let out a heavy sigh. "Listen, I need to get out of here."

"Are you okay?" He looked concerned.

"Not really. This place is a little too much for me today." She looked around the diner at all the mourners. "I keep expecting to see the old man come out of the kitchen, and it's going to drive me to drink." She focused on Jen, who was still sobbing. "You know what?" She looked at him. "Fuck it, I need to get wasted." Then turned her attention back to Jen.

"Good God, not you?" The sarcasm in his voice was very apparent. "Surely I misheard you? You want to get wasted?" He laughed.

Maria's body went tense. Her face lost all expression and she snapped her head back to stare wildly into his eyes. "What did you just say?"

"I was just joking." He fumbled his words. "Because you haven't been drinking . . . "

"No, seriously, what did you say?" she demanded.

He frowned and looked confused. "I said, 'Surely I misheard you—'"

"No, no that," she interrupted him. "What you said before that."

"What? The 'Good God, not you' thing?"

"That's it!" she said in a raised voice, which drew everybody's attention to them. She stared at him. Her mind was racing.

"Maria, are you okay?" he asked, as he put his hand on her shoulder.

She quickly looked around and noticed they were being watched, so she grabbed his arm to turn their backs on the room. "I heard Coop say that on the phone when he was shot, 'Oh God, not you'," she said in a lowered voice.

Travis had a blank expression. "I don't follow."

"Don't you get it? He knew who shot him!" She paused and looked around her surroundings. "Look, let's get out of here; I need to run something by you."

They turned around to see Andy walking towards them.

"Is everything okay?" he asked.

"Fine, I just think I need to get out of here." She embraced him.

"You sure you're okay?" He held her away by her shoulders.

"The… err… the emotion is getting to me." She looked at him closely for the first time that day. Perhaps Cathleen was right about him. He looked disheveled. His eyes had black rings under them and they were bloodshot.

"Okay. You know the old guy had a real soft spot for you," he said, and pulled her in for another hug. "Thank you, for being here today."

"You know I wouldn't have been anywhere else today." She hugged him tighter. "I'm so sorry for your loss, partner." She released her grip and stepped back.

"It's been a long day." He nodded to the rest of the family. "I'm about ready to get Mom and the girls out of here. Then I'm going to sit on my porch and get good and drunk."

"You want company?" she asked.

"Not today. Jack Daniels is the only person I want to talk to." He attempted a smile.

"I hear what you're saying, but if you change your mind, give me a call." She patted him on the shoulder. "See you on Monday."

"You bet." He winked at her. "You take care of her," he said to Travis, and walked away to join his family.

"Come on, let's get out of here," she said, and led them outside to the fresh air of the parking lot.

***

The waitress was speedy in both taking their order and returning with their drinks. She placed the beer bottles on the table and left Maria and Travis sitting in silence for a while, enjoying the cool, fresh air conditioning of the bar and the refreshing taste of their first mouthful of alcohol. An awkward atmosphere developed between them as she went into deep thought, frowning every now and again, as if arguing with herself inwardly. It was Travis who broke the silence.

"So, are you going to tell me what's going on?" he asked.

"Well, something has been bothering me about what I heard when I was on the phone to Coop," she began. "I've run it over and over in my head a thousand times, but it wasn't until you said that back there that I realized what I had missed." She picked up her bottle and took a good swill of beer. "That's when the light bulb went off. Two things struck me. First, Coop recognized his assailant. And, as far as I'm aware, no connection has been established between him and the dead guy." She stopped and had finished off her beer before looking around for the waitress. "You think we can get two more beers over here?" she asked after making eye contact with her.

Travis looked at her empty, then at his own, which was

still half-full, and quickly drained his in anticipation of the fresh ones arriving. "Okay, so what's the second thing?"

"According to the coroner's report, four shots were fired, which I heard." She stopped as the waitress deposited the fresh drinks on the table. "Can we get two shots of bourbon to go with these, please?" The waitress nodded and left; Travis looked worried. "I have to admit, things were hazy at the time," she continued. "What with the sirens blaring, screeching tires, and not forgetting I was on hands-free." She took a mouthful of beer. "However, I'm sure I heard movement after the fourth shot. Like footsteps walking away."

"Hmmm." He rubbed his hand lightly over his chin. "Could it have been the kid?"

"That would explain it; but why would the kid return to the scene, then disappear again before we got there?" she answered.

"That's a good point," he conceded.

"We need to find that kid, and fast." The shots of bourbon arrived. "He may have seen something that made him bolt the way he did."

"So let me get this straight," he said, as he put his elbows on the table and leaned forward. "You're not going with the shootout scenario that forensics has presented?"

"No." She shook her head. "I know I heard footsteps, and I'm certain this was staged to make it look like a shootout. Whoever did this had to make it look that way because Coop recognized him." She lifted her shot glass and fired the alcohol down her throat before slamming the glass back on the table and signaling to the waitress for two more. "If I'm right, I owe this to Coop. If someone else is guilty of killing him, then they need to be held accountable." She pointed to his bourbon. "Come on, drink."

Travis looked at the shots. "I take it we're *really*

drinking tonight?”

The waitress arrived with a full bottle of bourbon in her hand. “Excuse me, may I ask, have come from the funeral at Coop’s Diner?”

“Yes, ma’am, we have,” Maria replied.

“In that case.” She placed the bottle on the table. “This is on the house.” She reached into the pocket of her apron, retrieved a handkerchief and wiped the tears that welled in her eyes. “That man was a true gentleman, and it’s a crying shame what has happened.”

“Oh no,” Maria tried to protest her generosity. “You don’t have to do that.”

“Oh yes I do,” she said adamantly. “He helped us out so many times. The day we opened these doors he came in and introduced himself. He gave us a gift, a good luck horseshoe, which we hung over the bar. And he said if we ever needed anything to just call him.”

“And did you?” Travis joined in.

“Never needed to.” She shrugged. “Whenever we had a problem, he always showed up. We asked him if he had a sixth sense and he always used to smile, tap the side of his nose with his finger and say ‘I have my sources.’” She laughed. “And he never asked for anything in return. I tell you, that man was something special in this community.” She turned to leave, then stopped and turned back to them. “Let me know if I can get you anything else, and don’t forget, it’s on the house.”

Maria grabbed the bottle and poured two shots. Putting the bottle down she raised her glass. “To Coop, and the justice he deserves.”

Travis followed suit and raised his. “To Coop.” He touched glasses with her and they both fired down the shots. “So, what’s the plan?”

“First thing tomorrow, we find that kid. We’re going to

have to use all of your contacts, do whatever it takes. I need to talk to that kid." She pointed at him. "Before whoever did this gets to him first."

"You think that's a possibility?" he asked.

"If this guy is capable of gunning down an ex-cop and staging it like he did, he'll have no problem taking out that kid if he thinks he can ID him."

Chapter 32

Early the following morning, Maria sat outside in the screened-off pool area of her ground-floor apartment, studying the information she had pulled up on her laptop. The dark sunglasses and a half-empty gallon of fresh orange juice were a tell-tale sign of her delicate state. She and Travis had certainly completed their mission of getting wasted last night. Leaving a bar before closing time was an alien concept to her, but that is exactly what they had done. But the drinking hadn't stopped then. When they got back to her place she dug out the bottle of Jack Daniels she had kept in anticipation of a momentary relapse. With a mixture of heavy drinking and high emotions the inevitable happened, and they had slept well after their vigorous, drunken sex session.

When she awoke, the thought that she had heard footsteps and movement after the fourth shot was fired would not leave her mind. She got up to go over the report on the shooting and, so far, had read it three times, but still couldn't work out what she was missing. Ironically, the one person she would normally turn to at times like this was Coop.

She sat back and sipped her juice, staring at the screen. Her thoughts went back to that day. Why hadn't she put the blues and twos on earlier? Maybe she would have got there sooner and he would still be alive. The look on Catherine's face at the graveside flashed through her head. That woman deserved the truth, she told herself. And if someone else was involved she would bring them to justice. Her mind whirled with thoughts and memories until she was snatched back to reality by a noise from behind her. She turned around to see Travis at the patio doors that led to the kitchen, and burst out laughing.

He was wearing her pink robe that was at least two sizes too small for his muscular frame. His hair stuck up, which reminded her of a troll doll. His face was pale, the classic look of someone suffering from a monstrous hangover. He squinted and held his hand up to protect his severely bloodshot eyes from the bright morning sun.

"Morning," was all he could manage, in a voice deep enough to make Barry White envious.

"Wow! You look hot!" she teased.

"Shhh… I feel like shit," he whispered, and took her glass of juice from her. Before she could make any form of protest, the refreshing liquid was gone. "I need coffee." He gasped for air, and passed the glass back to her. "Lots of strong, black coffee." He eased himself into the seat next to her. "And food. I need food."

"Get dressed. We can get something on the way." She folded down the screen on her laptop.

"Okay. Wait; on the way where?" he asked.

"Sunny Glades." She poured some more juice into the glass.

"The theme park." He picked up the refilled glass. "Do I look in a fit state to be riding roller coasters today?"

"No. I want to check something out at the crime scene." She stood up.

"It's Sunday, I have the hangover from hell, and you want to go look at a parking lot?" He folded his arms and placed them on the table before gently resting his head on them.

"Yes. Are you coming or not?" She picked up the laptop.

He raised his head and looked down at the pink robe he was wearing. "I can't go like this. All I have is the stuff I wore for the funeral, and that's hardly appropriate for a Sunday morning in a parking lot."

“Relax.” She patted him on the head, making him wince. “We can swing by your place on the way so you can get changed.” She smiled and walked off. “Maybe you should pack a toothbrush for tonight, too?” She wiggled her ass as she swayed into the kitchen.

“Okay.” He smiled. “But I’m having a dip first.” He stood up, dropped the robe, ran bare-ass naked across the patio and dove into the pool.

***

It hadn’t taken them long to get to the theme park. After they had stopped at his apartment, Maria seemed possessed as she aggressively drove through the traffic. They flashed their badges to the toll attendant at the main entrance, who waved them through without hesitation. She drove straight to the Pink Flamingo parking lot and stopped in the exact spot she had stopped on the night of the murder. With some hesitation she turned the engine off and stared at the tarmac where Coop had lain.

“You okay?” he asked.

“Yes.” She nodded, and continued to look at the spot.

“Okay, so what are we doing here?” He looked around.

Without saying a word, she reached over to the back seat and grabbed her laptop, then exited the vehicle. He followed, and they walked around to the front of the car. She opened the laptop and placed it on the hood.

“Okay,” she said, pointing at the screen. “The crime scene report is on here. Read it out while I walk through it.”

He studied the report for a second. “The white van was parked somewhere there.” He pointed at an area.

“It was exactly here,” she corrected him, and placed herself in the spot.

“Okay.” He picked up the laptop and started walking with her. “Coop was over here, and the perp was slumped up against the van over here." He marched over to the point where the assailant had been found.

"Forget the report for a second. What do you think happened?" she asked.

He moved back to the car, placed the laptop on the hood and turned to survey the scene. With his arms folded, he stared at the area where the van had been.

"I think I agree with the report." Then he paused for a moment. "Yeah, the report makes sense to me. Coop comes around the front of the van and finds the kid struggling with the shooter. He pulls his piece." Moving around the scene, he began to re-enact what he thought happened. "The perp already has his gun out and panics, putting one in Coop's chest." Pretending to be Coop, he drops to his knees, clutching his chest with one hand and holding an imaginary gun with the other. "As he falls, he squeezes one off and hits the shooter. He slumps against the side of the van, but manages to get another one off, hitting Coop in the heart. Then, who knows; either with his last ounce of strength or out of sheer instinct, Coop fires a final round, hitting the bad guy in the head." He stood back up, putting his hands on his hips. He surveyed the scene again. "Yep. That all ties in," he said confidently.

"That does make sense, except for a couple of things." She walked around the scene. "There was a definite delay between the second, third, and fourth shot."

"But that's not in the report," he said.

"I know. I only remembered yesterday. There was a delay then I heard Coop say 'what the fuck are you doing?' and a 'shhh' before the third shot. Then there was another delay when Coop said, 'Oh God, not you' before the fourth and final shot." She stopped again as she surveyed the surrounding area.

"He might have said 'what are you doing' when he saw the perp taking aim at him again," Travis reasoned. "Then he might have recognized the guy when his cap came off."

"No." She stopped him. "Look at the position of the body, and look at where Coop was." She rushed over to the car and brought the photos up on the laptop. "See, the way the perp was found? There is no way Coop could have seen his face from the angle he was at."

He studied the pictures closely, then looked at the scene. "You have got a point there."

She nodded enthusiastically. "You know, the more I think about it, the more convinced I am that I heard footsteps and faint rustling after the fourth shot."

"You mean like paper rustling?" he asked.

"No. Trees or bushes," she replied.

"So maybe, and I'm only saying maybe, if your theory is right, then perhaps the 'second shooter' headed for the bushes over there." He pointed.

"Why there?" She looked at the area he was indicating.

He looked around at the scene, then back at the tree line. "Well, you have to figure that the sound of rustling wouldn't travel that far, especially over a phone, so that seems the closest place."

She scanned the scene one more time. "You should be a detective, with logic like that."

"I did think about taking the test, but it would just be my luck to get lumbered with a partner with a terrible sense of humor." He winked at her and started walking towards the area he had pointed out.

"Very funny. You're a funny guy." She glared at him as she followed. "I take it back; you would make a better comedian than a cop."

When they reached the edge of the bushes, he stopped and looked along curbstones.

"What are you looking at?" she asked.

He raised his arm to silence her while he studied the line of shrubbery. He bent down and peered into the darkness behind the greenery, then pointed into the undergrowth.

"This area has been disturbed, look." She bent down next to him. "See, there's broken twigs where someone has pushed through here, and indentations where someone has stood."

She looked at him with genuine curiosity. "Are you part Navajo?"

"What?" He looked at her, puzzled. "Oh, I see what you mean. No, I was a boy scout. Plus, I've done my fair share of hunting in my time. These are classic tracks."

"Okay, Pocahontas, I believe you." She frowned.

Dismissing her comment, he pointed to the right. "Looks like whoever was here headed in that direction."

"Okay, let's follow the trail." She pushed past him.

"No, wait." He stopped her. "Stay behind me. We'll stay to the left of the trail so we don't disturb any evidence."

They set off, carefully examining every inch as they slowly walked to make sure they hadn't missed anything.

"I think I have something." Travis bent down.

"What is it?" She peered over his shoulder and saw what looked like a discarded latex glove covered in blood.

He edged closer, craning his neck to make out what the object was. "Looks like a mask. A pig mask." He looked back at her and nodded.

"Okay, I'll call it in," she said, as she reached for her phone.

"Yeah. Come on, let's get out of here before we contaminate something." He paused. "Hello… what do we have here?" He pointed at the ground a few feet away from the mask. "That is a very clear footprint."

"Let's move. The CSIs are going to want to make a cast

of that." She edged backwards, retracing their steps carefully.

The midday sun was far too stifling to be standing around in, so they waited for the forensics team to arrive in the refuge of their air conditioned vehicle. Travis was going over the file from the slaying, and also the original crime scene pictures when he came across the one of the dead shooter.

"Did they ever get the name of this guy?" He held the photo up.

"No. Another one that's not in the system." She sighed. "It's pissing me off."

"What is?" he asked.

"The growing amount of people not in our system." She frowned. "I'm not buying that this guy has not offended before." She took the photo and studied the bloodied face.

"You know, the other mystery guys have turned up on my wall of shame," he said, looking at another picture taken from a different angle. "It might be worth looking on there."

"Good idea," she said, sliding the snapshot back into the file. "You get on that when we get to the station. I'm going to shove a rocket up someone's ass in the tech department." She looked out of the window as she saw the CSI van turning into the parking lot. "About time, too."

He returned all the documents to the file and they exited the vehicle. The van came to a stop a few feet away from them and a very disgruntled-looking CSI Palmer got out, followed by two junior investigators who didn't look too pleased, either.

"Good afternoon, Palmer!" she called over as the forensics expert opened the rear doors of the van to retrieve his kit.

"It was, until you two called." He slammed the door closed. "This had better be good. What are we doing here?"

"Sorry, but we found something," she said.

"We went through everything here, so what's new?" He

looked annoyed that his work was being questioned.

Travis pointed to the undergrowth. "Detective Hernandez remembered hearing something while she was on the phone." He started walking to the bushes. "We took a look over here and found a pig mask and a clear footprint."

"A discarded pig mask? In a theme park?" He looked disbelievingly at the detectives, who stopped and turned to face him. "You called me out on a Sunday to retrieve a fucking pig mask in a theme park?" His anger was obviously growing at the insinuation that he hadn't processed the scene thoroughly. "Do you know how many of these masks these places sell? Thousands of them every week!"

"Not covered in blood!" Her tone was aggressive. She wasn't in the mood to listen to his whining any longer. "Now quit bitching and do your fucking job." She pointed at the bushes.

Palmer signaled with his head for the other two CSIs to follow him, and silently they walked over to the designated area.

"You really are a people person, aren't you?" Travis said, squinting at her.

"Fuck him. This is about Coop. He should be bending over backwards, not whining like a baby." She was almost shouting.

When they got to the edge of the shrubbery, Travis stopped and pointed to where they had entered the undergrowth. "If you look here, this is where we spotted the damage, indicating this was the entry point."

"Thank you, Running Bear," the CSI sarcastically said. His underlings sniggered.

"He used to be a scout," Maria teased.

Travis scowled at his partner, who just smiled at him, then turned her attention to the forensics team. They had started photographing the area and placing marker cards by spots they found most relevant to their renewed investigation.

"Just to let you know," she told them, "we stayed to the left of the trail so as not to disturb anything."

"Okay, thanks." Palmer nodded to his two-man team to take either side of the trail.

With their cameras ready, they entered the undergrowth and began photographing and collecting evidence. The detectives waited, peering over the bushes at the activity.

After what seemed like an eternity for Maria, Palmer returned holding a clear evidence bag aloft. "I apologize, Detective. It looks like your instincts may have been right."

"Accepted." She nodded. "What do you think?"

"Well, this isn't the usual tat they sell in these places." He brought the bag down to examine the contents. "This has been custom-made, by the look of it."

"What? Why would anyone custom-make a pig mask?" She asked the question more to herself than anyone else.

"There are some freaky bastards out there. Your guess is as good as mine," he answered. "There's something else." He held the bag towards them so they could get a closer look. "Someone was wearing this when they were shot through the head."

"What?" she said in disbelief.

"The main blood spatter is on the inside of the mask." He pointed at a shredded part of the latex. "I'm guessing this was caused by a bullet exiting the head and passing through the mask."

She looked at the ground and frowned as she went into deep thought. Then she suddenly snapped out of it. "I think I can save you some time on the DNA match." She looked at Palmer. "I'll put money on it that the blood belongs to Hector Tobin."

"The guy from the alley?" The forensics expert looked surprised.

"Yes. He's not in the system, but he's on file in his office." She nodded to Travis.

"Thanks for the heads-up," he acknowledged. "I'll run a test against his corpse and get back to you ASAP."

"Okay, what now?" Travis asked.

"Well, the boys are taking a cast of the footprint. As soon as it's done they'll let me know the shoe size and try to assess a make on it." He paused and looked at Maria. "Just to clear something up. Coop was a man I admired greatly, as a cop and a friend. If I can help in any way to bring to justice the person responsible for his death, I will. But please, don't ever question my dedication again." He turned and walked towards his van.

"Well, he told you," Travis whispered.

"I guess so," she whispered back.

The disgruntled CSI stopped and turned round. "One more thing, Detective." Maria braced herself for another jibe. "Good work. Coop would have been proud of what you've done." He continued to his vehicle.

She didn't know how to take what had just been said to her. Mixed emotions of confidence and sadness washed through her mind.

"Come on, let's get out of here." Travis gave her a gentle pat on the arm and made his way to the car.

They were about to get in their vehicle when Palmer shouted over, "Hey, I forgot to mention. The cameras aren't working in this area because it's closed off to the public. But if the perp continued on that path," he pointed in the direction he was referring to, "we might be able to get footage from down there somewhere. I'll send my boys down there later."

"Thanks, Palmer, good work. Call me when you have something," she replied.

He gave a thumbs up in acknowledgement and

disappeared into the back of the van. They got in their car and drove away. "I have a feeling tomorrow is going to be a long day," she said, as she looked at the forensics van in the rearview mirror. He looked around the parking lot, making a note of one of the signs.

"Stop!" Travis shouted.

She slammed on the brakes, bringing the car to a screeching halt. "What?"

"Back it up," he said with some urgency.

"Have you left something behind?" she asked.

"No, just back it up to the scene," he insisted.

She put the car into reverse and backed up to the forensics van. Palmer must have heard them returning. He stepped out of the back of the van and stood with his hands on his hips, waiting for them to get out.

"What's wrong?" he asked when they got out. "Did you forget something?"

Travis didn't say anything. He marched over to one of the signs at the edge of the parking lot, looked at the ground, then at Maria. "Get the file from the car," he ordered.

She looked at Palmer, who in turn looked equally puzzled. She shrugged, and got the file from the car. "Here." She handed it to him.

He quickly scanned through the documents in the file and found what he was looking for. "You may want to take a look at this." He handed the open file to them so they could see what he was so excited about.

"It says the perp's cell had two text messages on it. More or less the same as the ones on Seaton's cell," she read aloud. "One about a pick up and the other a code."

"Read out the code," he insisted.

"P F dash R two six dash S one-one," Palmer read out.

They both looked at Travis, slightly bewildered.

"P F." He pointed at the sign depicting a pink flamingo. "R two six." He pointed at the number twenty-six painted on the ground next to the sign, and walked to the spot where the white van had been parked. The spot where Coop had lain. "S one-one."

"You really have got to be shitting me!" she gasped. "That's the code!" She looked at Palmer. "Do you know what this means? This was a designated drop-off point for the perp to rendezvous with the killer and hand over the kid. Like last time, with Seaton."

"This confirms there was someone else here then." He nodded. "Detective Travis, you are a fucking genius."

"Genesis!" she exclaimed. "Genesis is a person. And he was here." Her eyes widened. "He killed Coop."

"If you're right, Detective," the CSI said, "that completely dispels our shootout theory."

"You're damn right I'm right." She grabbed Palmer by the shoulders. "Bear with me on this." She positioned the CSI in the spot where the perp had been found, then positioned Travis in the spot where Coop had been found. "This is what I think happened." She started to act out the scene. "Coop follows them and comes around the front of the van. He stops the perp from throwing the kid in the van. The kid bolts, distracting Coop." She moves behind Palmer. "Genesis comes around the back of the van and pops Coop." She quickly moves next to Travis. "Coop fires back as he goes down, hitting the perp, who falls against the side of the van." She forces Palmer to sit down and goes back to Travis, pushing him down to lie on his back. "Genesis comes over to Coop, puts his gun in his hand. That's when I heard him say, 'What the fuck are you doing?' He tells him to shush, and fires at the perp, killing him with the head shot." She leans over Travis. "This is when Coop recognizes Genesis. Genesis stands up and fires the last shot into Coop. After that he places his gun in the hands of the perp and walks off in the direction of the bushes."

"If that's the case, then a GSR test on the perp's hand should tell us if he fired a weapon or not," Palmer informed her as he got up.

"Was he tested for that?" she inquired.

"If it's not in the report, then, no." The CSI looked embarrassed. "I'll get on the phone to the lab now and order a test."

"Okay, how long will it take?" Her enthusiasm started to kick in.

"It's a simple swab. Should only take a few minutes." He shrugged and went to the van to call the lab.

"Let me know when you've got the results." She turned to Travis, who held a hand out to help him up. She pulled him up, put her hands on her hips, and surveyed the scene again. "What do you think?"

"It certainly fits, and would explain the footsteps you heard after." He looked towards the bushes. "And the freaky shit we found over there."

"I'm going to have to report this to Regan and let Andy know, but I'll wait till Palmer and his team have finished here." She looked at her watch. "Probably won't get the DNA results till the morning."

"So, what's the plan?" he asked.

"When Palmer comes back I'm going to put the pressure on for getting some answers ASAP." She glanced at the van to see if the CSI was returning. "I'll call a meeting in the office first thing to bring everyone up to speed."

Palmer returned from his call to the lab. "Okay, Detective Hernandez, the test shows no sign of GSR on the perp's hands. He didn't fire any weapon. Looks like you're one hundred percent right."

“I knew it!” she shouted. “This thing just got a whole lot more serious.” She paused to catch up with her thoughts, which whirled around in her head. “This guy is good. If he can stage a murder scene like he did here, he’s a lot smarter than we think.” Her eyes grew wide. “I’ll bet he’s the one who tapped into our database and wiped the files.”

“You think?” Travis looked pissed.

“Yeah.” She nodded. “I’ll also put money on him being responsible for the Seaton murder at the station.”

“How the hell would he do that?” Palmer asked.

“If he can manipulate the computer system, he can wipe CCTV footage and gain access to the station. Think about it.” She held her hands out in a questioning pose. “All he needs is a code or key card to get in through the back door at the holding cell area, which, if he’s that good on computers, is going to be a piece of cake for him.”

“Jeez.” Travis was astounded. “This fucker could know our every move.”

“Yeah.” She stared straight at him. “And what’s worse is Coop knew him, which means there is a possibility that we know who he is.”

Chapter 33

"Come on, Palmer," Maria said impatiently. "I've called the meeting for nine thirty. That's fifteen minutes away!"

Palmer sat behind his desk, reading through his report for the third time to make sure he had covered every angle of the investigation. He finally got to the last page and signed the sheet at the bottom, closed the file, and passed it to the female detective.

"I've got to hand it to you, Maria, you were right about the blood on the mask matching Tobin's. The DNA is unquestionable."

"I knew it." She was elated.

"I personally retested for GSR on the perp; he didn't fire a weapon." He looked confident. "You should be able to light a fire under Regan's ass with the information in that file."

"That's what I'm looking for." She smiled. "When he finds out Coop was murdered by someone else he'll be gunning for the right result."

"Let me know if there's anything else you need." He nodded.

"Thanks, Palmer," she said, as she headed out of his office. "Will do." On the way to the meeting she called Travis on her cell. "Hey, how are you doing?"

"I'm making progress, but slowly," he told her. "This guy's face was pretty messed up by the gunshot wound. Trying to make a positive ID is not easy."

"I'm on my way to the meeting now so it would be good news if you could get something for me before we finish," she pressed him.

“Hey, I want to be there, but I know this is important to the case so I’ll keep at it and either call you or get to you ASAP,” he replied, and disconnected the call.

She looked through the information that Palmer had given to her as she walked to the briefing room. When she entered the homicide office the room was empty apart from Regan, who was waiting by her desk.

“Give me a rundown on what you’ve got, Detective,” he ordered.

“In short, sir,” she said as she continued walking, “The shootout scenario on Coop’s death was incorrect. We were going over the scene yesterday when new evidence was found. I called CSI Palmer, and his team have spent the last eighteen hours rushing through tests for me.” She waved the file in the air. “I have all the information here.”

“Okay.” He looked at the file in her hand. “If you’re right on this, Maria, I’ve told everyone that this takes priority. They’re in the briefing room waiting. Let’s see what you’ve got.”

“Thanks, boss,” she said, looking at the packed briefing room. “No pressure.”

They entered the briefing room. She felt an uneasy feeling in her stomach when she saw Andy calmly sitting in the front.

“Hey, partner,” she greeted him

“Hey, you.” He looked at her, then at the file in her hand. “You’ve been busy.”

She nodded. “You might not like what you’re going to hear, bud.” She put a hand on his shoulder. “But this is going to make more sense when I’m finished.”

He looked deeply into her eyes for a moment, then patted her hand that rested on his shoulder. “I know.” He nodded his head to the front of the room, indicating for her to continue.

She moved to the desk and turned to face her colleagues, who sat silently staring at her. She took a deep breath and commenced. For the following forty-eight minutes she presented the evidence. The disturbed undergrowth, the results of the mask that turned out to be homemade, the shoe print in the soil, and finally how she used two other detectives to re-enact the shooting as she now believed it went down. All the time she checked on Andy, monitoring his reactions.

"Right. Listen up," Regan said when she'd finished. "This case is now reopened. It takes priority over every other case you're working on. Detective Hernandez is lead investigator, so she will be letting you know what she needs." He stopped and waved his pointed finger across the officers present. "Make sure you give her your full cooperation."

"Sir," Andy said as he stood up. "I want to be in—"

"Detectives Hernandez and Cooper," he interrupted. "A word in my office," he barked, and marched out of the room.

Maria watched Andy follow the lieutenant to his office. "Okay. Our main priority is to find that kid," she said, as she straightened the documents on the desk and replaced them in the file. "I have Detective Travis from CACU reaching out to his contacts, and he's trying to ID the perp from his files. Until he gets a lead, I want you guys to get out there and ask questions." She paused to take a breath. "Let's go."

The room suddenly burst into life with the sound of chairs scraping on the floor and officers talking to each other as they filed through the door. Maria pushed her way past a few of them to get to the lieutenant's office as quickly as possible.

She could hear the angry exchange of words between Andy and Regan from the other side of the Homicide Department so quickened her pace. As usual, she didn't bother waiting when she knocked and just walked straight in. Regan was sitting back in his seat behind his desk, looking up at Andy, who had his hands on the desk, leaning over it to get his point across.

"Sit down, Detective Cooper," the lieutenant said sternly. "I won't tell you again."

The detective pushed himself away from the desk and put one hand on his hip and waved his other at Maria. "Can you tell him I need to be in on this?" he pleaded.

"I've told Detective Copper to take a backseat and stay out of your way," their superior informed her before she could say anything. "There is too much of an emotional attachment here, one that could jeopardize the case in court." He looked at her and nodded his head towards Andy to signal for some backup.

She put the file on the boss's desk and faced her partner. "He's right, Andy. We can't afford to take any chances on this. It's Coop we're talking about here." She gently put a hand between his shoulder blades both to calm and comfort him. "Your dad." She looked at Regan, then back to Andy. "When we catch this guy we have to make it an airtight case. No mistakes. He's going to get the needle for what he's done." She rubbed his back. "I promise."

The detective sighed, dropped his shoulders, and slumped into the chair opposite his superior. "You're right." He looked up. "I'm sorry, sir—"

"Andy." The lieutenant shook his head. "You don't need to apologize. I would be saying the same thing in your situation; but Maria is right. This case has to be airtight to secure a conviction. And I guarantee, I will personally push for the death penalty."

"I know, sir. And thank you." He relaxed into the seat.

"It's not me who needs thanking." He nodded towards the female detective.

He looked at his partner as she sat next to him. "Of

course. Maria, thank you."

"Hey." She put her hand on his shoulder again. "I'm your partner. This is what I'm here for." She looked at Regan, but continued to direct the conversation to Andy. "Why don't you take some time? Go and let Cathleen and the family know what's happening."

"Although, I would prefer it if you didn't mention any of this to Christopher or his staff at AppTech," the lieutenant insisted.

"Come on, sir." Andy looked vexed. "Surely you don't think my brother has anything to do with this."

"I'm not discounting anybody from this investigation, Andy." He lurched forward to lean on his desk. "There is still the question of how Maria's gun was used on Tobin when it was allegedly in the custody of your brother."

"There has to be some logical explanation for that!" he pleaded.

"Maybe so." He nodded. "But until we get this cleared up, I have to treat Christopher and Sinclair as suspects in the murder of Hector Tobin."

"Okay." The detective held his hands up in defense. "But please give me something to do. If I sit around doing nothing, I'll go crazy."

The lieutenant looked at the female detective for some approval. She acknowledged her agreement. "Maria will let you know how you can help. But, Andy, if either of us thinks you are at risk of jeopardizing the case, we'll pull you in and suspend you until we catch this guy." He glanced at the female detective again for confirmation. She nodded. "Do I make myself clear?"

"Absolutely," he approved. "One hundred percent, sir. Thank you."

"Now, please." He held his hand out to the detective. "Go and tell your family what is happening. They need to know before this gets out to the press."

"Yes, sir." He smiled, stood up, and patted Maria on the shoulder as a form of thanking her. "I'll call you later."

She patted his hand and watched him leave the office, then turned to the lieutenant. "Thank you, sir."

"Just find out who did this, Maria, and fast." He pointed at the door. "If Andy is anything like Coop, he won't be able to stay away for long. The last thing we need is for him to get impatient."

"I agree, sir," she said.

"What's your next move?" he inquired.

"We need to find that kid." She held one hand up, signaling for him to wait while she got her cell out. She dialed a number and waited for the call to connect. "Wilson. It's Hernandez. Have you traced where the kid got on the bus?"

"His journey originated at Fourteen and West Sussex bus stop," he informed her. "The assailant got on five stops later and sat four rows behind him, and two rows in front of Coop."

"We need a clear shot of the suspect's face. Travis is having a hard time trying to ID him because of the facial wounds. See if you can get one from the footage," she ordered.

"It's not going to be easy. He had that red cap on and kept his head down," the officer said.

"In that case, find the driver, pull him in, and sit him down with a sketch artist," she said, and disconnected the call. She looked at the lieutenant, who was staring at her. "What?"

"I'm impressed, Detective." He bowed his head quickly. "You're thinking on your feet now."

"Thanks." She stood up to leave. "I'm going to get Travis and get over to Fourteenth and West Sussex to look around for the kid." She turned to leave. "I'll keep you informed, sir." She closed the door behind her, leaving the lieutenant alone.

Regan thought for moment, then picked the phone up

and pushed a button. The call connected immediately. "This is Lieutenant Regan from Homicide… I need all information you can gather on a John Sinclair… He's head of security at AppTech… Send it to my office as soon as you can… Thank you."

He replaced the handset, leaned on the desk and rested his chin on his interlaced fingers as he went into deep thought.

***

By four thirty that afternoon, the two detectives had canvassed the whole area to no avail. They had talked to every kid they could find who pretty much matched the description of the victims from the earlier abductions.

"Come on, we might as well call it a day," Travis said, wiping the beads of sweat from his forehead with a paper towel he'd picked up from a hot dog stand when they had stopped for lunch. "We'll start again in the morning."

"Yeah, I think we've done all we can for today," she agreed.

"Can you drop me at my car? I need to stay at my place tonight," he asked, looking slightly nervous. "I'm expecting a delivery in the morning and I don't want to miss it."

"Sure thing." She shrugged. "I'm getting sick of the sight of you anyway." She smiled and lightly tapped him on the shoulder. "Come on, let's get going."

As they walked back to her vehicle, her cell started ringing. She quickly got it out of her pocket and checked the screen. "It's dispatch." She looked at Travis and pressed the button to accept the call. "Hernandez."

"Detective Hernandez, this is Julie at dispatch. I have a person-to-person call for you. The kid won't give his name," the voice on the other end of the line said.

"Kid? Are you sure it's a kid?" She looked puzzled.

"He certainly sounds like a kid," she replied.

Maria's mind began to race. "Get a trace on the call and put him through."

"Will do," she confirmed. "Connecting you now." The detective heard a few clicks. "Sir, you're through to Detective Hernandez."

"Hi, this is Detective Hernandez. What can I do for you?" she asked.

"You can stop looking for me," the obviously nervous young voice replied.

Her eyes opened wide as she looked at Travis. "Are you the kid that was at Sunny Glades?" she nearly shouted as excitement mounted.

"Yeah, I was there, and now I just wanna be left alone," he said.

"Can't do that; we need to talk to you." She tried to contain her excitement.

"I don't want to talk to anyone. I didn't see anything. I just want to be left alone." His voice wavered. "You've been looking for me for the last week, going all over the place asking questions. You aren't going to find me."

"Who's been asking questions about you?" She frowned.

"You guys!" he snapped. "The police."

She suddenly realized how much danger the kid was in. They had only started their search for him earlier that day. Genesis must be looking for him. She didn't want to scare him any more than he was.

"Listen, you have two choices, kid. First choice, you make this difficult and I have to find you. It might take a couple of days, but I will find you. I'll have to inform Social Services, which will make things very difficult for you." She paused to let that option sink in. "Second choice, you come to me, we talk, and I let you go on your way." She put her hand over the mouthpiece and whispered to Travis, "Get on to dispatch and find out where this call is coming from." He got his cell out. She removed her hand and went back to the call. "So, kid, which is it going to be?"

The line was silent. She thought she had scared him.

"I'll meet you in the morning." She breathed a sigh of relief when she heard his voice. "I'm at my dad's house tonight. I don't want my parents to know. I'll meet you at the park tomorrow at ten a.m." He paused. "Okay? But just you. If I see anyone else I'm gone, and you'll never find me."

"Okay, kid, but promise me one thing," she said adamantly. "You stay in your dad's house. Don't go anywhere until you meet me tomorrow. Promise."

"I promise," he hesitantly replied.

"Good. Now, if you're not there, I swear I will hunt you down and make your life hell," she said.

The phone line went dead and she looked at Travis.

"Tell me they got a trace." The urgency in her voice was obvious.

"Yes." He nodded, still holding his phone to his ear as they relayed the information to him. "Okay, thanks." He disconnected the call. "It's an address downtown. They're sending it to you via text message now."

"Yes!" she shouted.

"Are we going for him now?" he asked.

"No. We'll let him consider the first option overnight." She continued walking to her car. "I'll tell you one thing. If that little bastard is one minute late I will be knocking on the door of that address by ten thirty."

"I've got to hand it to you; you really know how to handle things with kid gloves," he joked.

"Bite me." They got to her car. "Okay, I'll drop you off and I'll call Andy to let him know about the meeting tomorrow." She started the car and pulled away.

***

She had called Andy immediately after dropping Travis off. He told her he would be at the diner, sorting some paperwork out in the morning if she wanted a coffee before work, so she agreed to meet him there at eight.

The evening light was fading as she drove alone. It had been a while since she had been on her own, and was quite enjoying the solitude. She had decided that the best thing to do that night would be to order a Chinese take-out, have a shower, and watch some mindless TV shows while relaxing on the sofa.

She pulled into her driveway thinking about out what food to order. Her ritual of unlocking the locks on the front door in a certain sequence was performed in a kind of autopilot mode. Even though she would have to unlock them again when her food order arrived, she reversed the ritual, ensuring she was secure in her abode.

Click. She flicked the light switch. Nothing happened. *Click, click.* Nothing.

"Oh great, a power outage," she muttered, and started towards the kitchen, where she kept a flashlight in one of the drawers. As she passed through the living room she never noticed two dark, shadowy figures standing near the sofa until she was in the middle of the room.

What was that? flashed through her mind as she realized someone was in her apartment. In one swift movement she spun around and whipped her gun up to point it directly at the intruders. Without warning, a hand appeared from the behind her and pushed her weapon down, causing her to fire a round into the floor. She tried to bring the gun up and get another shot off but the person had a firm grip on her wrist. Thinking quick, with all her strength she brought her left hand up and slammed the palm upwards under the chin of the attacker, sending him flying backwards, releasing his grip.

She swung her gun up. *Wham!* The force of a right hook sent her to the ground. She sprawled across the floor and a well-placed foot on her wrist stopped her attempting another shot.

"Enough!" she heard a voice shout. "Get her up and put her in the chair."

The shadowy figures descended on her. One grabbed the weapon from her grip while the other dragged her up. The sudden raising of her already spinning head sent her into a semiconscious state. Unable to make any kind of protest, she flopped into the chair and passed out.

***

When she came to, she instinctively tried to stand up, but couldn't. Her hands had been handcuffed behind the chair back and her ankles had been secured to the legs of the chair with duct tape. She tried to shout, but a piece of duct tape over her mouth suppressed the sound to a muffled mumble.

Through blurred vision she looked around the dark room. After a few moments she realized she was in her living room. *Well, I haven't been kidnapped,* she thought. She could just make out a figure sitting on the sofa opposite to where she sat, and could sense that there was someone standing right behind her.

"If we remove the tape, are you going to shout?" the figure in front of her asked.

She shook her head, her eyes staring straight forward in defiance of the intruder. The man waved his fingers to the person behind her, who leaned forward, grabbed the corner of the tape and ripped it off, leaving her lips with a burning, tingly feeling.

"Ouch! You mother fucker." She turned to glare at the tall, muscular figure. "What the fuck is going?" She moved her mouth around, trying to get some feeling back.

Click. The figure on the sofa turned a table lamp on and leaned forward. The light hurt her eyes, and she squinted to focus on the person. As the realization of who it was sank in, she sighed.

"Franco Baresi. Thank fuck it's you." She smiled.

"Well, that's not the usual response I get." He looked confused.

"That's because most people don't know what a demented fucker you are, and the fact that I'm still alive means you want something from me." She sat back in her chair as best as she could.

"Very astute, Detective Hernandez. You are, of course, correct. Let me reassure you that I am not here to harm you. On the other hand, if you call me a demented fucker again, I may have to re-evaluate the situation." He laughed. Pointing at her, he looked at the man standing behind her. "Can you believe the balls of this one?"

"Yeah, huge balls, boss," the man mumbled through a snigger. "Nice tits, too." He looked at the man standing at the side of him and nudged him. "Am I right?"

"Hey, hey, hey, Tony! Show some fucking respect!" Baresi ordered.

"Sorry, boss," he sheepishly replied, lowering his head like a scolded schoolboy.

"You want to cut to the chase and tell me why you're here?" she snarled, as she looked around to see if there was any way to get out of this situation.

"I like that; straight to the point. Okay, first of all, I apologize for the manner in which this meeting is taking place." He held his arms out with the palms of his hands face up. "I was concerned you might say no if I just called you up and asked to meet."

"No problem. I much prefer it this way; getting jumped and knocked out in my own home gives me a warm, fuzzy feeling inside." Turning towards Tony she smiled. "Was that you that did that, Tony?"

"Sorry about that," he muttered, and shrugged. "Just doing my job."

"No problem, you did an excellent job." She nodded to his crotch. "Although, the minute I'm free I am going to kick you in your peanut-sized balls."

Franco laughed. "I fucking love this girl!"

"I think you're great too. Shall we go to a bar and continue this conversation there? Have a few cocktails, maybe some chicken wings? Spend some time, get to know each other? Who knows where it might end." She rolled her eyes. "Or, you could tell me what you want, then untie me and get the fuck out of my house."

Franco stared at her and edged forward on the sofa. "I'm here to find out about a mutual friend… Coop."

"What about Coop? Are you responsible for his murder?" Her eyes widened. Her muscles tensed and she pulled at the restraints.

"Whoa, calm down. Coop was my friend." He signaled to the bodyguards to back away. All three took a step back. "He was my best friend. I'm here to find out what happened to him." Leaning his elbows on his knees, he clasped his hands together, pointing both index fingers at her. "So, what happened to him?"

"Coop was friends with a piece of shit like you?" she huffed. "Do me a favor. Don't bullshit me."

He edged even closer to her and lowered his voice. In a calm tone that made it seem even more sinister he iterated, "So far I have been reasonably pleasant. I am giving you leeway, as we have intruded into your home and, to a certain degree, forced you into a conversation. However, if you continue to insult me with vulgarity, that will change very quickly. Do I make myself clear?"

She realized she had pushed him too far. So far she had

disguised the fact that she was scared so much that even she had started to believe her charade. But now his chilling tone shook her to her core. She knew of this guy's reputation and therefore, knew it was time to cooperate as much as possible.

"I just find it hard to believe that Coop would be friends with you." She shrugged.

"We grew up together. I went into the family business and he went…" He paused and shrugged. "Well, he did his thing. We kept in touch, obviously away from prying eyes. He was like a brother to me, and the only person I would ever listen to."

She looked at him, really studying his facial expressions. The way his eyes dilated and contracted when he spoke. He was speaking with real emotion and genuine feelings. "My God, you're serious!" she exclaimed.

"Why else would I be here?" He raised one eyebrow. "He told me he was working on something with you. Looking for guys that hurt kids. Is that what got him killed?"

Maria stared down at her knees. She still felt responsible for the old man's murder. A solitary tear rolled down her cheek. She tried to wipe it on her shoulder, not wanting to show any weakness to her captors. "Yes."

He pulled a silk handkerchief from the breast pocket of his suit, leaned forward, and wiped her cheek. "When you find out who did this, I need to know before you take him in."

She looked at him to make sure she understood what he was suggesting. "I'm a fucking cop, not a vigilante. I can't do that." She pulled away from his hand.

"If you want justice for Coop, *proper* justice for him," he sat back on the sofa, "then that is exactly what you will do." He pointed at her again. "He spoke very highly of you, said you were good people."

Maria was confused by this whole thing. It was becoming too much for her.

"We're going to leave now. Let's keep this meeting between us." He pulled out a card from his inside pocket and placed it on the sofa and tapped it. "My card is here. You need *anything*," he emphasized, "anything at all, call me. I sometimes come across information that the police don't." He sat forward again. "I want to be very clear about this. Finding this guy is my priority right now. Coop was family, and nobody whacks a family member without paying the price."

He nodded to the three men behind her. They moved forward and began cutting the tape and unlocking the cuffs. Franco stood up and held out his hand. She reached out and he helped her to her feet.

"Sorry it had to be like this, but I needed to make sure I had your attention." He kissed the back of her hand. "Make sure you call me."

She was still confused and scared, but continued to act nonchalant about the whole thing. "I'll see what turns up." She nodded towards the door. "Now get the fuck out of my house."

Franco smiled and shook his head. He signaled for his men to follow. As they walked to the door, Maria followed them. The nearest one to her his rubbed his chin.

"You've got a damn good left hand there, girlie," he said in appreciation.

They reached the door when she called out, "Just one more thing."

They all stopped and turned around. She walked straight up to Tony and with a smug smile on her face swiftly connected the toe of her shoe in the delicate area with great velocity, sending the thug to his knees in excruciating pain.

Franco laughed out loud. "I told you that girl has balls. I fucking love this girl!" He pointed at her. "You make sure you call me." Then he signaled to the other bodyguards. "Pick him up and let's get out of here."

He walked down the driveway, still laughing.

Chapter 34

Coop's Diner had lost all of its charm since his passing, as far as Maria was concerned. It just wasn't the same without the man himself there. The food was still good; if she was honest, it was better. Beth had taken over the day-to-day running of the place while the family decided what to do with it. Since she had been in charge, she had employed three new chefs, taken on four new waitresses, and organized a work schedule. The new girls were young and attractive, and were already a massive hit with the regulars and new customers that seemed to be frequenting the place more and more. It didn't go unnoticed to her that since Beth had been in charge, the place had gotten a lot busier.

As she sat waiting patiently for Andy, she went in the pocket of her summer jacket and pulled out the card that Franco had given her the previous evening. She toyed with it in her hand, reading the information on it occasionally. Aside from the dull ache in her jaw from the punch, this was the only evidence she had to say she had been visited by the mobster. She had decided to keep the incident to herself, for the time being at least. She didn't know why; maybe it was her instinct, but she had a feeling she could trust this guy. Perhaps it was because he had been a close friend of Coop's. Even if that is what it was, it was a weird instinct for a cop, trusting a known mafia boss.

As she thought about how surreal the whole situation was, her eyes wandered around the busy diner again. She guessed there were nearly eighty people in the place, but a lone male diner caught her attention. He stood out from everybody else because of his immaculately tailored suit and patent-leather shoes. *He looks out of place in here*, she thought. *He's not here to jack the place; nobody wears patent-leather shoes to pull off a robbery.*

He was busy reading the morning paper, and for the briefest of moments he looked up from the paper and they made eye contact. He immediately diverted his eyes back to the paper and shifted sideways, like he was trying to hide something. Her mind went into overdrive. *Am I being paranoid?* she questioned herself. Here was a guy having a coffee and reading the paper before a hard day at the office. *Stop turning everyone into a criminal*, she chastised herself. She looked again at the card in her hand.

"Morning," Andy said. She hadn't seen him come in and was surprised to find him sitting next to her with a stack of papers in his hand. "Wow, you look tired," he commented.

"Didn't get much sleep last night," she answered discreetly, putting the card in her pocket in case he saw who it was from.

"You should slow down a bit," he said, placing a comforting hand on her shoulder. "You're going to burn yourself out before you know it."

"Maybe I will as soon as I've solved this case." She glanced at the suited male and caught him looking back at her. He quickly went back to the paper. *Is he watching me?*

"I'm sorry I couldn't speak when you called last night. I was busy sorting this out and getting nowhere." He waved the papers in her direction. "So, what's going on?" he asked, but she hadn't heard him due to being distracted.

"What?" She looked at him.

"Are you sure you're okay?" he inquired, looking concerned.

"Yeah, sure. It's… it's this case. It's a strange one." She finished her coffee in one mouthful.

“Aren’t they all?” He got the attention of one of the waitresses and signaled for more coffee. “What’s the latest developments?”

“Oh, yeah, the kid made contact. I’m meeting him at ten at Richmond Park.” She looked over at where the guy in the suit had sat, but he had left.

“The kid that was at Dad’s shooting?” he asked.

“The very same.” She looked at her watch and got up. “Listen, I’d better get going. I’ve got to get to the office and let Regan know what we’re up to today.”

“We?” he probed.

“Yes, we.” She looked sheepish. “Travis has been temporarily transferred while this case is open.”

“Have I lost my partner?” he queried.

“No. Not at all,” she reassured him. “You’ve got things to sort out here, and you know you can’t get too involved in this one.”

“I know.” He smiled. “I’m just playing with you.” He stood up and kissed her on the cheek. “Make sure you get this fucker for us.”

She smiled and walked out of the diner, looking around to see if she could spot the suited guy. He was nowhere to be seen.

***

By the time she arrived at police headquarters, it wasn’t long before she had to be at the park to meet the kid. So she quickly informed the lieutenant of the latest findings, and collected Travis from the CACU They got to the meeting place in good time, so they sat in the comfort of the air-conditioned vehicle.

“So, I’ve been thinking,” he casually said, while looking out of the window. “When this is over, how about you and me go on vacation?”

“Why would I want to go anywhere with you?” she replied, without taking her attention away from looking for the kid.

He turned to face her with the look of a kid who had heard the ice cream truck but had been told no by his mum. “I just thought it might be nice to get away from it all for a while.” He turned his head back to looking out of the window.

“Don’t start sulking.” She smiled to herself. “I’ll think about it later. At the moment this case is my only priority.”

“I bet you look fantastic in a bikini,” he said, without turning his head.

“I do,” she said nonchalantly. Her attention was drawn to something she had spotted in her rearview mirror. “I think I have a visual on the kid.”

He turned in his seat to get a better look out of the rear window. “Yeah, he matches the description. Let’s go talk to him,” he said, as he unbuckled his seatbelt.

They simultaneously opened the doors and exited the vehicle. The kid stopped in his tracks when he saw the two cops walking towards him.

Maria saw the look of panic on his face. She knew instinctively by the way he quickly scanned the area that he was looking for an escape route. Sensing he was about to run, she pointed at him.

“Hey, kid, police!” she shouted.

The boy looked directly at her, then at Travis.

“He’s going to run,” he said under his breath.

“I know, but which way?” she said.

“We’re about to find out,” he answered, as they quickened their pace.

As they got closer the kid continued to look for a way out. He made eye contact with Maria for a split-second, then turned and ran.

"Stop! Police!" They both shouted in unison.

"We just want to talk to you!" Travis called out, but the kid wasn't stopping.

They gave chase but as fast as they ran, the kid was managing to pull away from them. He was like a whippet, weaving through the other pedestrians on the sidewalk. He made it to the intersection and ran straight across the road, ignoring the blaring horns from the frustrated drivers who managed to swerve him. When he reached the other side he stopped and turned around. The safety of the traffic lights ensured the cops couldn't get to him without having to dodge the oncoming traffic.

"Don't come any closer!" he shouted at the out-of-breath detectives as they stood on the opposite curb. "Are you really cops?"

"We're staying here!" Maria said through heavy panting. "Yes, we are cops." She pulled out her badge to show him and waved it at him. "I spoke to you on the phone yesterday!"

"I told you to come alone!" he shouted back.

"I didn't think it would be a big deal if I brought my partner!" She quickly looked around to see if she could find a way they could get to him without him running again. She held her hand up to signal for him to stay where he was. "What's your name, kid?"

"Ralph!" He squinted at them with suspicion.

"Ralph, we need to ask you about the other person that was at the shooting!" she shouted.

"The one in the wolf mask?" he asked.

Maria's ears perked up. She held her breath and looked at Travis, then back to the kid. "Yes! Just give us ten minutes! If you like we can go get a burger and a shake." She nodded to confirm what she had said. "You tell us what you saw and you can go."

"You promise that my parents won't find out?" He tilted

his head and put his hands on his hips.

"We promise, kid!" Travis said, still trying to catch his breath. "Let's go eat. I need to sit down after running like that. You know, you're pretty good! You should think of taking on Usain Bolt."

"You think so?" Ralph smiled.

"Absolutely!" Maria added. "What do you say, shall we eat?"

"Okay. You got it. But then you leave me alone, right?" He waited for some reassurance.

"That's right, Ralph!" Travis shouted. "Come on, let's go."

Ralph smiled, shook his head, and stepped off the curb. He had taken a few steps when the sound of squealing wheels got the detectives' attention. They turned their heads to see a white panel van speeding towards the kid, who froze as it got closer and closer.

Travis lurched forward in attempt to get the child out of the way but only managed to reach the middle of the road as the van hit Ralph head on. The air filled with screams from other pedestrians who witnessed the collision. Unable to stop through his momentum, Travis hit the side of the speeding van. The force sent him flying sideways, hitting the tarmac and rolling several times. He looked up to see Ralph's limp body going under the back wheels of the fast-moving van.

Through instinct, Maria drew her gun and caught a glimpse of the driver as he passed. He stared at her from behind a mask. A wolf mask. What horrified her was she was sure he was sadistically smiling at her.

She ran into the middle of the road to try and get a clear shot. Making the decision to aim for a rear tire, she took aim and emptied an entire clip, to no avail. The van sped off and screeched around the next corner

She quickly turned around to see Travis limping towards the kid, who lay motionless in the street. She holstered her weapon and got her cell out as she rushed over to them.

"This is Detective Maria Hernandez!" she shouted in urgency. "I need an ambulance to Richmond Park and an APB on a white panel van. Florida plates Zero, Fiver, Niner, Oscar, Sierra, Golf, Quebec. Approach with caution and apprehend the driver. Please be advised he could be armed."

By the time she had reached them, Travis was only a few feet away from the kid. He suddenly fell to the ground, holding his left arm with his right hand. Blood was running from his forehead. She knelt down to support him.

"I'm okay. Check on him," he mumbled.

"Lie down." She slowly lowered him down. "There's an ambulance coming."

She leaned over the boy. He had blood coming out his nose and ears. His legs were bent upwards in an unnatural position. It was too late.

"How's he doing?" Travis asked.

Maria looked at him and shook her head, then took another look at the body in the road. "This fucker is going to pay."

Chapter 35

Limping heavily, and with his left arm bandaged, Travis followed Maria into the Homicide office wearing sunglasses to hide the black eye. The cut on his forehead was held together by butterfly stitches, and dark bruising on his cheekbone made him look like he'd gone a few rounds with "Iron Mike." They had taken no more than two steps into the room when the familiar bellowing voice of Regan resonated, causing the injured detective to wince.

"You two." He pointed a finger at them. "Get your asses in here, now!" He disappeared into his office, slamming the door behind him.

"I really fucking need this today." Travis stopped, looked at his bandaged arm, then grimaced as he began to hobble towards the lieutenant's office.

"This is going to be a perfect start to a Tuesday morning." Maria sighed and shrugged, resigning herself to the fact that they were about to get a roasting. "Oh well, here goes nothing."

She knocked on the door and waited to be summoned in. She didn't have to wait long.

"Today is not a good day to fuck with me, Hernandez. Get in here now!" her superior growled from inside.

She grabbed the handle and turned to Travis. "I can't imagine any day would be a good day to fuck with him." She smiled.

"Please don't; it hurts when I laugh," he said, trying to contain a smile.

She opened the door, entered, and spotted Andy sitting in a chair opposite Regan, who was perched behind his desk looking extremely vexed. As soon as the door was closed he started his tirade.

"So, Cagney and Lacey, do you want to explain to me why I have to call the parents of a fourteen-year-old boy and tell them that at the time of his death, their son was being pursued by two of my homicide detectives?" he fumed.

"Technically, sir, I'm not a homicide detective," Travis said quietly, causing his partner to glare at him in disbelief, knowing full well a comment like that was going to infuriate the beast even more.

The lieutenant didn't respond immediately, just scowled at them, his face turning a deep scarlet as his anger built. Unable to contain his rage, he let rip.

"Are you a clown? A funny man? A joker in the pack?" He banged his fists on the desk. "I tell you what, funny man; *you* make the call to the kid's parents. You tell them how their son died because of *you* and your incompetence. Maybe drop in some of your rib-cracking wit to break the ice, you fucking idiot!" As he vented his rage, Regan had raised six inches out of his seat while berating the young detective.

"I was just saying—"

"Hernandez!" He cut him off and glared straight at her. "Advise your partner to shut up from here on out or I will kick him all over this office that he, technically, doesn't work in." He returned his stare to Travis.

"Sir, we are both upset by this." She tried to calm the rising tension. "We had the kid's trust. He had stopped running and was crossing the road to come and talk to us." She looked at her injured partner; he really did look like a schoolboy who was being chastised by his father, she thought. She looked back to her boss. "Sir, this was no accident."

"What?" he asked in disbelief.

She glanced at Andy then at Travis, waiting for a nod to confirm she had the go ahead tell them what had happened.

"The killer was waiting for the kid, sir. I'm one hundred percent sure of it." She paused and let the information sink in for a moment. "I, err… also, I caught a glimpse of the driver. He was wearing a mask. A wolf mask."

"Like the one you found at the theme park?" Regan asked.

"That was a pig mask, sir, but yes, sir." She nodded.

"What's the deal with the animal masks?" he inquired, and looked at Andy. "What do you make of it?"

"Not sure," he replied with a puzzled look. "But I would imagine someone driving around in a van with a mask on would garner a lot of attention."

"Sir," she grabbed his attention. "We did get some information from the kid. He confirmed that there was another shooter at the scene." She looked at Andy. "Sorry, partner, but this is by no means over. Someone else shot your dad."

"The kid said that?" He looked at her, mouth agape. "Did he give you a description?"

She shook her head. "He was crossing the road to give us all the details when he got hit. All he said was that the other guy there was wearing a wolf mask."

The lieutenant rubbed his forehead. "Okay, let's get the facts down as we have them so far." He picked up a pen and opened up a notepad on his desk. "What have we got?"

"We know there have been kids going missing after arranging meetings through a mobile app Chat Around Me…"

"What happened with the search warrant for AppTech?" he interrupted her, and looked up from his writing.

"We got the warrant but we haven't executed it yet, sir," Travis spoke. "We're heading over there today to seize the records."

"Good. Get on that as a matter of urgency." He started writing again.

"Yes, sir," she agreed. "We're hoping to find something that confirms my theory."

"And what theory is that?" the lieutenant asked.

"That this is some kind of pedophile ring," she said as a matter of fact. "They make contact with the victims using this app, and promise them some sort of fame or fortune, then they lure them to the theme parks and kidnap them." She stopped to think of everything pertaining to the case. "Palmer has confirmed that these animal masks are homemade, so that leads us to think they have a significant relevance to the kidnappings somehow—"

"Why?" Regan stopped her again.

"Well, why go to the bother of making a mask that you could easily buy from any costume or joke shop?" She looked around the room at the others to make sure her point was valid.

"Good reasoning," the lieutenant agreed, and continued writing.

"We think the red baseball caps might be relevant too—" She was halted by her superior suddenly raising his hand.

"Red caps? Why is that ringing bells?" He tapped his pen on his pad and went into thought for a moment before a look of euphoria spread across his face. "Andy, didn't your shooting victim have a red cap on? The shooting where the kid got caught in the crossfire?"

"Erm . . . Yes, now that you mention it, I think he did." The senior detective nodded.

"Yes." He pointed at Andy. "Pull the file on that. We'll go over it again to see if we missed anything." Andy stood up and walked to the door. "Pull the file on the assassination case, too. I'll bet they're connected in some way."

"Will do, sir," Andy said, and left.

"What's your next move?" Regan turned to Maria.

"We're heading over to AppTech to execute this warrant, sir—" She was interrupted again, this time by her phone ringing. "Hernandez... Hi, Palmer… Are you serious . . .? Send the information to my cell." She disconnected the call and looked at the lieutenant, excitement etched across her face. "They've found the van that was used to kill the kid."

"Have they run the plates?" Regan asked.

"Palmer said it's registered to a little Mom and Pop operation so they don't have computerized records. Anyway, you're not going to believe this. The van in question is on a long-term lease to AppTech." Her enthusiasm was obvious. "A lot of shit is getting linked back to that place."

There was a knock on the office door. "Enter!" the lieutenant ordered.

The door opened. Andy entered carrying the two files, which he placed on the desk, then realized everyone in the room was looking at him.

"What's wrong?" he nervously asked. "What did I miss?"

"There's no easy way to say this, Cooper." Regan cleared his throat. "Maria has just received a call from Palmer. The van used to run the kid down was on a long-term lease to AppTech."

"No. Are you sure?" He looked horrified. "There must be some mistake."

"I'm afraid not, Andy." His superior paused to think for a second, then continued. "Look, because of your connection to the company, I'm afraid I'm going to have to pull you from this case altogether." He looked apologetic and shrugged his shoulders. "I have no choice."

Maria turned to the senior detective, who looked like his

whole world had been crushed. “Andy,” she said, putting a comforting hand on his shoulder. “I’m sure Chris is not a part of this. That slimy bastard Sinclair or the other one… err… Miller, they are more likely candidates.”

“Sinclair!” Regan sat forward, waving his finger at Maria and Travis. “I did some checking up on that guy, and I’ve got a feeling he let the press in on the Seaton murder downstairs.”

“Do you think he’s behind all this?” Andy asked.

“Well, he certainly knows his was around computers and a CCTV system,” he said, as if convincing himself of his theory. “You can bet your life on it he knows how to hack into a database and erase files. You two get down there. Execute that warrant, and have a good sniff around while you’re there.” He glanced briefly at Andy, then back to the duo. “Treat everyone as a suspect.” He paused. “No exceptions.”

“Right away, sir.” She signaled for Travis to follow her and started towards the door.

“Maria,” the senior detective called after her. She turned around. “Do me a favor; make sure Jen is safe, please.”

“Of course, partner. That goes without saying,” she reassured him.

He shook his head. “I can’t believe the person who shot Dad could be this close to the family.” He took a deep breath. “You find this fucker and you nail him, you hear me?”

“Roger that! Hopefully he’ll resist arrest when we get him.” She smiled.

Regan looked at Travis, who had been holding his injured arm the entire time.

“Are you okay for duty, son?” he asked out of concern. “I don’t want one of my best detectives going into a situation with a guy who can’t back her up.”

“I’ll be fine, sir,” he insisted.

"Hernandez, are you okay with this guy like this?" He waved his hand at the injured officer.

"Yes, sir, he'll be fine." She nodded.

"Cooper." He closed the notepad on his desk and put his pen in the breast pocket of his jacket. "You and I will go down to the tech guys and light a fire under their asses. I want to know where those files are, today. Then we're going to go over these files again." He pointed his finger at the other officers again. "You two, be careful. Anything you find, you call me. Any problems, you call me. Anything at all, you call me. Understood?"

"Yes, sir," they said in unison.

"We all meet back here tonight and run over everything again." He dismissed them by nodding towards the door. "Now get out of here and get this bastard."

Chapter 36

As they headed towards AppTech, Maria drove at her usual breakneck speed. Travis sat holding his injured arm, occasionally lifting it just to see how far he could move it before it hurt.

"Are you going to be a baby about that all day?" She shot him a sideways glance.

"I never said anything. I'm just seeing how much movement I have in it." He paused, raised one eyebrow and looked at her. "I could do with a massage, just to ease the pain a little." His words fell on deaf ears.

"I've been thinking." She swerved to avoid a car that had stopped suddenly. "I know the lieutenant said to treat everyone as a suspect, but I think we should take Chris into our confidence."

He put his hand on his shoulder and rolled it a couple of times. "It's your call. I don't know the guy, but, what from I have seen of him, he doesn't strike me as the kind of man that would shoot his own dad." He grimaced, obviously in pain. "Or the kind of guy to be involved in a pedophile ring, for that matter."

Concentrating on the traffic, she nodded her head. "That's what I'm thinking, too."

She pulled the car into the AppTech parking lot and stopped the car in a 'Reserved For Employees Only' spot. They exited the car and entered main reception. John Sinclair lifted his head behind the reception desk as they approached.

"Good morning, Detectives. What a lovely morning." He greeted them with a smile. "How can I help you?"

“We’re here to see Chris.” She walked straight through the checkpoint and headed towards the elevator. Travis was right behind her.

“Wait, Detectives!” He ran around from his position to chase after them. “You haven’t signed in, and you haven’t got your name badge.” He lightly placed a hand on Maria’s left shoulder.

With lightening reflexes her right hand reached across and grabbed his hand. She spun around, bringing her arm underneath his armpit and before he knew it, Sinclair was on the ground, looking up at her firearm, which was no more than six inches from his face with the safety clicked off.

“Take this is as your one and only warning. Touch me again and I will shoot you dead.” She stared at him a few seconds, deliberately put the safety back on, and returned the weapon to its holster. Then she pointed at the gold shield on her belt. “As for a badge, this is the only one I need.”

She straightened up, stepped over him, and signaled for her partner to follow, leaving the embarrassed head of security to slowly get to his feet.

“Is that your idea of keeping a low profile and discreetly asking questions?” Travis asked, as they waited for the elevator to arrive.

“That mother fucker is lucky I didn’t double tap him.” She glared at Sinclair, who had returned to the reception desk and was on the phone. “Fucking guy assaulting a police officer. I have half a mind to arrest him right now.”

Ding. The elevator arrived and they boarded.

When they reached Chris’s office, they found the door ajar. Maria pushed it open as she knocked and they entered. Chris was on the phone behind his desk.

“It’s okay, John,” he said, looking up at them and smiling. “They’re here now.”

On the opposite side of the desk sat Jen, holding a tablet, looking at her uncle. She turned around when she heard him say they had arrived.

"Hey." She smiled broadly. "Morning, Maria. Is Dad with you?"

"No, he isn't, but he said to say hi." She returned the smile. "Are you okay?" "Yeah, I'm really enjoying it here and, I'm learning loads." She brimmed with excitement and turned back to her uncle. "I have a pretty cool teacher to thank for that."

Chris put down the handset, turned to the detectives and shook his head, while pointing at the phone.

"That was John." He rubbed his forehead and smirked. "He said you didn't see the need to wear visitor badges today."

"Simple misunderstanding." Travis stepped forward. "He didn't realize how much of a rush we were in to speak to you."

"That guy is a dick. He grabbed me so I had no choice but to take him down." Maria was indignant.

"Oh. My. God. Maria!" Jen put a hand to her mouth. "Have you beaten up another one of Uncle Chris's employees? You really don't like the people, here do you?"

"I don't like the weird ones." She looked at Jen, then focused her attention on Chris. "Is there anywhere we can talk in private?"

"Sure, close the door, we can talk here." He shrugged his shoulders. "Jen is okay, she won't say anything."

"No, not here." She looked up at the camera. "Walls have ears and eyes."

He quickly glanced at the camera. "Oh, don't worry about that. It's just the internal system. As a matter of fact, the only places not covered are the restrooms."

"Even so, I'd like to talk to you away from prying eyes and ears," she insisted.

"This sounds serious." He tilted his head to one side and gave her a questioning look, but she just stared at him. "In that case, may I suggest we talk in my private bathroom?" He held his hand out, gesturing to the door behind his desk

"That will do." She marched over to the door. "Come on you two. Jen, would you mind waiting here for a moment? This won't take long."

Chris looked at Jen, shrugged, and hesitantly made his way to the bathroom, followed by Travis. Maria held the door open until they were all inside the bathroom, then closed and locked it.

"Well, this is weird." Chris looked around the confined space. "You want to tell me what this is about?"

"We have a problem." She looked at him. "Oh boy, this is difficult." She took a deep breath. "New evidence has come to light in the killing of your dad."

"What do you mean? I thought you had the guy, the dead guy?" He looked back and forth between the two of them.

"Like I said, we have new evidence." She glanced at her partner, then awkwardly back to Chris. "Not only that, we have a connection that leads us back here, back to AppTech."

"What!" The software mogul was looking concerned. "What kind of evidence?"

"A witness was killed yesterday in an apparent hit and run," the injured officer interjected. "The vehicle used has been traced back to AppTech through the leasing company."

Chris looked completely horrified, then suddenly held his hands up and looked at the female detective. "Wait. We don't have any vans on lease."

"According to the lease agreement you do," Travis contended. "Can you go through your financial records and see who hired it?"

"If you're sure, of course. I'll get Sinclair on it

immediately." He took a step towards the door. Travis stepped sideways, blocking the exit.

"Wait!" Maria said. "The thing is, Chris, everyone who works here is under suspicion." He stared disbelieving at the two cops. "You honestly think someone who works for me is responsible for killing my dad?" He shook his head. "Who do you think it is?"

"If we knew we wouldn't be having this conversation," she said. "We have our suspicions, but the truth is, we just don't know. That's why we need your full cooperation."

"Absolutely," he said with some enthusiasm. "What exactly do you need?"

The detectives looked at each other, then back to Chris. "Anything that will give us a clue as to who hired this van," she said.

"I need to be at my computer to access the financials." He looked with pleading eyes at the male officer to let him through the door.

"Okay," she agreed.

"Wait." Travis held his hand up to stop them. "When we get back out there, anything you need to tell us, don't speak. Write it down."

Chris nodded in agreement.

As they went back into the office, Maria noticed that the camera had been repositioned to look directly at the bathroom door and was now following Chris as he sat behind his desk. He started typing frantically on his keyboard, so she positioned herself directly over his shoulder to block the camera's view of the computer screen. Jen looked on in bewilderment.

Chris stopped typing, looked up at Maria, and shook his head. Meanwhile, Travis wandered around the office, looking at the photographs and awards that adorned the walls. He came across one particular photo of the entire AppTech staff.

Checking he couldn't be seen by the camera, and that the others weren't paying attention, he slipped the snapshot in his pocket.

"What's going on?" Jen broke the eerie silence.

"I'll explain later," Maria said. "How are you getting home, by the way?"

"Martin is giving me a lift," she informed them.

Chris looked at the male detective to confirm that it was okay. He shook his head.

"Erm… There's no need, sweetheart. I'll drop you off," he said.

"It's okay, Uncle Chris. I'll wait for him," she maintained.

Thinking quickly, Maria produced the warrant from inside her jacket. "I'm afraid Miller is going to be some time." She handed the document to Chris. "Here's that warrant you requested. We're going to have to go through your databases. Specifically the ones for the Chat Around Me app." She turned her attention to his niece. "Why don't you go and collect your things while I have a quick chat with your uncle."

"Oh. Okay." Jen looked perplexed. "I'll be back in a minute."

Maria wasted no time. As soon as Jennifer left the office, she leaned down to talk quietly to her uncle. "Here's what I want you to do. Get Jen out of here as quickly as possible. Don't do or say anything to alarm your staff."

"What about the warrant?" he asked.

"We'll deal with that later. But right now, we're going to go to the leasing company." She glanced at her partner, who nodded in agreement. "We'll have a better idea who and what we're looking for if we can ID the person who hired that vehicle."

"Okay." He started to get up. "I'll take her home and come back to help out with the search on the databases."

"No," she adamantly said. "Go home. At least we know you're safe there."

"Okay, I'm ready when you are, Uncle Chris," Jen cheerfully said as she came back into the office.

"I'll be right with you, sweetheart." He smiled and started to close down his computer.

"We'll leave you to it, Chris." Maria signaled to her partner to leave. "Let me know how things go."

"What?" He looked baffled. She tilted her head towards his niece. "Oh, yes. I'll call you later."

"Okay, you three." Jen put her hands on her hips. "Will someone please tell me what is going on?"

"Nothing. We just have a little business to sort out." The detectives walked towards the door. "By the way." Maria stopped and turned around. "Have you got my number?"

"Yes, of course." She nodded and dropped her hands off her hips.

"Good. If you have any problems," she looked at the camera, "anything at all, you call me straight away."

"Sure," the youngster confirmed.

"Good girl." She smiled. "I'll see you later."

The detectives left and headed for the elevator. As they walked through the main reception area, Maria and Sinclair glared at each other.

"We'll be seeing you soon," she snarled at him.

"Looking forward to it, Detective!" he shouted back, and smiled.

"He's our guy, I'm telling you," she said to her partner as soon as they were outside and out of earshot. "I'm so going to nail that fucker."

"Let's get to the leasing company and see if they can ID him from this." Travis produced the photo from his pocket.

"You sneaky bastard." She smiled as she realized what

he was holding. “Nice work, Detective.”

“I know.” He broadly smiled as the got in the car and drove away.

Chapter 37

"Have you got the picture?" Maria asked Travis over the roof of the car. They had got to the Central Florida Car Rental office in good time, considering it was getting close to rush hour.

The *tinkle-tinkle* of the small brass bell above the door had barely stopped when a woman appeared behind the service desk. The female detective estimated her to be in her early sixties although clearly, the woman herself thought she was much younger, judging by the long, curly, peroxide-blonde hair, thick, powdery makeup, and Barbara Cartland blue eye shadow and youthful dress sense. The twenty to thirty gold chains around her neck and numerous bangles and bracelets on her wrists continuously made a metallic clinking sound every time she moved even slightly.

This woman has never heard the expression 'less is more,' Maria thought to herself, *and obviously believes in her own mantra of 'more is more'.*

"Good morning, y'all." The woman spoke with a thick southern drawl.

Maria took a deep breath and glanced at her partner, who took the lead.

"Good morning, ma'am. I'm Detective Travis, and this is Detective Hernandez." He gestured towards the female detective. "We're with Orlando PD." He stopped and studied the woman. "And you are?"

"I'm Reba Mae." She smiled and coyly dipped her head, batting her eyelids at the detective. "But everyone just calls me Missy. Now, how can I help you folks today?"

"Well, Missy," Maria was hesitant to call the woman

Missy, but went with it anyway. “We need information on a vehicle that’s registered to this company.”

“Oh, is this the same vehicle the other officers were inquiring about?” The receptionist seemed quite upset.

“Yes, the white panel van,” she confirmed.

“I do believe I sent all the vehicle documents by fax to a . . . errr… Officer Palmer.” She started to look around the desk in search of something. “I’m sure I have the copy of the fax confirmation ticket here.”

“Oh, that’s okay, we don’t need that.” The male detective put his hand on hers to stop her searching unnecessarily. “We were wondering if we could talk to the person who actually made the booking and handed over the keys.”

She looked up and smiled broadly as she let him hold her hand a little longer.

“Well, you surely are in luck today.” She flipped her hand over so she could hold his. “That would be me. I signed the agreement on that there van. And I sent the copies of the leasing contract with the other documents. So, how can I help you today?

Despite the way she looked, and her constant batting of her eyelids as she openly threw herself at Travis, Maria was warming to this woman very quickly. Her aura made her feel very at ease, like they had known each other for years. “Would you be willing to take a look at this picture and see if you recognize the person who hired the vehicle?”

“Absolutely,” she said, still gazing at her partner. “Although I did give the other officer a full description of the guy.”

Travis attempted to pull his hand away but came up against some resistance. For an elderly lady she obviously had a strong grip, judging by the amount of force the male detective had to use to get away from her. He produced the picture and held it out for her to take a look. She fumbled behind her desk for a moment, eventually bringing out a pair of reading glasses, which she perched across the bridge of her nose and peered closely at the photograph. There was a long silence as she pored over the snapshot featuring the AppTech staff. The longer she looked, the more the detectives held their breath in anticipation, until she suddenly pointed at a face in the crowd.

“That’s him. Right there; that’s the guy.” She held the photo closer for another look. “Yes, sir. That’s him.”

The female detective rapidly moved around the reception desk to stand by the woman and peer at the person she was indicating. She looked at her partner in disbelief, then back to the photo and placed her own finger in the same spot. “This guy?”

“That’s right, darlin’. I never forget a cute face.” She looked at Travis and winked. “I will certainly remember you for a long time to come.”

He smiled back awkwardly and leaned over the desk to see who had been pointed out. It took a second to sink in what he was looking at then looked at his partner for some reassurance. She just looked at him blankly shaking her head not wanting to believe what she was seeing.

“Missy. I need you to be clear on this. The man you are pointing out is this one here.” She tapped the face in the picture with her index finger.

“That’s right, sweetie. As a matter of fact, he was wearing a red cap, but that’s the guy.” She looked concerned. “Is everything okay?”

A horrified look came across the female detective’s face and nodded to the door as she looked at Travis, signaling for them to leave, quickly. “Yes. Thanks. You’ve been a great help.”

Travis snatched the picture back and they raced outside to the car.

"Y'all have a nice day now!" Missy shouted after them. "Don't forget to call again."

***

"You drive, get us to AppTech, now!" she ordered, as she tossed the keys at him. "I need to make some calls."

He fired up the engine, hit the gas, and turned on the blues and twos.

"Holy shit, this is fucked up," he said, not taking his eyes off the road. "What's the plan?"

"I need to get hold of Jen." She fumbled in her bag, pulled out her phone, dialed her number and waited. "Fuck! It's gone straight to voice mail... Jen, it's Maria. Call me as soon as you get this. Urgent!"

She tried to stay composed and dialed another number as the car weaved in and out of traffic. "Come on, Andy, answer your fucking phone." The call rang and rang, eventually going to voice mail. "Fuck me, why don't people just answer their phone? Andy, it's me. Call me. Urgent. You're not going to like this." She hung up.

She braced herself when she saw the oncoming red light; it was obvious they weren't stopping. They sped through the intersection, causing cars around him to skid to a stop.

"You do realize we need to be alive when we get there." She frowned at him, repositioned herself in the seat as she scrolled through her contacts. Finding what she was looking for, she pressed call. The call was answered after a few rings.

"Kim, it's Maria," she said in a firm tone. "Is Jen with you?"

"No, she's at work." There was a moment's silence. "Is everything okay?" The mother sounded a little concerned.

"I'll explain later." She looked at her partner, not knowing what to say. Should she tell her what happened? Or try and sort the situation out without worrying her? Say nothing, she decided. “Listen, Jen is on her way home with Chris. As soon as she gets there, can you get her to call me?”

“Yes, of course,” Kim replied. “Are you sure everything is okay?”

Maria paused for a moment, questioning if she was doing the right thing by not letting her in on what the developments were. “Positive… Hey, can you try to get hold of Andy and ask him to meet me at AppTech?”

“Maria, you’re scaring me.” She raised her voice. “What is going on?”

“I have to go, Kim.” She grabbed the dashboard to steady herself as the car weaved through the traffic. “Just get in touch with Andy.” She was about to hang up when she heard Kim shouting something and put the phone back to her ear.

“Maria! Maria! Please make sure my daughter is all right!” The sound of sobs quickly followed the plea.

“She’ll be okay, I promise,” she reassured her. “Now get calling Andy. Call Jen, too. Let me know if you make contact. I really have to go now.” She hung up before Kim could make any more pleas and continued to call Andy, with no success.

“I’ll call Chris’s house.” She scrolled through her contacts and pushed the number to connect the call. The call rang a few times before Amber answered.

“Hello, Amber Cooper here,” she said in her pretentious English accent.

“Amber, it’s Maria Hernandez,” she informed her. “Listen carefully, I’m trying to get hold of Chris. Is he there?”

“Hi, Maria. No, he’s not.” The accent started to slip. “He’s normally home by now. I did try and call him but there’s no answer.”

“When was the last time you heard from him?” she asked.

“About an hour and a half ago,” she replied. “He called

and said he couldn't talk because he had Jennifer and had something to sort out."

Maria glanced at her partner and shook her head. "And you haven't heard from him since?"

"No. Is everything okay?" she inquired.

"I'm sure everything is fine." She hesitated. This was getting serious now. Her suspicions were becoming increasingly confirmed as time went on. "Okay, Amber, do me a favor. Try to get hold of Chris. If you can't get hold of him, try and call Jennifer. If you contact either of them, let me know."

She thought about calling for backup and tried to decide if it was the right call given the circumstances. If she had read the situation wrong, the repercussions could be massive for her and Andy. Their relationship would undoubtedly be damaged beyond repair. However, it was procedure, and the right thing to do. Concluding it was the only option, she grabbed the mic of the police radio and was about to call it in when her cell rang. She checked the screen and dropped the mic. It was Kim.

"Kim, have you heard from Jen?" she asked.

"No, but Andy has called." She had calmed down since their previous conversation. "He said he'll meet you at AppTech, and to get there as quickly as possible."

"Okay, we're on our way." She nodded to Travis. "Keep trying to get hold of Jen for me."

"Please, Maria, tell me what's happening," Kim pleaded.

"I'll get Andy to call you when we get there," was all she could think of to say. "Keep calling Jen." She hung up. "Andy is meeting us at AppTech. You'd better step on it."

Travis shifted down a gear and floored the pedal, sending the car lurching forward, the sound of screeching tires filling the air.

***

As the car swung into the parking lot, Maria spotted

Andy's car parked next to Sinclair's pickup truck.

"There's Andy's car. Get next to it." She directed Travis to the spot with her pointed finger.

He pulled the car to a screeching halt next to the open vehicle and they got out. Maria went straight to the senior detective's vehicle and peered in to see if there was any sign of him. Nothing. Travis went around the back of their car, popped the trunk, leaned in, and pulled out two bulletproof vests.

"Here," he said, as he tossed the vest to her. "Put this on."

"Andy must be inside already." Daylight was fading fast as she looked up at the darkened building, and noted the only light that was on was in the vicinity of Chris's office.

They secured the protective clothing to their bodies and checked their firearms, then he checked that they had a few spare clips for their weapons before leaning back into the trunk and pulling out a shotgun and offering it to her.

She holstered her weapon and patted it. "I'll be okay with this."

He nodded, then leaned into the trunk again to grab two handfuls of shotgun shells, which he placed in his pocket. "You ready?"

"Wait. I'll call Andy." She got her cell out and dialed his number. Again, there was no answer. "Shit." She looked up at the building. "Okay, let's assume Andy is in there. He doesn't know Chris is involved, so let's be careful."

"Right," he agreed.

"We should separate," she continued, taking the lead and looking at the reception area. "There's no sign of Sinclair. He has a private apartment in the building. It's over that way." She pointed towards the right of the building. "If you find him, detain him in a secure place."

"What about you?" He looked concerned.

"I'm going in the front way." She nodded to the main entrance. "Whoever finds Andy first, call the other. Okay?"

"Okay."

"Make your way to Chris's office. I'll meet you there." She nodded at him and looked back to the building. "Come on, let's move."

They separated and walked towards their chosen entrances. "Hey!" he said in a loud whisper. "Be careful in there."

She didn't acknowledge him. Instead she drew her weapon and held it at the ready as she approached the main entrance doors. Surprisingly, they weren't locked. Her gut instinct told her this wasn't right, but she had to push on and get to Andy before his brother did.

Chapter 38

On the upper floor of AppTech, in an office that was dimly illuminated by a single desk lamp, Martin Miller typed frantically on the keyboard in front of him. He had to finish what he was doing before anyone came in.

He frequently stopped to glance at the door, thinking he had heard movement in the corridor outside. Pausing for a moment he listened, then returned to his work, satisfied he was still alone.

He suddenly stopped working and sat back in his seat, glaring at the open door. Something wasn't right. He needed to make sure he was alone. Silently, he stood up and walked to the door. He listened for a moment to see if he could hear anyone approaching before he popped his head out and looked left to right, checking either end of the passageway.

He took a quick look back at his computer screen to make sure he had put it into sleep mode, then hesitantly stepped into the corridor and stood motionless, eerily half-lit by the emanating light from his office.

***

The outside streetlights filtered through the glass partitions separating the offices from the corridor, giving Maria just enough light to systematically edge her way through the building.

She opened another door and shined her flashlight in, following the beam of light with her gun as she swept the room. Another empty office, Lord knows how many to go, she told herself as she switched the flashlight off, closed the door, and moved on to the next office, making sure she stayed low and close to the partition in an attempt to conceal herself from anyone waiting inside the next office.

The sound of a door closing further along the corridor stopped her from opening the door she was reaching for. *Shit, who's there?* she asked inwardly. Peering into the darkness and squinting hard to try and make out what could have made the noise, she thought she saw someone move at the end of the corridor.

"Andy!" she whispered as loud as she dared. There was no reply. Her mind began to race. *Call him on the cell.* She quickly got her cell out and pressed redial. Instead of hearing a ringing tone, the constant beeping let her know the receiving cell had been turned off.

Another door opening at the end of the corridor grabbed her attention. Again she strained her eyes to see who was there. Was that someone standing in the doorway, watching her? She grabbed her flashlight, flicked it on, and directed it down the passage in time to see the door leading to a stairwell close.

"Mother fucker," she cursed under her breath. Adrenaline coursed through her body faster than before. She could hear and feel her heart beating in her chest.

"Okay, move," she urged herself, and rapidly advanced along the hallway towards the door, aiming her weapon and flashlight straight at the door. She took a deep breath, opened the door, and stepped into the stairwell, aiming her weapon first down the stairs, then up.

The door on the next landing was slightly ajar. Shining the flashlight at the gap between the door and the frame, she caught sight of someone looking at her.

She instantly froze, the hairs on the back of her neck standing on end. "Freeze! Police!" she shouted.

The door slammed shut. Instinctively she sprinted up the stairs, grabbed the handle and pulled. The door wouldn't open.

She peered through the wired glass panel into the darkness on the other side. Unable to make anything out, she shined the flashlight through the window. The sight of the wolf mask suddenly appearing sent a shockwave through her body. Before she could react, the door slammed into her face, sending her flying backwards. She hit the opposite wall and slumped to the floor, dazed.

By the time she had shaken her head to clear it and got to her feet, the door had been closed again. *Take your time.* She leaned back against the wall and pointed her weapon at the door, anticipating the wolf's return. *Come on, think.*

"Travis," she said out aloud. *Call him now.*

***

Travis had found and thoroughly searched Sinclair's private quarters; there was no sign of the head of security. He didn't have the advantage Maria had of being semi-aware of the building layout due to being there on previous occasions, so he was mainly using instinct to guide himself to the upper level, where they had seen the illuminated office from outside.

So far he had managed to work his way through the basement, which consisted of broom closets and stationery supplies, but hadn't come across anything worth being alarmed about.

His cell ringing snapped him out of what was becoming routine. He looked at the screen and accepted the call.

"Maria, have you found anything?" he asked with some urgency.

"Travis, where are you?" she was whispering.

"I'm checking the basement," he replied. "Where are you?"

"In the stairwell at the east end of the building. He's here. The guy in the wolf mask is here." She spoke with labored breath. "I've followed him up to the top floor."

“I’m on my way!” he shouted.

“No, wait.” She stopped him. “There’s a stairwell at the opposite end of the building. Come up that way; he may try and get down that way.”

“What if he uses the elevators?” he added.

“I’ll try Andy again. If he doesn’t answer this time I’m calling this in.” She paused. “Fuck it, we need backup now.”

“Okay,” he agreed. “I’ll get to you as soon as possible.”

“Be careful. I don’t know if he’s armed,” she added, and disconnected the call.

He put his cell away, pumped the shotgun, and headed towards the west stairwell. Once inside, he stood looking up through several flights of stairs into the darkness. After a moment to allow his eyes to adjust, he slowly started ascending the stairs, checking the door leading to every level as he passed.

***

Maria took a deep breath and steadied her aim at the door. *Call it in.* She held her cell up so she could see the screen, at the same time keeping an eye on the door. Scrolling as quickly as possible, she found the number for dispatch and pressed the call button.

“Dispatch,” a voice abruptly answered.

“This is Detective Hernandez,” she announced, holding the cell to her ear and staring at the door. “I need full backup at the AppTech building on Oakrun Boulevard.” Her tone was precise and clear. “I’m unable to make contact with Detective Cooper, so assume there is an officer down. I’m in pursuit of a suspect in the building.”

“Okay, Detective Hernandez, hold the line,” the voice answered. “All units in the vicinity of Oakrun Boulevard, respond immediately to report of officer down at AppTech building. Detective Hernandez is onsite and in pursuit of suspect.” There was a pause for a few seconds. Maria could still hear her own heartbeat as she waited in the unnervingly dark stairwell. "Officers are on their way, Detective. Stay on the line so we can guide them to you."

She was suddenly startled by the sight of a light coming on in the area behind the closed door. Holding her breath in anticipation of something or someone coming through the door, she pressed the phone harder against her ear. "I'm on the top floor. Get them here now."

She disconnected the call, put her cell away and edged towards the door with her weapon concentrated on the door. Hesitating for a moment, she grabbed the handle, flung the door open, and stepped into the passageway in one swift movement. She waited for a few seconds to let her eyes adjust to the light.

The light dimly lighting the hallway was coming from an open office door. *Is that Chris's office? No, his is nearer to the elevator. Whose office is it?* She quickly surveyed the area; there was no sign of the wolf mask. *Move, come on, move.*

Gripping her gun in both hands and aiming directly at the light source, she eased her way along the corridor, staying as close as possible to the dividing partition and being careful not to let her concentration slip.

After what seemed like an eternity, she made it to the open door. Her mind was working overtime. *Who's in there?* Her heart was racing and her palms had become sweaty from the tight grip she had on the weapon. In quick succession she wiped the palm of each hand on her jeans to dry them, then assumed her stance, prepared for any surprise attack. *Okay, relax.* She paused for a moment to compose herself.

No matter how many hours she had put in on the firing range, or the endless scenarios she had gone over on the simulator that had been recently installed at the station, allowing cops to act out scenarios on an interactive big screen, this was different. This was real.

Okay, I'm good. Go! She swung her body around the door frame and entered the office, scanning the room with her pointed handgun. Her heart felt like it was going to burst out of her chest. There was no sign of anyone.

Her attention was drawn to the nameplate on the desk. Martin Miller. She glanced back at the door, lowered her weapon slightly, and took a few steps towards the desk.

What was that? She froze and snapped her weapon up at the sight of a leg jutting out from behind the desk.

"All right, get up nice and slow," she ordered, but the person didn't respond.

"Police! Get up!" she shouted. There was no movement.

She edged around the desk, her gun trained on the suspect. He was wearing a red baseball cap. Confusion set in when she noticed a pool of blood seeping from under the suspect, who was lying face down. Affording herself another quick look at the doorway, and scanning the room again to make sure nobody else was in there with her, she knelt down and placed her index and middle finger on the neck, checking. *He's dead all right. Let's see who you are.* She rolled the body over and removed the baseball cap, fully expecting to see the face of Martin Miller staring back at her. She was wrong.

"Fuck me, this can't be right," she said aloud.

She was completely confused as she stood up, staring at the body, then caught sight of someone standing behind her in the reflection of the widow. A shockwave blasted through her body. *Shit! He's behind me!* She tried to spin around but it was too late.

The wolf was immediately behind. Before she had chance to completely turn around, his forehead connected with the bridge of her nose and he had a grip on her wrist, stopping her from raising the gun any higher. The impact and searing pain made her body tense up, causing her to squeeze the trigger, firing a round into the floor.

Dazed, she fell backwards, stumbling over the body behind her. But the hold on her wrist from the wolf stopped her from falling to the floor. He pulled her back.

"I've been waiting for you," he hissed in his thick, Southern drawl as he landed a right hook square on the jaw, instantly knocking her unconscious.

***

Travis heard the muffled shot from the stairwell. He instantly started sprinting up the stairs as fast as he could. He got to the top floor and burst into the corridor, spotting the light coming from the open door.

"Maria!" he shouted as he ran along the passageway. There was no reply.

He was nearly at the open door when he noticed a figure standing in the doorway leading to the stairwell at the opposite end of the building. He slowed down to a steady pace and aimed the shotgun at the person.

"Identify yourself!" he shouted, as he kept advancing. But the figure calmly stepped into the darkness of the stairwell and let the door close. Travis fired a round at the door, instantly knowing there was no way he had hit the figure.

He reached the door and looked into the office to see his partner lying on the floor, her face smeared with blood.

"Fuck, Maria!" He raced in to see if she was alive, and noticed the body behind the desk.

The sight of the blood-stained shirt and entry wound in the chest of the body let him know the person was dead. He turned his attention back to the injured detective and bent down to see if she was alive. She started to come around as he lifted her head and called her name.

"I'm… I'm okay," she mumbled. "It's the wolf mask guy. Go after him."

"Are you sure you're okay?" He was concerned about her.

"Go after him!" she ordered in a raised voice.

He didn't need telling again. He lowered her down, picked up the shotgun and raced after the wolf. Without hesitating he burst through the door leading to the stairwell and rapidly descended the stairs in pursuit of his quarry.

He had gone down two flights of stairs and was halfway down the third flight when he was suddenly halted by the sound of two gunshots. Pinning himself against the wall, he waited to see if the shots were being fired at him. He could hear shuffling below, then the sound of an emergency door being opened and closed. *Think, quick.* He looked around. *The window.*

He pounced towards the window on the landing and peered down to see a body slumped over the shoulder of another person, being carried towards the area where they'd left their vehicle.

No! He'll be gone by the time I get down there. His mind raced, trying to come up with some way of stopping the wolf. *Wait... the office windows.*

He ran into the nearest hallway and raced to the office he guessed was in the middle of the building so he could get a clear shot of the suspect. Kicking the door open and rushing to the window, he looked down in time to see the figure dumping the body in the back of Sinclair's pickup truck. The body rolled over. He looked closer. Horrified by what he saw, he banged on the window.

"Stop!" he shouted as loud as he could, and banged vigorously with his fist.

The figure below looked up and stared at him for a brief second. *Is he smiling at me?*

The thought of the suspect taunting him sent Travis into a rage. He stepped back from the window, raised the shotgun and fired, shattering the glass, sending it raining down into the parking lot below. By the time he had stepped forward to take aim, the wolf had turned the truck around and was accelerating away.

Travis took aim and was about to fire but thought better of it. The last thing he wanted to do was risk hitting the person in the back, who could still be alive.

Indeed, the last thing he wanted to do was to take a shot and hit the incapacitated Andy Cooper as he lay in the back of the pickup truck.

Chapter 39

Travis gently lowered Maria onto the sofa in Regan's office and gave her an ice pack to take the swelling down on her bruised cheek. She had refused medical attention at AppTech, opting for a few painkillers to relieve the pounding headache that understandably made her feel a little woozy.

"You okay, Hernandez?" the concerned lieutenant asked as he stood over her.

"I'm fine, sir," she replied, although her posture told another story. Resembling a withered man in his nineties, she sat slumped on the sofa, looking down at the floor while she let the ice pack slowly numb her face.

"Are you sure?" Travis persisted.

"I said, I'm fine!" she snapped.

"Okay, Detective," the lieutenant said calmly. "Take it easy."

"I'm sorry, sir," she said, looking up at him. "I had that fucker right in front of me and he got away."

"You're lucky to be alive, Maria," her superior reassured her as he sat on the front of his desk.

"That's what I don't understand, sir," she continued. "This guy is pooping people all over the place. Why didn't he kill me?"

"Maybe he panicked after you fired a round off and knew it wouldn't be long before I got there," her partner reasoned. "Although, this guy has got some balls."

"Why's that?" Reagan asked.

"When I got to the passageway it was like he was taunting me. He just stood there, looking at me, before stepping into the stairwell." He looked at the lieutenant. "If I had fired without asking him to identify himself he'd be in a body bag now, sir."

"And if you'd fired first we might be putting your partner in a body bag," the superior officer informed him. "You did the right thing."

His usually immaculate appearance had gone. He had his shirt sleeves rolled up and his jacket and tie had been discarded. The dark circles around his eyes were a tell-tale sign that he had been in the office for a long time. He eyed the female detective pressing the ice pack against her cheek, then looked at her partner holding his injured shoulder and shook his head.

"Going on the condition you two are in, I would normally take both of you off the case. But the truth is, I have nobody to replace you." He pushed himself up off the desk and moved around to sit behind it. "Andy is missing—"

"I'm sure it was him in the back of Sinclair's pickup, sir," Travis interrupted.

"But Sinclair is dead; is that right, Hernandez?" He looked at her for confirmation.

"Yes, sir." She nodded. "I checked his pulse before rolling him over. At first I thought it was Miller, what with it being in his office."

"Okay, run me through what happened again. What can you remember?" he asked.

"I walked in and saw a body on the floor." She shook her head and sat upright, groaning as the change of position sent waves of pain through her head. "I must have missed an area when I swept the room because when I stood up I saw the wolf mask in the reflection of the widow. Before I could turn around he had my wrist so I couldn't take aim, and he head butted me. That's when I fired a round off. That's the last thing I remember until Travis was talking to me." She pressed harder with the ice pack. "Has anybody got any Tylenol?"

"Where was Andy when this was going off?" Regan rummaged around in his desk drawer as he spoke. He pulled out a bottle of Tylenol and passed it to the male detective, who gallantly attempted to get around the childproof lid, with no success.

"He'd gotten there before us," she told him, while scowling at her partner and signaling to give her the bottle of pain relief tablets. "He must have been looking around on the lower levels when the perp ran down the stairwell."

"That's when I heard two shots and what sounded like a struggle," Travis interrupted, and passed the unopened bottle to her. She flipped it open with ease, drawing a disbelieving look from him. "He must have subdued Andy, then carried him to the pickup," he continued, turning his attention back to the ranking officer.

"So, who are we looking for?" the lieutenant asked.

"Chris Cooper, sir," the male detective informed him. "The woman at the van rental place positively identified him as the one who hired the van."

"You are fucking kidding me! Chris Cooper is in on this?" Regan shouted. "Why are you only telling me this now?"

"It was information we received earlier sir," he informed him. "That's why we were heading to AppTech."

"I know this case is pretty fucked up, but, Chris?" He shook his head, leading the detectives to think he was finding it difficult to believe what he was being told.

"Or Martin Miller!" Maria sternly said, as she looked around the office for some water to wash down the painkillers. Spotting a half-full bottle on the desk, she held her hand out and wiggled her fingers at it. Regan tossed it to her partner, who again tried to be chivalrous, but struggled to open the bottle.

"But the woman at the van rental place—" her partner

started, but was cut short.

"I know what she said, but the guy who took me out had a heavy Southern accent. Just like Miller's." She snatched the bottle from him and looked at the lieutenant. "He said 'I've been waiting for you,' just before he punched me." She glanced back at Travis and held the bottle up, emphasizing how easy it was to open. "As far as Chris is concerned, we don't know his full involvement yet, sir. He could be part of it, or, he could have been forced into cooperating."

"Okay." The lieutenant sat forward. "Sinclair is dead, Andy and Jennifer are missing, Chris could be involved but we don't know to what extent." He paused for a moment. "Are we naming Miller as the main suspect?

Maria launched the tablets into the back of her throat and washed them down with a mouthful of water, wincing as she swallowed hard. "He's on the top of my list, sir." She looked him straight in the eye. "I came so close to nailing him."

"All right. We've put an APB out on Sinclair's pickup truck and I've had the rest of the Cooper family brought in for their own protection." Regan looked at the female detective. "I'm sorry, but I'm going to have to cover all the bases here." He picked up his phone and tapped on a number. "This is Lieutenant Regan. I want warrants issued for the arrest of Christopher Cooper and Martin Miller immediately in connection with the abduction of Detective Andrew Cooper and his daughter, Jennifer Cooper. Make sure all units take this as a priority and call anything in ASAP." He put the phone down and shrugged. "That's about all we can do at the moment." He looked at the detectives. "Unless you have any ideas?"

"Have we got anything? Any sightings? Anything at all to go on?" Maria was exasperated.

"Nothing at all. They've disappeared." He sat back, twiddling a pen between his fingers. "I've got all our tech guys in going over the personal computers of Sinclair and Miller." Regan paused. "I'd better add Chris's name to that list, too."

"Something isn't right here; I just can't accept that Chris is involved in this," Maria said, as she rolled her head around her shoulders to loosen up. The pain relief was really starting to kick in now, making her feel much better. "He must have been blackmailed, had a threat made against him. Or he just hired the van for something, then forgot about it." She stood up and started stretching and moving her body, trying to wake her tired and aching muscles.

"Where would you go if you potentially had three hostages?" Regan asked her out of the blue.

She stopped moving and thought about the question. "Somewhere isolated."

"Why isolated?" Regan pointed at her.

"Because, if I know Andy, he'll be putting up a hell of a struggle if he's conscious, and even more so because of Jen." She stopped. "If he's incapacitated, carrying an unconscious body around is going to draw a lot of attention." She thought again. "Then there's moving Jen and possibly Chris around as well."

"That's a good point." Travis looked at her. "So, are we looking for abandoned warehouses?"

"This fucker has been too methodical." Maria shook her head. "Abandoned warehouses leave too much to chance." She took a moment to rethink. "Get the tech guys to see if Miller has taken out any leases on isolated properties since moving to Florida.

"They're already going over all his finances. It's going to take time though," the lieutenant told her. The phone rang on his desk and he literally banged the speaker button, allowing everyone in the office to hear the call. "Regan."

"Lieutenant, it's Palmer. We've had a ping from

Detective Cooper's phone," he said with some urgency.

"What's the location?" the ranking officer shouted. Both detectives suddenly sprang nearer to the desk in an attempt to hear exactly what was being relayed.

"It briefly showed up on a triangulation on, or around, Old Neptune Road," the forensics officer informed him. "Looks like the edge of the swamp."

"That's where he's going to dump the bodies," the male detective interjected.

Maria shook her head. "That makes no sense." She put both hands on the desk to steady herself. Although her faculties were returning quickly, she still felt a little disorientated. "If he wanted them dead, then why not kill them at AppTech and leave the bodies there?"

Regan raised his hand. "Maybe he didn't have time."

"He has a ritual," Travis muttered. "That's it. He has a ritual." He looked wide-eyed at the others. "He takes them, does whatever he does, kills them, and dumps the bodies in the swamp."

The horror of what her partner had just said sent a shockwave rippling through her body. "That's where the kids are." She glared open-mouthed at the lieutenant. "He's dumping the bodies in the swamp." She turned to the map on the wall and rushed over to it, looking for the location of Old Neptune Road. She found it and slammed her finger on the spot. "There!"

The other officers joined her at the map and examined the area.

"Palmer!" Regan shouted.

"Sir," he responded.

"Narrow your search to this area for properties leased out by Miller," he ordered.

"Check out if there are any leased out to AppTech," Maria added.

"Do it now, and get back to me!" the lieutenant barked.

"Yes, sir." The line went dead.

All three continued to scour the map for anything that would indicate where they should be searching for the missing detective and his daughter.

"Hmm." She looked at her superior. "Did you say you brought the rest of the Cooper family in?"

"Yes." He nodded. "I thought it was for the best."

She looked back at the map. "Let me go talk to them. It's possible Amber might know if Chris has got any property in that area."

"It's worth a try," He agreed. "I'm going to breathe down Palmer's neck, just so he stays on his toes."

"Okay, I'll call you if we get anything from the family." She signaled for her partner to follow.

***

Kim rushed to them as they entered the conference room. "Maria. Please tell me what's happening. Where are Jen and Andy?" she asked between sobs.

"I don't know is the honest answer." The detective looked around at the women. "But I'm hoping you ladies may be able to give me some information." Not fully knowing how to deal with this situation, she quickly decided that the no-nonsense approach was going to be the best way forward. "Do any of you know of any buildings that AppTech owns or leases around the Old Neptune Road area?" she asked, looking directly at Amber.

Chris's wife looked bemused. Her usual exquisitely turned out appearance had been forgotten, possibly through the rush to get to the station and not having time to go through her two-hour beauty routine, a thing she did every morning before getting to the breakfast table. Her hair was disheveled, there were no signs of any makeup on and she was reduced to wearing sweatpants and a hoodie.

"I don't know. I don't get involved with Chris's business, and he never talks about things like that." Her eyes were red and puffy, an indication that she had shed her own fair share of tears recently.

Cathleen stepped forward. "Is that near the swamp?"

"Yes, has Chris mentioned anything to you?" the detective asked.

"No, but Coop owned a fishing lodge out on the swamp," the matriarch informed her.

Maria looked at Travis, then back to the elder woman. "Do you have an exact location?"

"I've only been a couple of times, but I think I could give you directions," Cathleen added.

Maria turned to Travis. "Get hold of Regan. Tell him to assemble a SWAT team. I'll meet you downstairs." He nodded, and rushed out of the conference room. She turned back towards her, putting her hands on her shoulders. "Okay, Cathleen, where is it?"

Chapter 40

Jen sat on the floor in the pitch-black room, with her knees tucked under her chin and her arms wrapped round her shins, pulling her lower legs in as tightly as possible to offer some comfort to the frightening situation she was in. She had taken to rocking back and forth slightly while humming random tunes in her head to distract her thoughts from her mounting anxiety.

She had been so engrossed in her self-imposed meditation the she hadn't heard the clinking of keys unlocking the door, and was only brought into the moment by the shaft of light that partially lit the room.

Startled, she looked up at the blinding light and scrambled backwards to the nearest wall, squinting as hard as possible to stop her eyes from hurting. She hit the wall harder than she wanted to and scrambled to the left into the outstretched arms of the other person held captive.

Once in the relative safety of the embrace, she quickly glanced around the room, noticing that the walls were covered with old bed mattresses, providing makeshift soundproofing. The brilliant light flooding the room was suddenly dimmed by the appearance of a seemingly impossibly large figure standing in the doorway.

She raised one hand to shield her eyes from the lights in an attempt to make out who it was standing there, silently looking at them. She concentrated on the face, but from what she could make out it was disfigured. What was wrong with it? Why couldn't her mind comprehend what her eyes were seeing? Her sight focused a little more. The face wasn't disfigured; it was a mask. He was wearing a wolf mask. Then she noticed the gun in his hand, pointing towards the floor. A wave of fright flashed through her body, causing her to press herself against her fellow captor.

The wolf silently raised the weapon until it was pointing directly at her. "You!" He barked in his Southern drawl, making her jump. "Come with me."

It was only then that the person offering her comfort spoke.

"Leave her be," he said, and shuffled forward enough to move in front of her, putting himself in the line of fire. "Take me instead."

The wolf pulled back the hammer on the firearm. "I will not be repeating myself again. She either comes with me, or I shoot you and she comes with me anyway." He slowly moved his aim between the two hostages. "Which is it going to be?"

"Don't shoot!" Jen pleaded. "I'll come with you." She stood up and tentatively walked towards the door.

The wolf stepped aside, allowing her to pass, his gun trained on the figure still in the room. "I will be back for you real soon."

Jen looked back at the lonely figure on the floor. "Don't worry; I'll be okay, Uncle Chris," she said, as the wolf closed the door and locked it.

***

As soon as the door had locked, Chris got up and felt his way along the wall until he reached the door, putting an ear up against it to see if he could hear anything. For a few seconds all he could hear was his own breathing, then he could make out shuffling, then the muffled Southern accent of their abductor. But he couldn't make out what was being said.

Think, think, think, he told himself. *Do something.*

Carefully he edged his way around the room as best he

could, feeling for something, anything, that might help him get out of this situation. He fumbled around in the darkness for a few minutes but found nothing. His search was cut short by the sound of the lock on the door being opened. He scrambled back to his position on the floor and was settled into place by the time it opened. The light flooded the room once again, causing Chris to squint to let his eyes adjust. The wolf stepped in, pointing his gun at Chris.

"Come with me," he ordered.

"Where is Jen?" the captive asked.

"Do not test me, Christopher." The Southern drawl was thicker than before. "Now get up and come with me."

"Miller? Is that you, Miller?" Chris scowled. "What the fuck is this all about?"

"You'll find out soon enough, now come with me!" he snapped.

"No! I'm not going anywhere until you tell me where Jen is, Miller." He folded his arms in a childlike act of defiance.

"I'm taking you to Jen," Genesis snarled. "You defy me one more time and I'll put a bullet in your head, then I'll go put one in that pretty little niece of yours."

Chris slowly got to his feet, maintaining eye contact with his captor the entire time. He moved slowly towards the door, shooting a quick glance at the weapon. A thought shot through his mind; could he disarm this guy? Surely he could overpower Miller. What if he didn't, though? Surely that would mean the end for him and Jen. His mind was racing. *Should I make a move or not?* Then, as if he was reading his mind, the wolf spoke.

"Don't even think about it," he calmly said. "I will not hesitate to shoot you."

As Chris got closer, the wolf stepped back out of the room and to one side to allow him to pass.

"Stop!" the kidnapper ordered, and held the weapon

against Chris's temple. He closed the door to the soundproof room. "Over there!"

Chris looked around. The only light in the room was coming from a small spotlight, illuminating a hanger that had a neatly pressed beige jacket, beige trousers, beige shirt and a red baseball cap resting on the hook above the garments. There was a single metal frame chair beneath the light, with a pig mask resting on the seat and pair of brown loafers neatly placed on the floor.

"Get changed." The wolf removed the gun from his temple and shoved him towards the clothing.

That was when he noticed that the garments matched the wolf's attire. Everything was identical. He hesitantly pulled the jacket off of the hanger.

"Why are you doing this, Miller? Is it money you want? I can give you money if that's what it is," Chris pleaded, while looking at the jacket.

"Enough with the questions." He waved the weapon, signaling he wanted him to hurry. "Just get changed and maybe, just maybe, you and your precious niece will make it out of here alive tonight." The accent slipped.

This made Chris think. He noticed something else, the way he moved his arm. "Wait, you're not Miller, are you?" He peered at his kidnapper. "Who are you?" he asked.

"I would like to tell you, but let's just say right now I'm not Abel." He laughed.

"You think this is funny?" Chris shouted. "Think this is a fucking joke?"

"Genesis!" He barked back, startling the captive. "I'm Genesis! Now, enough with the questions. Just fucking get changed."

Chris put the jacket on the chair and began to undress. He suddenly stopped when he realized that his captor was staring at him. "You going to watch me get dressed? Is that how you get your kicks?" He tried to get a rise out of him. Anything that would give him a clue as to his identity. It didn't work. The aggressor merely waved his gun to signify he wanted more haste from him.

When he had finished getting changed, he turned to face the wolf.

"Now the pig mask," he growled.

"What?" He looked confused.

"Put the mask on!" He pointed the gun at the latex disguise on the chair.

He reluctantly removed the baseball cap and slowly put the mask on before replacing the cap.

"Perfect." He beamed. "Now, it's time to reunite you with your niece." He paused. "Yes, a nice little intimate family reunion." He laughed, then loudly grunted and squealed like a pig. "Come on, little piggy."

Chris was thinking that whoever this guy was, he had finally gone over the edge. He quickly decided if an opportunity arose to overpower him, he would take it.

Genesis stepped into the darkness halfway across the room. "Don't do anything stupid, Christopher. Remember, I still have your niece."

Before he could react to the comment a light came on, illuminating a table. What was more horrifying was the sight of his niece bent over the table, with her ankles tied to the table legs at one end and her body stretched across the top, with her wrists tied to the legs at the opposite end. She lay there staring at him through tear-filled eyes.

His anxiety rose. He looked around the room, desperately searching for something, anything, that would suffice as a makeshift weapon. As he looked around the room he had a sense of familiarity coming over him. He knew this place.

He had been here before. Then he realized where he was; his dad's cabin.

"Christopher!" the aggressor called out. "We're ready for you."

"What the fuck have you done to her?" he screamed, and made a move towards her.

"Hold it right there." Genesis stepped closer to Jen, lifted his arm, and placed the gun on her temple. "Let's not be making any sudden movements like that, because I get very jumpy." He looked down through the sinister wolf mask at the gun in his hand. He then looked back at Chris. "Accidents happen when I get jumpy, and we don't want that, now do we?"

"Jen, are you okay?" He glared at the weapon as a feeling of helplessness swept over him.

"I'm okay," she spluttered through sobs. "As soon as Dad gets here he's going to kill this bastard."

"I wouldn't count on your father being part of a rescue mission." He laughed behind the mask.

"What does that mean?" Chris looked at him.

"Nothing for you to worry about right now." He calmly reached over and stroked the back of Jen's head. "You shouldn't worry either, little girl. As long as Uncle Christopher cooperates, you'll be fine."

"Of course I'll cooperate. Just let her go. She has nothing to do with this," he pleaded, then turned his attention to his niece. "It's going to be okay, sweetheart. I'll do whatever he wants. I love you."

"Do you, Christopher?" he asked, and tilted his head to the left, inquisitively looking at the concerned relative.

"Do I what?" he answered, somewhat confused.

"Do you love her?" He tilted his head to the other side.

"Of course I do, she's my niece." Chris was puzzled by the question.

"How much?" he pressed.

The varying thickness of the Southern accent made the questioning seem even more sinister to the struggling software executive. The heat of the Florida swamp, the wearing of the latex mask, the intense questioning, and the general fear he was experiencing from the whole situation had caused Chris to sweat profusely. He lifted his mask in an attempt to wipe his brow.

"Leave the mask alone and answer the question. How much do you love your niece?" Genesis barked.

He slowly replaced the mask. "To answer your question, I love her immeasurably. What is this? Why are you asking ridiculous questions?" His eyes began to sting from the sweat, but trying to rub them through the mask didn't make much difference.

"What would you do for her?" he continued.

"Anything!" he snapped back.

"Show me." He nodded towards the girl.

"What?" he exclaimed.

"Show me how much you love her," Genesis ordered.

"I don't follow you; what do you mean?" He was blinking frantically beneath the mask, trying to clear his eyes of sweat.

"Show me how much you love your darling niece." He removed the weapon from Jen's temple and waved him over with it. "Get over here and fuck her."

"No!" Chris protested. "Are you completely insane?"

Jen, who had been crying the entire time suddenly stopped. "You're one sick fucker. Dad is going to kill you when he gets here," she said through sharp intakes of breath.

Genesis sighed. "I've warned you before. You say no to me one more time and I will shoot both of you." He pushed the gun barrel hard into the back of Jen's head. "Starting with her."

Chris looked at his niece and noticed her face had visibly

changed. She struggled momentarily when the muzzle of the gun touched her skull.

"Shhh!" the aggressor hissed. "Calm down, Jennifer."

"Fuck you!" she screamed at him.

"You should tell your princess to take it easy." He looked at the uncle, who stared in disbelief.

Under his mask, Chris was open-mouthed. The stinging sweat in his eyes began to make his head reel. He couldn't believe what was happening. Moreover, he couldn't comprehend what he had been ordered to do. "Jen, I can't do it."

"You said you would do anything for her, Christopher," their attacker said to him. "You said you loved her and would do anything."

"Yes, but—" He didn't get to finish his protest.

"Then fuck her!" the wolf shouted. "Now!"

The uncle tried to force himself forward but was frozen to the spot. "I can't." He quickly shook his head.

Genesis reached under his jacket and pulled out a knife. Keeping the gun pressed into her head, he moved around to behind the girl, lifted up the hem of her skirt, and holding the knife an inch away from her body, slowly moved his hand down. When the blade neared her buttocks, Chris feared she was about to be mutilated.

"No, stop!" he yelled, shaking his head.

Genesis looked at him. He moved the knife closer to her skin. "I told you what would happen if you disobeyed me again."

"Stop! I haven't disobeyed you!" Chris pleaded.

The aggressor ran the blade under the waistband of his niece's panties and jerked the blade up, cutting through the flimsy material. The panties dropped to the floor, leaving Jen naked from the waist down. "That's why I'm not shooting yet."

Jen began to cry even louder. She tried to wriggle her hips to try and get her skirt to fall back into place.

Genesis looked at the girl and saw what she was trying to do. He slipped the knife back into his pocket, and in one swift movement he pulled the skirt completely away, leaving the young girl totally exposed. "Now, get over here and fuck her."

"Please don't make me do this," Chris cried beneath his mask.

Genesis raised his gun. A loud bang echoed around the cabin as he fired a shot into the ceiling. He then pressed the barrel of the gun hard against Jen's temple. The youngster screamed in pain at the hot metal, and the smell of searing skin filled the room.

"Please, Uncle Chris, I don't want to die!" she screamed as the intense burning pain grew.

"Jen. I just can't do it," Chris sobbed uncontrollably. "I just can't."

"Please make it stop!" she squealed. "It hurts!"

He glared at his niece being tortured, but how could he do what was being asked of him? On the other hand, failure to comply would almost certainly result in both of them being killed. As he toiled with his conscience, he heard her voice.

"Uncle Chris. Just do it. I don't want to die!" she screamed.

Unable to take it any longer, he snapped out of his daze. "Okay, okay. I'll do it. Just don't hurt her."

Chapter 41

Chris reluctantly stepped forward, unzipping his trousers, and dropped them, along with his underwear, to the floor as he did so. He tried one last-ditch attempt to reason with their captor.

"You don't have to do this. I have money. I'll give you everything if you just let us go," he begged, and pointed at Jen. "If not both of us, let my niece go. She hasn't done anything wrong to you."

"Stop sniveling, Christopher," Genesis snapped. "I'm getting bored of repeating myself. My trigger finger is warmed up now, so, either fuck her, or you both die. Right here, right now. The choice is yours."

With a shaking hand he leaned forward to whisper in her ear. "You do know I don't want to do this. I love you, sweetheart. I promise I'll be gentle." He stood more upright, placed a hand on her shoulder and, staring straight into the wolf's eyes through floods of tears, he carefully entered his niece.

Jen let out an undistinguishable sound as her uncle penetrated her. Her sobs filled the room and tears rolled down her cheeks.

Suddenly she fell silent, and turned her head to look at the captor. Through bloodshot eyes she glared deep into the eyes. She had stopped crying, her face enraged.

"Is this what you wanted to see?" she scowled. "You limp-dicked fucker?" Her fear had well and truly transformed to anger. "That's it. Come on Uncle Chris, give it to me."

Her uncle, incessantly sobbing, kept his rhythmic hip

movement going. "Don't, Jen. Don't say that. Please don't."

"Ooh yeah, that's it, Uncle Chris." She wasn't listening. "Fuck me harder!" she shouted, still staring at the wolf mask.

"Do as she says, Christopher," the aggressor urged. "Give it to her harder." He laughed out loudly.

"You sick bastard!" Chris snarled at him.

"I'm a sick bastard?" he huffed. "You're the one fucking your niece, and enjoying it too, by the looks of things. Ah, the irony," he tormented Chris.

"He's not the only one enjoying it," she said, maintaining her stare. "Come on, Uncle Chris, do it to me."

"I knew you two wanted to do this by the way you act around the office." The wolf laughed.

"My God, you were so right. Harder, do it harder. Give this fucking pervert a proper show." She licked her lips while letting her eyes burn into the mask of the imposing figure standing above her.

Her uncle, meanwhile, experienced a varied amount of emotions. Fear, guilt, embarrassment, and worst of all, as much as he hated himself for it, enjoyment.

"You are enjoying yourself more than you care to admit, aren't you, Christopher?" the aggressor teased.

Chris tried to focus on him through tear-drenched eyes. "You're going to pay for this."

The kidnapper raised the weapon to within an inch of Chris's face, who instantly froze. The faint sound of intermittent buzzing could be heard. With his free hand he went into his pocket and pulled out his cell. He held the phone up so he could check the screen while still keeping his victim in sight, then pressed the answer button and slipped the phone under his mask. As he did so, Chris strained to see if he could get a glimpse of the face. No good; the mask hadn't been lifted high enough.

The thick Southern drawl returned as Genesis began to

speak. “Hello... There are no more deliveries; there will be no more deliveries, ever. This business has closed down.”

Chris thought about shouting for help to whoever was on the other end of the phone but dismissed the idea quickly, figuring that the caller was probably in on the whole thing. Plus, shouting for help would only agitate their aggressor further.

He did have one act of defiance in him. As the call was ended, he pulled out of his niece, bent down, and pulled his trousers up.

Genesis put the phone on the shelf immediately behind him and pressed the gun into the captive’s cheek, pushing his head sideways. “I didn’t tell you to stop.”

“I’m done,” he said, afraid to make eye contact.

“Well, I’m not,” he hissed, and pulled out the knife.

“No. Wait.” Chris panicked. “You said you would let her go if we did what you said.” Pressing the weapon harder into the uncle’s face, he looked down and slid the length of the blade slowly over Jen’s exposed buttocks. Menacingly, and yet, at the same time strangely seductive, he continued to run the knife down the inside of her upper thigh. He looked back at the trembling detainee. “Move back. Over there.” He removed the firearm from his face and waved towards the chair where he had earlier changed clothing.

“What are you going to do? Don’t hurt her,” he pleaded again.

“I’m a man of my word, Christopher,” he said, keeping the gun pointed at the hostage’s head as he slid the knife down to Jen’s ankle. With a quick flick of the blade, he cut one ankle restraint, then quickly moved to the other one.

“You’re not a man of anything, you piece of shit!” Jen shouted, trying to kick out at her assailant. Her legs were almost useless from being tied to the same place for so long. Her attempts to strike out were hindered by the restraints on her wrists.

"You need to calm down, young lady, or I'll leave you there." Genesis moved out of range of the flailing limbs and flicked the weapon, signaling to her uncle to move around the table. "You, untie her arms, then put her in the room over there. You and I need to have a private chat."

Thinking quickly, Chris shot a glance at the discarded phone and adopted a nervous manner. He slid past his captor and slowly walked around to the front of the table, swiping the phone up as he did so, and quickly secreting it in his jacket pocket. He held his breath for a few moments, waiting to see if he had been caught taking the device. No, he was in the clear. Satisfied he had gotten away with it, he proceeded to untie his niece's wrists and help her stand up. As she stood up, she pressed herself into her uncle's chest for some form of protection.

"I'm so sorry, sweetheart," he whispered. "I'm so, so sorry," he repeated.

She burst into tears and held on tightly to her uncle. "It's okay, it wasn't your fault," she sobbed. "You did what you had to do."

He loosened the grip the girl had on him and took half a step back, took off the jacket he was wearing and wrapped it around her shoulders, pulling it down slightly to hide her modesty.

"Aww, how touching," Genesis mocked. "Now put her in that room. We have things to discuss."

He huddled his inconsolable niece into his chest again and led her to the door, briefly stopping to pick up her skirt and panties. He opened the door to the soundproof room, gave her a reassuring hug, then gently pushed her into the dark room.

"Please don't leave me here, Uncle Chris," she begged through streaming tears.

His heart sank at the sight of his niece in such a state.

"It's going to be okay, sweetheart. Your dad and Maria will figure out where we are."

"Yeah, the legendary Detective Cooper will save you." Genesis laughed out loud. "Now close the fucking door."

He took one last look at his terrified niece. "If you get cold in there, sweetie, wrap yourself in the jacket and put your hands in the pockets. Don't be scared; just keep telling yourself your dad is coming. He'll save us." He took a deep breath and closed the door.

"Move away from the door," the attacker ordered.

Doing as he was told, Chris shuffled awkwardly to the area where he had changed clothes earlier, keeping his gaze on the aggressor continuously.

Genesis locked the door and put the key in his pocket. "We have a lot to go over, Christopher." He waved the gun in his direction. "You have no idea at all how much worse your day is about to get, do you?"

Chris closed his eyes and said a silent prayer. *Please, God, let Jen find that phone. And quick.*

Chapter 42

Genesis pointed to a couple of chairs at the far side of the room. "Grab those two and sit at the head of the table," he ordered.

Chris was deflated. He was beginning to lose hope that he would get out of this alive. Nonetheless, he reluctantly dragged the chairs to the table and awaited further instructions.

His aggressor took one of the chairs and placed it at the head of the table furthest away from the door to the room containing Jen. "Sit down." Once his captive was seated, he sat at the opposite end and deliberately placed his gun on the table. "Now, you and me are going to have a nice little chat and clear a few things up."

The software executive's attention was suddenly piqued. The annoying Southern drawl had gone completely. He recognized the voice, or at least he thought he did. He must be imagining things; fatigue must be playing games with his mind. *I can't give up,* he told himself. *Fight back.*

"If you're going to kill me then just pull the fucking trigger!" he shouted. "Just let Jen go! She has nothing to do with this."

"You are in no position to be demanding anything," the antagonist sneered, and banged his hand down on the table. The accent was back.

"Whatever you say." He leaned forward, his newfound anger rising. "My brother will find you. He will make sure you suffer when he finds out what you have done to his daughter." He paused. "If Andy doesn't get you, one of my associates will. Either way, you're a dead man walking."

“Associates? What are you talking about? And, as for your brother.” Grabbing the weapon and standing up in one fluid movement, he walked over to a darkened corner, almost disappearing into the blackness. “I don’t think Andy is going to be a major concern of mine.” He laughed.

Chris was suddenly blinded by the bright light that illuminated the corner. He rubbed his eyes to let them adjust, then focused on the area. What was that? Is that a body? He squinted in an attempt to make out what the bundle was. Then, as his mind registered what he was looking at, his whole world collapsed.

Slumped on a chair was the lifeless body of his brother. “Andy!” he shouted, and launched himself out of the seat to get to his sibling, but was halted by the firearm being brought up to point directly at his head.

“Stop!”

“You fucking animal.” He stood still, looking at the body. The two gunshot wounds on the chest and expanded blood stains on the shirt left him in no doubt that there was no chance the victim could be alive. His mind whirled at what seemed like a million miles per hour. He felt dizzy, and reached out for the chair he had been sitting on to steady himself.

“Sit down before you fall down, Chris,” Genesis advised. “Besides, he’s long gone. There’s nothing you can do for him.”

He staggered around the chair, lowered himself into it, and rested his arms on the table, taking deep breaths to try and clear his head. A thought suddenly flashed through his mind. He looked up and was surprised to see his captor had sat back at the other end of the table with his firearm facing him.

“Did you kill my dad?” he asked through gritted teeth.

“Yes,” he confirmed, with no sign of remorse. “That interfering old fool should have kept his nose out of my business."

"Why? Why kill a defenseless old man?" he snarled.

"He wasn't exactly defenseless," he nonchalantly said, as he put the gun down on the table and sat back in the chair. "He had to go; he was getting closer."

Chris spied the weapon. *Could I get to that before he can react?* He ran the scenario through his mind. *Don't let him know what you're thinking. Distract him. Keep him talking.* "He was just a cop doing his job."

Genesis seemed to momentarily lose his cool. He lurched forward and snarled at his victim. "No! He was a nosey old fucker, sticking his beak in where it didn't belong."

Startled by the sudden change in manner, Chris sat back in his chair. "No, you're wrong." He glanced at the gun. *Keep talking.* "Maria told me about the case she was working on with my dad. They were tracking a pedophile." He sat forward and pointed at the aggressor. "They were tracking you." He paused. "You killed him in cold blood to save your pathetic, cowardly ass." His confidence began to rise; insulting the killer was really making him feel invincible. "They love pedophiles in prison. You are going to be very, very popular with guards and inmates alike," he taunted.

"It makes no difference what you think of me!" he snapped and stood up, sending his chair scraping across the floor. "But I'm no pedophile."

"Yes, you are. You lured kids to meet you. Then you raped them and killed them." He continued, "Your family must be so proud of you."

That final comment got the reaction he was looking for.

"Family?" he screamed, and banged his fist on the table, making the weapon bounce a little further away from him. "Family? Don't preach to me about family. You have no idea what happened to me."

"You're right, I don't. And you know what else? I don't care." He wasn't sure what was happening, but he felt somehow he was beginning to get the upper hand in this situation. If he could keep agitating his assailant, maybe he would get a chance to make a grab for the gun.

"I wonder how you would have turned out if you were raped at twelve years old and strangled to within an inch of your life." His breathing became heavy beneath the wolf mask. "Then left for dead. By a family member. Someone who should protect you, not hurt you." He banged the table again with both fists. "Then, when you tell your father what happened, he takes his belt to you. Tells you it's your fault for being in an area he told you not to go to." He took a deep breath and straightened up, moving a little further from the weapon.

"So that gives you the right to rape and murder other kids?" He shook his head. "You are just a pervert trying to validate your actions."

The killer leaned forward, placing his hands on the table again. "I didn't rape those kids." He shook his head. "I was present, but I didn't rape them." He pushed himself upright again, looking up at the ceiling as if recalling a memory. "I did rape a boy once." He spoke hesitantly. "I was nineteen years old. When I had finished, I strangled him." He looked back to Chris. "The rape did nothing for me. If I'm honest, I felt disgusted with myself." He sighed. "But, taking someone's life. Well… Ooooh!" He shuddered as if a shiver had gone down his spine. "That really is something else."

Chris looked at him, slightly horrified at the way he recited his story. "You really are fucking deranged." He leaned forward in his chair. "You need help. Give up, hand yourself in. Go and get the treatment you need," he pleaded.

Genesis slammed his hand down on the table. "No!" he shouted. "I don't need treatment. I need a fucking medal. I put those kids out of their misery."

"That's your reasoning? You killed all those kids as an act of mercy?" he snapped back.

"Yes, exactly! They don't have to live with what I've had to live with!" he shouted again. The accent was becoming less and less apparent the angrier he got.

Chris laughed. "You can't justify any of this, you sick fuck. You were there. You could have stopped those kids from being raped, but you didn't." He pointed his finger at him and snarled. "You stood by and watched. Then you took the lives of those innocent kids." He slapped his palm on the table and stood up. "You're nothing more than a child killer. A pathetic excuse for a human being."

"I was absolving them of their sins. I gave them absolution." His voice was calmer and the accent was back.

"Absolution? From what? From the sins you and your pervert friends inflicted on them?" Chris paused, his mind racing again. A thought suddenly entered his head. "Wait… does this mean you're going to kill Jen, too?" he asked, as he glanced at the gun still positioned at the far end of the table.

"No, I would never hurt Jennifer. She is family to me." He laughed.

"Family? Are you fucking serious?" The hostage shook his head in disgust.

"I haven't done anything to Jennifer," he replied.

"You made me rape her, you sick bastard." He slammed his hands down on the table, using the distraction of the noise he made to nudge his chair a little closer towards the end of the table.

Genesis clenched his fists, then raised one hand and pointed at Chris. "You wanted to do that. I've seen you two together."

"Are you seriously that broken?" He was exasperated.

"Jen is my fucking niece; I have done nothing but show her the appropriate love and affection that a doting uncle should." He paused. "Until now, you sick, twisted fuck."

The wolf mask shook. "You wanted her for yourself."

"What?" Chris asked. He was more confused than ever. He was also sure that this guy could snap at any time, and he had to get himself closer to the gun without making it obvious.

"You heard me. You wanted her for yourself. You wished she was your daughter to make up for your slut of a wife being barren," he sneered.

"What the fuck are you talking about? I love my wife." He edged his arm along the table. *Could I reach the gun if I stretched my arm out fully?* He wasn't sure. He needed to get himself at a better angle to make a lunge for it. He knew he would have to be careful and not draw any attention to his plan because it seemed his aggressor was becoming more unstable.

The wolf sighed again. This time he overemphasized it by dropping his shoulders in an over-exaggerated way. "Oh, dear, you just don't get it, do you, Christopher?" He paused as if giving himself time to find the words he wanted. "Let me try to explain it to you." He straightened up. "Do you ever read the Bible?"

"Never felt the need since I was forced to read it at school." Chris shifted in his chair, moving it half an inch closer. He suddenly noticed the eyes looking at him from behind the mask. *Those eyes… They look familiar. Concentrate. Had he noticed the movement? If he had noticed he wasn't saying anything about it.*

"That's a shame, because it holds great significance to our present situation," Genesis broke the momentary silence and sat down at the table.

"Really? My religious studies teacher, Mr. Turner, must have bypassed the chapter about psychopathic pedophile child killers." He raised an eyebrow.

"I'm not a pedophile!" he shouted, springing to his feet and slamming his fists on the table again. Then, he took a deep breath and outstretched his arms. "All this is staring you in the face. The answer is in the Bible," he said in a much calmer tone.

"Really? Tell you what." He moved in the seat, shifting it again. "Why don't I give Mr. Turner a call? I can't help but feel that he is responsible for all this. If he had made more of an effort teaching me about this . . ." he waved his arms around, "religious stuff, then maybe we wouldn't be here." He put his elbow on the table and rubbed his forehead.

The eyes glared down at him from behind the mask. "Very droll, Christopher. Let me enlighten you. Genesis, chapter four, verse two. Does that ring any bells?"

He shook his head and looked at his captor. "No, no it doesn't." He sighed. "Look, I've had enough of this. If you're going to kill me, then just get on with it. But, please, let my niece go."

Genesis stood upright. "Now Abel kept flocks and Cain worked the soil. In the course of time Cain brought some of the fruits of the soil as an offering to the Lord and Abel also brought offering, fat portions from some of the firstborn of his flock—"

"Is this going to take long?" Chris asked, faking a yawn.

He ignored the interruption and continued. "The Lord looked with favor on Abel and his offering." As he recited from the Bible, he slowly moved over to the limp body on the chair and stood over it. "But on Cain and his offering he did not look with favor, so Cain was very angry and his face was downcast." He lowered his hand and grabbed under the chin. With one fluid motion he pulled up hard, pulling a mask off, revealing the true identity of the dead person.

Chris tried to speak, but nothing came out. His whole body was paralyzed with shock. The recital continued. "Then the

Lord said to Cain, 'Why are you angry? Why is your face downcast? If you do what is right will you not be accepted? But if you do not do what is right, sin is crouching at your door, it desires to have you, but you must rule over it. Now Cain said to his brother Abel, let's go out to the field.' While they were in the field Cain attacked his brother Abel and killed him." As he moved closer he lifted the deflated mask up, making it look like it was eerily floating towards the captive, eventually stopping inches away.

Shocked behind his pig mask, Chris was entranced by what he was looking at. *This can't be right,* he thought. *I'm looking in a mirror.* His head raced, trying to make sense of what he was seeing. *Snap out of it. This isn't real.* He blinked and looked up to once again see those eyes burning through the wolf mask, bearing down on him.

Chapter 43

Chris's wild-eyed gaze was transfixed on the mask as Genesis casually dropped it on the table in front of him. He couldn't take his eyes off it for a few moments, then he slowly lifted his head to regain eye contact with the menacing figure standing before him. His mind struggled to grasp the situation. None of it made sense.

His aggressor silently returned his gaze, then slowly reached for his own mask, slipping his thumb under the latex façade, and began to take it off.

The captive's stomach churned and knotted as he watched, riveted to the seat. Finally the mask was off and placed on the table next to the one resembling his face. For the second time that night, his world imploded. He gawked, open-mouthed, into the eyes of a familiar face. A face he knew as well as his own. The face of his own twin brother.

"Andy?" he gasped, and removed the pig mask he had been ordered to wear. "What have you done?" His head reeled, trying to make sense of what was happening. "Please tell me you're not behind all of this. For God's sake, you're a cop! You're supposed to uphold the law."

"And that is exactly why I will get away with it." He pounced forward, banging the firearm on the table. "Do you think we have arrived at this juncture by accident?" Shaking his head, he stood up, seemingly towering over his sibling. Chris sank back further into the seat, unable to speak. "Oh no, brother, this is no accident. This is a well thought out and executed plan that has been years in the making."

"What? You planned this whole thing?" He looked at the

floor as if searching for some answers. Then, like a lightning bolt, it hit him. "You made me rape your daughter, you sick fuck."

"A sick fuck?" he huffed. "A sick fuck who is about to inherit everything you own. As for Jen, that was a necessary evil." He shrugged. "She'll get over it." His face was stern.

Chris thought he saw a glimmer of remorse, but he couldn't be certain. He wasn't even sure he knew who the man in front of him was at all. "She'll get over it? You made me rape her! How the fuck is she going to get over that?" he raged. "If this is about the money, why didn't you just ask? I would have given you anything!"

"This isn't about the money." Andy smiled. "Although that sure is going to be a nice little bonus."

Chris sighed. "You're not getting a dime of my money. I've set up a trust fund for Jennifer, including a percentage of the company, and the rest goes to Amber." He returned his brother's smile. "So you see, you get nothing."

Andy picked up the mask of his face. "You know how being a twin has always been a bit of a hindrance to us? Even our own father not being able to tell us apart?" Chris was unsure where his evil brother was going with this, but he nodded his head in acknowledgement. "Well, I used that to my advantage for once. I went to visit your attorney about eighteen months ago. I posed as you, and told him I was going through some marital difficulties and that I wanted to change my will, leaving everything to my loving, caring brother." He smiled again, and sat back on his seat.

"You bastard! You won't get away with it," he said.

"I think I will." He leaned forward, resting his elbows on the table. "You see, I had our devoted father come along with me to witness the new will. Stupid old fool never had a clue." He sat back in his seat with a smug smile and ran his hand through his hair. “Super cop and devoted father couldn’t even tell us apart.”

“Did you really hate him that much?” Chris asked.

Andy bolted out of his seat, sending it flying backwards. “The day he took his belt to me as punishment,” he nodded, confirming what he was saying was correct, “when I told him I had been raped by that sick redneck, was the day he stopped being my father,” he sneered.

Chris struggled to keep his cool. Should he just make a leap for the gun? He considered it for a brief moment, but quickly realized it would be futile. “So, because Daddy didn’t love you enough, it gives you an excuse to punish the rest of our family that have always been there for you?”

“I’m not making excuses!” he bawled back. “Everything I ever did wasn’t good enough for him.” He held his arms out, emphasizing what he was saying. “Even when I became a cop it didn’t please him.” He paused and pointed at his brother. “Yet you, on the other hand, got praised no matter what you did?”

“You could have had everything I have.” Chris rose from his chair, putting his hands on the table. “You were always far more competent on a computer than I was. In fact, I remember begging you to become a partner with me when I first set up AppTech, but no, you had to become a cop to prove to Dad that you could.” He looked around the room. “And where has that gotten you?” he mocked.

“It’s gotten me exactly where I want to be,” he huffed again. “All the IT knowledge enabled me to hack into the police database and manipulate the files, erasing criminal records and CCTV footage.”

“Is that what you did at my house with Maria’s gun?” His anger rose.

“Oh no, no, no, brother.” He laughed. “Something far more simple. You see, the weapon deposited in your safe was mine. I switched them before we got to your office. This was all a setup for you to give me an alibi." He paused, letting his brother take it all in. "You just don't see the big picture. I'm going to walk out of here with my daughter wanting to be my daughter, all of your money, and, to top it all, I'll be hailed a hero cop for bringing in Genesis." He paused and rubbed his chin. "Don't worry; I'll make sure Amber is provided for. You never know; she may even show me her appreciation." He winked. "If you know what I mean."

That was one comment too much for Chris. He slammed his hands down hard on the table and pushed it into the groin of his brother, sending him backwards. Unable to gain his balance, Andy had to go with the momentum of the table pushing him into the wall with great force, the impact making him lose his grip on the weapon, which bounced across the tabletop and into the hands of his brother. He slumped to the floor, winded, and gasping for breath. When he regained his faculties he looked up to see the weapon pointed straight at him.

"Stay right where you are," he snarled, with the gun trained on his brother's head. Andy slowly got to his feet and rested his back against the wall. "So, you going to shoot me now?"

"Not unless I have to." His hand was shaking. "But make no mistake, I will pull the trigger if you force me to." He signaled to one of the chairs. "Now it's your turn. Sit down." He backed away, keeping the weapon trained on his brother, and watched as he pushed the table back into position and calmly sat down before retrieving the chair he had been sitting on and placed it opposite to him. They sat in silence, staring at each other. "You know," Chris broke the silence. "Thinking about it, this may be the opportunity I need." He nodded to himself. "You see, you're not the only one with secrets, brother. I've got myself into a situation, and this could be my way out."

Andy tilted his head to one side in an inquisitive manner.

"I don't follow."

"No, you probably don't." It was Chris's turn to laugh. "It's no concern of yours, but let's just say, killing you and taking your identity might be the perfect solution for me. Kim gets to think I'm her loving husband, and Jen gets to call me Daddy. Plus, if what you say about changing my will is true, then I get to keep all of 'my' money." He smiled at his brother. "I suppose I should be thanking you, really. It's a win-win situation for me."

"There's just one problem." Andy stared his brother in the eyes. "You don't have the stones to pull the trigger." He lunged out of his seat.

Chris instantly took aim. "Fuck you." The loud bang of the weapon being fired reverberated around his head, causing his ears to ring. "Who doesn't have the stones?" he said under his breath.

Chapter 44

Jen screamed when she heard the muffled sound of the gunshot in the adjoining room. Whimpering, she huddled up under the jacket, taking the only security that it had to offer. As she enveloped herself in the garment, she heard something drop to the floor. In the pitch-black darkness of the cell she fumbled around and touched something solid.

What was that?

She grabbed at the object and brought it up to her face, trying to make out what it was. With both hands she felt around it and realized it was a cell phone. Frantically she pushed one of the buttons. The screen illuminated her face, making her squint at the sudden light.

Without hesitation, she started dialing as quickly as her fingers could tap on the digits.

Chapter 45

The smell from the gunshot still hung in the air. Chris had fired a shot over his brother's head, putting a bullet into the wall. They had remained in silence, glaring at each other since the shot had been fired. The tell-tale buzzing sound of an incoming call on Andy's phone in his pocket momentarily broke the silence. He reached down to retrieve it.

His brother instantly reaffirmed his aim. "Don't give me an excuse, Andy."

Andy froze, and then slowly moved his hand back above his head. "It's only my phone; I'm going to reach for it slowly." His hand slowly made its way back to his pocket. He held his hand up before it disappeared into the pocket and showed him his thumb, index and forefinger.

"Nice and easy." Chris pointed the gun at his brother's hand.

He slowly pulled out the phone and held it purposely in front of his brother. "No need to get jumpy." He glanced at the screen, and a look of realization hit his face. Then he looked over to where he had placed his Genesis phone, the phone he used to arrange the meetings. It was gone. He afforded himself a smile of appreciation. "Very good, Christopher. You really are a dark horse, aren't you?"

"You don't know the half of it," he replied.

"It's Jennifer. I'm going to answer it, okay?" he asked, as his finger hovered over the accept button.

"Don't do anything stupid." He pulled back the hammer of the gun and steadied his aim on his brother's head again.

Andy accepted the call and held the phone to his ear.

"Hello, Detective Cooper."

"Dad, it's me," Jen desperately said. "Miller has gone mental. He's holding me and Uncle Chris and I think…" she blubbed, "I think he may have shot him."

"It's okay, stay calm, sweetheart. I know where you are." He looked his brother dead in the eye as he spoke. "I'll be there soon."

"Please, Daddy, hurry." Her words were almost inaudible due to her sobbing. "I'm scared. I don't know what he's going to do."

"I'm on my way." He looked over at the body of the software geek in the chair. "And don't worry; I'll make sure Miller pays for this."

He smiled at his sibling as he cancelled the call and lowered the phone slightly, then, with a rapid explosion of speed, he flicked the phone at his brother's head and propelled himself forward.

Another gunshot echoed around the room.

Chapter 46

In the dark, isolated room, Jen screamed down the phone.

"Daddy, please help me!" She looked at the screen and saw that the call had been ended.

Panic set in. Still clutching the cell, she put her hands over her face and screamed. Realizing it was a pointless task, she curled up in a ball under the jacket and squeezed into the corner as far as possible, mentally trying to make herself invisible. She froze when she heard a gunshot and held her breath, listening, straining to hear any noise. Then she heard two more shots, in quick succession. Frightened and alone, she pushed harder into the corner, pulling the jacket over her head, maintaining her hold on the phone as tightly as possible. Her head was spinning, and she began crying uncontrollably. Then, she heard the door being unlocked.

"Oh please, no, no!" she yelled out between sobs.

The door opened, flooding the room with light. She was beside herself with fear as she lay beneath the jacket, holding her breath. The knuckles on her right hand turned white caused by the grip on the mobile device.

"Jen?" a familiar voice bellowed out.

Cautiously she pulled the jacket down from her face, just enough to get a look at the figure that was standing in the doorway. "Daddy?" she asked nervously.

The figure walked towards her. "It's okay, sweetheart. It's over."

"Daddy!" She flung the jacket to one side, jumped up and ran towards him, breaking down in tears again as she threw her arms around him, holding on as tight as she could.

"Uh… gently, sweetheart," he said uncomfortably.

She looked up into his face and saw that he was wincing in pain. Relinquishing her grip a little, she moved away slightly, allowing the light to illuminate him further. His blood-soaked shirt sent her into a panicked frenzy.

"Daddy, are you okay?" she screamed.

"I'll be fine." He held her by the shoulders and looked her up and down. "Are you okay, did he…" He hesitated. "Did he hurt you?"

"No!" She looked embarrassed, and wondered what her father would do if he found out what had happened. She couldn't tell him, ever. "No, he didn't."

"Are you sure?" he pressed.

She looked into his eyes and noticed there was something different about him. He had changed ever so slightly. She stepped back and studied his face. Had he changed, or was she imagining it? Maybe it was her that had changed. The only thing she was certain of was that she was exhausted. But still, the look in his eye bothered her. Her thoughts were suddenly interrupted when she remembered something.

"Daddy, where is Uncle Chris?" she slowly asked.

He looked deep into her eyes, then, without saying a word, he shook his head.

She exploded into a flood of tears and threw her arms around him. This time when he grunted in pain she ignored it, and continued to hold on as tight as she could.

After a few moments he gently broke her grip. Holding her by the shoulders again he bent down to look her in the face. "What do you say we get out of here?"

Through controlled sobs, she nodded. He picked up the jacket, wrapped it around her, then put his arm around her shoulder and guided her out of the room.

She buried her head into his jacket to stop the light hurting her eyes. As her vision slowly adjusted, she peered around the Genesis Chamber, spotting the body of Miller on the chair in the corner. Then, she saw the body of what she believed was her Uncle Chris, strewn over the table, posed in the same position she had been in earlier. She began to shake and burst into tears.

"Don't look, sweetie." He placed his hand on the side of her face and buried it into his jacket again to stop her from looking at the scene.

They continued to make their way to the door when suddenly, it exploded open. In no time at all the room was filled with armed police wearing SWAT jackets.

"Down, down, down!" the lead officer shouted out.

"We're unarmed!" he yelled, and threw his hands up in the air, encouraging Jen to do the same.

Three heavily armed officers stood a few feet away with their guns trained on them. Jen froze, her heart pounding; she couldn't move through fear. It was a weird momentary standoff until Maria came through the door, her gun held in front of her.

"Lower your weapons. That's Detective Cooper!" she shouted out, and rushed forward to help the pair, placing her gun in its holster as she did so. "Are you okay?"

He fell to his knees and just stared at her.

"He's been shot! Please don't let him die!" Jen cried out.

"Get me a medic in here, now! Officer down," she ordered, when she saw the blood-stained shirt. "You guys secure the building."

The lead cop spoke into his radio fastened to his bulletproof vest at the shoulder. "We need a medic at our location, officer down." He then signaled with his head for two of his team to search the soundproof room that Jen had been held in.

"I've got you, partner," Maria said, as she knelt down and supported him. "There's a medic on the way, just stay with me, okay?"

Travis entered the chamber and pushed his way past the armed officers to survey the room. "Holy shit!" he exclaimed, when he saw her attending to the injured Cooper. "Is he okay?"

She looked up at him and shook her head. "Get Jen out of here. An ambulance is on the way. See if she needs medical attention." She paused. "Call the station and let Kim know that they're safe."

He waved to Jen to approach him. She was still frozen to the spot, staring at the body on the table.

"Jennifer!" Maria snapped her out of her trance. The girt jumped and turned to her. "Go with Travis. I'll take care of this.

The youngster hesitantly shuffled to the waiting detective, who put an arm around her shoulder walked her out of the chamber. When he got to the door he turned back to the female detective. "What about Chris?"

"Uncle Chris is dead. Miller killed him!" Jen said, before bursting into tears again.

Maria nodded her head, signaling her new partner to leave. Alone with Cooper, she leaned over and applied pressure to the wound on his shoulder in an attempt to stem the bleeding. "Come on, partner, stay with me. Today is not your day to go."

"Tell Jen I'm sorry and… I love her," he said.

"Where's the fucking medic at?" she screamed out over her shoulder. "You will be able to tell her yourself, this is only a flesh wound. And as for being sorry? You just saved her life."

He looked into her eyes. "Thank God it's over."

She quickly looked around the room, then turned back to him. She could see the pain in his face, and figured if she kept him talking it might take his mind off of the pain. "What the hell happened here?"

He closed his eyes, took a deep breath, then opened them slowly. “I don’t know. One minute I was in AppTech heading for Chris’s office. The next thing I woke up here.” He swallowed hard and grimaced. “That fucker Miller must have jumped me.”

She tried to hold him still. “Don’t move,” she said. “Then what happened?” Keeping him distracted was becoming more difficult for her.

“When I came around I was laying on the floor. I looked around and saw Chris on the table.” He nodded at the lifeless body. “I jumped Miller but he had a gun, and put one in me. I don’t know how, but… I kept going, and managed to overpower him.” He shook his head slightly and his voice wavered. “I had him in the corner over there when I heard Jen scream. He tried to rush me. I had no alternative; I had to shoot him.” A tear rolled down his cheek.

“You did the right thing, partner.” She wiped the tear away. “It was you or him. If it had been you, he would have got to Jen,” she reassured him.

One of the SWAT had been checking for any signs of life from the body on the table when he pointed at the discarded masks. “Detective Hernandez,” he said, pointing at the latex facades.

“What’s that?” she asked.

“Some weird shit. There’s a wolf and a pig one, but this one . . .” He leaned forward and examined the homemade mask closely. He suddenly glanced at the body nearby. “This one looks like this guy or… Detective Cooper.”

She peered at the eerie-looking mask. “I bet he wore that when he hired the van.” Then she directed her look to the cop. “Can you find out where that medics is?”

“Sure thing.” He nodded and walked towards the exit, stopping before he got there, and turned to them. “Good work, Detective. Between you and me, if it had been my daughter, I would have emptied my entire clip into that fucker." He nodded and left the room.

"You're going to be okay." She took a closer look at the wound. The blood flow had slowed considerably. "It's all over now."

"But at what cost?" he said, then looked down.

Two medics rushed into the room, signaling to the female detective to allow them access to the victim. She obliged and got out of the way as they set about tending to the wound. It wasn't long before they had him bandaged up on a stretcher and wheeling him out of the door. He glanced around as they got to the door, taking a last look at the bodies.

As the stretcher was wheeled to the waiting ambulance, Jen rushed forward. "Daddy!" she called out.

"It's okay, sweetheart, I'm going to be fine." He smiled as best he could. "You go with Maria. I'll see you at the hospital, okay?"

As the medics loaded him into the back of the ambulance they maintained eye contact. He nodded to her, and she smiled and nodded back as the medics closed the doors.

"I love you!" Jen shouted through the closed doors.

Maria appeared behind her and put her arm across her shoulder. "Come on, let's get you back to the station. Your mom is waiting for you there."

Chapter 47

Franco Baresi sat in a crowded bar, dabbing the sides of his mouth with a napkin. It wasn't the kind of place people normally associated the mobster with, but, he insisted the meatballs they served there could rival those served in any of the finest Italian restaurants.

He had just finished his meal and was enjoying a large glass of the finest Chianti while observing the clientele in the intimate establishment when the TV behind the bar caught his attention.

A female reporter was depicted standing on Fifth Avenue, New York. These were streets he knew so well, but somehow looked so different; they were deserted. It was the banner at the bottom of the screen that grabbed his attention more than the report.

"Up next. Hero cop fatally shoots serial killer and exposes pedophile ring" the banner read.

"Hey, Mikey," he shouted to the bartender. "Turn up the TV over here."

"Not a problem, Mr. Baresi." The bartender jumped into action, frantically searching for the TV remote. After a few seconds of rummaging around he located the device and pointing it directly at the box, turning up the volume. The news reporter was still in New York, finishing off her update.

"So, just to recap, New York is on lockdown. FBI and NYPD sources are staying tight-lipped at this time, although this is all almost certainly connected to an appearance on live TV this morning of known international terrorist Maleek Al Rakeem. We will keep you updated on this situation as it develops. This is

Alex Wood, in New York. Back to the studio."

Franco looked puzzled; he turned in his seat to one of his bodyguards who was sitting in the booth behind him. "Make contact with our New York associates; see what's going on up there."

"On it, boss." The bodyguard slid off of his seat and walked towards the door, pulling his cell phone from his pocket as he did so.

Franco turned his attention back to the TV.

"Back to central Florida now. An Orlando PD Detective is being hailed a hero after a bizarre situation led to the tragic murder of his twin brother and the shooting of the man responsible for his slaying."

A photograph of Andy Cooper in the top left corner of the screen wearing his police uniform came into view.

"Detective Andrew Cooper, an eighteen-year veteran of the Orlando PD, shot dead suspected child serial killer Martin Miller. Miller, from New Orleans, is suspected of infiltrating the software company owned by Detective Cooper's brother, and developing an app to lure young boys to their deaths. It's thought that Detective Cooper's identical twin brother, Christopher Cooper, owner and CEO of AppTech, based in Orlando, got suspicious of Miller's activities, confronted him, and paid the ultimate price."

"But, there is a further twist to this story," the second news anchor cut in. "It is believed that Miller is also being linked to the kidnapping of Detective Cooper's daughter three days ago and the slaying of his father, James Cooper, four weeks ago. James Cooper was a very well respected retired police veteran of the Orlando PD."

"Detective Cooper was himself kidnapped by Miller, and held captive in the family's isolated log cabin until he managed to overpower his captor in a struggle that resulted in the officer being wounded, and the unfortunate death of Christopher Cooper." The first anchor picked up the story while the images showed the cabin taped off and swarming with forensics experts. "The latest we have on the condition of the injured officer is that his wounds are not life-threatening, and he is expected to make a full recovery."

"As is his daughter, Jennifer, who remains in the hospital by her father's side as she is treated for shock and minor abrasions. Investigators are not looking for anyone else in connection with this truly fascinating case. We wish Detective Cooper and his family a speedy recovery, and will follow this story with great interest, I'm sure."

Franco looked incredulously at the screen for a few moments, then looked at his remaining bodyguard. "Something ain't right here."

"Boss?" The stooge looked quizzical.

His employer didn't elaborate. He simply put his hand inside his jacket and pulled out a money clip, peeled off a hundred dollar bill, and placed it on the table. "Hey, Mikey, I'm out of here. Keep the change!" he shouted to the bartender.

"Everything all right, Mr. Baresi?" the barman asked with a look of concern on his face.

"We'll see, Mikey," he answered, as he walked towards the door without looking back. "We'll see."

Chapter 48

It was an overcast morning as Maria and Travis pulled into the parking lot of the Orlando Sunny Vale Crematorium. Even though it would be another hour before the service began, the place was quite busy, with a large number of mourners milling around, waiting for the Cooper family to arrive so they could pay their respects and pass on words of comfort.

As she got out of the passenger side of the vehicle, she noticed well-suited men heading in her direction. She immediately recognized one of them as Tony, the stooge she'd had the pleasure of grounding with a swift kick to the groin at her house. She glanced around to her partner, who was making his way around the car to join her.

"Who are these two?" he asked, as he stood next to her.

"It's okay, I think," she muttered under her breath to him. "Just keep calm."

Unsure as to what they wanted, she quickly assessed the situation while casually placing her hand on the handle of her gun. As the thugs got closer they eyeballed the male detective, then turned their attention to Maria.

"Detective Hernandez." The larger one of the two stepped forward. "Mr. Baresi would like a word with you." He paused and looked at her partner. "Alone."

"Franco Baresi?" Travis asked, while trying to look over the man's shoulder in the direction of a stretched Mercedes limousine that was parked away from all the other vehicles in the lot. "Sorry to disappoint you, and Mr. Baresi, but anywhere Detective Hernandez goes, I go."

Tony stepped forward to get in the detective's face. "Mr.

Baresi said he wanted to speak to the organ grinder. He never mentioned her monkey." He started laughing and turned to his associate to encourage him to join in.

"Tell you what, guys." The officer squared up to him. "How about this monkey arrests you and Mr. Baresi for threatening a police officer?"

The two thugs looked at each other, then back to Travis. "We didn't threaten anybody, Detective Travis."

"That's not the way it sounded to me," he said through gritted teeth.

"I think you have the wrong idea here." The goon smiled at him and took a step back and held his hands up to diffuse the growing tension. "Mr. Baresi merely wants to extend his congratulations to Detective Hernandez on a job well done."

"Okay, that's enough, you guys." She stepped between them. "Travis, wait here with your new friends, I'll be right back." She looked at the thug who had previously knocked her out. "Tony, watch your balls; he kicks like a mule." She gave him a cheeky wink and walked towards the black limousine.

As she got closer, the rear passenger window slid down and Franco Baresi came into view for the first time. He signaled for her to get in the other side.

She entered the vehicle as instructed and sat back in the plush leather seat. The mobster was watching the developing news story regarding the terror attack in New York on a TV in the headrest of the seat in front of him.

He casually pointed at the screen. "Terrible business, this. Some people just baffle me, Detective." He shook his head and watched the end of the report before turning off the TV and giving her his full attention. "So, how are you holding up, Detective Hernandez?"

"Well, I've been better. It's been one hell of a few weeks. What do you want?" she abruptly said.

"Coop said you were direct." He laughed and looked out of the window. His eyes narrowed and for a brief moment, she thought she could see tears forming. "I really miss that guy. One hell of a man."

She sat quietly, studying him for a few seconds. "What was the deal with you and him?"

He turned his attention back into the car. "There was no deal. He was my friend, my best friend. It's as simple as that."

"I can't get my head around it. Coop was a good cop. How did he end up being friends with a notorious gangster?" she asked.

"Wow, he wasn't exaggerating about your bluntness," he exclaimed. "Don't spare my feelings over here." He smiled at her. "What you have to bear in mind, Maria... is it okay if I call you Maria, by the way?" He awaited an answer.

"Sure, why not." She shrugged. "I mean, you've already been a guest in my house, so why not dispense with the formalities altogether?" She looked him in the eye.

"Again, sorry about that. But I had to make sure you were as on the level as Coop said you were." He looked back out of the window. "Back to your question about how Coop and I remained friends. He knew what I did, and I never flaunted it in front of him. What you have to bear in mind is, it was a different world back in our day. It wasn't like these gangbangers today, killing indiscriminately. We kept the streets free of the scum; innocent people felt safe. The only bodies that ever turned up . . ." He looked back at her. "I'm not claiming responsibility here. I'm just saying, that might have been traced back to me, were all bad guys." He smiled and winked at her. "We were friends long before we took to our chosen professions. We looked out for each other. To the point where if Coop had someone he couldn't touch legally but knew they were guilty . . ." He paused and nodded. "He would call me with a name, and I would take care of it." He faced her again.

"You were a hit man for a cop?" She shook her head. "And what price did he have to pay for that?"

"No price, Maria. Like I said, I ran the neighborhood. It was in my best interest to keep low-lifes out. Coop's only reward was from the PD as the crime rate went down." He laughed.

"So, what is it you want from me?" She was starting to get bored with the conversation.

He rubbed his chin and stared out of the window again. "Coop said you were good. He said you could be trusted." He paused and turned back to her. "He also said if anything happened to him, he wanted me to keep an eye on you."

"I'm a big girl, I can look after myself." She laughed.

"Yes, you certainly can." He nodded. "But let's just say, you may be needing my help in the not too distant future, and I just want you to know that I'll be at your disposal."

Her eyes narrowed. She looked at him questioningly. "Why me? Why not Andy?"

He took a deep breath. "Just because he is his father's son, it doesn't make him the same man." He paused for a moment, as if giving her a moment to think about what he had just said. "Coop had his reasons for asking for me to look out for you and not Andy. I have my reasons for obliging."

"This whole thing sounds very intriguing. Why me and not his own son?" she persisted.

"Today is not the day for explanations, Maria. Just know that anytime you need me, you just call me. Okay?" He handed her a card. It looked different than the one he had given her previously. "That's my personal number. You can get me on that anytime." He slid the window down a little more. "The remaining Cooper family will be arriving shortly. You never know who is watching, so it's probably best you return to Detective Travis now, before we're seen together."

She studied the card, then slipped it in her jacket pocket. She opened the car door and put one leg out, ready to leave.

"Just one more thing, Maria," he stopped her. "Be careful who you confide in. There is a lot going on that you are not aware of. Detective Travis seems to be above board, from what we can ascertain. But, I would think long and hard before revealing anything to any of your colleagues."

Maria shook her head as she got out of the car. Once outside, she ducked her head back in. "This is all a little too cryptic for me." She half-laughed. "As for watching out for me, if I see you or any of your goons around me, my partner or my friends, I will put several bullets in you." She stepped away and closed the door.

She walked back to her partner, who was standing, peering over the shoulder of Tony.

"Everything okay?" he asked her as she got closer.

"Everything's fine," she said, not breaking her stride. "Like they said, Mr. Baresi just wanted to congratulate me on my outstanding police work. Isn't that right, Tony?"

The bodyguard turned around to make his way back to the waiting limousine. "That's correct, Detective."

Before he could take a step, she landed her foot in his groin again, sending him to the ground.

"Holy shit, Maria!" Travis was flabbergasted. "What the fuck?"

"That's just to be perfectly clear." She leaned over him. "Stay away from me and everyone associated with me. Understand?"

The stooge rolled on the ground, groaning in agony.

Franco could be heard laughing loudly from inside the vehicle. He loved this girl already! he shouted to his driver.

She straightened up and walked past her partner. "Next time, don't pussy around. That's how you deal with these numb nuts."

There was an overwhelming look of joy on the male detective's face as he backed away from the writhing goon and caught up with his partner. "You are so cool." He beamed in admiration.

"Shut up!" she snapped, and continued to join the gathering mourners.

***

For the second time in just over a month, Sunny Vale Cemetery was filled with mourners attending a service for the Cooper family. The service was drawing to a close, and the sound of bagpipes filled the air, creating an even more somber atmosphere and drowning out the continuous sobbing and weeping from the anguished congregation.

The attendees seemed to be segregated into two groups. The Cooper family and close relations, and the AppTech staff. All were there to mourn the fallen computer executive.

Cathleen sat feet away from the casket, flanked by Kim and Amber. Standing behind her were her surviving son and granddaughter, holding each other's hand tightly for comfort.

The instrumental salute came to an end, and the mourners began to file past the grieving mother and his widow, offering their condolences. When the congregation had passed, Kim and Amber helped Cathleen to her feet and guided each other towards the waiting funeral cars, followed by her offspring.

Maria walked briskly to catch up with Jen and her guardian. "How are you two holding up?" She spoke with sincerity.

"We're okay," he replied, without taking his attention away from his mother. "I just want to get today out of the way."

"I've got some good news," she informed him.

He stopped and looked at Jen. "Why don't you catch up with Grandma, I'll be with you in a minute."

She didn't speak. Instead, she nodded and carried on, with her head bowed. The female detective watched her walk away.

"Is she okay?" The concerned look on her face signaled she was genuinely worried about the girl.

"She'll be fine." He looked her in the eye. "This is a hard time for her. What's the news?"

"We've officially closed the case," she answered. "Millers family didn't want anything to do with him when they found out what he had been doing, so the state has cremated the body."

"That's a load off." He afforded a half-smile and continued walking.

"So, when are you thinking of coming back?" she continued, scurrying after him. "We all miss you in the office."

"I'm not sure I'm coming back," he calmly said as he marched on, keeping an eye on his family. "After all my family has been through in the last few weeks—"

"You can't leave the force!" she interrupted him. "What will you do?"

"I don't know." He stopped and looked at her. "Chris… Chris has left me everything. I need to spend some time with the family." He gazed into her eyes for a moment, then walked on to catch up with his clan.

He caught up with them as they reached the lead vehicle and helped his mother into the back. He stepped aside to let Jen get in next to her grandmother when Cathleen held her hand up, stopping the youngster from going any further.

"Would you mind if I spent some time with my son, sweetheart?" the matriarch said calmly.

"Oh, of course." Jen sounded a little perturbed. "Is everything okay, Grandma?"

"Yes, fine, sweetie." She gave her a reassuring smile. "I

just need a moment with him."

Jen backed out of the car and into the arms of her mother. "Come on, we'll follow in the car behind."

Cathleen signaled for her son to get in and sit next to her. He slowly entered the car and positioned himself between his mother and the open door.

"Close the door," she ordered, as she looked out of the opposite window.

He closed the door and sat back in the seat. "You okay, Mom?" he asked.

"Oh, I'm fine," she answered, continuing to gaze at the mourners as they made their way to their own vehicles.

There was an awkward silence, which made him shift slightly in his seat. "What's on your mind?"

"It's been a terrible time." She waved at a mourner who bowed his head as he passed. "This family has had a lot of heartache of late." She paused, making him feel a little more uncomfortable. "I've buried my husband. I've buried one of my sons. It would be unbearable if I lost you, too."

He turned to look at her. "That's not going to happen, Mom."

"And I'm going to do everything in my power to make sure that it never happens." She spoke assertively, still watching the outside world. Then, without warning, she turned to look him straight in the eye. "You know, I've been going through some of your father's papers I found in the garage." She looked deeper into his eyes. "What happened in the cabin is very similar to a case file he had there. Almost identical. Would you know anything about that?"

He shook his head. "No. You know Pops never talked about his work to anyone, let alone me."

"Well, you know what he was like." Her harsh gaze mellowed. "He would only ever discuss his work with other cops." He looked a bit unnerved. "One more thing," she continued. "There was only two ways I could tell you two apart."

He shifted uncomfortably in the seat. "How's that?"

She looked deeper into his eyes. "Glasses."

His heart began to beat faster. "And the other?"

"Wedding bands." She said calmly. He suddenly moved his right hand over his left hand to hide his wedding finger. "You may want to address that at some point." They maintained eye contact for what seemed like an eternity. "When your brother passed, I spent a lot of time with him at the funeral home."

"I know you did mom." He was starting to get really unnerved.

Opening her purse, she produced a wedding band and handed it to him. "You may need this. When you decide who you want to be, make sure you wear the right one." Then turning to the chauffeur. "Drive on, please," she ordered.

Cathleen returned to indignantly looking out of the window as the vehicle pulled away, followed by the rest of the funeral procession.

THE END

12240421R00219

Printed in Great Britain
by Amazon.co.uk, Ltd.,
Marston Gate.